Supernatural Consultant, Volume One

Dragon Consultant

Dane, a supernatural consultant, is hired by the FAA to look into a series of reported dragon attacks on their planes. What Dane finds in the wooded area where the attacks took place is not quite the problem he expected: a group of dragon kits and their sick father hiding from the authorities.

When he learns the real reason the family was in the woods, his case grows more dangerous, and though Dane is experienced at both crime solving and watching his own back, taking care of baby dragons and their ill father makes everything else look easy.

Dragon Deception

A life full of children and mysteries to solve doesn't leave much time for relaxation or each other, something Lumie wants to help fix for Dane and Mercury by way of arranging a picnic. But good intentions and life rarely cooperate, and Dane knows it's only a matter of time before all hell breaks loose.

Hell turns out to be someone using Quicksilver's name to destroy buildings, but there's no way to tell whether the enemy is an impostor or a trap. Hopefully it won't mean missing the picnic.

Dragon Dilemma

Dane hasn't spoken with his mother in years and he's never met his father. But somehow his mother finds out about Mercury and the kits anyway, and it's difficult to throw one's mother out when she happens to be a powerful, dangerous witch.

She isn't the only uninvited guest, and the others are even less likely to take no for an answer—and much more likely to leave everyone dead if they don't get what they want.

Supernatural Consultant

Volume One

Mell Eight

A NineStar Press Publication

www.ninestarpress.com

Supernatural Consultant, Volume One

Printed in the USA

Print ISBN:

First Edition, September, 2020

Table of Contents

Dragon

Consultant

Chapter One

The phone started ringing out in the main office just as Dane was finishing up with his last client of the day. He had to suppress an eager smile—Dane could only think of one reason for the phone to ring so late—and refocused his attention on his current client. Dane had been expecting the client on the phone to call a week ago; he could wait ten more minutes.

"Mrs. Hempstead, I assure you the pixies are not the ones harming your prized roses. In fact, I'm fairly certain that the pixies are the only reason your roses are still alive, given the extensive damage in your garden." Dane tried to speak slowly and calmly so the elderly Mrs. Hempstead would understand and hopefully not get angry. It was probably a lost cause, though. She screamed pretentious and arrogant from the large pearl necklace around her wrinkled neck to the expensive mink coat she was wearing on a warm spring evening. She was used to hearing yes to everything she asked, so Dane telling her she was wrong would probably not go over well.

"If it isn't those disgusting pixies, then what is destroying my roses?" she snapped, her back regally straight and her eyes flashing with anger. Dane was shivering with fear in his chair...not. "You are supposed to be the premier consultant on everything supernatural. I expect results!"

Dane kept his face pleasant through sheer force of will. He had known this reaction was coming, but that didn't make it any more fun.

"The teeth marks on the bushes were quite distinctive," Dane continued gamely. "I would suggest that you keep your dog away from that part of your garden if you want your rosebushes to bloom at all this year."

She gasped, one silk-gloved hand flying to her chest as if Dane had uttered the most offensive thing she had ever heard. "Diamond would never do something like that!" The Chihuahua in question chose that moment to fart loudly in its carry-purse on the floor next to her chair, an action Mrs. Hempstead completely ignored.

"I have found the pixie family from your garden a new home where their abilities will be properly appreciated. You shouldn't be bothered by their presence any longer."

She sniffed in disdain. "Well, at least you've done as I asked. I'm sure my rosebushes will recover now that they're gone. Contact my solicitor for payment." She got to her feet smoothly, turned, and walked out of his office without a single word of thanks. Her roses would be dead by the end of the week; he'd bet that damned ankle-biter currently destroying her designer purse would ensure that.

Mrs. Hempstead didn't dawdle on her way out of the office. Barely thirty seconds later, Dane heard the outer door shut with a click. The phone on his desk lit up, and his secretary's voice sounded through the speaker.

"You have a call on line two. It seems important; he insisted on holding until you were done with your meeting."

"Thanks, Becky," Dane replied into the speakerphone. The lights on the phone all vanished as Becky hung up, except for the button blinking for line two. Each line belonged to a different type of client thanks to a nifty spell that made his life so much easier. Mrs. Hempstead would have gone to line three, as an ordinary human. Supernatural creatures lit up line one. Line two was for anything remotely associated with the government.

Dane picked up the phone, hit the button, and held the handset to his ear. He already knew who would be calling and why, but a touch of professionalism never hurt.

"This is Dane, your local supernatural consultant," Dane said, his voice stiff with formality. "How may I help you today?"

"Why aren't you already traveling to the mountain in question?" the voice on the other end snapped.

"Why, hello, Jacobson. So nice to hear from you!" If he was going to give Dane flack, Dane would give it right back. Jacobson was the ignorant fool in charge of the local division of the SupFeds, or the Federal Bureau of Supernatural Investigation, the branch of the federal government that oversaw all supernatural issues that had to do with the police or military. Jacobson was a human without the slightest magical ability. He relied on those who had power, like Dane, with far too little foresight. He simply didn't understand just what he was dealing with whenever he called Dane.

If he did, he would be a whole heck of a lot politer.

"You know exactly why I'm calling. The FAA is talking about calling up the Air Force for a strike."

"All for a dragon harassing a couple of airplanes?" Dane asked, skeptical that things would be so bad for such a little problem.

"How about multiple dragons? We've had sightings of at least one red and one blue dragon in the area." Now that was an interesting fact that hadn't made the news. "They've attacked three planes and forced an additional dozen to turn back. We're diverting flights right now, but it's not sustainable. We need those dragons contained as soon as possible. If you don't step in, we're going to have to take drastic action. I've sent all the information we've been able to gather to your email."

The phone clicked and Jacobson was gone. He had hung up on Dane. What a bastard. One of these days someone was going to eat him, and Dane would get a nasty phone call from his successor asking Dane to figure out how, who, and why. Dane occasionally wondered how he would explain that Jacobson was an ignorant dick while still maintaining his professionalism. It really wasn't a phone call he was looking forward to.

It only took a few clicks of Dane's email to find the information Jacobson had sent. The laptop whirred loudly as it downloaded the files, which made him frown. It wasn't exactly a standard-issue laptop. It was top of the line in human technology and magical spells. It was hackproof, spellproof, and near indestructible. The file Jacobson had sent must be huge.

Pictures popped up first, which explained the size of the file. Most of them were grainy, shot through a plane window with a smartphone by a bystander, but there were enough professional-quality shots included in the package that Dane could clearly see three different dragons. The professional shots worried him the most: they meant the government had taken the time to investigate their potential targets in case they had to be taken out. However, those shots also raised a more peculiar question.

Dragons were generally solitary creatures. They lived and hunted alone in territory they didn't share with anyone else. The only exception was when they mated; it took ten years for a dragon to form, lay, and hatch a clutch of eggs that the two parents worked together to keep from harm. Once the kits could manage on their own—which was when they learned how to fly properly —the parents left, and the kits happily went to find separate territories of their own.

The need to find and protect their territories from all invaders meant that dragons also spent most of their lives in the wild. It was a rare moment when a dragon got close enough to humans to cause a problem. However, that distance meant that dragons were overwhelmingly ignorant creatures. Dane knew the dragons couldn't help their ignorance, but the stigma against them was pervasive. They were considered to be uneducated, unmannered, and generally dislikeable by humans and other magical creatures that participated in normal society's norms and rules.

So why were three different dragons all living in the same airspace so close to human cities and towns?

That was the mystery Dane had to solve.

He shut down his computer and closed his office for the weekend. Becky was doing the same in the main office when he stepped out.

"I'll lock up if you want to head to those dragons now, Dane," she offered. At first glance, Becky looked like an old woman. Her hair was gray and pulled into a tight bun at the base of her neck, her back was bent, and her face deeply wrinkled. After a blink of Dane's eyes, her form changed into a beautiful young woman, strong and supple, with smooth skin and enough beauty to ensnare anyone who swung that way. She appeared in whatever form she needed in order to accomplish her calling as a banshee. At night she could be seen screaming, but during the day she worked as a secretary to pay her rent. She was perfect as the first line of defense of Dane's office, too, since her scream could paralyze almost anyone with fear.

"Thanks, Becky," Dane replied. "I'll call you if I won't be back by Monday. Have a good weekend."

She harrumphed in reply and started digging in her purse for her keys. Dane trusted her to lock the door and set the protection wards, so he left her to it. He started walking toward the front door, but he never reached it. Between one step and the next, he allowed his magic to pull him away. When Dane next put his foot down, it landed in the heavy debris of leaves and dirt that littered the ground of the forest around him. He was in the foothills of one of the nearby mountain ranges.

The dragons had claimed territory somewhere between four major international airports—Bradley, Logan, Albany, and Burlington—and were disrupting any flights whose path went through their territory's airspace. A half dozen or so regional airports nearby were also forced into diverting or canceling flights. Dane would need a map to be certain of which airport was closest to him at the moment. Large swaths of land in the area were deserted in terms of human habitation and would have been perfect for a dragon to claim as territory if it weren't for those pesky airplanes flying low overhead. Dragons didn't share any of their territory with anything large enough to be a threat, airplanes included.

But they also didn't share well with other dragons, so something strange was definitely occurring.

Dane tamped down on his power so he wouldn't advertise his presence and started walking in the direction where most of the dragon sightings had occurred. He'd stumble upon something eventually.

The forest was peaceful, which was really the only warning Dane needed to know something large and dangerous was living there. Normally a forest would be filled with the sounds of birds calling to each other and other wild animals scampering by, but all he could hear was the wind rustling the leaves overhead and the occasional bug scurrying around.

It took about five minutes of walking before Dane heard the crunch of old leaves behind him. He kept walking as if he didn't know he was being followed and started gathering his magic for a stunning spell just in case whoever it was tried to jump him. The rustling was too loud to be made by even the most unskilled human. Four dragon paws would certainly explain it, but for some reason Dane suspected there was more than one creature behind him.

"I don't think he'll scare away like usual," one voice whispered behind him. It sounded young and very unsure, which had Dane recalculating the strength of his stunning spell. "He's not dressed like the hikers from before."

"We could bite him?" a second, even younger-sounding voice asked.

There were two kits behind Dane. It seemed as though at least one was definitely old enough to be flying. Why hadn't he gone off to find his own territory by now? *The mystery thickens*, Dane couldn't help thinking dramatically.

"I don't think that would work," the first voice replied sardonically despite still sounding slightly unsure.

"I still want to bite him," the second voice grumped.

"You want to bite everything," the first voice responded in a scathing tone. "How do we get rid of him?"

It was time for Dane to figure out what was going on, preferably before the kits got inventive. Between one step and the next, he let his magic pull him away. He reappeared behind the two small dragons just as they were gasping at his sudden disappearance. They were crouched low behind a bush, still staring at the space between the trees where Dane had just been standing.

The larger of the two was a blue dragon and the smaller a brown. The scales covering their bodies were still small, emphasizing just how young they were. The ridge of spikes on adult dragons that ran down the spine in a straight line were still little nubs, as were the two horns growing over their pointed ears. Both had wings that were too large for their bodies, which was normal for very young dragons. They were born with wings capable of flight; they just had to grow into them. Only the blue had grown large enough to manage that. What was odder was that two different types of dragons would be willing to work together. If two blue dragons could only spend enough time together to have kits, a blue and a brown dragon would immediately start fighting should they meet. Age didn't matter when it came to territory.

"Just what is going on here?" Dane asked in his most severe voice. Both kits gasped and spun around. The younger one let out a little whimper and huddled into the side of his companion.

"He's going to hurt Daddy, Nickel!" the younger one cried.

"I won't let him!" the older one declared, his wings flaring out aggressively. He growled, and Dane could feel the pull of magic in the air as water started to coalesce around the dragons.

Dane waved his hand through the air, canceling the kit's magic with his own. Nickel gasped again, and his wings drooped.

"I don't want to hurt you or your daddy," Dane insisted, gentling his voice so he wouldn't scare them too much more. They were his key to figuring out what was going on here, so Dane couldn't afford to alienate them. "You can't stay on this mountain for much longer or people are going to get angry. I just want to help you find a new territory."

"We can't leave right now!" the little brown dragon insisted. "Daddy's sick, and we have to protect him!"

"Chrome, shh!" Nickel hissed.

"I'm here to help," Dane reiterated. "Maybe I can find a doctor for your daddy? To help him feel better?"

"Nickel?" Chrome whined. "What if he can help?"

Dane was the recipient of Nickel's fierce, piercing, blue-eyed stare for a few long seconds as he was evaluated and no doubt found wanting. Despite that fact, Dane was the only one available who might be able to help their father and them. Nickel didn't have a choice except to trust Dane. Finally Nickel relented, but not without a fight. "If he tries to hurt Daddy, you and 'Ron can bite him all you like."

"Oh boy," Chrome giggled. Both dragons turned and started walking in the same direction Dane had been headed earlier. He followed meekly behind, aware that Nickel kept glancing suspiciously over his shoulder. It wasn't long before the trees in the area began to display signs of dragon inhabitants. The bark showed scratches from dragon scales and claws, and distinctive, taloned footprints covered the ground. One glance around confirmed that Dane was dealing with a lot of children. The trees were all disfigured low to the ground, and the prints were too small for an adult. Besides, an adult would take better care of their territory.

Eventually they reached a clearing. At least three trees had fallen recently, opening the area to the sky, which was essential for dragons. The fallen trees had also created a natural cave off to one side. Dane could sense at least two dragons inside. Another brown dragon in human form was tottering unsteadily on her short baby legs. She was holding a large, curved piece of bark in her hands and seemed determined not to spill the water carefully held inside.

She was walking toward an adult dragon lying in the sun on the far side of the clearing. After she lay the piece of bark down, the adult dragon weakly lifted his head to drink. The water was gone in an instant, barely a sip for a dragon of the size collapsed there. The girl immediately snatched up the bark and hurried off.

"Daddy's sick," Chrome whispered to Dane. That much was obvious to see. It looked like an advanced case of dragon fever to him, something that in humans was called the flu. Dane walked closer, keeping his hands behind his back as the ever-suspicious Nickel paced him closely.

The adult's eyes were glazed with fever. He couldn't even differentiate Dane from Nickel, and after a few seconds of trying, his eyes slid closed. Dane turned to Nickel, who was apparently in charge until the adult got better.

"I can take him to a doctor," Dane tried to explain. "He'll be better in a few weeks if I do."

"What about the rest of us?" Nickel asked. There was fear there, most likely from the idea of being separated or left to fend for themselves. That was unusual in a dragon, but then nothing was usual about anything Dane had seen so far.

"You'll have to come with me, of course," Dane replied in as gentle a voice as he could manage. "Your dad won't get better without all of you with him."

Nickel thought for a long moment. Chrome whispered something about more biting in Nickel's ear, which seemed to appease Nickel somewhat. Oh, joy.

"Fine," Nickel finally relented.

Dane nodded. "Gather everyone. I can take you all with me at once, but you have to be touching me for the magic to work."

Chrome dashed across the clearing and into the cave. Nickel went in the other direction toward where the little girl had gone. He returned first.

"This is Iron, but we call her 'Ron," Nickel said as she placed the piece of bark filled with water near the adult dragon's head. It had tadpoles swimming in it, which were probably a nice snack for the kits. Dane had little doubt they had been living off of frogs and other small critters since Dad had gotten sick. "She's very good at biting."

'Ron bared her teeth, which even in human form were exceptionally sharp. If it weren't for the fact that she was naked, she would have looked like an ordinary human girl. Little brown scales covered her stomach and chest. Had she been wearing clothes, most of the scales would have been hidden, and only someone who could sense her power would know what she was. 'Ron was maybe three or four years old, the same approximate age as Chrome, and just on the cusp of learning to fly.

"Hello, 'Ron," Dane said very politely.

"You smell funny," she replied before focusing her attention on Dad.

Okay, then? Kids were really weird creatures, and kits were apparently no different.

It was another minute before Chrome returned. He had shifted into human form, his only covering the same brown scales as 'Ron wore. Two red dragons in human form, their red scales and hair almost identical in color, accompanied him. One was very small. If Dane had to guess, he wasn't long out of his egg. The other boy was approximately Nickel's age, so about seven or eight. All three of them were very carefully carrying a fire-red dragon egg. The egg was easily the size of the baby red trying to hold it up. What the heck were five young dragons and one very sick adult male doing with a red dragon egg? Dane hurried over and took the egg from them before they could drop it.

"Everyone make sure you're touching me," Dane insisted. Four small hands clutched at his clothes. Nickel huffed and shifted into human form, too, his small body only covered in blue scales, and his hand joined with the others. Dane cradled the egg in one arm and reached out to place the other on Dad's back.

Magic shifted around everyone. When it settled down again, they were standing on the expansive front lawn of Dane's home. The kits all gasped, staring at the field of grass and the two-mile-long driveway cutting through the middle.

The kits didn't wander far from Dad as they went to explore. Only the baby red remained with Dane, one thumb in his mouth as he sat at Dane's feet. Dane moved the egg to his other arm and dug into his pocket for his phone. It only took a few seconds to scroll through Dane's contacts and hit Call.

"Dr. Krantz?" Dane asked when someone said hello on the other end.

"Dane, my boy!" Dr. Krantz said jovially. "What can I do for you?"

"I have a very sick adult dragon down with what looks like dragon fever and five young kits that have been exposed."

"Say no more, my boy," Dr. Krantz interrupted. "Give me five minutes." He hung up.

Dane scrolled through his contacts again until he found Daisy's name. She didn't pick up until the third ring, and when she did, she sounded distracted.

"What can I do ya for?" she asked just as someone screamed loudly in the background. "No, you do not pull each other's hair! I said no! Do not hit me with that tail, young man!" Her phone was put down with a *thunk*, and Dane patiently listened as she corralled two squalling kids and got them situated in time-out. "Sorry 'bout that," she said sheepishly. "What's up, Boss?"

'Ron was eating a dandelion she had pulled from the ground. Nickel and the other red dragon were playing leapfrog with a very frightened cricket, although neither had actually taken their eyes off of Dane yet. Chrome was also watching with his teeth bared, as if he were waiting for a chance to bite. The baby red was using one of Dane's feet as a pillow.

"I have five young dragon kits on my front lawn, and I don't know what to do with them," Dane admitted.

"What're ya doing with so many dragons?" Daisy yelped.

"Your guess is as good as mine," he replied. "Anyway, I have one girl and four boys who need clothes and food."

"Let me round up the husband to watch my own brats, and then I'll hop right over." Daisy sounded far too curious on the phone for Dane's own peace of mind, but then it would be good if she could get answers out of the kits about their unusual situation. She hung up on Dane too; it appeared to be the day for it.

The kits eventually wandered back to their dad and Dane. They flopped down onto the grass to wait. The egg was starting to feel heavy, and its constant warmth under the setting sun was making him sweat.

The ground lit up suddenly near the driveway, causing all the kits to jump to their feet in surprise. It was a transportation spell circle, and as the light faded, two figures emerged. Dr. Krantz and his assistant hurried over toward where everyone was standing. Nickel and the older red—Dane really needed to learn his name—surged to their feet and transformed into dragon form with loud growls.

"It's all right, kits," Dane called as teeth were bared and claws extended. "This is the doctor!"

Dr. Krantz stopped short just in front of the boys. His glance took in all the young kits, the egg in Dane's hands, and the dragon laboring for breath at Dane's feet. He turned to his assistant and murmured something. The young man spun on one heel and hurried back to the circle. He vanished a second later.

"The bronze dragon needs medicine immediately," Dr. Krantz explained to the kits. He said it a gentle tone, but Dane could still see the urgency in his eyes, and if Dane could see it, Nickel could too.

"It'll help?" Nickel asked, still defensive.

Dane was still struck by the bronze part of Dr. Krantz's comment. What the heck was a precious dragon doing with a bunch of elemental kits? Every new thing Dane learned about these dragons just confused him even more. Thanks to the layer of dirt, sweat, and grime, Dad could pass as a brown elemental dragon. Upon closer inspection, however, Dane could just barely see the gleam of bronze peeking through.

There were two different types of dragons. The more common type was the elemental; their powers corresponded with their colors of fire red, earth brown, water blue, and air white. The only elemental dragon not represented by the kits was air, but they tended to be fairly elusive. The less common type was known as a precious dragon. There were three different types—bronze, silver, and gold—and regardless of their color they had the ability to work magic without a specific element. If Daddy weren't felled by dragon fever, he would be quite a formidable foe.

"Yes, son," Dr. Krantz insisted. "It will help a lot."

"Okay," Nickel said. He slowly backed away to give Dr. Krantz room. "But I'll be watching closely."

"Thank you," Dr. Krantz replied. He moved slowly as he approached Dad and knelt in the grass at the dragon's side. "It would be easier if you twiddled your fingers and turned this bronze into human form, Dane, my boy."

It was a bit more than just twiddling his fingers, but to a healer-witch like Dr. Krantz, that might have been the best explanation he was able to give. Dane felt for the streams of magic surrounding the dragon and began to pull here and twist there until the bronze's magic took over from muscle memory. His gigantic dragon form faded, replaced by a human adult male who looked to be about thirty years old.

His face was red with fever, but despite that he was probably the most handsome man Dane had ever seen. His lips were full, his nose small and pert, and his lashes thick over his closed eyes. His hair was a beautiful bronze color that echoed the large scales that covered most of his very naked body.

It took Dr. Krantz a few moments of searching before he found a bit of skin not protected by the scales that was adequate for his purpose. "I'm going to give him a shot," he explained to Nickel as he pulled a syringe and a vial full of liquid out of his medical bag. He prepped the needle as he continued to speak. "Inside this liquid is a mix of human chemicals and magic. It should have your dear dad up and about in only a few hours."

"That fast?" Dane asked, wondering if calling Daisy for help had been too preemptive.

"It will take him a few days before he's strong enough to walk farther than from his bed to the bathroom and back, but the fever will be gone." Dr. Krantz stuck the needle deep into the muscle of the bronze's inner thigh, where the scales thinned to reveal human skin, and depressed the plunger. It was over before Nickel could cry out in shock. "Do you have a bed, dear boy?" Dr. Krantz asked as he carefully capped the needle and dropped it into a biohazard bag.

Dane nodded. "I'll make sure he gets to one soon."

"Don't make holes in Daddy!" 'Ron whimpered. "That's not nice, and he wouldn't like it!"

Dr. Krantz nodded solemnly. "I'm very sorry; you're right. Of course, if he were awake he would get a lollipop for taking his medicine so bravely." He pulled five plastic-wrapped suckers out of his bag, all in different colors, and displayed them to the kits.

"I take medic-stuff," the baby red insisted from where he was still sitting on Dane's foot. Dane hadn't known he was old enough to talk just yet, but then dragon development wasn't something Dane had ever made a study of. He would have to remedy that, since he was apparently watching over a herd of them for now.

"You are very brave, little red. What's your name?" Dr. Krantz asked as he knelt on the ground in front of Dane where the kit was still sitting.

"I Lumie." He made grabbing motions toward the red sucker.

"Well, Lumie, I need you to drink this medicine. Once you've swallowed all of it, you may have the lolly." Dr. Krantz poured a purple liquid out of another bottle he pulled from his bag into a small cup. Lumie downed the liquid without hesitation, although he did grimace at the taste. The sucker replaced the usual thumb in his mouth. Dane could never trust a stranger that easily, but then the innocence of youth wasn't a luxury he had ever been allowed. With Lumie happy and unhurt from the experience, the rest of the kits hurried forward in human form to take their own medicine and get their lolly too.

The transportation spell flashed twice while the kits were lining up. Dr. Krantz's assistant reappeared first, wheeling an incubator covered in protective spell runes and large enough to hold the egg Dane was still cradling. Daisy was only a few minutes behind the assistant. She started cooing at the kits the second she saw them, exclaiming over their naked state and how dirty they were.

"Baths right away, then dinner 'n bed. I have the cutest pj's for the scamps, ya know," Daisy insisted. She had 'Ron cuddled in her arms. 'Ron was fascinated by Daisy's green skin and the thick lizard's tail that poked out of the bottom of her skirt.

"Then let's get them all inside," Dane replied. Lumie had eaten the lollipop stick, too, and his thumb was back in his mouth, but that didn't stop him from rumbling unhappily when Nickel poked him until he got to his feet. The other red dragon was growling at Dr. Krantz as the egg was situated in the incubator. It took some doing, but eventually all the kits started heading toward the front door of Dane's house. That left Dane, the bronze dragon still lying in the grass, and Nickel, who had remained behind to watch over his dad.

Nickel really was cute in a slightly murderous way. His stare would have sent chills up Dane's spine if he hadn't already experienced much worse in his lifetime. Dane didn't want to know what Nickel had faced in his life to teach him that look either.

"I'll have to carry your dad," Dane told Nickel first so he wouldn't get upset; then Dane stooped down and got one arm underneath the bronze's shoulders and the other underneath his knees and stood back up. He wasn't nearly as heavy as he ought to have been for a dragon, and that was worrying.

Daisy had been in and out of Dane's house for years, so she knew exactly where to take the kits to get them scrubbed clean. This wasn't the first family of strays Dane had helped find their way, although so far they were his most confusing. She was his main go-to whenever children were involved. Nickel closed the front door behind them and then followed closely as Dane walked up the stairs and down the right-hand hallway. They passed the bathroom where Lumie was squalling about not liking water and 'Ron was giggling loudly to a chorus of splashing. The last door in the hall was the master bedroom for the wing. It had a king-sized bed, a large sitting area, and a private bath. It would be more than enough space for the dragon family when they were spending time with their dad.

"In the bottom drawer over there," Dane told Nickel, using his chin to point to a dresser along one wall, "is a pair of sleeping pants that will fit your dad." Dane headed into the bathroom, because there was no way the dragon was sleeping on Dane's sheets smelling like he did. It wasn't pleasant, to say the least.

The bronze's heavy wheezing was evening out slightly, which was a welcome sign. His breathing returning to normal was the first indication the dragon fever was breaking. Dane lay him down on the bathmat and started the water in the tub. Nickel returned while Dane was waiting for the water to heat up.

"You're going to have to get a bath of your own, too, you know," Dane told him. The water finally heated up, so he plugged the drain and watched as the tub began to fill.

"After I'm sure you're not about to make dragon stew," Nickel replied without the slightest trace of humor in his voice. Dane had to hide a grin; Nickel really was the cutest little potential murderer when he sounded like that.

Dane shut the water off when the tub was only half full. With Nickel's help, he got Dad into the water.

"Your job is to make sure his head doesn't go underneath the water," Dane told Nickel sternly as he wet a washcloth and started up a lather with some sweet-smelling soap and set to the task of getting the beautiful bronze clean.

The bronze scales washed clean easily with just one swipe of the washcloth. The human skin required a bit more scrubbing, but it eventually came clean too. It took both of them to scrub the long bronze hair that fell messily to the dragon's shoulders. When they were finally done, Nickel held out a towel as Dane pulled the drain in the tub and lifted the dragon free.

A few minutes later, the dragon was dry, in pajama pants, and tucked into bed. Nickel helped the entire time. He knew how to tighten the strings on the pajamas and how to fold down the sheets on the bed. Those weren't skills normal dragons came by; there weren't beds in the wild where they lived.

The door opened before Dane could ask about it.

"There ya are!" Daisy exclaimed as she stepped into the bedroom. "I've got pants for ya. Go on and take yer bath; dinner'll be ready in twenty." She held out a pair of loose, green, child-size pajama bottoms for Nickel to take. He snatched them from her with a glare, turned the glare on Dane with a sharp warning in his eyes, and then stomped back to the bathroom. Dane heard the water start running a few moments later through the door Nickel hadn't bothered to close.

"That's a rascally one, right there," Daisy sighed with a shake of her head. "Copper's gone and made himself a nest with the egg, Chrome and 'Ron were testing their teeth on your banister, and Lumie's wandered off. I'll get dinner into them and get them into bed. Then I'll be back in the morning."

Dane's poor banister, although they couldn't do more damage than that teething werewolf cub had a few years back. "Thanks, Daisy," he replied fervently. Her help was invaluable. Dane knew he couldn't do this without her.

The bronze was slumbering peacefully in the bed. His damp hair spilled over the pillow, and the covers were pulled up tight to his chin. His color was better and his breathing even. Dane forced his eyes away from the dragon's pretty face and walked into the hallway. He closed the door behind himself to give Nickel some privacy when he finished in the bathroom.

There was a soft thump and weight suddenly deposited on Dane's foot. Lumie looked up at him, grinning around the thumb in his mouth. He was sitting on Dane's foot, and he wrapped one arm around Dane's ankle when Dane didn't immediately dislodge him. Here was another strange kit. Lumie wasn't afraid or wary of Dane, and unlike most young dragons, hadn't protested the change in territory.

Dane lifted his foot experimentally, and Lumie giggled and clung tightly. He didn't seem inclined to move, but Dane had a phone call to make. Dane walked down the hall, heading toward the other wing of the house with Lumie giggling happily from his position on Dane's foot the entire time. The two hallways for the two separate wings of the house met in the center where Dane had created a pleasant sitting area. There were two double couches and a deep armchair circled around a coffee table whose legs looked chewed as if a puppy had been teething on them. Dane and Lumie quickly bypassed the furniture and headed down the hallway toward his office.

Jacobson's number was written in Dane's address book. Dane only kept friends on speed dial on his phone, and Jacobson most definitely wasn't a friend. It was probably too late to catch him at the office—he didn't seem the type to work any more hours than he had to— but Dane should leave a message at least.

The phone rang six times before the answering machine picked up. Dane waited while bouncing his foot up and down, causing Lumie to giggle even more.

"Jacobson," Dane said into the phone once the usual beep ended. "I have relocated your dragon problem. Feel free to contact the FAA and tell them regular flights can resume. My office assistant will submit my usual invoice to your office first thing Monday morning." Dane hung up without saying goodbye.

Lumie and Dane left the office and headed down the stairs toward the kitchen. Dane was sure Daisy would appreciate an extra pair of hands getting dinner ready, and maybe she could detach his new leech. The kits' bedtime couldn't come soon enough.

Chapter Two

Mercury woke slowly, awareness returning to him in stages. Feeling came first: the softness of the bed underneath him and the warmth of the blankets covering him. Then a touch of mystery surfaced. Why wasn't he lying on the ground in the middle of a forest in his dragon form? Worry came afterward. Where was he, to be in a bed, and where were his kits?

It was the worry that propelled Mercury's eyes open. He was met with the sight of a well-appointed room. The walls were a generic off-white color, complemented by light-blue curtains closed over large windows. There was furniture along the walls, too, but Mercury was more interested in the kit snoring lightly where he was curled on the end of the bed.

Chrome was in human form, strangely enough. He preferred his dragon shape because it made it easier for him to bite things, yet someone had convinced Chrome to stay in his more defenseless shape. Chrome was even dressed in loose sleeping pants and a T-shirt, another thing Mercury hadn't thought possible. Chrome snuffled in his sleep and rolled over. Sleepy brown eyes blinked slowly open, but they eventually focused firmly on Mercury's own bronze-colored ones.

It took a second for comprehension to kick in, and then Chrome's eyes widened comically.

"Daddy's awake!" Chrome yelled at the top of his lungs, making Mercury jump in surprise. Chrome clumsily fell off the bed with a thump and ran to the door. He yanked it open and yelled out into the hallway Mercury could see through the open door. "Daddy's awake!"

More thumps and bangs could be heard farther down the hall, and then a stampede of small feet pounded closer. Nickel was in the lead. His short blue hair was flattened slightly on one side from sleep, but his gaze was sharp as he took in Mercury's open eyes and the way Mercury was awkwardly propped up on his pillows. 'Ron was just behind Nickel. She giggled happily and bounced onto the bed to give Mercury a clutching hug around his middle. Copper strolled in, saw that Mercury was okay, and turned back around. Mercury hadn't missed the fleeting look of relief that crossed Copper's face, but the most aloof of his kits wasn't about to openly declare that fact. He would probably tell the egg Mercury had little doubt he was heading back to curl up with all about it.

All of his kits looked clean and cared for. Someone had taken the time to give them baths and to get them into clothes, a feat Mercury didn't envy. All of his kits except one. Mercury looked around, half expecting Lumie to have snuck in somehow, but he didn't see his baby red.

"Where's Lumie?" Mercury asked. He untangled one hand from the covers so he could stroke 'Ron's hair. She was still hugging him tightly, and it didn't seem like she was going to let him go any time soon.

"He's gotten attached, and I can't get him off," a new voice said from the doorway. Nickel didn't tense, so this stranger wasn't a danger, but he still looked wary. Mercury let a little magic flare between his fingers, the warmth fizzing welcomingly against his skin as he sat up a little straighter and turned to face the stranger.

Mercury recognized the look on the stranger's face even if Mercury didn't actually recognize him. The perplexed twist to his lips as he looked down at Lumie sleeping in his arms was one Mercury had seen on his own face in the mirror plenty of times. There was nothing quite like going to bed alone and waking up to find Lumie had somehow managed to sneak past his considerable defenses and latch on without waking him. Lumie had his hands fisted in the stranger's nightshirt, and Mercury knew that if the man removed his arms where he was gently holding Lumie in place, Lumie wouldn't drop an inch.

The stranger looked bemused, but also resigned. He had apparently spent enough time with Lumie to get used to his quirks. Mercury wished he knew how much time had passed since he had fallen asleep in the woods. What exactly had happened to his kits that they had managed to find hospitality?

"You wouldn't know how to get him to let go?" the man asked, his voice and eyes pleading to Mercury for help.

Mercury shrugged. "Not a clue. When he wakes up, he'll wander off somewhere." Now that he could see that Lumie was safe, Mercury refocused on the stranger. He was a gloriously beautiful man, almost too beautiful to be human. His nose was a thin blade between prominent cheekbones and wide blue eyes. His blond hair trailed in messy waves past his shoulders, emphasizing how broad and muscled they were. The tips of pointed ears poked through his hair, the ends pierced with silver rings that jingled as he shifted in place. He looked like a man from an age where hair was long as a fashion statement and cravats had more lace than sense, except he was wearing comfortable and functional-looking cotton sleepwear instead of formalwear. Mercury knew he looked like a man who had spent years in the woods: unkempt and ragged. His hair was long because he needed a haircut, not because of any fashion. Although, Mercury didn't think he would look as good in pajamas as the stranger did even if he were properly groomed.

'Ron finally released Mercury and found a comfortable spot in his lap to curl up. "You don't look the same?" she asked, tilting her head slightly to the side as she studied the stranger curiously.

The stranger flushed, his cheeks turning slightly red as if he were embarrassed. "Ah, my apologies, 'Ron." All of a sudden an inner light vanished, as if a light bulb inside the stranger's body had been abruptly switched off. His skin and hair lost the ethereal glow that had mesmerized Mercury, and his pointed ears shrank until they were hidden behind his hair. The stranger looked ordinary— still far too beautiful for a mere human—but he could pass as one now.

Seeing a glamour tossed about like it only took a thought to utilize such advanced magic told Mercury exactly whose house his kits had invaded. There was only one person in the area purported to have that much strength.

"You're the Genie of the East?" Mercury asked, although it was more of a statement of fact than a question.

A slight frown flittered across the stranger's face. "I have been called that," he said grumpily, "but since I'm not a genie, that's hardly accurate."

Not a genie? Then how could he have the power the rumors suggested he did? "You are the supernatural consultant though?"

"I am," the stranger replied. "Please call me Dane."

"He found us in the woods and brought you to a doctor!" 'Ron explained eagerly. Her eyes were shining with hero worship as she gazed eagerly at Dane before looking up at Mercury as if she needed assurance that her awe wasn't misplaced.

Mercury couldn't help smiling at 'Ron despite his misgivings. Doctors were...the simplest way to put it was bad. He didn't think the Genie of the East would be working for the enemy—at least, he hoped not. It was why he had been traveling through the mountains toward Dane in the first place.

"He gave us lollies, and then the green lady helped us get clean," Chrome added, eager to be included in the conversation.

A fleeting look of frustration crossed Dane's face as Chrome and 'Ron both began explaining Dane's appearance and how they had magically gotten to his house. There wasn't any room for Dane to interject, which he clearly wanted to do. Mercury could easily guess why, too, given the strange gathering of dragons he had taken in. The entire situation was against normal dragon behavior, but then their reasoning for banding together was drastic enough to warrant it.

Dane wanted to know that reason, but he also appeared to know that interrupting the kits would be a bad idea.

Mercury was fighting off a wide yawn by the time the awkward and twisting story arrived at the present. The kits had been in the forest without his protection for an entire week. They knew how to survive, particularly Nickel, but they shouldn't have had to. They were still kits, and dragon fever or not, he had failed them.

Despite his guilt, the flu still had its horrible claws dug deep. Mercury's eyes were sliding closed involuntarily, and he felt too weak to fight against it. Even the magic he had gathered in defense fizzled away.

"Back to bed, everyone," Dane insisted. 'Ron whined something Mercury was too tired to interpret, but he felt the bed shift as she climbed down and Chrome followed.

"I'll keep an eye on Dane," Nickel's voice whispered softly into Mercury's ear before his footsteps followed the other kits out of the room. Nickel was certainly capable of that. It was a relief to know that someone wasn't blindly trusting Dane not to be in league with the enemy. Given Dane's excellent reputation, Mercury and the kits believed it was very likely Dane could be trusted, but it still didn't hurt to be cautious. Mercury slipped back to sleep hoping nothing would go wrong while he was unconscious.

*

Sunlight was shining through the windows when Mercury blinked his eyes open again. Time had passed, but without a clock Mercury didn't know how much. He was alone in the room, but 'Ron's distinctive laughter could be heard somewhere outside.

It took a lot more effort than Mercury expected to throw the covers back and turn so his feet were planted on the floor. He had to pause for the room to stop spinning before he let his leg muscles propel him into a standing position. He wobbled his way to the bathroom, holding on to furniture to stay upright. By the time he had finished using the facilities, his legs were shaking, and he wasn't entirely confident he would make it back to the bed without crawling.

It wasn't a dignified position to be in, especially when he had kits to be taking care of. He wrestled the bathroom door open and leaned against the jamb, his fingers digging into the edge for balance, as he looked hopelessly at the distance between him and the bed.

"There ya are!" a woman's voice said chidingly. "Thought you'd run off for a sec." She hurried over and slipped her shoulder under his arm, forcing him to lean on her as she guided him back to the bed. Her skin was very green, which could only mean she was Daisy, the woman who had been taking care of the kits.

Daisy got him sitting up in bed with the covers pulled comfortably up to his waist. Only once he was settled did she turn away to grab a tray from the bedside table that held soft-poached eggs on toast with a large glass of orange juice. Daisy carefully situated the meal on his lap.

"I'll let Dane and the kits know yer awake," she said. "Eat up." She swiftly left the room, giving Mercury a glance at the green tail, which 'Ron had so eagerly told him about, poking out from the bottom of her skirt.

Mercury found silverware and started eating. He was starving. All three eggs and the slices of toast were long gone by the time anyone stopped by to interrupt. Mercury was working on his orange juice when Dane's knock came.

Mercury would have liked to assume that the gorgeous man from the night before had been a figment of his fevered imagination. That wasn't the case at all. Dane's glamour was still in place, but that didn't diminish his good looks in the least bit. He was walking funny, almost stilted, as he moved across the floor toward the bed. A glance downward revealed Lumie standing on Dane's foot, thumb in his mouth. Lumie squealed, his words too garbled to understand, and threw himself at the bed. It took a couple of tries, but he somehow managed to climb onto the mattress. He copied 'Ron's move from the previous night, clamping his arms around Mercury's middle with no intention of letting go. Mercury moved the empty tray out of the way and pulled Lumie close. His youngest kit was the most needy, but Mercury loved that about Lumie.

"I'm sure you have some questions," Mercury said when Dane continued to stand awkwardly next to the bed.

"A few," Dane said with a small smile that twisted his lips to emphasize the understatement in his tone. "I should probably ask for your name first. I can't keep calling you 'the kits' dad' in my head."

That was easy enough to answer. "Mercury."

"You were traveling to see me?" Dane continued.

Mercury nodded. "I was hoping you would be able to help us."

One eyebrow lifted in curiosity. "You needed supernatural help?" he asked. "You're a precious dragon. Your magic is one of the strongest of all supernatural creatures. What would you need my help with?"

"To save the dragons," Mercury stated, his voice dark and serious.

That clearly wasn't what Dane was expecting; Dane took a step back in surprise and shock filled his face. "What's wrong with the dragons?"

That wasn't a question that was easy to answer. It required going back three years to when Mercury had first been yanked into the middle of the fracas.

"I was walking home from work one evening," he began slowly, the memory far too fresh in his mind, "but I never made it. I don't know what happened. My magic didn't alert me that I was under attack, and I didn't see or feel anything, but one moment I was walking past the pizza place and the next I was waking up strapped down on a gurney. Four humans were wheeling me down a white hallway, and all I could smell was dragon's bane."

Dane winced. He obviously knew just how debilitating the herb dragon's bane could be to dragons. Mercury had seen it do terrible things: in minor cases, it set off sneezing and coughing attacks, but it quickly became more debilitating the longer the exposure. Some dragons ended up with severe asthma attacks, while others became paralyzed to the point that they couldn't move to escape the affected area. 'Ron, for example, got both asthma and paralysis, which made it potentially deadly should she be exposed, but Mercury just got a nasty case of the sniffles.

"I'm not as allergic as most, so I started gathering my magic. I don't think the humans knew what type of dragon I am. I was in human form, and bronze dragons are mistaken for brown very often. They didn't notice when the straps holding me down unhooked, but they did notice when I knocked two of them out. I got free just in time for a section of wall to blow out of a nearby room. This tiny blue dragon kit flew through the opening, killed the six guards who were responding, and then turned on me. He couldn't have been more than four or five years old, but the second he realized I was also a dragon and was handling the guards in the hallway, he turned around and went back into the room. I eventually followed."

Mercury had to catch his breath and swallow bile as memories from that night played like a movie in his head. The blood staining the walls and the tiny claws of the blue kit. The screams of humans and of dragons. By the time he had been able to follow the kit into the room, four other blue dragon kits were dead. A fifth was on her way to death as she bled helplessly on the floor, and a sixth was so disfigured that it was a mercy for him to die. Two eggs were smashed open, their innocent contents dead on the floor.

"They were experimenting on blue dragons," Mercury tried to explain. "Injecting something into their eggs before they hatched and performing experiments on the kits. It was horrible. Nickel showed me everything that night, and I destroyed that building and all the research inside. They were going to send me somewhere where they were researching brown dragons. I found that out from a chart hung on the end of my gurney. Nickel and I teamed up to find and save the other dragons."

"And then Daddy came and got me!" Lumie insisted with an eager grin on his face.

Mercury couldn't stop a gentle smile from forming on his lips as he looked down at Lumie's earnest red eyes. Even his worst memories couldn't overcome that good one. He and Nickel had been dismantling the research station at the red dragon compound so Mercury could destroy it properly when behind them came a scream. A guard had been trying to sneak up on them, and the tiniest dragon kit Mercury had ever seen had latched his teeth into the guard's ankle.

Copper had killed the guard and scooped Lumie safely into his arms. They were the only two surviving kits, along with an egg that Mercury wasn't sure would ever hatch.

"I went and got 'Ron and Chrome first, but yes, then I got you." Lumie beamed at his answer.

Dane looked outraged at Mercury's story. His lips were pinched, his eyes hard, and he was losing a little control over his glamour as he glowed slightly with fury.

"I will figure out who's doing this and put a stop to it," he snarled.

"We have to find the air dragon research lab first," Mercury insisted. "I know it's somewhere in the east."

Dane frowned. "In my territory?" He sounded even angrier at the idea. "I'll take care of it."

He spun around and stomped out of the room.

Lumie sighed and snuggled closer. "I like him," Lumie insisted, "even if Chrome really wants to bite him."

"Is there anything Chrome doesn't want to bite?" Mercury replied.

Lumie giggled. "No." His eyes slid closed as a yawn split his face. Mercury liked the idea of a nap. He couldn't chase after Dane, not with his legs still feeling like wet noodles, and there wasn't much he could do from inside a bed except nap. Mercury rearranged Lumie so he was under the covers, too, then curled around his baby kit and slowly fell back to sleep.

Chapter Three

It was all there, right under Dane's fricking nose. Three years ago he'd heard of a government science lab getting bombed, but that event had gotten lost between the pearl snatching from a naiad, the fight to save a dryad family's forest from a greedy developer, and dozens of other cases Dane had been involved with at the time. Besides, there hadn't been any indication that the bombing had any supernatural connections, which meant he wouldn't have had any interest in it. At the time, he had chalked it up to human terrorism and went on with his life.

The bomber called himself Quicksilver, Dane found as he read through old news reports of all three bombings. The bomber would write the very biblical *Let My People Go* statement on one of the few walls still standing when he was finished destroying the building, sign it with his pseudonym, and vanish until the next attack.

There had only been a total of three attacks, and they were spread out enough that the multitude of news articles was a little odd. None of the articles had any information on what the labs were researching, just that someone had the gall to bomb them. Dane clicked to another webpage with a column detailing the most recent attack that had occurred just over three months ago. The story was only a week old. Three months was a very long time for the news stations to still be interested in the story—their viewers had a shorter attention span than that—which meant someone from higher up the food chain was pressuring the news agencies to keep the story fresh in the citizens' minds. Someone in a position of power wanted the unequivocal support of viewers who had been bombarded with the media-released version of the truth for too long. Should Quicksilver be caught, any jury would already be biased against him. Dane had seen it happen before, and it was a damned effective tool used far too often—and usually by the government—for nefarious means.

Quicksilver was another name for Mercury. That connection wasn't hard to find, given that Mercury had already stated he was behind the attacks. What was hard to fathom was who was behind the labs and the news articles. Who wanted Mercury caught and convicted by the viewing public without a long trial that would expose the truth behind those labs?

They were government labs, but just because the government was funding them didn't mean the employees knew what type of research was being conducted inside. However, not just anyone would be cruel enough to conduct experiments on helpless dragon kits.

Speaking of kits, there was a small hand on Dane's knee. Dane looked down and saw Lumie staring imploringly up at him. Lumie's eyes were wide as he waited for Dane to pick him up and show him what he was looking at on his computer.

Dane's office was warded. Even Mercury, an adult dragon with precious magic that Lumie would never have access to, would have trouble getting through without Dane's permission. It also wouldn't be a quiet process: Dane's wards were supposed to let off a siren should anyone try to breach them. Despite all that, Lumie had somehow gotten past his wards, through the closed door, and across the room without Dane noticing him.

"How did you get in here?" Dane asked sharply.

His tone went through one ear and out the other without Lumie acknowledging he had even heard Dane. The damned kit was sucking his thumb, and when Dane showed no signs of picking him up, he whacked Dane's knee with his free hand again.

Dane sighed. Why had he let the kits into his home in the first place? He could still throw them out and let them create a territory in the forest portion of his property instead of inside his house. Lumie whacked Dane a third time, and in the interest of remaining bruise-free, Dane had no choice but to relinquish his misgivings and pull Lumie up into his lap.

"You're very strange," Dane told him. Lumie ignored Dane again, the damned brat, in favor of angling Dane's computer screen so he could see it better. Lumie made a distressed sound in the back of his throat when he saw the picture. He had been recently rescued from the facility in the photos, Dane remembered, and probably recognized the images.

Lumie glanced upward from the computer to look at Dane. His eyes were imploring, but also slightly accusing, as if he couldn't decide if Dane's interest was a good or bad thing.

Dane had to explain, if only to keep Lumie from deciding he hated Dane. Dane had a bad feeling that despite his superior knowledge, magic, and strength, it wouldn't end well for him.

"Your dad asked for my help finding the facility holding the air dragons hostage," Dane reminded Lumie. "I was just reading up on the other labs to see if I could find a clue. We have to save them too."

Lumie nodded solemnly, the suspicion gone from his eyes. He angled the computer screen back to Dane's height before curling up in Dane's lap. He tucked his head against Dane's stomach and proceeded to fall asleep right there.

Dane looked around the room warily, checking to make sure there weren't other kits prepared to pounce. Aside from Lumie, the room was dragon-free. Dane shut his computer off with a sigh. There was no way he could wade through the mystery of the government labs with a kit in his lap. He slid one arm under Lumie's body and stood. Dane needed to find Mercury.

He wasn't hard to find, luckily. Mercury was getting stronger every hour, but he still spent most of his time in bed. Dane knocked on the propped-open door perfunctorily before letting himself in.

Nickel was curled at the end of the bed, thankfully in human form; Dane would fear for the state of his sheets otherwise. Scales ripped cotton very easily. Nickel popped one suspicious eye open, saw it was Dane, and went back to sleep. Mercury was sitting up in bed reading a book. He tucked a bookmark into the pages and set the book aside as Dane walked over to his bedside.

"Tell me about Lumie," Dane said, settling into a chair that one of the kits had no doubt dragged there. Lumie was still sleeping comfortably in his lap.

Mercury tried to hide a smile, but he failed. His voice was full of suppressed laughter as he spoke. "Where did he magically appear this time?"

Dane's own voice sounded overly grumpy, even to his ears, when he replied. "Inside my locked and warded office."

This time Mercury could not stifle his snort of laughter. "The first time Lumie did that to me, I was inside what should have been an impenetrable spell circle trying to locate an air dragon I thought might have helpful information. I finished the spell and looked down to find Lumie sucking on his tail at my feet. I about jumped a mile."

"Wards don't affect him?" Dane asked, staring down at Lumie incredulously. If that was true, he was one of the most dangerous creatures in the world. The little bundle of clingy cuteness curled in Dane's lap could go anywhere, infiltrate anything, and no one could hold him captive should he be caught.

The mirth in Mercury's eyes faded as he looked at Lumie. "I don't honestly know. He was in an egg for most of his time at the facility. I know they were running experiments on the eggs, but I have no idea what chemicals and magic they injected him with. He hatched only a few days before I arrived, but he's been jumping through wards and spells for as long as I've known him."

"And the other kits?" Dane had to ask, his throat tight as he suppressed a snarl. Those bastards deserved to die for what they'd done to Lumie.

"They were all hatched before they were brought to their facilities. I know there were some experiments with dragon's bane—'Ron is inordinately allergic—but I think they were mostly pincushions for the blood and bone needed in the experiments on the eggs."

"So the egg Copper is inseparable from?" Dane led, curious, although the weight in his heart already told him the horrible answer.

"Might never hatch," Mercury growled, "or the creature that comes out of it might be better off dead.

There's no way of knowing what they did to the poor thing, and Copper is so damned hopeful that he'll have a little brother or sister to nurture that I don't know what he'll do when it hatches."

"It'll be really sad," Nickel added softly. "I don't think I want that egg to hatch."

Lumie yawned widely around the thumb tucked in his mouth. He sat up slowly, wobbling unsteadily as he crawled across Dane's lap and onto the bed without actually opening his eyes.

"It'll hatch," Lumie mumbled as if he were talking in his sleep. He slipped into Mercury's arms and pressed his face into Mercury's chest. "And he'll be the most beautiful dragon you'll ever see." His breathing evened out as he slipped back to sleep.

And that wasn't cryptically creepy, not in the least. Dane told his sarcastic side to shut up and focused on Nickel rolling his eyes in exasperation, as if Lumie interrupting his sleep like that was a common occurrence.

Dane had met plenty of seers and prophets in his lifetime; Lumie was neither. Dane couldn't say what Lumie actually was, aside from a red dragon with very strange magical powers, but he lacked the omnipresent air of someone who could see the future. There was only one way to see if Lumie did have a touch of prescience: wait for that egg to hatch.

Mercury resettled Lumie in his lap with a fond sigh, but before anyone could think of something more to say, Chrome walked into the room.

"I found him," Chrome crowed into what Dane recognized as his own damned cell phone. He had left the thing in his bedroom, in his own territory. Didn't any of these kits have some semblance of the territorial urge?

"Your pants were ringing," Chrome explained as he held the phone out toward Dane.

Dane took it from Chrome, but he didn't know what to say. Should he scold Chrome for going through his things or thank Chrome for actually bringing him the phone instead of eating it? Dane just held it up to his ear and said, "Hello?"

"Sounds like you're having an interesting weekend," Becky said. She was laughing at Dane.

"You could say that," Dane agreed dryly. He patted Chrome on the head before heading out of the room so he wouldn't disturb Lumie.

Becky continued to chortle. "Dragons, dragons everywhere, and not a spell to stop them."

"What do you want, Becky?" Dane asked, his temper fraying slightly. She wouldn't have called without good reason, and making fun of Dane wasn't a good one, no matter what she might think.

She sobered up almost immediately. "I was in the area, and since I wasn't sure if the office would be open tomorrow, I thought I might as well stop in to at least check the phone messages. There were two. The first one was from Mrs. Hempstead. According to her rather irate message, the creature that has been destroying her rosebushes pulled one clear out of the ground last night. She's refusing payment. I've already forwarded the case on to your lawyer."

That wasn't enough of a reason for Becky to have called Dane at home. Mrs. Hempstead was a minor annoyance. The centaur he employed as a lawyer would rake her across the coals without Dane's help. Dane waited somewhat impatiently for Becky to get to the point.

"The second message was from Mr. Jacobson. He is threatening to revoke your private investigations license over what he's calling false business practices. He's talking about having you arrested, Dane."

Now that was surprising. "Did he say why?" Dane asked, incredulous.

She snorted, so Dane took that as a no. "He babbled something about how you were supposed to apprehend the dragons, not move them. I'm not really sure."

"I see," Dane replied slowly. He thought he really did see. Those military-grade photographs hadn't been about identifying a target to take out. No, they were just about pure identification. It sounded to Dane like the enemy had wanted to know which dragons were running loose in order to tuck them back into the labs they had escaped from. Mr. Jacobson had clearly gotten far more involved than Dane had originally thought. "Are you still at the office?"

"Yes," she said immediately.

"Do me a huge favor and call Mr. Jacobson back. Act like I'm very concerned about his threats and that I want to make amends. Tell him I could still apprehend the dragons if he would like me to and beg for a face-to-face meeting so I can express my apologies in person."

Dane could practically hear her smug smirk through the phone line as she spoke. "Right away, sir." She hung up, and Dane turned his phone off and tucked it into his pocket.

"You're going to turn us in to the bad guy?" Chrome asked as tears began to form in eyes growing large with betrayal. He had followed Dane into the hall and overheard his conversation. Chrome sounded heartbroken as if Dane had broken his trust.

"I'm not," Dane insisted. He knelt to Chrome's height. "I'm making the bad guy think I could in order to get him to like me."

"And then Dane's going to bite him when he's not looking," Nickel said fiercely from behind Dane, who jumped again. How did these damned kits keep sneaking up on him?

"Biting is good," Chrome agreed. He hurried back into the bedroom, no doubt to explain everything he had just overheard to Mercury.

"I'm going with you to that meeting," Nickel said softly so Chrome wouldn't overhear another private conversation.

Dane was at a loss for words again. How did he explain to Nickel that he was still a kit and kits should be playing? Dane had seen Nickel play with a grasshopper and run around with his siblings; Nickel knew how to act his age and enjoy it. Yet the look in his eyes at that moment was cold and calculating. There was nothing childish about him aside from the fact that his body hadn't hit puberty. It was the face of a man who had hunted down his prey and killed it cruelly and without remorse.

All of the horrible experiments the scientists were conducting, stealing children and eggs and chemically and magically altering them for an unknown final purpose, were nothing in comparison to what they had done to poor Nickel. All of Dane's joking aside, no child should ever have that look in his eyes.

"I'll have to see what Mercury says," Dane replied finally. Mercury knew Nickel better than he did. Dane still didn't know enough about dragon development to be able to say for certain that Nickel wasn't old enough to handle it all. Lumie was barely a few months out of his egg, and he was walking and talking like a three-year-old human child. For all Dane knew, Nickel might be emotionally and mentally fully grown and was waiting for his physical body to catch up.

There had to be some information about dragon development that Dane could get his hands on. If the Internet didn't provide a reliable link, he was certain the library would have something. Dane needed to find that information before the kits drove him insane.

*

Monday morning rolled around without any further word from Becky. Daisy, on the other hand, had made it quite clear multiple times that Dane wasn't properly providing an adequate play area for the kits. His answer had been to point outside where the plants were flowering, animals were building nests, and bugs were creeping along just waiting to be pounced on. It was the perfect playground for younglings of many different species, and it wasn't Dane's fault that the kits were more interested in staying close to Mercury than going outside to enjoy it.

Daisy's answer hadn't been repeatable in polite company, but luckily her own brats had decided to catch a nasty stomach bug at school, and she had gotten distracted. Still, Dane knew that if he hadn't addressed the issue before she came back, she would blister his ears again. It also meant she wasn't able to come to his house to feed and clothe the kits. Lumie was sitting in his favorite spot on Dane's foot while 'Ron and Chrome waited impatiently at the table. Dane gave the oatmeal bubbling happily in the oversized pot on his stove another stir and mentally willed it to cook faster before the kits started eating his kitchen furniture. 'Ron's head barely reached the top of the table when she was sitting, and that, unfortunately, put her teeth at the perfect height to start chewing the luckily already-scratched wood. It had been a nice table before that werewolf cub had gotten to it, and although Dane could afford to replace it, should the kits get destructive, he didn't really want to have to make that effort. There were too many other things he needed to focus his attention on at the moment.

Finally, Dane deemed the oatmeal softened enough to be yummy and began filling the colorful plastic bowls Daisy had left in his kitchen. Dane added a spoon to each bowl and handed them out to the three kits. Luckily, Lumie decided to let go of Dane's foot so he could sit on the floor and eat. Dane filled two more plastic bowls and two regular ones, put them on a tray, and headed upstairs where the rest of the dragons were hiding.

Copper barely left the bedroom he had commandeered for himself. The incubator was tucked into a corner. Dane thought Copper put the egg there the few times he ventured out, but for the most part he and the egg stayed curled in a nest he had built of blankets and pillows on the full-sized bed. Dane knocked on the bedroom door first before opening it and stepping inside.

"I have your breakfast," Dane called into the darkened room. Two eyes popped open from the direction of the bed. They glowed slightly, reflecting the light in the hallway. Dane felt the magic in the room shiver briefly and watched as those eyes changed position on the bed as Copper shifted from dragon form to human. *His scales must have shredded my poor sheets*, Dane thought with a wince.

A boy with brilliant red hair and bright red scales covering his chest untangled himself from the blankets.

Copper hopped off the bed and strode quickly over to Dane, as if he didn't trust Dane enough to allow him near his precious egg even though Dane had held it briefly not too long ago. Copper was wearing a pair of loose pajama bottoms—red, of course—that Daisy had forced him to wear, and he took the red plastic bowl from Dane's tray without asking which was his.

"Thanks," Copper mumbled perfunctorily as he spun around and hurried back to his nest with his prize in hand.

"Make sure that ends up back in the kitchen," Dane admonished. He knew Daisy had been trying to instill some sense of propriety into the otherwise wild kits and that she would be appalled to learn Dane had allowed Copper to keep dirty dishes in his room.

Dane closed the door when he left and headed down the hall to Mercury's room. This time he waited for the okay after he knocked before he opened the door. Dane walked inside and shut the door behind him so the other kits would hopefully stay out. Nickel was sprawled on the end of the bed, and Mercury was tucked under the blankets. They both sat up and took their bowls. Dane sat in the chair still pulled up to the bedside and took the last bowl on the tray for his own.

"There's still no word from Jacobson," Dane began after everyone had had a chance to eat a few spoonfuls. "But I think I should go to the office anyway. He probably thinks that letting me sweat will make me more repentant and eager to do his bidding, so I want to be there to pretend anxiousness when he finally calls."

"Sounds like a good idea to me," Mercury replied after a moment of thought. "Bring Nickel with you," he added.

Nickel scowled, but he didn't argue. Apparently, they had already had this conversation. There was no way for Dane to know whether Nickel was coming along just in case Jacobson did get in contact today, or whether he was there to watch Dane closely to see if he was an enemy. Clearly, Dane would have to work hard to convince Nickel he was only going to help.

"Finish your breakfast; then change into some outdoor clothes." Dane knew Daisy had outfitted the kits with at least one pair of jeans and a few matching shirts. "Meet me in my office when you're ready." Nickel nodded in agreement, but he didn't get up to dispose of his empty bowl and get changed. Dane knew he would remain at Mercury's side until Dane left the room first or Chrome wandered in to take over guard duties. One glance at Mercury showed Dane that Mercury had noticed how overprotective his guard dog was being and that he didn't have the heart to send Nickel away. Mercury's beautiful lips were twisted slightly as he shook his head sadly when Nickel wasn't looking. Dane agreed completely. No kit should have to ensure such a heavy burden, yet Nickel did it like it was his duty.

Dane stood up first. He wanted to stay and speak with Mercury about something happier. He longed to see Mercury smile and Mercury's eyes light up again. Dane wanted Mercury as more than just a client or a friend, and he was pretty sure Mercury wanted him, too, but Nickel wouldn't allow Dane the private time to find out for certain. Dane doubted he would find that time until after Jacobson was dealt with and they had rescued the air dragons, at which point Mercury would be healed and on his way back home with his kits. It would be better for Dane if he found a way to push his lust aside and forget about being with Mercury altogether.

He would run screaming from Dane eventually anyway, just like all Dane's past lovers. Why put himself through that pain again, especially since he already knew Mercury would be leaving soon enough?

"I'll take your bowls back to the kitchen," Dane said, holding out his hand for Nickel and Mercury's empty bowls. They passed them over, and Dane stacked them on the tray before turning and leaving the room. His resolve would have to start now. Right this minute. He had to stop thinking about Mercury in a romantic sense. Instead, he thought about Nickel's face if he were to catch them in bed together and the murderous rage that would no doubt follow.

Dane was laughing softly to himself when he reached the kitchen. Three bowls had been left on the floor, and there was no sign of the kits who had left them there. Dane stooped to pick them up and stacked everything in the dishwasher. Copper hadn't brought his bowl down yet, not a surprising fact, so Dane waited to start the wash cycle.

Nickel met Dane in his office a few minutes later. Nickel was wearing jeans and a blue T-shirt, and it looked like Mercury had made him comb his blue hair. He didn't look nearly as wild now, Dane couldn't help thinking, except then he glared up at Dane. His eyes were still as serious as a serial killer's.

"Are we going?" Nickel snapped. He held out one hand imperiously for Dane to take so Dane could transport them both to work. How could Dane not obey his command? Dane took Nickel's hand while trying to hide a grin and pulled them both toward work.

Becky was already sitting at her desk when they arrived. She stood up with a wide smile when she saw that Dane wasn't alone.

"Who have you brought with you?" she gushed. Becky might have been a banshee, but she liked kids. She was too busy to help out at Dane's house like Daisy, but she never minded when Dane brought them to work.

"This is Nickel. He's waiting on the phone call from Jacobson with me."

"And the little one?" Becky asked. She walked around her desk and knelt on the floor. She was looking at Dane's feet. Confused, he followed her gaze to see Lumie. He had the thumb of one hand in his mouth. The other hand was fisted around the cuff of Dane's pants. Dane should have noticed Lumie. There was no possible way Dane could have missed him. Hell, even Dane's magic hadn't noticed that he was transporting a third person.

Lumie smiled happily up at Dane and gave his thumb another contented suck. That damned brat!

"I Lumie," he chirped at Becky with another smile.

Chapter Four

The kits could never stay away for very long. Mercury knew that. Even Nickel, his most independent kit, and Copper, his most aloof kit, had to stop by to see him at least once a day. All dragons had some form of separation anxiety thanks to the genetic behavior of parents abandoning their kits once they had physically grown enough to survive on their own. It was a terrible practice, but the territorial urges that all full-grown dragons experienced meant that parents would be just as likely to accidentally view their kits as territory intruders as protect them. Dragons spent too much of their childhoods alone, something his kits were all too aware of.

Mercury had learned to fly at nine years old and had been lucky enough to eventually wander into a city where he was tossed into the local orphanage. Too many kits died because of a practice that dragons couldn't help repeating. Nickel and Copper, for example, had barely been surviving in the woods when the enemy had taken them. 'Ron and Chrome were too young to have experienced that firsthand, but they had been through the government labs and were equally scarred. Dragon kits needed the chance to grow up. To be fed and clothed and hugged even after they had learned to fly. It was an issue Mercury had thought about asking whether the Genie of the East had a possible solution to, not that he had high hopes someone could change a territorial need. Besides, he had to save the dragons from the enemy first before he could even think of a more long-term solution.

Chrome and 'Ron ended up sprawled across his bed not even an hour after Nickel and Dane had left. 'Ron whined and crawled under the covers, her head resting on Mercury's knee. Chrome took up the end of the bed with a grumble.

"It's not fair!" 'Ron moaned. She rolled over, pulling the covers with her as she moved. Chrome snarled and yanked on the blankets to flatten them back out underneath him, which made 'Ron squawk and flail to move the blankets back where she wanted them.

Mercury let out a snarl and sent a pulse of magic through the blanket. Both kits froze in place. "That's enough," Mercury admonished. He preferred their antics to sitting alone and bored, but allowing them to continue would destroy the bedroom and might accidentally also destroy Dane's house.

Dane seemed very prosaic about the kits running roughshod around his house. Mercury doubted the banister would ever be the same, given Chrome's stories about chewing on it, yet Dane had not complained even once. Dane was such a beautiful man with or without his glamour, but Mercury couldn't help also admiring Dane's easygoing personality. Plus, Dane's fury—his eyes flashing with power and his fists clenched in anger—when Mercury had told him about the labs had been both deadly and stunning. It wasn't an image Mercury would ever forget, nor did he honestly want to. Beautiful men whose power was equal to Mercury's own weren't a dime a dozen. Mercury wanted to savor every moment and every memory so that when he was healed and had moved on with his kits, Mercury could take advantage of his fond memories of Dane in his few, private—kit-less—moments.

"Sorry, Daddy," Chrome and 'Ron both grumbled simultaneously.

"But it's still not fair!" 'Ron reiterated with another whine.

"What isn't fair?" Mercury asked, wondering if he was going to regret asking. 'Ron had complained about the fact that she couldn't hop like a frog just as fervently as when she was pointing out the poisonous snake Lumie was about to investigate.

"That Nickel and Lumie both got to go to the office with Dane. I wanted to go too!"

"And Lumie?" Mercury repeated sharply. He knew Lumie fairly well after watching over him for a few months and couldn't help wondering when Lumie had decided to go too. The real question Mercury had was whether Dane had noticed Lumie tagging along. And the answer was probably not. Mercury sighed.

Mercury knew that Lumie's powers were above average, so if something did happen, Lumie could take care of himself. Hopefully, Dane would also notice Lumie before Lumie got into trouble. Unfortunately, all Mercury could do at the moment was worry.

"If you ask nicely, Dane might bring you to his office next time," Mercury replied, hoping he wasn't putting words into Dane's mouth.

Chrome and 'Ron immediately brightened. 'Ron crawled up Mercury's chest and stuck her head out of the end of the blankets right below Mercury's chin.

"Really?" she gasped excitedly. "I have to tell Copper!" She bounced off the bed and dashed for the bedroom door.

"Wait for me!" Chrome yelled as he jumped up and ran after her. The door slammed shut behind them, leaving Mercury alone again. He groaned tiredly as he levered his body into a sitting position. Dragon fever sucked royally. Aside from the fact that he had probably been well on his way toward dying in the woods before Dane had rescued them, which would have left his poor kits alone and none of the other dragons saved, the recovery was a long and annoying process. He was a precious bronze dragon, strong in magic and body. His magic had recovered, of course, but he didn't have the strength or stamina in the rest of his body to handle the stress using his magic caused. He could barely walk to the bathroom and back.

He had made enormous improvement since he had made that first short journey, though Daisy had needed to support him back to the bed then. He could do it on his own now, but it rankled that Dane had promised to return in time to make lunch for the kits because Mercury couldn't even get downstairs to the kitchen. He couldn't take care of his own kits!

Mercury pushed away his depressing thoughts. He only needed a few more days to recuperate; he reminded himself. He would be back to full strength soon enough, and then he and his kits would leave Dane's house to continue on their journey. There was no need to impose on Dane for any longer than they needed to, even though they could, hopefully, continue working together against the government stooge hurting the dragons.

Yet the thought of leaving sent an unhappy pang through his chest. He would still see Dane, Mercury reminded himself, even if it wouldn't be multiple times a day.

Mercury threw his legs off the side of the bed with a snort of disgust and slowly levered himself to his feet.

Maybe a bath would take his mind off Dane's pretty face. He had been lying in bed for too long if he couldn't get his mind off the man he wanted to join him in bed. Dane was the Genie of the East. He had said he wasn't an actual genie, but to get that reputation he had to have a lot of influence and power in the supernatural community. He wouldn't need to stoop to Mercury's level to find a bit of pleasure; hell, he probably had dozens of lovers eagerly waiting for him. Mercury was a precious dragon, which meant his magic was far stronger than most other magical creatures, but even he wasn't a match for someone with Dane's overwhelming abilities. Dane wouldn't appreciate Mercury's infatuation, Mercury knew, and he tried to force that resolve into his brain where lust had taken over.

His progress across the room was slow, but steady. His feet were sturdier than his thoughts, to be perfectly honest. Mercury reached the bathroom doorjamb and leaned tiredly against it. His eyes saw the bathroom—the sink, toilet, and bathtub unchanged since his last visit—but his mind was still stuck on that morning, eating oatmeal with Dane. It was difficult to wait on an invalid and his kits, yet Dane hadn't seemed to mind the extra effort.

And, damn it, he was thinking about Dane again. Mercury stumbled the rest of the way into the bathroom and yanked on the lever to turn the hot water on in the tub. He spun back around to shut and lock the door. Only Lumie could get through that without making an inordinate amount of noise and damage, which meant Mercury had a private space for a few moments. He made sure the tub was filling and shucked his clothing, then sat down on the toilet cover to wait for his bath to be ready.

His scales were dull, Mercury noticed as he ran a hand down his chest. It was the clearest indication that he was still unwell—aside from the fact that he had to take a bath instead of a shower because his legs wouldn't hold his body up long enough to get clean. He wasn't looking his best, which was another reason Dane would never deign to look twice at him.

Mercury snarled at himself. He needed to get Dane out of his head! He was losing objectivity. His focus needed to be solely on finding and destroying the last of the government labs. He needed to save the dragons, not assuage his libido.

The tub was full, so Mercury shut off the water and carefully climbed in. It was nice and warm; the steam gently caressing his face as he leaned his head back against the wall behind him. The bar of soap was green and smelled faintly of jasmine as Mercury leisurely washed off his scales. The heat and the nice scent combined began to relax his tight shoulders. The bath could only be better if he had someone to massage the last of the tension from his muscles.

So much for forgetting Dane and moving on. Every thought led back to him; even the most mundane sent Mercury's mind spinning in the direction of the gutter. It was ridiculous, and yet, at the same time, it made Mercury all warm inside. He couldn't remember the last time he had felt this strongly about anyone. Who else had dragged his thoughts away from more important tasks, had made him lose himself so thoroughly? They needed to figure out a way to save the dragons, and here Mercury was, wondering how amazing Dane's fingers would feel pressing and caressing along Mercury's back in a massage.

Mercury snorted to himself and forced his mind back onto the task at hand: getting clean. He rinsed off the soap, glad to see his scales regaining some of their luster, and grabbed some shampoo for his hair. He desperately needed a haircut. He was so unkempt; between that, his unhealthy state, and his kits destroying everything, it would be no wonder when Dane did ask them to leave.

When he was finally clean, Mercury pressed the valve over the drain to let the water out. He carefully stood and reached for the towel hanging from the nearby bar.

The towels felt soft and fluffy as he dried off. The towel rack probably didn't appreciate him using it to stay upright, but he was quickly coming to the end of his endurance. The order of the day was to find fresh pajamas and climb back into bed. He needed a nap, and hopefully when he woke up again, his brain would be back in working order.

"Daddy?" 'Ron said as she knocked on the door. Mercury wrapped the towel tightly around his waist and cautiously stooped down to pick up his dirty clothes.

"Yes, 'Ron?" he called as he slowly made his way to the locked door. "I'm coming."

"There's a man outside on Dane's front lawn," 'Ron continued. "He doesn't look happy, and Chrome says we need to make him go away before he comes into our territory."

Sudden strength filled his legs as adrenaline shot through his system. He flipped the lock and threw the door open.

"Where's Chrome now?" he snapped.

"Getting Copper," 'Ron replied, her eyes filling slowly with tears at his harsh tone. "Copper can fly, so he can help!"

Mercury hugged her quickly in apology, but pulled away after a few short seconds. They might not have the time to spare for hurt feelings at the moment, depending on who was on Dane's lawn.

"Go to Copper and Chrome and tell them to stay put. I'll go check this guy out." Mercury gave her a little shove toward the door, and 'Ron obediently scurried off. He let the towel drop to the floor and pulled on the dirty pajama pants in his hands with a few sharp yanks that almost sent him toppling sideways. He had to hold onto the walls as he left the bedroom and walked in the direction of the grand staircase he could see just ahead.

There was a shivering feeling in the air that definitely wasn't entirely natural. The smell of magic was burning his nose. Mercury hadn't been able to explore the house over the last few days like his kits, so he didn't know what the rest of the house was supposed to smell like, but Dane didn't smell nearly so caustic, and dragon magic from the kits couldn't cause what Mercury was sensing. It felt tainted and unnatural, like the bitter aftertaste on the back of his tongue he always got from breathing inside a recently scrubbed and bleached bathroom.

He sensed the air flexing around him, like the tainted magic was pushing against a dome covering the entire house. The intruder was trying to breach Dane's shielding—the only viable explanation—and without Dane home to reinforce his shields, it was only a matter of time before the intruder broke through. Mercury had to hurry to find a place where he could see the intruder and make a stand, but his damned legs couldn't move any faster. He only needed a few more days to recover; couldn't the enemy have waited that long so he could trounce them properly?

Copper's door was firmly shut when Mercury stumbled past. He could sense Copper, Chrome, and 'Ron's magic behind the sturdy wood. Copper apparently could feel him, too, because a second after he had walked past the door, it swung open and Copper stomped out.

"They'll protect the egg," he insisted, although the way his eyes shifted uncertainly toward the door told a slightly more pessimistic story. "I can lend you my shoulder, even if I'm not strong enough to fight." He matched actions to words and slipped underneath Mercury's arm, forcing Mercury to lean on him instead of the wall. Mercury wanted to protest and send Copper back to his precious egg, but at the same time, he knew if he did Copper would be devastated. If he could send Nickel off with Dane, then he ought to also be able to trust Copper with his weight.

Copper was different than Nickel, of course. He had been glued to the egg for all the time Mercury had known him. He, Lumie, and the egg had all come from the same facility, but where Lumie had quickly identified himself as quite a personality over the last few months, Copper had hid himself away. Mercury honestly didn't know what Copper was capable of, but he was willing to find out.

He moved faster with Copper's help. The air felt oppressive and sick. It swirled as they passed through it, leaving behind nausea in the pit of Mercury's stomach. The tainted magic was growing. It was almost as if it was building up to something terrible. Mercury wanted to reach out with his own magic to see if he could figure out what was happening, but the thought of touching the tainted magic with his own sent a shiver of disgust down his spine. It would be better to look to see what was happening so Mercury didn't blindly waste his magical reserves.

The grand staircase opened into a furnished landing on the second floor. Large picture windows overlooked the extensive backyard. Mercury didn't see anything amiss outside those windows, so he let Copper turn them both toward the stairs. The banister continued down to the first floor and the entrance hall, where large, locked double doors centered the space. Above those doors was a massive window with veined edges and designs and colored glass in the shape of leaves and flowers, but the center was clear. Mercury could see a long driveway leading from the left side of the house through an expansive green lawn and out into the distant forest.

A man was standing in the driveway approximately halfway between the house and the forest. Mercury couldn't make out exact facial features from such a long distance, but he could see the snarling contortion the man's lips and teeth were in. It was almost as if he were growling at his enemy or holding in a scream of pain behind his clenched teeth. Maybe it was both. He wasn't physically moving forward, but if the tainted magic was his, then he was doing something.

Slowly, ever so slowly, the man lifted one of his feet off the ground and pushed it forward as if he were trying to take a step through a pool of molasses. It took a while and Mercury thought he heard the man scream, but eventually he completed one step forward. As his foot touched the ground again, Mercury felt his ears pop. The weight in the air vanished, but the touch of the tainted magic tripled.

Dane's shields around the house had fallen. It was the only explanation Mercury could come up with for the way the magic around him was reacting.

The man outside took two more steps forward. This time he was completely unimpeded. His grimace was replaced by a wide smile as he strode toward the house with confidence. Mercury saw death coming closer in that grin and knew he had to kill the intruder before he destroyed everything.

Chapter Five

Becky had sweets in the bottom drawer of her desk. Dane learned something new every day. After Lumie had introduced himself and Becky had finished cooing over him, she had reached into her desk and pulled out a large handful of candy. Apparently, the best way to get Lumie's attention was to bribe him with sugar, because he let go of Dane's leg and dashed to Becky's side as quickly as his little legs could take him.

Lumie had picked all the red-colored candy out of Becky's hand and was currently sitting on the floor in the middle of the office, carefully tasting each one.

"Any messages?" Dane finally asked Becky, tearing his attention away from Lumie carefully separating out all the red gummy fish from a packet of multicolored ones.

Becky was smiling at Lumie, but it faded as she looked up at Dane. He hated to remind her of the bad deal they were fighting with Jacobson, but at the same time as Lumie was in hog heaven—or was that fire dragon heaven?—Nickel was glaring a hole into Dane's back. Did it say something weird about Dane that he wanted to hug homicidal Nickel more than adorable Lumie? Probably, but Dane's messed up mental state wasn't a recent realization for him.

"Gregory called," Becky began. She flipped through a stack of papers on her desk until she located the message from Dane's centaur lawyer. "He wanted to know why you were sending him to hound an old lady and if you were going to give him a challenging case any time soon. I called him back and asked whether he had met the crazy old bat and her dog yet. When he said he hadn't, I told him to call and complain once he had." She put the paper aside and pulled another forward. "A Madame Boothby called. Her son is molting out of season, and she thinks he's allergic to something. She would like to hire you to find out what's causing it."

"Call her back and set up a meeting time next week," Dane replied. Nickel's glare was intensifying on Dane's back as impatience set in, but there honestly wasn't anything Dane could do until Jacobson called first. "Ask if she can bring her son with her as well as any medications or health spells he might be using."

"Of course," Becky began, but she turned away from Dane before she could finish her sentence. "Honey, I don't think you want to eat that one," she said in a gentle voice to Lumie. "That's a Cinnamon Bomb. I'm not sure you'll like it."

Lumie was holding a round, fire-red candy between two fingers. It was about a half inch in diameter. Dane recognized it as one of the candies he avoided if he wanted to have working taste buds for the rest of the day. Lumie sniffed it hesitantly, but before Dane could voice his own protest, Lumie popped it into his mouth. Lumie gasped at the initial taste—Dane was already cringing in sympathetic memory—and then Dane swore Lumie purred like a contented cat. Lumie dug through his pile of uneaten candy until he found a second Cinnamon Bomb, pulled it out of the wrapper, and stuck it in his mouth with the first one.

We have a winner! Ding, ding! Dane foresaw pounds of cinnamon candy in his pantry in the near future. Maybe finding a candy that Nickel liked would soften his disposition too? Dane would have to look into that at some point.

The phone rang, which made everyone except Lumie jump in surprise. Line two lit up. Becky let it ring a second time before hitting the button for the speakerphone.

"Supernatural Consultants. This is Becky speaking; how may I help you?"

"Is Dane there?" Jacobson asked, his voice barely more than a snarl as he spoke.

"Yes, he is," Becky replied, her voice still perky and happy even as she was scowling at her phone. "Give me a moment to redirect your call. Dane would like to speak with you personally." She reached out to hit the button that would send the call to the phone in Dane's private office, but before she could touch it, the call died with a hard click. It sounded like Jacobson had purposefully hung up on her.

Lumie moaned. Dane looked at him to see if Lumie was about to throw up Cinnamon Bomb all over his carpet, but Lumie was glaring at the door. Dane followed his gaze and saw a strange distortion. The lines of the door looked wavy as if they were made of water in a current. It wasn't natural. Dane reached out with his magic and slammed into a wall.

"There's a shield around the office," Dane snarled, reaching as far around him as his magic could go and running into the wall in every direction. It didn't feel like a normal shield to Dane. For one thing, it was actually blocking his magic. Very few creatures had the power to do that.

"It's not dragon magic," Nickel said slowly. His unsure tone made Dane turn to look at him. He was biting his lip uncertainly. Dane felt Nickel's water-based magic swell around him only to splash against the same shields Dane was stuck behind. "I don't think it's dragon magic," Nickel repeated awkwardly.

It wasn't dragon magic. Dane could tell that much. But then again, he was familiar with almost every kind of magic around the world, and he couldn't identify the shield spell. It could be dragon magic, then, only a form Dane had never encountered before. There were two types of dragons in the world, elemental and precious, but this magic didn't belong to either. It felt more elemental than not, but it also felt strangely tainted. It was almost as if someone who wasn't a dragon was using dragon magic.

Dane forced himself to stay still and keep his face blank as that realization rang true. Someone who wasn't a dragon, yet could still use dragon magic? Dane couldn't help looking at Lumie, who was swaying slightly side-to-side as he looked at the door, and at Nickel who was still trying to force his way through the shield with his magic. Dane had assumed those poor dragon kits had been experimented on so the government could breed a superweapon of some sort within the unhatched eggs. But it wasn't inconceivable that the labs had multiple purposes. Humans were the only creatures on earth who didn't always have magic. Some were born with it and some had the ability to learn it, but there were far more humans who never had an ounce of magic to their names. What if those labs were trying to genetically and magically change what humans could do? Dane didn't know why they had chosen dragon magic—he wasn't a scientist and he didn't know the ins and outs of genetics—but it explained Nickel and Dane's confusion.

All of Dane's swirling thoughts had passed through his brain in only a few seconds. Becky was on the phone with what sounded like Jacobson's long-suffering secretary. Jacobson wasn't available as he was out of the office, but hadn't he just called from there? Lumie was still sucking on his Cinnamon Bombs while staring at the wavering door while Nickel continued to batter at the shield with his magic.

"Nickel, stop. I can bring down the shield. Just give me a few minutes to finish gathering my magic," Dane told Nickel, mostly to get him to stop wasting magic and distracting Dane as water dripped from the ceiling. Dane always had a large supply of magic at hand in case of emergencies, but he would need more to bring down the shield. Dane's magic was slippery and hard to hold on to. That was the trade-off he suffered for being so powerful. Dane could do just about everything with his magic, but the more magic a spell took, the more difficult it was to perform. Breaking the shield spell would not be easy.

Dane had just started gathering magic when he was slammed in the chest with a magical backlash. Magic, his magic, returned to him abruptly as a large spell he had cast was shattered. It felt like a rubber band being snapped against his skin, only a hundred times more violent. Dane staggered at the impact and gasped in pain.

"What is it?" Nickel asked, before starting to worry his lip with sharp teeth. Dane could feel him gathering his magic again, although he didn't unleash it.

"The shields around my home were just destroyed. We need to break out of here fast." Dane no longer had the time to leisurely gather his magic together. Instead, he started grabbing it out of the air and shoving it into his storage reserves. It was painful, but Dane shuddered to think of what might be happening at home. Chrome and 'Ron were there, and they would be helpless against the sort of tainted magic Dane was fighting against. Dane didn't know Copper well enough to really say what he might be able to do, but he would die protecting that egg. And Mercury. Dane's heart leapt into his throat at the thought of Mercury, helpless in bed. His beautiful face contorted in rage as he fought against an enemy he didn't yet have the strength to defeat. Dane had to hurry.

"Up!" Lumie insisted suddenly, breaking Dane's concentration, which allowed for a string of magic to slip through his fingers and escape. "Up!" Lumie repeated. Lumie was standing by the twisting door with his hands in the air. He glared at Dane imperiously and waved his hands in the air as if he were waiting for Dane to pick him up.

"Not right now, Lumie," Dane replied through his teeth as he tried to regain the concentration he needed to gather magic.

"I help! Up!"

"I think he means the doorknob," Nickel gasped. He dashed forward and bent down so he could pick Lumie up. Lumie immediately reached for the door. His hands passed effortlessly through the obscuring spell, and his fingers wrapped around the doorknob. He turned the knob as hard as he could, and with a pop the shield dissolved.

It took Dane two strides to reach the door and another half second to ensure he had both kits safely in his arms. Dane's magic pulled them away from his office. They reappeared on his lawn just inside the edge of the forest. Dane didn't know what had happened at the house or where it was safe to land. He chose a spot and hoped for the best. The transportation spell faded away quickly, so he put Nickel and Lumie down.

A dragon roared, and the earth underneath their feet shook. Dane could sense magic running through the ground and the air. It felt like Mercury's magic, except it was thin and reedy. As a bronze dragon, he should be able to wipe the floor with any intruder, but he was still recovering from the fever. That he had held on this long spoke of his desperation to save his kits.

Dane ran out of the forest and out onto the open expanse of lawn. The first thing he noticed what that his house was still standing. The great window over the front door was shattered, but this wouldn't be the first time Dane had needed to replace it. The second thing Dane noticed was Mercury standing on the front lawn. He was beautiful in dragon form with his bronze scales gleaming in the sunlight. His snout was long and his teeth sharp. There were two horns on the top of his head and a line of deadly-looking spikes down the center of his back. Mercury was also as tall as Dane's two-story house with his leathery wings flared at full length.

Magic sparked through the air, Mercury's own battling with the tainted magic Dane recognized from the shield spell, and the ground shook again. A flare of sparks erupted between Mercury and what looked like a human man. That any human, even one with magic, could withstand Mercury's onslaught spoke of just how weakened Mercury was by his illness. It also probably said something about how strong the intruder was, but Dane wasn't feeling magnanimous enough to give him the benefit of his admiration.

A smaller, adolescent red dragon was creeping along to the intruder's left. Copper, Dane felt safe assuming, kept his body low to the ground and was moving soundlessly through the short grass. Dane felt a swell in fire magic mere seconds before the intruder was engulfed in a column of flame. Dane was still too far away to see the results, but he heard the intruder's scream and saw Copper's body jerk suddenly as he was flung violently away. The fire faded quickly as Mercury roared and the intruder staggered back a step.

An inexperienced eye might think Mercury and Copper were winning. Dane wasn't inexperienced. Copper was hurt, and he was too young to have full control over his powers anyway. The intruder was singed, but it wasn't life-threatening or even anything more than mildly distracting. Mercury's eyes kept closing and abruptly popping back open as if he were fainting from exhaustion and was staying conscious only through an extreme act of will.

Enough was enough. Dane stopped running and let his magic take him to where he needed to be. Dane reappeared between Mercury and the intruder with his hand pressed against the intruder's chest.

"Jacobson," Dane said sharply, looking at the government weasel he occasionally worked for. Jacobson gurgled helplessly in response, and his magic battered against Dane's as if he could actually get free. "Mercury," Dane continued as he studied the idiot in front of him, "get Copper and go back inside my house. I'll handle this."

Mercury moved at an achingly slow pace, but he obeyed. He clearly knew he had reached his limit and that getting out of Dane's way as he continued the fight was the better course of action. He was smart as well as pretty.

The stasis spell Dane had caught Jacobson in wasn't unraveling because Jacobson's magic, though strong, couldn't touch Dane's. Instead, Jacobson's magic was beginning to fray at the edges, which was odd. Dane looked closer, trying to identify the cause, and saw something Jacobson couldn't be aware of or he wouldn't be using magic so injudiciously. Magic had limitations. There were a few things that even Dane couldn't do. Jacobson's stolen magic's limitation was that it had a finite end, and it was powerful until the moment he reached that end. It was like a line of string. Jacobson could pull and pull until suddenly the spool was empty and there wasn't any more string to pull on. Dane helped it along, drawing on Jacobson's magic, dumping it into the ground as quickly as he could summon it from within Jacobson's body. Dane would have very green grass for the rest of summer.

"You injected liquid power into yourself?" Dane asked Jacobson as Jacobson struggled against him. Dane didn't expect Jacobson to answer, and he didn't even try. Instead, he kept trying to use his magic to stop Dane, which only unrolled the spool of power even faster. "I'm guessing it's still mostly untested, but you took some anyway in order to get back the dragons Quicksilver has been taking from you. I always knew you were too arrogant to understand you are not the top dog in our relationship. I never knew you were stupid enough to move against me." Dane's glamour had dropped when he was fighting against the shield around his office, but he let his power swell around them to prove a point as the spool of Jacobson's magic finally came to an end.

Jacobson gurgled at the end of Dane's stasis spell as his eyes rolled into the back of his head. Too late, Dane saw the green skull and crossbones hidden at the end of Jacobson's magic.

Foam dripped from Jacobson's mouth as his body jerked with seizures. It only took milliseconds for him to die. There was no time to combat the death spell someone had added to the magic injected into Jacobson's system. As a failsafe, it was ingenious. Jacobson wouldn't talk now.

"Damn it!" Dane swore. He tossed the body aside and let his magic take it away before it could touch the ground. Jacobson's body would be found eventually, but not today and not before all traces of what he had done to himself had fully dissipated. Dane didn't want any coroner's office to stumble on the terrible magic Jacobson had taken in and try to emulate it. Jacobson's magic needed to die with him, which meant Dane needed to find the lab where the testing was being done. Someone had added the death spell to Jacobson's magic. The idiot might not have even known it was there, although Dane wouldn't be surprised if Jacobson had known and had been foolhardy enough to think a little magic made him invincible. It meant there were additional people who needed to be stopped before more dragons were hurt.

Dane needed to go dig through Jacobson's office and home to find what information he had before his associates could hide it, but first Dane needed to get his own home back in order.

Copper was sitting up. One of his arms looked abraded as if the grass had given him a nasty case of rug burn as he'd slid across it, but otherwise he looked unharmed. Mercury was kneeling at Copper's side in human form, but his body was swaying back and forth like he was caught in a stiff wind. Copper reached out with his good arm to steady Mercury and was joined a few seconds later by Nickel.

Lumie was... Dane looked around and didn't see him until a small hand yanked on Dane's pants.

"Up," Lumie insisted. Dane bent and picked Lumie up and walked over to Mercury. As Dane walked, he formed his magic into a new shield for his home. He made it larger in diameter. Before, someone could walk along the edge of his wards and catch glimpses of his house. That was probably how Jacobson had known Dane had taken the dragons in; he had seen them playing in the yard. The new shield terminated well in the forest where no one could get a free show.

When they reached the three dragons, Dane passed Lumie to Nickel and bent down to pick up Mercury. Dane had one hand under Mercury's shoulders and the other under his knees—just like the last time Dane had carried Mercury—as he led the way toward the house. Mercury let out a tired sigh as he let Dane carry him. His head tilted on Dane's shoulder with his long hair gently brushing against Dane's neck.

Dane looked down, unsure of what he was expecting to see. Mercury's big bronze eyes were looking at Dane. There wasn't any calculation in Mercury's gaze. Once most people found out just how powerful Dane was, they always started thinking about what great things Dane could do for them. Except for Mercury, apparently. Dane also didn't see any fear, which was even more surprising. Mercury was just looking, taking in Dane's facial features and whatever expression he was wearing at the moment. In fact, Dane wasn't certain if he didn't catch a touch of lust there, although that could just as easily be from his libido playing with his imagination. Mercury's eyes slowly slid closed and his head tilted until he was using Dane's shoulder as a pillow, and then he fell asleep in Dane's arms. Dane had to swallow hard in reaction; the intimacy was almost too much for him to handle.

"Watch out for the glass," Dane warned the kits following him, trying not to get ahead of himself when it came to Mercury. What Dane thought he saw in Mercury's eyes might just have been delirium. There was no way Mercury felt safe enough in Dane's arms to relinquish control to him. There was no way Mercury wasn't judging him and his abilities and already planning his escape route. Too many other men in Dane's life had proven how relationships with Dane worked over and over again. They got what they wanted and then left, often in fear of what Dane could do. When Mercury woke up again, he would come to his senses.

Dane tried not to let himself dwell on any possibility that Mercury might somehow be different from all the others, but damn, it was hard. It had been so long since Dane had held a man in his arms and even longer since he'd had real feelings involved. Still, this wasn't the time or the place. There was too much to do to let himself drool over Mercury now. Once he was able to toss Jacobson's place and then start laying plans with whatever he found there, he could return to letting his foolish hopes dominate his thoughts.

"I need to follow up on Jacobson," Dane explained to the kits as they traversed the field full of broken glass and approached the front door. Dane would have to get a cleanup crew here before the kits got themselves hurt. "He might have information in his office or his house about where the air dragons are being kept. We need to get to it before anyone else does."

Copper hurried forward to open the door, and everyone trooped inside. The banister overlooking the foyer was shattered. It looked like Mercury had thrown himself in dragon form from the sitting room up there and through the front window in order to confront the intruder before he could get near the kits. Dane needed a new banister anyway, given how quickly Chrome and 'Ron had been chewing through it. Mercury had only accelerated the process.

They walked up the stairs and down the hallway. Copper's door was flung open as they got close and Chrome and 'Ron spilled into the hallway. 'Ron was crying and Chrome didn't look too far off from following her.

Chrome swallowed heavily to clear his throat. "Is Daddy okay?" he asked, his soft voice rough with suppressed tears. "We heard the glass shatter and Daddy yelling."

"He's fine," Dane reassured them both. "He's just sleeping. He worked too hard at keeping you safe. How's Copper's egg?" he asked to distract them. Copper had already slipped past them into his room to check.

'Ron looked proud of herself. "We held it tight so it wouldn't roll when everything started shaki—"

"It's hatching!" Copper screamed.

Dane couldn't help dashing forward, careful of Mercury slumbering in his arms as he fit through the door. The rest of the kits scrambled into the room around Dane. Copper was kneeling on his bed amid the nest of blankets and pillows. In the center was the red egg. It was rocking back and forth as a spiderweb of cracks formed and grew on the surface. It wasn't long before it was more crack than shell, and with a sudden pop, the shell fell to pieces around a dragon even tinier than Lumie.

The dragon blinked as it looked at everyone watching it. One eye was red and the other blue, Dane saw with horror. The dragon's scales matched. Some were red, others were blue, and even more had both colors swirled together as if a painter had tossed paint recklessly at a canvas and called it art. The oversized wings curled on the dragon's back were also swirled with both colors. There wasn't any purple on his body, so the colors hadn't mixed at all. It was beautiful, but terrible. Dragons didn't come in multiple shades.

It sneezed as the dust from the disintegrating egg fell around it. A gout of flame erupted from its mouth. Everyone instinctively jumped back, even Copper, despite the fact that his own magic should have taken care of any fire hitting him. The flame froze in midair and fell, shattering on the floor like an ice sculpture. The baby yawned next, curled up in Copper's nest with its head resting on Copper's knee, and then fell asleep.

"What's his name?" 'Ron asked softly. There was awe in her voice. She clearly didn't understand what those bastard scientists had done to the dragon. Fire and ice mixed together in one. It was unnatural, and yet she was right all the same. He was a dragon just like the rest of the kits. He had a terrible past and his magic was messed up, but then so was Lumie's, and Lumie was adorable.

"I don't know," Chrome whispered back, sounding just as reverent. "He's so pretty. Why couldn't my scales look like that?"

"Alloy," Dane decided, looking again at the flames melting on the floor. He was a mix of two different elements to create one whole: an alloy.

"Alloy," Copper repeated with a firm nod. He and Nickel were old enough to understand why Alloy was different, but they were young enough and stubborn enough not to care. Dane would have to emulate them, he decided. Yes, Alloy was a different sort of dragon, but Dane was a different sort of creature himself. Alloy had a difficult life ahead of him, but they could be his loving family and support him when things got rough. Dane had never enjoyed that luxury, so it would be nice to provide it to Alloy and the rest of the kits.

Which reminded Dane. "Let me put Mercury in bed. You guys stay with Alloy while I go after Jacobson's notes." He turned and left the room, heading farther down the hall to Mercury's room. Dane got him safely situated under the covers and forced himself to walk away. He wanted to climb into the bed with Mercury and hold him while he recovered, but Dane had a feeling that might get him punched in the face when Mercury woke up. Instead, Dane walked back into the hall and firmly closed the bedroom door behind him.

"We're going with you," Nickel said abruptly. Dane jumped in surprise and spun around. Nickel and Lumie were standing together in the hallway. Nickel looked stubborn, as if he was going to get his way regardless of what Dane wanted. Lumie was sucking on his thumb.

"Fine," Dane sighed. Mercury had wanted him to take Nickel with him anyway, and Lumie was Lumie. If Dane didn't take Lumie with them, he had a feeling Lumie would find some way to follow anyway. Dane walked up to them and bent to place a hand on each shoulder, and then he let his magic take them away.

Dane had snuck into the regional headquarters of the SupFeds before. The local government had wizards and other creatures on their payroll that had shielded the building, but these shields Dane could work his way through. With Lumie in tow, he didn't even need to try. The shields didn't register their presence. Once Lumie was old enough to fully understand how his powers worked, he really would be a formidable and dangerous person.

They reappeared inside Jacobson's private office. As the director of the SupFeds, he had all the privileges someone of his rank had earned, including a private office. A large wooden desk dominated the space. Dane zeroed in on the stack of files next to a sleeping laptop. Nickel wandered toward a large filing cabinet on one wall while Lumie toddled in a different direction.

The computer required a password to access, so Dane closed the top and tucked it under his arm. Dane had spells that would crack the laptop open in a few hours. The stack of papers was mostly red tape and trash reports that were passed around government offices to keep all the employees informed of various policies and events. Dane moved to the desk drawers next.

"Anything?" Dane whispered to Nickel as Nickel rifled through the bottom drawer of the filing cabinet. He wasn't quite tall enough to reach the top, although he had shattered the lock keeping the drawers closed.

"Unruly selkie," Nickel read slowly. "Mad werewolf. Nothing about dragons." He was probably reading the regular supernatural cases Jacobson was in charge of overseeing.

Dane turned back to the desk, pulling open the first drawer to find a stapler and other basic office supplies. The second drawer was just as useless, and after feeling both drawers for their dimensions, Dane realized there wasn't a secret compartment. He stood to go help Nickel when he noticed Lumie standing by a blank stretch of wall. Lumie was staring upward, thumb still in his mouth. His free hand reached out, and he slapped the wall in front of him. A panel popped open above his head. It had been so well concealed Dane hadn't even noticed it was there, but Lumie had seen it easily. The little scamp. Dane ruffled Lumie's hair as he hurried over to see what Lumie had found.

There was a small glass bottle full of a shimmering, rainbow-colored liquid on top of a pile of full file folders. Dane sensed a strange miasma to the liquid, like tainted dragon magic, which meant Lumie had found Jacobson's stash. Dane tucked the bottle into a pocket and the folders under his arm with the laptop. One last look through the compartment showed Dane had emptied it. He shut the panel.

"Do you see anything else?" Dane asked Lumie, who shook his head. Nickel had closed up the filing cabinet when he saw what Lumie had found. He also shook his head. "Then let's go to Jacobson's house and see if he left anything there." Dane took hold of both kits and let his magic pull them away.

Chapter Six

He's a god. That was Mercury's last thought before he had fallen asleep. Dane wasn't a genie; he wasn't any other supernatural creature Mercury had ever encountered, and there was a good reason for that. Gods didn't descend to earth very often, and when they did, they usually didn't stay and open up a consulting firm. But there was no other explanation for the sheer amount of power Dane had let off when he so decisively and easily ended the battle.

After that last thought, Mercury had fallen asleep. He had been too exhausted to stay awake and wonder. Now that he was awake again, Mercury still didn't want to think about it. Dane was beautiful and powerful. He was a god. He could have anyone he wanted. Why would Dane want a lowly bronze dragon who had spent most of their acquaintance asleep while his kits had done their best to drive Dane mad?

Instead of dwelling on the impossible, Mercury focused his attention on his surroundings. He was back in bed, warm under the covers, but he wasn't alone in the room. He could sense Copper as well as a dragon he didn't recognize. Dane and Nickel were in the sitting area near the bathroom door, their low voices filtering over to Mercury, although he couldn't hear what they were saying.

Mercury slowly opened his eyes and even more slowly sat up. He didn't feel any worse than he had the last time he had woken up in bed. His body still felt like it was recovering from a bad illness. His magic was also depleted from the battle, but it was slowly recovering with the rest of him.

"So you think it's a warehouse on the Chesapeake Bay?" Nickel asked Dane sharply, his voice rising loud enough that Mercury could overhear them.

"There's a good chance," Dane replied before their voices dipped lower again. They were bent over a stack of papers while a laptop smoked alarmingly next to them. Since the smoke was alternating between the colors of pink and orange, Mercury felt it was safe to assume Dane had a hand in whatever was destroying that poor piece of technology. Copper was sitting at the end of the bed. He was holding something, Mercury realized, and was looking at it avidly.

"What are you holding?" Mercury asked, wincing at how rough his voice sounded. He had been screaming during the battle, he remembered, as his spells fought against the intruder's encroaching magic. It was no surprise he was hoarse now.

Copper jumped in surprise, but he eagerly moved closer so Mercury could see. "This is Alloy," he explained, holding out the small kit so Mercury could see. "He hatched yesterday after the battle was over."

"Oh," Mercury gasped, looking at the red-and-blue dragon in shock. Alloy sneezed, and a piece of ice shaped like a flame fell onto the bedspread and started melting. "Oh," Mercury couldn't help repeating. Alloy was certainly beautiful, just as Lumie had insisted. Lumie stirred in the bed next to Mercury, not that Mercury had known he was there until just that moment. He was asleep with his thumb in his mouth.

Mercury reached out to run his hand down Alloy's scales, marveling at their color. He would curse whoever had done this to poor Alloy later. For the moment he enjoyed the fact that Alloy had hatched at all and that Copper had the little brother he'd always wanted.

"Dinner's ready!" Daisy's voice called from the hallway. "Anyone who wants to eat needs to come now!"

Nickel put down the papers he was studying with Dane and hurried to the door. Lumie also popped up, fully awake, and scrambled down the bed after Nickel. Copper carefully moved off the bed with Alloy in his arms and slowly left the room. After a few seconds, all of his kits were gone, leaving only Mercury and Dane.

"I think we've found the facility where they're holding the air dragons," Dane said softly as he stood and walked over to Mercury's bedside. "We're going to check out the site early tomorrow morning, before the employees come in to start work and end up getting in the way."

"I have to come with you," Mercury insisted. If there were any dragon kits there, he and Nickel were the only ones they would trust. They were more likely to attack Dane than listen to him.

Dane didn't argue, which meant either he had come to the same conclusion or Nickel had explained it to him. Before either of them could say anything more, the door opened and Daisy bustled inside. She was carrying a large tray with two equally large steaming bowls perched on top. She pushed the smoking computer aside with her elbow and placed the tray on the table in the sitting area.

"Up, out of bed," she said sternly to Mercury. "Ya won't get yer strength back lying there all the time. Ya can make sure he doesn't go splat, ya hear, Boss," she added to Dane before hurrying back out of the room to return to where she had left the kits momentarily unsupervised.

Mercury was hungry, and eating would help his magic and his physical strength replenish. He pushed back the covers and slowly climbed out of bed. Someone had dressed him in a fresh pair of pajama pants. He had shredded the old pair when he had changed shape. He had also destroyed Dane's front window, he remembered with a pang of guilt.

"I'm sorry for destroying your house," Mercury said softly. He had been so worried about what his kits were doing that he had never thought what he might do.

Dane just shrugged. "It's happened before, and I'm sure it will happen again. Don't worry about it."

Mercury's progress from the bed to the sitting area was slow, but he felt stronger than yesterday. It gave him time to think of a response. Once he was sitting and Dane had removed the papers and smoking laptop so they had the table to eat on, Mercury turned to Dane.

"You have to let me repay you for the damages," Mercury insisted. "I could have used the front door."

Dane passed over one of the bowls of stew and a large chunk of bread before replying. "I have a feeling if you had taken the time to use the door, the house wouldn't have been standing at all by the time I got here. Besides, I'm fairly certain you and your kits will do much worse to my poor house over the next few years."

"Years?" Mercury asked, unsure if he was hearing Dane correctly. Surely he didn't expect or even want them to stay for that long.

"Only if you want to," Dane added quickly.

"Want to?" Mercury repeated awkwardly. Did Dane want them to stay? Dane's shoulders had slumped at Mercury's words as if he was hearing rejection. He was practically hiding behind his bowl as if embarrassed for assuming Mercury would want to stay.

"I didn't think you would want us around for much longer," Mercury said, repeating his own thoughts out loud. "After all the trouble we've caused you, I would think you would want us as far away from you as possible."

Dane lifted his head away from his stew to look at Mercury. "I like having company," he said hesitantly. "And your kits aren't the worst critters I've had running around."

"Would you like us to stay?" Mercury asked boldly, suddenly aware that Dane didn't feel he had the right to ask Mercury that question. It was as if Dane was imposing on Mercury instead of the other way around.

"Would you want to?" Dane asked, his voice still hesitant and unsure. "I'm not exactly good company."

Dane wasn't talking about his personality. He also didn't seem to know just how devastating his smile could be to Mercury or about Mercury's thoughts on whether Dane would be very good company in and out of bed. He was talking about his powers, Mercury realized suddenly.

"I don't care that you're a god," Mercury insisted. It was the truth. He didn't care about Dane's powers in the least. All he knew was that he wasn't worthy of being Dane's companion. He was only a bronze precious dragon. Dane should find another god to love.

"I'm only the son of a god," Dane said sheepishly, "but that usually scares people away."

"Doesn't scare me," Mercury replied around a mouthful of stew. It was good stew, too, fragrant with spices and tender beef. Dane was blushing, Mercury noticed quickly as Dane turned back to his stew with a touch too much haste. "It doesn't," he reiterated. "I... You're too pretty to be scary." Mercury had almost said he liked Dane before he had caught himself. He wasn't ready to admit that just yet, especially when he had no business liking the son of a god.

Dane dropped his spoon back into his bowl and stared at Mercury in surprise. "I'm pretty? Have you looked in a mirror lately? You're the pretty one. I'm the one who has to hide behind a glamour so I don't scare everyone around me away!"

Mercury returned his own spoon to his bowl as he stared incredulously at Dane. "You don't look scary to me," he said softly, aware that he was apparently hitting a very sore spot by continuing their conversation. "I like you," he finally admitted. "If you weren't too good for me, I would prove it."

"Too good for me? It's the other way around! I'm the son of a god, so everyone runs away from me screaming in fear. I'm the one who's not good enough for someone as perfect as you! Mercury, I know all the negative stereotypes about dragons, but you embody none of them. You are proof that dragons are far better than the stigma they've been stuck with."

Mercury shook his head in denial. Surely Dane's words couldn't mean what his heart hoped they did. Yet Dane was leaning forward, and Mercury felt his own body responding without reference to his brain. Their kiss wasn't earth-shattering. Mercury didn't see fireworks or feel faint. The press of soft lips against his was just that, and yet it was so much more. Dane was kissing him! Dane, who shouldn't be having amorous thoughts about a lowly dragon, had chosen to kiss Mercury.

It was an affirmation of reciprocal feelings and that made the kiss so much sweeter. There would be fireworks and shaking earth later, Mercury knew, but for now it was enough to know that Dane liked him back. He pressed harder into the kiss, wanting to indicate his interest and excitement without words. Dane whimpered and tilted his head so they could get a better angle.

The door slammed open, and Nickel hurried into the room. Mercury and Dane jumped apart, Dane reaching for his stew almost reflexively, but his cheeks were still pink and his breathing slightly heavy. Mercury's own breath wasn't exactly even either, but he tried to hide it from his kit.

"What do you need, Nickel?" Mercury asked.

"Miss Daisy was feeding Alloy, and he burped. I thought you should know the kitchen is on fire and the oven is melting."

Mercury jumped to his feet, but he was a touch slower than Dane. "I'll handle it," Dane said. He placed his hand on Mercury's shoulder as he passed and squeezed a little more tightly than was strictly necessary before letting go and hurrying out of the room to save the rest of his house from dragon destruction. They would finish their conversation later, Dane's touch told Mercury. Nickel cast Mercury a suspicious glance—his kit didn't miss much, did he?—before following after Dane.

*

The warehouse at four in the morning didn't look any different from any other warehouse at any other time Mercury had ever seen. Still, Dane and Nickel were certain that the air dragons were being kept inside. Mercury hadn't had the energy to go through Jacobson's notes, but he trusted Nickel and Dane. He believed them even more when he saw the first high-tech security camera a block away. These were dock warehouses; places rented to sailors going crabbing in the bay. There was no reason for more than a cursory security system.

Water splashed behind them from the Chesapeake Bay, hitting the concrete cement wall of the long pier. The air smelled fishy, damp, and generally unpleasant. There were places to dock boats along the wall, but all the spots were empty. It was still dark out, and there wasn't any security lighting. The moon was long set, and dawn was at least an hour away.

Mercury let Dane zap the cameras. He was staying on his feet well enough, but his knees were still shaky. Mercury wanted to conserve his strength for later. Nickel had his game face on and was clearly ready for anything; Mercury could do no less, even though he still wasn't feeling his best. Dane's spell on the cameras was supposed to show a constant loop of the last twenty minutes instead of their bodies as they walked up to the warehouse. On the long wall closest to the water were three oversized garage doors, no doubt ordinarily used to store boats. It was a safe bet that they were firmly locked, as was the lone door on the short end of the warehouse. Dane squinted at the door, and not only did the lock pop, but the door slid open.

No one yelled in surprise inside. Mercury also didn't hear running footsteps as someone watching came to investigate. Dane waited to make sure no one was coming before stepping into the building first. Mercury felt a subtle swell of magic as Dane dealt with whatever cameras and other security measures were inside. Nickel hurried forward next, able to move faster than Mercury. He vanished inside only steps ahead of Mercury who was quick to follow.

The warehouse was completely empty. The floor was solid concrete, the walls corrugated metal except where the garage doors broke up the monotony. Mercury could see a half-dozen cameras along the roof, but there was no other sign that the warehouse was in use. The air smelled stale as if no one had been inside for a long time.

"This is the right place," Nickel insisted as he walked farther into the room. His voice echoed in the empty space. Dane's magic ruffled Mercury's hair almost playfully as it swept through the room. It bounced back just as easily as Nickel's voice. A little too easily, considering how strong Dane was. Mercury called on his own magic, but instead of letting it sweep the room, he let it creep along the walls and across the floor.

The walls were plain metal, but the floor wasn't uniform. His magic rolled over cement everywhere except for the far left corner where it felt like wood. Mercury hurried over and bent down to feel with his hands what his magic was telling him.

"There's a trapdoor," he explained to Dane and Nickel who had followed him across the warehouse. The door was colored the same gray as the concrete, and Mercury didn't feel any hinges or a handle. Either there was an electronic hinge underneath that they didn't have the switch for, or someone with magic knew how to remove the door.

"Let me," Dane said as he knelt next to Mercury on the floor. His hands brushed over Mercury's for a brief moment, sending a shiver down Mercury's spine that was completely inappropriate for the time and place, before they flattened against the surface. He pulled upward, but kept his hands pressed flat with a touch of magic. The door came free with a screech of metal grating against metal. Dane tossed it aside so they could all look down. A stepladder was set up below them, leading down into a dark hole of indeterminate length. It wasn't wet despite its depth and the proximity to the bay, but a little bit of searching told Mercury that the construction crew had had a witch on staff when the concrete was poured. The spell was an old one; it might predate the enemy taking control of the warehouse, but there was no way for Mercury to be certain. "I guess we have to go down," Dane sighed. He was staring into the dark hole with a look of disgust. "Nickel, we need you to stay here and guard our retreat."

Nickel grimaced, but he didn't argue. He wasn't being shuttled off on a chump job. Mercury knew that, and Nickel was also smart enough to know how important guarding their exit was, especially when they didn't know who else might be coming to deal with any air dragons hidden below. A rear guard was necessary. Nickel didn't have to like being left behind—Mercury could tell he didn't like it at all—but he would do it and do it well. Nickel backed away from the trapdoor, putting his back against the wall so he could see the main door, the garage doors, and the trapdoor without being ambushed from behind.

Dane stepped onto the ladder and began to descend. His magic flared and light appeared below his feet.

"Stay safe," Mercury admonished as he waited for Dane to clear the ladder.

Nickel grimaced and flexed his fingers, water magic swirling around him. "Let them try me," he growled. Mercury grinned at him and then followed Dane down the ladder into the depths of the warehouse.

The ladder was seventeen feet high, about one story, and Mercury was on the ground beside Dane quickly. Dane held a small ball of light in one hand, which revealed that they were in the terminating end of a long white hallway. The space was unadorned and otherwise unremarkable. They followed the hallway slowly, watching for any potential traps. It led underneath an adjacent warehouse, which made Mercury wonder just how large the facility might be, and eventually opened up into a pleasant sitting area. The walls were still a uniform white, but the couches were a tasteful shade of blue. They were situated around a low coffee table. There weren't any magazines or coffee mugs lying around. In fact, if it weren't for the couches, Mercury would have thought the building to be long since abandoned. They had made more than enough noise opening the trapdoor, and stepping onto the hard metal of a marginally stable ladder wasn't exactly quiet. Someone should have come to investigate the noise.

"They've abandoned the facility," Dane murmured, echoing Mercury's own thoughts. "They've already got what they wanted."

"What about the dragons?" Mercury replied, fear tightening his voice. The enemy had wanted the dragons to create their magic serum. Now that their goal was complete, they didn't need the dragons they had been experimenting on.

Dane grimaced, no doubt his own thoughts echoing the morbid direction Mercury's had been taking. "There's only one way to find out."

The sitting room had two more doors along two separate walls across from where they were standing. Dane chose one at random and pulled it open. It led into a steel and glass lab that looked modern to Mercury's admittedly ignorant eyes, just like the labs in the last three facilities had looked. There were machines everywhere, although none of them were beeping or lit up like they'd been in the previous active labs. Dane tossed his ball of light toward the ceiling to illuminate the room. It was empty of people and dragons, and there weren't any other doorways. Dane moved the light around to ensure they could see every corner. In the center of the room was an incubator with one white egg nestled into the lining. Mercury gasped and hurried forward, but skidded to a stop the second he came close enough to see what had been done to the poor egg.

Some idiot had drilled a hole through the shell. They were probably either planning to inject or remove something for one of their horrible experiments. What they didn't know was breaking the shell so heavily destroyed the magic that allowed the kits to grow properly. A small needle's pinhole wasn't large enough, but the one Mercury saw in this egg was the size of a silver dollar. The poor kit had died almost instantaneously, at least, and hadn't had to suffer any longer. Mercury turned away with a growl of disgust and stalked from the lab.

The other door in the sitting room was shut as well. Mercury flung it open angrily, but had to wait for Dane to catch up with the light before he could see what was behind the door. The light revealed another hallway, although this one was much shorter than the one where the ladder had been. There were five heavy metal doors on the right and blank wall on the left. Four of the doors had been left open, but the fifth at the very end was closed tightly.

They looked like cell doors, something Mercury confirmed when he glanced inside the nearest one and saw a small cot on one side of the five-by-five space and an even smaller toilet on the other side. He couldn't help glancing into each open door as he passed, just so he didn't miss anything, but they were all empty. Only the closed door at the end was different.

A heavy bar kept the door secure. Dane helped Mercury lift it and toss it aside, but he let Mercury pull the door open on his own. Light shined into the small room, illuminating the same small cot and toilet. It also revealed a small figure wrapped in a threadbare blanket on the bed.

The figure slowly sat up and let the blanket pool around her waist. She had the white hair and gray eyes of an air dragon and the tight look caused by fear and torture that Mercury remembered from Nickel and Copper's faces when he'd first rescued them. The older the kit, the more scars they had accumulated in the facilities. The girl looked like she was also seven or eight years old, the same age as Mercury's older kits.

"They said you might come," she rasped. Her voice was beyond hoarse, as if she had been screaming for hours and days with no one to hear her.

"They did?" Mercury asked, hoping for a clue as to who had kept her here while also trying to act friendly so she would relax enough to trust him to bring her to safety.

She nodded in response. "They said they were leaving me here and either you would come and get me or I would die. They didn't care which, but they thought it would be interesting to find out whether you would find me in time."

"I'm glad we found you in time," Mercury replied, but he shared a sharp look with Dane as he spoke. The enemy had to be watching the warehouse if they wanted to know whether Quicksilver could save the helpless kit. She had been locked up and left to a horrible death of starvation all so the enemy could get a read on Mercury and Dane.

Which meant they knew Mercury and Dane were inside the facility. They had to get back to Nickel, now, before something terrible happened. "It's time to get you to safety."

He held out his hand for her to take. Mercury wanted to lunge forward and grab her, then make a run for Nickel, but if he scared her now she would never learn to trust him.

"What's your name?" he asked when she hesitated.

Finally she pushed the blanket back and swung her legs over the edge of the cot. "I'm Zinc," she replied, "and I don't think I'm strong enough to stand right now." She put her feet on the floor and then grimaced. "I've been alone for a very long time."

There was no telling when they had abandoned the facility. It had been twenty-four hours since Dane had killed Jacobson and almost four days since Dane had snatched them all from the woods. Zinc was just a kit, and she had been deprived of food and water for far too long. Of course she didn't have the strength to stand.

"Do I have your permission to carry you?" Mercury asked, hoping that none of his impatience leaked into his voice.

"Yes," she whispered, her words choking and halting as she forced them out. "Please get me out of here."

Mercury stepped forward and gathered her into his arms. She was far too light for a kit of her age, but his weakened legs still protested. Despite that, Mercury gritted his teeth and carried her out the cell door, down the hallway, and out into the sitting room.

"There's magic in the air," Dane warned with a hiss when Mercury would have continued blindly hurrying to the hallway that led to the ladder. Instead he froze in place and let his magic search out what his eyes couldn't see.

There was magic in the air, he quickly confirmed, and it smelled destructive. *Like a bomb*, his brain supplied unhelpfully.

"I think we need to run," Mercury gasped, following his words with actions. His legs found new strength as he dashed through the sitting room and into the long hallway, Dane hot on his heels. The magic continued to swell around them, but it soon became mixed with more familiar water magic. Nickel had fought or maybe was still fighting above them. Mercury's legs moved even faster as fear for his kit buoyed his adrenaline. He reached the ladder in record time, but he couldn't climb with Zinc in his arms.

"I'll go first," Dane said. He climbed the ladder, no doubt unwilling to teleport into the unknown situation above, and vanished through the trapdoor.

The ground started shaking underneath Mercury's feet while he waited for Dane to reappear. It took a few seconds, during which time Mercury's heart started beating double time. What had happened to Nickel that Dane was taking so long? But then Dane reappeared. He was lying on his stomach with his head and arms through the trapdoor.

"Pass her up," he called. Mercury lifted Zinc upward. She reached for Dane until their hands clasped, and Dane pulled her up and out of sight. The floor was shaking even more now as if an earthquake was rumbling by. Water dripped down from the trapdoor as Mercury started climbing the ladder. It was wobbly, rocking side-to-side with the movement of the earth. He had to shift his weight to compensate so the ladder didn't tip, which made it even harder to climb. He tried to hurry, but he also didn't want to slip.

Dane's head reappeared above Mercury when he was only halfway up the ladder. He held his hand out for Mercury to take once he got high enough to reach. Dane's light was flickering as the earth-shaking magic continued to grow. The light abruptly went out just as the most violent shudder yet rippled through the floor. The ladder tipped and Mercury gasped, unable to see where to put his feet to keep himself upright. He lunged upward blindly, grasping for Dane's hand or anything that would get him out.

For a few seconds, he was certain he was dead. He was going to fall hard on the cement floor below, the ladder would fall on top of him, and then the ground would collapse and bury him in an unmarked grave—unless the water from the bay rushed in and drowned him first. There was nothing but air beneath his fingers until, suddenly, skin met skin with a hard clap. Fingers clasped around his wrist, and Mercury couldn't help desperately digging his nails into the hand holding him up.

"I've got you," Dane gasped. "Just hold on."

There was light above him. It illuminated Dane's face, wild even with his glamour in place as crazed fear twisted his features into something almost alien. It also showed the open square of the trapdoor. Dane pulled Mercury upward until Mercury could reach out with his free hand to grasp the edge of the door and finish pulling himself safely away from the long drop below him. He collapsed into Dane's arms when he was back on the solid concrete of the warehouse floor. He wrapped his arms around Dane's waist without thinking as he held on tightly and panted for breath with his eyes squeezed closed.

It took him a few long seconds to realize that he wasn't the one shaking. Yes, he was still shivering in remembered fear, but the warehouse itself was swirling with the destructive magic that had taken down the ladder and almost killed him.

"We have to go!" Nickel yelled—not for the first time, Mercury realized. He pulled away from Dane and pushed himself to his feet, firmly ignoring the way his knees and hands were trembling. Dane also jumped up. He bent to grab Zinc, who had been sitting at Nickel's feet while Dane rescued Mercury. The door was too far away, given how strong the magic around them had grown. Dane waved one arm and the nearest garage door was flung back. Mercury heard it splash into the water of the bay, and he hurried after it. He stepped outside and kept running. Metal screeched and Mercury heard the low rumble of the ground collapsing, which only made him move faster. How far until they reached the outside of the spell's zone of destruction?

Dane came up behind him, wrapped his arm around Mercury, and grabbed Nickel, and magic pulled them away.

Never before had the front lawn of a house looked so damned inviting, but Dane's house with the awkwardly boarded-up window and the torn grass from Mercury's claws was a welcome sight.

"That was fun," Nickel lied darkly with a growl.

"What...what happened?" Mercury asked. He slowly slid to the ground as his knees finally gave out. Dane slid to the ground next to him, and Mercury couldn't help leaning against him for support.

"Three of them tried to jump me," Nickel grumbled. "As if that's enough to catch me. When they failed, they left. I guess they decided that if they couldn't take me in, they would let me die with this kit," he finished with a wave of his hand toward Zinc. She was looking around them with awe in her shining eyes. Mercury didn't want to know how long it had been since she had seen the sky or any trees. He really, really didn't, yet at the same time he knew he would eventually have to ask her for all the information on their enemies she could provide.

"Why would they try to capture you?" Dane asked, curious.

"He's one of the original kits," Mercury replied when Nickel just scowled heavily. "Eggs are always guarded by their parents, but kits are left to run around as they please. We think the scientists originally grabbed a few kits from each element for their initial experiments, and only once they got a little braver, and perhaps a little stronger thanks to their first experiments with stealing dragon magic, were they able to start working with eggs. Nickel, Copper, and probably Zinc, too, were all also changed and strengthened by those original experiments. The enemy would take any of them back in a heartbeat if they thought they could."

"Yet they left Zinc behind to die?" Dane asked.

"I was bait," Zinc answered pragmatically. "I also wasn't the only older dragon there. Platinum was taken when they cleared out the facility. They didn't need me anymore." Which meant there were still dragons in need of rescue.

"We'll go through Jacobson's notes again. See what we can find," Dane insisted, no doubt reading Mercury's fears on his face.

"There's nothing else there," Nickel snarled. "We've been through them enough times that even I know that. That warehouse was the only viable location he mentioned." Probably for a reason, Mercury realized, since it set up such a convenient trap.

The front door of the house was flung open before anyone found a reply. Chrome and 'Ron rushed out.

"You're back!" Chrome yelled happily. "Why'd you bring back a girl?"

"Yay!" 'Ron exclaimed. She skidded to a stop in front of Zinc. "Hi, I'm 'Ron. Who're you?"

"This is Zinc," Mercury explained when Zinc appeared to be overwhelmed with 'Ron's exuberance. "She needs food and a bath. Will you make sure she gets both?"

'Ron immediately reached out to yank on Zinc's arm. "Come on. I'll show you the kitchen. We can't use the oven, but Miss Daisy left lots of cereal to crunch." Zinc let herself be pulled to her feet, but she stumbled at the first step and fell back into the grass. Nickel sighed, but he lent Zinc his shoulder as they headed into the house.

Mercury turned to look at Dane now that they were alone and found Lumie standing between Dane's legs. Dane's look of disconcerted surprise was priceless.

"You'll get used to it eventually," Mercury said with a laugh. He reached out to pull Lumie into a hug.

"Cin Bomb?" Lumie asked, looking at Dane expectantly.

Dane laughed and reached out to ruffle Lumie's hair. "I don't have any right now. I'll give you two in the morning, okay?"

Lumie tilted his head as he thought this offer through, then nodded. He pulled out of Mercury's arms and followed the other kits into the house.

Now finally and actually alone, Mercury let himself relax exhaustedly against Dane's shoulder. "I don't want to think right now," he insisted. He didn't want to think about the enemy or the dragons they still held captive. He didn't even want to think about the growing possibility that he and Dane might be starting a relationship of sorts.

"So don't," Dane replied with a shrug that nearly dislodged Mercury. "You're still recovering. We don't know where to find the next clue to the enemy's location, which means there isn't anything more we can do today. Let's eat something and go to sleep." He hesitated, then turned his body so Mercury was leaning against his chest instead of his shoulder. When Dane bent down, Mercury was happy to surge upward. Their lips met, and this time Mercury definitely saw fireworks.

Of course, that might have been caused by whatever had also made a terrible crashing noise from inside the house. 'Ron was screaming in fury and Chrome laughing hysterically, so Mercury didn't worry. It was just business as usual for his kits. He pressed his lips against Dane's one last time before sighing and climbing to his feet.

"I think it's naptime for some unruly kits too," he grumbled, stalking into the house with Dane beside him.

Epilogue

Mercury was still sleeping when Dane's alarm went off first thing Monday morning. All Dane wanted to do was curl closer to Mercury's warm body. Maybe Dane could wake him with a kiss, or by doing something even more fun, but the clock told Dane that if he didn't get into the shower now he would be late, again, and Becky would laugh at him, again. Besides, Dane wasn't going to wake Mercury even with a kiss until after he had ensured that Lumie wasn't hiding somewhere. Searching for Lumie required that Dane get out of bed anyway, so he climbed out from under the covers, but his shoulders were slumped the entire way into the bathroom.

It hadn't taken long to convince Mercury to switch bedrooms and join Dane in the other wing of Dane's house. Mostly it was that Mercury wanted to share his life with Dane, which included sharing a bed, but the fact that all of his kits had rooms on the other side of the house had also played a part in his decision. Dane couldn't resent Mercury for that given how much magic Dane was using to ensure they didn't bring his house down around their own ears. Zinc had fit right in with the insanity, of course. She and Copper were in some sort of feud, which only made Mercury snicker and say something about Copper combining with Zinc to make Brass, which made absolutely no sense.

Dane finished his shower and toweled dry quickly. He got dressed in the dim bedroom while Mercury slept on. Dane couldn't leave without at least saying goodbye; he walked over to Mercury's side of the bed, leaned over him, and pressed his lips to Mercury's.

"Mmm, morning," Mercury rumbled as his eyes blinked slowly open.

"Morning," Dane replied. "I'm about to go get breakfast. Want to come?"

"Not a chance," Mercury replied immediately without even glancing at the clock. "You have fun. I'll see you tonight," he added with a grin that made butterflies flitter in Dane's belly.

"Your loss," Dane joked, but he let Mercury go back to sleep without protest. Dane had to pause by the door to gather himself before opening the door and heading downstairs to the kitchen.

Lumie was standing in the middle of the kitchen waiting for Dane. When Dane walked in, he immediately held out his red plastic bowl. Lumie's favorite cereal had a lot of cinnamon in it, not that Dane was in any way surprised when he learned that fact. Dane dug it out of the cabinet and the milk out of the fridge. He filled Lumie's bowl and handed him a spoon before turning back to the cabinets to find his own bowl and cereal.

"You coming to work with me again?" Dane asked as he filled his bowl with cereal that contained a lot less sugar than Lumie's did.

"I think we both are," Nickel answered as he joined them in the kitchen. Nickel was determined to find the missing dragons and had apparently decided that working as Dane's sidekick at Dane's consulting firm was the answer. Lumie was Lumie; Dane had no idea what, if anything, went through his head. Sometimes he joined Dane at work with Nickel, and other times Dane didn't see him for an entire day. The kits certainly made Dane's life interesting, which he couldn't complain about in the least.

When they finished eating, Dane helped Nickel and Lumie rinse their bowls and put them in the dishwasher. Mercury and Daisy were working on teaching the kits how to do chores in order to instill some sense of responsibility into the otherwise crazy creatures. It was a fool's errand as far as Dane was concerned as Copper, Nickel, and Zinc were barely old enough to understand why, but Mercury persisted with it, so Dane had to support his efforts.

Lumie latched onto Dane's leg, his arms and legs wrapped around Dane's ankle as he used Dane's foot for a seat. Nickel just put his hand on Dane's elbow. Dane let his magic sweep them away. They reappeared inside Dane's office a moment later.

A new, child-sized desk had appeared in one corner of the room a few weeks ago. Dane didn't know when Becky had gotten it, but it was covered with Nickel's paperwork. Becky had him doing research for some of Dane's own cases, which he tackled with the same persistence as he had his continuing search for the dragons. Lumie also detached himself from Dane's leg. He hurried over to Becky and stuck one hand out.

"There's a man on hold on line two," Becky told Dane as she dug into a candy jar that had also appeared on her desk in recent weeks. "He insisted on waiting until you got to the office." She turned to Lumie as Dane walked into his private office. "What do we say?"

"Please!" Lumie chirped with a grin. Becky immediately grinned back and dropped a wrapped Cinnamon Bomb into Lumie's outstretched hand. "Thanks!"

"You're very welcome, Lumie," Becky replied.

Lumie took his sweet off to a corner to suck on. Dane closed his office door, sat in his plush chair, and picked up the phone.

"This is Dane. How may I help you today?" he asked politely into the receiver.

"My name is Ames Stockton. I'm the regional deputy director of the Federal Bureau of Supernatural Investigations. As I'm sure you saw on the news, the body of Miles Jacobson, the regional director, was found last week. Your agency comes highly recommended in these sorts of issues, and I was wondering if we could hire you to supplement our own investigation." Stockton's voice was deep and graveled. Dane thought he had met Stockton once at a SupFeds convention. He was a big man with deep black skin and sharp eyes. Dane didn't remember Stockton being as idiotic as Jacobson. If he was the one promoted to director, which was very possible, Dane could expect a very different relationship between the SupFeds and his firm. Dane needed to tread carefully here, yet he was also holding back ironic laughter. Not too long ago he remembered thinking to himself that Jacobson's successor would be calling to have Dane investigate Jacobson's death. Dane never thought at the time that he would be the one who killed Jacobson, or why.

"I'm not going to take that case," Dane began. There was no way he was going to investigate himself, but he couldn't leave Stockton hanging after their first business conversation. Dane still wanted Stockton to call back with a different case. "But I will give you some free advice. Have you read the news reports on the magical earthquake that destroyed a large part of the pier along the Chesapeake Bay about two months back?"

"I have," Stockton replied slowly as if he were wondering where Dane was going with this and why.

"Some stations and papers have also started reporting about one warehouse where what appears to be a lab and some jail cells were hidden below," Dane continued despite Stockton's growing distrust.

"Those news agencies believe that the government has been hiding the fact that they've been doing illegal experiments on dragons." Stockton's voice sounded scathingly disbelieving.

"Those news agencies aren't wrong." Something Dane knew they had gotten correct because he was the one who had leaked that tidbit of information to them. "All of Quicksilver's attacks on government labs have been to save dragons that were being experimented on in secret. You might want to look into Jacobson's involvement in those labs as I'm certain that is why he was killed."

"Experimenting on dragons," Stockton scoffed. "You really expect me to believe that?"

"When you find the connection between Jacobson and those labs, I would appreciate it if you could forward me a copy of those findings. I'm trying to find the rest of the dragons they have imprisoned."

"Why do I think you had a hand in Jacobson's death and now you're trying to distract me from the truth with this fool's errand?" Stockton snarled. The phone clicked as he hung up on Dane.

Dane sat back in his chair and smiled. Skeptic or not, half correct or not, Stockton would still have someone look into what Dane had said if only to disprove him. When Stockton found the evidence, he would call back. Dane had no doubt of that.

With that handled, Dane pulled forward the paperwork Nickel had left him for Madame Boothby and her molting son. Spending the afternoon trying to figure out how to tell her that her son was experiencing the normal male pattern baldness that came with hitting middle age was going to be an interesting and aggravating task for the afternoon.

Luckily, Mercury was waiting for Dane at home. Dane smiled involuntarily and picked up the phone to call Madame Boothby's secretary to set up a meeting.

DRAGON

DECEPTION

Chapter One

"A picnic?" Dane repeated, looking down at Lumie and Alloy's eager faces with skepticism and disbelief. These were Mercury's outlandish kits. Why couldn't they have waited to ask Mercury when he got home? Daisy, once his part-time housekeeper and more recently his and Mercury's full-time nanny, was at a parent-teacher conference for her own kids, so she wasn't a possible savior for at least five more minutes. Dane couldn't stall that long, and Mercury hadn't yet gotten home from work. It looked like Dane would have to save himself. "Why a picnic?"

"You and Daddy work too much," Lumie explained solemnly as Alloy nodded in agreement. "You go, relax, and the answer will come to you."

"Like magic!" Alloy chirped eagerly.

Lumie and Alloy were in a neck-and-neck race for which kit was Mercury's strangest. Alloy should win for his looks alone. Unlike most dragons, he had hatched with two powers: fire and water. All other elemental dragons could only use one element, but Alloy was different—and that difference was reflected on the outside too. In human form, he had one red eye and one blue. His hair and his scales when he was in dragon form were an even mixture of the two colors. That the red and blue hadn't mixed into purple was odd, but Alloy actually enjoyed having two colors.

Alloy was the result of a cruel experiment done by humans looking to harness dragon magic for their own selfish use. One day Dane was going to crush those humans, as soon as he could find them, but that didn't mean he couldn't love the results. They had made Alloy into something different, something special—but even he wasn't as special as Lumie.

Lumie was also the result of experimentation. He looked normal for a fire elemental dragon. His hair in human form was flame red, as were his eyes. His scales in dragon form were a universal red as well. Whatever had been done to him wasn't reflected on the outside, but rather with his magic. Lumie had fire magic like all dragons of his kind, but he was also impervious to the magic of others. He could walk through wards that would stop Dane without feeling a twinge and sneak around Dane's house without Dane knowing he was there. Sometimes Dane wondered if Lumie was prescient as well, but since he didn't walk around prophesying all the time, Dane couldn't say for certain.

Both boys were five years old, although since Alloy liked to cuddle and play while Lumie had grown to be more aloof, it often felt like there were multiple years between them. They were just two of Mercury's seven kits, all adopted. Unlike the kits, who were all elemental dragons, Mercury was a bronze precious dragon. His kits were all young dragons he'd rescued from secret government labs. It was unusual for dragons to mix between elements, never mind between elemental and precious, but they somehow made it work. All of the kits— even Lumie and Alloy—were beyond the age most adults would allow them to share territory, but Mercury wasn't most adults. He, and now Dane, were committed to raising them to full adulthood. Which meant occasionally entertaining the whims of five-year-olds.

Dane could tell that Alloy and Lumie were both eager to help, given that they continued to stare expectantly at him, and he found himself unable to say no.

"Tomorrow," Dane said, caving into their wide puppy-dog eyes. "Mercury and I will have a picnic lunch. Will that be okay?"

They cheered and smiled. "I have to tell Copper!" Alloy exclaimed, spinning on one heel and dashing out of Dane's office door. Dane could hear him yelling Copper's name all the way down the hall.

"I'll make sure you have all the right picnic foods ready," Lumie said before he followed Alloy at a much more sedate pace. Dane hid his grimace until he was certain Lumie was gone. Lumie and edible foods weren't exactly synonymous. He liked food with cinnamon in it, the more the better, and he couldn't quite grasp the fact that other people would throw up and die if they ate as much as he did.

Also, what were the chances that Lumie actually knew what foods belonged in a picnic? Pretty low, dammit. Maybe Dane could order a pizza and sneak it to the picnic spot without Lumie noticing. That way Mercury and Dane would be able to eat something and Lumie would still be happy.

It would take some finagling to get a pizza past Lumie, since he noticed everything, but Dane wasn't the son of a god for nothing. He would find a way or, knowing Lumie, die trying. Mercury would need to be warned, too, Dane reminded himself. Still, that was a problem for tomorrow. Dane had a lead on his current case that he wasn't about to let grow cold.

Two weeks ago, a mother dragon and her three very young kits had been attacked. She managed to get safely away with all three kits, but her mate was badly injured. He sent word to Dane, since Dane had made it widely known over the past five years that he was very interested in helping any dragon in need. The enemy had left the father dragon for dead, uninterested in a full-grown dragon when they had three kits to snatch. Dane needed to find the kits and their mother before the enemy did and get them to safety with the still-healing mate.

Dane's newest lead was from a werewolf who'd stopped by Dane's office to tell Dane about the strange bag lady he'd run into two nights previously. It had been the full moon, so some of what he had seen was a little shaky in his memory, but he clearly recalled a harried-looking woman wearing what looked like two dresses and three coats pushing a shopping cart through the woods where he and his pack were hunting. He remembered three children in the cart, he told Dane, but none of them had smelled like prey, so he and the pack had moved on.

Either that was the mother dragon ineffectively trying to hide by wearing human clothing, following customs that she didn't quite understand—she was a wild dragon from the forest, not one taken in as a kit by humans like Mercury had been—or Dane had a lamia hunting in his territory. A lamia would need to be destroyed at once before she started eating children, so it was imperative Dane locate whoever the werewolf had seen.

Dane pushed his chair away from his desk and stood. He couldn't do anything more from home, and his kits were in Daisy's care. The answer was somewhere in that forest. Dane had already done one grid search of the area, but this time he would widen his search. It was impossible to keep three young dragons corralled for long. Dane knew that from experience; Lumie and Alloy hadn't been easy to deal with when they were only a few months out of the egg, not that they were any easier five years later. The missing kits would have caused a mess somewhere that their mother couldn't hide. Dane just had to find it, especially before the enemy did. Dane heard Daisy talking in the kitchen, so he knew the kits were being supervised and he could leave to continue his search.

Magic came to his call easily, and as Dane walked forward, he let it pull him away. The first step was on the hard floor of his home office, but a second later his feet crunched on leaves as he walked into the forest. The trees above were showing off their autumn colors of red, orange, and yellow, while the leaves on the ground were turning an ugly shade of brown. They hid the paw prints from the werewolf pack that Dane remembered from his last time here a day ago, but autumn was really starting to progress now and many of the tracks he had followed before were obscured. Dane hoped fervently there would be new tracks now.

He directed his magic to send feelers out around him, allowing him to sense more than his eyes could see alone. The magic delved up into the trees and down hills. Dane used it to dig underneath large piles of leaves so he wouldn't have to search them by hand. He wasn't searching for dragons like Lumie, who had been experimented on and therefore had the ability to hide from magic at will. These were ordinary, wild elemental dragons. When Dane got near them, he would know. He would also know if he found a lamia: their magic was even more distinct than a dragon's and always felt slightly warped to Dane. Any creature that did something as vile as eat children pinged wrongly on his magical radar.

The sun was setting earlier and earlier as winter approached. Soon it was difficult to see the difference between a pile of leaves and other debris and what was simply a shadow thrown by the trees. It was even more difficult thanks to the irregular shapes of the trees overhead. Some of them still had all of their leaves while others were nearly bare. The worst were the trees that had only lost half their leaves; they threw both bulky and barren shadows, their strangeness catching Dane's eye.

He spent two hours walking a large grid, back and forth through the forest, while his magic swept an even larger grid around him. There was plenty of evidence of the werewolf pack. Fallen leaves hid the visible evidence of footprints and claw marks, but Dane could sense lingering pack magic around the trees. Anyone with a hint of magic would be able to sense that the woods were owned and know to stay away. Which would tell a dragon with territorial urges to pass through quickly and quietly, of course.

Dane froze in place and called himself eighty different kinds of stupid. How had he missed something so obvious? He shouldn't be trusted with helping an old lady get her cat out of a tree, let alone saving dragons from an unknown enemy. Hell, Dane shouldn't even be allowed to leave the house if he kept making stupid mistakes.

Two days of exhausting work wasted, all because Dane hadn't bothered to think.

Elemental dragons, like the mother and kits he was searching for, would immediately know they had encroached on someone else's territory. When Dane's werewolf contact had seen her on the last full moon, she was probably trying to get out of the werewolves' hunting ground as fast as possible. And Dane, in his idiocy, had confined his search to the hunting ground. Dane would have been amazingly, impossibly lucky to find the tracks of a shopping cart underneath all the leaves, but he had kept up with his wild goose chase for far too long. The dragons were an additional two days ahead of him, and Dane doubted the enemy had made the same stupid mistake he had.

Dane needed a map and he needed to begin figuring out where he should have been searching. He strode forward and let his magic pull him away again. Dane reappeared at home in his office and hurried over to his desk where his laptop sat waiting for him.

He almost sat on Lumie before Dane noticed he was sleeping in Dane's desk chair. Lumie was upside down, his messy red hair flopping toward the ground while his feet were hooked over one of the armrests. His thumb was firmly planted in his mouth. Lumie had grown a lot in the five years Dane had known him, but Dane knew the one thing about Lumie that would never change was how strange he was. He was odd even for a dragon, but that honestly only made him more loveable. It also made him one of the more annoying kits living under Dane's roof, but it was an annoyance Dane was happy to live with.

Instead of waking him, Dane took his laptop and left his office. All the wards that kept everyone else out were still up and running. Dane double-checked them as he softly closed the door behind him and stepped into the hall. An ominous crash sounded from downstairs before Dane could move more than a few feet down the hall toward the bedroom he shared with Mercury. He rushed into the bedroom and dropped his laptop onto the sitting table by the fireplace in the corner, then turned around and quickly retraced his steps until he reached the stairs.

No one was screaming and Dane didn't smell smoke, but that didn't always mean much in his household. Dane reached the kitchen and Daisy wordlessly pointed to the set of double doors that led to the dining room. He followed her directions and pushed through the doors. The centerpiece of the room was a massive sixteen-seater oak table. It had been flipped over, and the sixteen chairs had been scattered around the room. Dane sent his magic toward the table and lifted it in one swift motion, hoping he didn't find a squashed kit underneath. When Dane didn't see blood, he rotated the table and put it back where it belonged. He sent his magic after the chairs too. As Dane flipped the last chair into place, he found Alloy clinging to the cushion.

The room had looked like a giant gust of wind had blown through it, which meant Zinc, the lone air dragon living under Dane's roof, was the culprit. Alloy would have to serve as Dane's witness.

"Alloy, what happened?" Dane asked, kneeling on the floor next to him. "Are you okay?"

Alloy popped his blue eye open, saw who was talking to him, and opened his red eye too. "Are Zinc and Copper done yelling at each other?" he asked.

"For the moment," Dane replied with an inward sigh. Their flirting had been cute when they were eight years old. Now that they were thirteen and hormones were making them even stupider about it... Dane didn't understand how Mercury could laugh over the sheer amount of destruction they caused. Dane was really glad Copper hadn't been the one to lose this round. Instead of flipping the table, he would have set it on fire.

Since Dane couldn't hear anything else getting smashed around the house, he felt it was safe to assume that Copper and Zinc had concluded this particular fight. Or they had taken it outside and were busy destroying his lawn. That was also possible.

Alloy sighed in relief and climbed off the chair. "Okay. It's time for dinner anyway." He grinned and wandered off in the direction of the kitchen. Dane followed. There was research to do, but leaving Daisy alone with all the kits when he didn't have to was cruel. She usually left right after cooking dinner so she could spend the evening with her own family, but was staying later tonight because she had started work today after her kids' parent-teacher conferences.

Daisy had set plates along the kitchen island where Dane had bought high stools for the kits to sit on. Lumie, 'Ron, and Chrome were already seated and waiting eagerly for dinner to be served. Alloy climbed onto his stool next to Lumie. Copper's stool was still empty, but he would be joining them soon, as would Zinc and Nickel.

'Ron and Chrome were both earth elemental dragons. They were nine years old and they shared the same brown hair and eyes, but the similarities ended there. 'Ron had embraced being a girl from the very first moment Daisy had introduced her to dresses, and now 'Ron was looking forward to puberty so she could start filling out. Chrome had decided to embrace being a boy instead. He wore ratty shirts and played every sport he could, and 'Ron avoided him like the plague, something Mercury insisted meant that he and 'Ron were eventually going to have a lot of kits of their own together. Mercury said that a lot, though, and Dane wasn't entirely certain he believed him. Then again, dragons were a bit odd when it came to finding their mates. If Mercury thought that 'Ron and Chrome would realize they had that connection after puberty, Dane knew Mercury would encourage them to be happy together. It wouldn't matter to them or to Mercury that they were being raised as siblings. They weren't related by blood, and the mating bond trumped adoptive family ties.

Nickel was the most serious of Mercury's kits. He was a water dragon with blue hair and eyes, and he had made it his mission to personally rescue the dragons. Nickel was Dane's assistant at Dane's consulting firm, and he worked there every day instead of staying behind to play with Copper and Zinc, who were both his age.

Daisy clicked her tongue unhappily at the empty seats, but she started serving food to the kits that were present. Her green skin was bright and vibrant, which meant the parent-teacher conference had gone well. Her own kids were a handful, too, which only meant that she was experienced enough to handle Dane's. He had doubled her salary when he invited Mercury and the kits to live with him permanently, and she had obligingly doubled her work hours.

"Lumie, are ya done in the kitchen tonight?" Daisy asked once everyone present had been served, Dane included. Dane usually waited for Mercury to get home to eat on the few nights he had to work past dinnertime, but it was nice to eat with the kits on occasion too.

Lumie nodded. "I made everything for the picnic," he insisted. "I'll put it in the basket tomorrow." Lumie had done the cooking? Dane suppressed a wince and a groan. He was five years old, for Pete's sake. What the hell was he doing cooking a picnic for Mercury and Dane? And how horrible would it taste? Ordering a pizza to eat instead of Lumie's picnic was sounding like a better idea every minute.

Nickel strolled into the kitchen just moments after the food was served. He was reading from a packet of papers, either schoolwork or, more likely, casework from Dane's firm as he took his stool. Daisy frowned pointedly at him, and Nickel tucked the papers away and let 'Ron draw him into conversation. Copper and Zinc slunk in moments later. They wouldn't look at each other, and their stools were on opposite sides of the kitchen island. Copper immediately started grilling Alloy about his day. Copper was essentially the one raising Alloy, not Mercury or Dane, and he took being Alloy's big brother very seriously. Zinc pulled her long white hair away from her face and joined 'Ron and Nickel's conversation.

Daisy had been trying to teach the kits table manners, but even though they all managed to use a fork and knife to eat, they stuffed their faces quickly and dashed off.

"Bath time!" Daisy yelled after Lumie and Chrome, who both ran out of the kitchen pretending they hadn't heard her. Daisy sighed, but collected dishes from the counter. "I'll catch up with the scamps," she insisted when Dane stood and began helping gather the dirty plates. "I'm sure ya still have work to do."

"I don't know what I would do without you," Dane told her seriously. With both Mercury and Dane working, there was no way they could have raised all the kits without Daisy's help. "How were your parent-teacher conferences?"

Daisy sighed. "Good. My brats are passing middle school, although Jeremy wants to take up football." Dane winced, thinking about her rambunctious kids running around learning to tackle people. It would only be worse if Chrome were the one who wanted to play. Dane made a promise to himself to never let Chrome even try. Although Dane couldn't get any of his kits into school at all.

Nickel had heard just how long the school day was, asked Dane how he was supposed to get any work done when he was stuck in a horrible classroom all day, then informed Dane that he wouldn't be attending. Luckily Dane had gotten a compromise out of Nickel that he would study for three hours every day with a tutor Dane had hired for him and spend at least one hour every night on homework. Once the other kits had learned that Nickel wouldn't be attending school, they had also refused, but thanks to Nickel's compromise, they spent the better part of the day in a classroom. When Mercury, the tutor, or Dane could catch them first, of course. Dane was going to make certain that they would all get their GEDs at the very least.

"Yeah, it's a mess," Daisy finished, echoing Dane's own thoughts closely, "but I'll figure it out. Now, ya git. We've both got stuff that needs doing." She was smiling as she made shooing motions, so Dane allowed himself to be pushed from the kitchen.

He walked up the stairs and turned toward his bedroom where he had left his laptop. Dane could hear splashing from one of the bathrooms down the other wing of the house, so at least someone was obeying Daisy. Probably 'Ron or Zinc. Nickel would finish his work first while Copper would avoid the water for as long as Daisy let him. Daisy would have to catch Lumie and force him into the water, and Alloy's bath depended on whether he was embracing his fire or water half that day.

Dane left them to it and headed into his bedroom. His computer was where he had left it, so he settled into one of the armchairs, popped it open, and called up a map of the Great Appalachian Valley. It stretched from Alabama all the way up into Newfoundland. Dane's territory was a small part of that. He controlled from north of the Mason-Dixon line—although his territory did stretch down the Chesapeake Bay into Maryland in a few places, so that wasn't exactly an accurate description—and ended at the Canadian border. Dane watched over the Northeast primarily, the boundary of which depended on which map he looked at. Some said the Northeast began in Virginia and followed the coast to Maine; others said it began in Pennsylvania; and yet more insisted it was everything east of New York, which was essentially New England. Regardless, in Dane's opinion, north of the portions of Maryland that he controlled was all his.

The werewolf's pack territory was in the Lehigh Valley in Pennsylvania. The mother dragon wouldn't have traveled south or west, as an extremely territorial Minotaur had set up his maze in the mountains there. She couldn't have gone east because she would have run into human civilization, the very creature she was running from. Which only left north. Given the amount of time she had been on the run and the distance Dane calculated she could have traveled with three kits in tow, she must be in the Hudson or the Mohawk Valley in New York. It was a large geographic area, but aside from the lone cat shifters setting up small territories throughout, there wasn't anything to keep her from feeling safe. Therefore, this was the most logical area for Dane to resume searching. He would start walking a grid in the Hudson Valley, keeping away from the suburbs of New York City, and head toward Albany. She and her kits had to be somewhere in between the two big cities.

First thing tomorrow, Dane would start walking through the valleys.

"Almost done?" Mercury asked, leaning over Dane's shoulder to look at what he was researching. Mercury's long bronze hair brushed Dane's arm as he settled his chin on Dane's shoulder. Dane loved the way Mercury looked with his full lips, small and pert nose, and his thick lashes over his bronze-colored eyes. Mercury's hair was also a beautiful bronze color that echoed the large scales that covered most of his body.

"Yeah," Dane sighed. He had his starting point, so he didn't need to keep looking at maps. Going out searching in the dark in those mountainous woods was dangerous. Dane had to at least wait for first light.

"Good," Mercury breathed. He tilted his head and took the point of Dane's ear in his teeth. "Because Daisy has Lumie in the tub right now. She's running the water faster than he can evaporate it, but they'll still be a while."

Which meant that they didn't have to worry about Lumie walking through the wards and locked bedroom door and seeing something he shouldn't. Dane grinned and shut his laptop, then turned his head to take Mercury's mouth in a proper kiss. Sometimes it was awkward finding time to be together, but Daisy had informed Dane that he was only living the hell of any parent. In a way, it made the time they did find together more special.

Dane loved Mercury, and it was nice to know Mercury loved Dane too, even after five years together.

Chapter Two

Mercury reclined on the pillows, happy to relax in bed. Dane was tracing circles on Mercury's stomach with two fingers. He wasn't glowing any longer now that the fun had ended, but he hadn't put his glamour back on. His long blond hair was splayed behind him in tangles. The color of sunshine, it mesmerized Mercury if he looked at it too long. He preferred to get lost in Dane's eyes, but the blue orbs were closed as Dane fought to even his breathing. Instead, Mercury reached out to run one finger along the pointed tip of Dane's ear, jingling one of the silver rings pierced through the cartilage.

"Lumie wants us to go on a picnic during lunch tomorrow," Dane said out of the blue. He opened his eyes to look at Mercury. There was a pinched line between Dane's eyebrows that made Mercury laugh. Dane was very worried about what Lumie had planned.

"Sounds like fun," Mercury replied with a shrug just so he could see that line deepen and Dane frown. "I can leave work for an hour around one o'clock."

Dane saw the smile on Mercury's face and buried his head in a pillow with a groan. "It's Lumie's picnic. Something is going to go wrong," Dane insisted. He peeked one eye out to look at Mercury, who couldn't help laughing even louder.

Lumie was a menace, admittedly, but it was far too much fun watching Dane try to handle Lumie's quirks.

Dane was smart in that he knew offending Lumie wouldn't end well for him, and trying to dance around the delicate line between upsetting Lumie and appeasing him was going to slowly drive Dane insane. Mercury was enjoying every moment of it, and he thought Lumie might be too.

"You're sure you can get off work?" Dane asked hopefully after a moment of thought.

Mercury's smile grew at the plaintive note in Dane's voice. Dane was an amazingly powerful person, both in magic and personality, and a five-year-old dragon had felled him.

"I've taken lunch at my desk while working for the past few days," Mercury explained, much to Dane's consternation. "No one will complain if I leave the office for a bit tomorrow."

Mercury still wasn't entirely certain how he had gotten a job with the local division of the SupFeds, also known as the Federal Bureau of Supernatural Investigation. He had applied on a whim, joking with Dane at the time that he would make an excellent spy inside the SupFeds to see if they still had any hand in the dragon abductions and cruel experiments. Mercury never expected to be called in for an interview and was even more surprised when he was offered the job.

He was a low-level analyst whose job was to comb through alleged supernatural crimes to find out which ones actually had magic or a magical creature involved. The various police departments in the region handled most local crimes, even the supernatural ones, but it didn't hurt the SupFeds to stay abreast of what was going on. Mercury looked for patterns, repeat offenders, and crimes with enough magic that the local police wouldn't have the resources to handle them. Then he passed everything he found to analysts higher on the food chain. This job meant that he recognized when a dragon in distress caused a disturbance, and he did break his security clearance to point Dane in the right direction.

Sometimes Mercury thought he had been hired so the SupFeds could prove how diverse they were in their hiring practices. He was the only dragon on staff, and the vast majority of his colleagues were human. Other times Mercury wondered if they were using him to watch Dane. Someone had to know that Dane wasn't a mere human or an ordinary supernatural creature, and once they had realized that Dane was involved with Mercury, they probably thought they could somehow keep better watch on Dane's activities through him. Mercury wasn't certain whether that meant they thought he would disclose information about Dane—which he wouldn't—or whether they just wanted a firmer connection with Dane. Mercury wondered if they also realized Dane was using Mercury to keep a better watch on them in return.

"Yay, we're going on a picnic," Dane deadpanned with a heavy sigh. "You bring Lumie's picnic basket, and I'll sneak us a pizza."

"You don't think Lumie's picnic is going to be delicious?" Mercury asked. He couldn't help teasing Dane. It made Dane's beautiful face scrunch in the most interesting expressions of disconcertion and disgust.

"Lumie cooked it himself," Dane groaned. He buried his head in the pillow again as he spoke. "There's no telling what's actually in it or whether anything will be edible. I think Daisy just left Lumie to it and only supervised enough that I wouldn't need to replace another oven."

"It'll be an adventure," Mercury declared. Dane just grumbled incoherently into the pillow.

It certainly would be, Mercury knew. Dane was right: there was no telling what Lumie had put into the picnic basket. It could be something dangerous or poisonous for all he knew. Yet, if they ditched the food somewhere and got a pizza instead, Lumie would somehow know and hate them forever.

"So how did your search go today?" Mercury asked, hoping that changing the subject would get his own mind off of his fears over Lumie's picnic.

The pillow covering Dane's face didn't move, and Dane's breathing halted for a long moment. It was almost as if Dane was embarrassed, which wasn't an emotion Mercury saw from him a lot. He mumbled something so softly that Mercury couldn't hear what he said through the pillow.

"What?" Mercury asked. This time he kept his smile in check. As funny as it was to see Dane out of his element, the topic was far too serious to tease him over. They had to find those dragons before the enemy did.

Dane slowly pulled the pillow away. "I'm a fool," he repeated scathingly. "The mother dragon wouldn't stay in pack territory. She moved on while I've been uselessly searching the wrong area."

Mercury hadn't thought of that either. It was common sense that a dragon would want to leave someone else's territory as quickly as possible, and Mercury hadn't thought to mention it, or honestly even thought of it at all, the last time Dane had mentioned his search.

"So you were figuring out where to restart your search when I interrupted you?" Mercury wiggled his eyebrows to let Dane know exactly the type of interrupting he meant. Dane's grin was a little sharp as memory quickly surfaced.

"I've got it all figured out. Now, come here so I can figure you out too."

Mercury laughed and let Dane pull him close. Mercury bent down to kiss Dane, and when Dane's hand landed on his back, Mercury smiled.

*

Dane put on his sturdy boots with his outfit that morning while Mercury was contemplating actually wearing a tie. His kits would tug on it and choke him. Besides, he only wore a tie when he had a meeting with his boss. Wearing it today just because he was going to take a long lunch would probably raise some red flags.

Mercury got away with dodging the business professional dress code because he growled at anyone who mentioned it to him. It probably fell under some species awareness law, so the HR department couldn't force someone of another species to conform to human standards. He tossed the tie he was holding on to the back of a chair with a growl of disgust and left it where it lay. He was wearing a pair of nice dress pants and a collared shirt, which was good enough as far as he was concerned.

They both went down to the kitchen together for breakfast. Lumie and Alloy were waiting for them. Both kits were holding their breakfast bowls in their hands and standing patiently, hoping for someone to come and help fill them with food. Lumie had just allegedly cooked an entire picnic, yet he couldn't get the cereal down from the cabinet and pour himself and Alloy some breakfast? Something didn't add up, and unfortunately the answer was locked up somewhere in Lumie's head, which meant Mercury would never know.

Between Mercury and Dane, they were able to get Lumie and Alloy happily crunching on cereal. Nickel wandered into the kitchen yawning widely and fixed himself a bowl on his own.

"I'm not bringing all of you to work today," Dane grumbled ineffectually. If Lumie and Alloy wanted to go to Dane's office, they would go. Nickel went to Dane's office every weekday and did his schoolwork and some easy office work. It kept Nickel happy and gave Daisy fewer kits to look after during the day.

Lumie made a face. "Just want breakfast. Don't want to walk in the woods. Make sure you come back for your picnic!"

Dane sighed tiredly, and Mercury had to suppress a laugh. "I won't forget," Dane replied.

"Neither will I," Mercury echoed.

Dane gripped Nickel gently on the shoulder, and they both vanished with a whoosh of magic. Mercury ruffled Lumie's and Alloy's hair. Daisy would get the rest of the kits up in time for school, so he only had to worry about these two for the moment.

"Try to behave today?" he asked them both. He got reluctant nods in return, which was probably the best Mercury was going to get out of them. "I'll see you for dinner."

Mercury's magic was different than Dane's magic. He couldn't just vanish into thin air. Dane emulated a basic transportation spell by using enough power to do what he wanted it to. Mercury, on the other hand, needed to recall how the magic had to be shaped around him so the transportation spell would work properly before he cast and magic pulled him away. The kitchen vanished around him, and the front entrance of his office building appeared.

The building had magical shields around it that prevented someone like Mercury from appearing inside his cubicle at will. Instead, he had to walk through the front entrance just like every other employee. Mercury didn't need to carry car keys, though, which made walking through the metal detector a quick process. His badge was scanned by the guard, and then he was waved toward the elevators as the guards tried to hurry the morning line along.

There was more than one federal department inside the building. Mercury's office was on the sixth floor, the entirety of which belonged to the SupFeds. His space was a small cubicle amid a floor of small cubicles. The outer edges of the room were lined with windowed offices for people with considerably more clout than Mercury. He didn't want an office like that; it just brought more scrutiny and more work hours. Daisy did an amazing job corralling Mercury's kits, but it wasn't fair to keep her from her own family just because Mercury's job required more hours. He would apply for a promotion to get a slightly larger cubicle, but going into a private office was too much.

The fuzzy walls of Mercury's cubicle were an ugly gray. Some of his coworkers had plastered their cubicle walls with family photos and awards certificates. Mercury had one lone picture hanging next to his computer. He studied it while he waited for his computer to boot up.

Alloy was hanging over Copper's shoulder, grinning widely. Lumie had his thumb in his mouth and was clinging to Dane's leg. Copper and Zinc were glaring at each other from opposite sides of the frame. Nickel was in the center of the picture next to Mercury. His smile was small and hesitant, as if he was still unsure of his place in the world. The picture had been taken before Dane had finally relented and Nickel had become a permanent fixture at Dane's office. 'Ron was clinging to Mercury's arm and beaming, and Chrome was standing on Nickel's other side glaring sullenly at the camera.

Daisy had only gotten the one shot before the kits started wandering off to play in different directions. Dane had a copy at his office too.

The computer beeped softly to let Mercury know it was finally on. He input his password and settled into his chair to begin sorting through his work email. Most of them were junk or the usual reply to alls that accidentally went viral. Mercury had to delete all of those first before he could get to work on the real emails.

"Mercury, if I might have a word?" a voice asked from outside the cubicle. Mercury jumped in surprise, and a fizzle of magic sparked between his fingers. He quickly moved his hands away from his keyboard and mouse so he didn't fry another motherboard. His work computer wasn't as sturdy as Dane's spelled laptop.

"Director Stockton!" Mercury gaped, standing up abruptly when he saw who had interrupted his work. Ames Stockton was the Director of the Federal Bureau of Supernatural Investigations. He was so far above Mercury on the food chain in terms of work that he should be locked in his office on a pedestal while peons like Mercury did his personnel fetching. Stockton was a big man, tall and thickly muscled. There wasn't an ounce of extra fat on his body, but Mercury had little doubt he had to go up a suit size or two in his shirts just to accommodate his shoulders. His skin was dark and his eyes sharp with intelligence as he looked at Mercury.

"This way, please," Stockton said, waving his arm toward one of the conference rooms. Most of Mercury's coworkers were probably still fighting through the crush of people downstairs trying to get through security, but enough people poked their heads around their cubicles to see what was going on that he knew the gossip would be flying once he was out of earshot.

"Is something wrong?" Mercury asked as he obeyed Stockton's directions. There were two other people that Mercury didn't recognize in the conference room and a very large stack of papers covering one end of the long table. Mercury walked inside. Stockton followed and closed the heavy door.

"Nothing is wrong, per se," Stockton began as he took a seat at the head of the table. He gestured that Mercury should sit too, so Mercury pulled out a chair further down the table and perched awkwardly on the edge. "We just have some questions for you."

"Okay?" Mercury asked, wondering where this was going and if he should be contacting Dane to break him out of the office.

"As you know, we performed our usual extensive background check prior to your hiring," one of the other men Mercury didn't recognize said. "Because you were raised in a government-funded foster home, you have a Social Security number and identification we can track. School records, work locations, etcetera. Except one day you simply vanished and only reappeared three years later. You explained the missing time as going dragon in your interview. You realized you needed time to embrace your cultural heritage by spending time in the wild. There were people who believed your story, enough that you were hired, but those few who still had concerns kept digging."

He pulled a piece of paper off the top of the stack and pushed it across the table for Mercury to see. It was a printout of a news article from eight years ago. *"Terrorist Bombing! Government Lab Set on Fire by a Terrorist Calling Himself Quicksilver."* Mercury could make out the destroyed remains of the lab that had held the water dragons captive in the grainy photo.

"You were living in Chicago at the time of this attack, and the facility in question was only ten miles outside the city. You did not arrive at work on the day this attack occurred and did not reappear until the day after the fourth attack in Maryland occurred three years later."

Three additional pieces of paper were placed in front of Mercury, each an article detailing Quicksilver's attacks. Mercury looked up at Stockton, whose face was as blank as Mercury hoped his own was. Inside, Mercury was wondering if he should demand to contact a lawyer before the interrogation continued. Gregory, Dane's centaur lawyer, would be tickled pink to be given the chance to go after the SupFeds.

Mercury was guilty of the bombings, although he hadn't used any actual explosives. He had woken up after being kidnapped strapped to a gurney in a lab where scientists had been conducting cruel experiments on dragon kits and eggs. He still didn't know why someone wanted an adult dragon, but he felt safe in assuming that someone had noticed what he was, and that he was in his less-protected human form, so had taken him. The first attack in the newspaper articles had occurred when Mercury escaped from his bindings and started killing the bastards that had kidnapped him. Then Nickel had blown open a wall for his own escape attempt, and together they had brought the entire building down around them. The following two attacks had been Mercury rescuing the earth and fire dragons from their own separate labs, and the final attack had been a trap laid to stop him and Dane from pursing the government and the scientists. They had barely escaped with their lives and with Zinc. But he wasn't going to tell the SupFeds any of that.

The government had funded those labs, and there were some who were also benefiting directly from the experiments being conducted there. Jacobson, Stockton's immediate predecessor, had been one of those people. Jacobson and others had forced the media to keep the findings of smashed dragon eggs and the bodies of dead kits mixed in with the dead scientists a secret, one that had only gotten out when Dane leaked it to the media five years ago. Stockton knew the terrible truth about the labs and hadn't confronted Mercury about it, although he had to have his suspicions about Mercury's involvement.

Another piece of paper was dropped in front of Mercury, this one unfamiliar. "*Quicksilver Strikes Again! Terrorist Bombs Another Government Facility.*" It was a printout from an online news site dated just that morning. The article said the blast had occurred at six o'clock in the afternoon the previous day while Mercury had been at work.

His alibi was airtight, recorded on the cameras scattered throughout the sixth floor and on every exit and entrance into the building. Mercury had arrived at work at eight in the morning. He had to work late to finish a report and hadn't left until six fifteen that evening. He wasn't sitting in an interrogation, Mercury realized—he was in a debriefing.

"Was any evidence of experiments conducted on dragons found in the destroyed facility?" he asked calmly.

"Nothing specific," the third man, who had yet to speak, answered. "The responding officers found a few rooms that might have been used as jail cells, but the facility was too destroyed. We can't be entirely certain."

"And the signature?"

"Different," the man replied immediately. "Handwriting analysis of the first crime scene photos show we are looking at a copycat of some sort."

A destroyed facility with no evidence of dragons could mean two things. Either the copycat had heard about Quicksilver's bombing attacks and had decided to emulate them for his or her own purposes, so saving incarcerated dragons wasn't part of the plan, or it was the enemy blowing up their own emptied facilities in order to draw the real Quicksilver out. The enemy had been on the run ever since Mercury had started destroying their labs and Dane, the Genie of the East, had declared to the supernatural community that he was on the side of the dragons and anyone experimenting on them would be punished.

"And you want me to look into this?" Mercury asked, wondering if the SupFeds were laying a trap to connect him to Quicksilver too.

Stockton sat forward in his chair and caught Mercury's eyes with his own piercing ones. "We know you had something to do with Quicksilver," he said, the sharp tone of his voice brooking no arguments. "You can't deny that, and I don't want to hear you even try. We both also know that the person calling himself Quicksilver in this new attack is a copycat. You're the only analyst in this department with enough experience with the issue to understand what's going on." And his connection to Dane would ensure Dane got involved without the SupFeds having to pay him for his work. "We're putting you on a field assignment with one of our special agents. She's waiting for you at your cubicle and has been fully briefed on your connections to the case."

That was a dismissal, so Mercury hopped back to his feet and hightailed it out of the conference room. His cubicle looked empty at first glance, but as he approached, a woman straightened up. She had been leaning over to get a closer look at Mercury's lone picture. Her hair was a nondescript color of brown, pulled into a no-nonsense tail at the base of her neck. Her makeup was light, just a touch of eyeliner around her brown eyes and gloss on her lips to keep up a professional appearance. She was completely human as far as Mercury could tell, which meant that she couldn't get away with skipping the female version of a tie, i.e. makeup. Her pantsuit was off the rack, navy blue, and her blouse ordinary white.

He approached her quickly, not wanting to keep her waiting. When he got close enough, she eyed the bronze scales where they peeked out of the collar of Mercury's shirt for a moment before meeting his eyes. Her own eyes were cold, and Mercury knew he had been found wanting solely because of his species. It was something he was used to. Most dragons didn't attend any school, let alone have any eligibility for jobs at a government facility. The vast majority of dragons never left the forest at all. Humans, apparently including the woman in his cubicle, had developed prejudices against magical creatures deemed uneducable. Admittedly, most dragons weren't interested in attending school. Mercury had seven kits at home that were prime examples of that fact, and putting himself through high school and then college hadn't been easy, but it was doable if the right motivation was involved.

"I'm Mercury," Mercury said with a small smile. He would try to be friendly first, and if that didn't work, he would hope for a cordial working relationship at the very least.

"Valerie," she grunted in reply. Her severe face didn't soften into anything resembling a smile.

"I guess we're working together, then?" Mercury asked. He let his smile fade away, but he forced his voice to remain friendly. He refused to be the reason their partnership failed.

"Let's get some things straight right away," she snapped. "I'm the lead on this case. You will listen to what I have to say and do it as I say it. Understand?" Mercury nodded wordlessly, feeling his eyes grow round in surprise as she continued to snarl. "Good. Shut down your shit and meet me downstairs in five. We have a crime scene to investigate."

She stomped off, and Mercury sagged against the edge of his cubicle. He glanced at his watch and winced when he saw it was only eight thirty. One o'clock lunch with Dane couldn't come soon enough.

"So you're the one stuck with Crazy Valerie this time?" Cheng asked as he stuck his head over their shared cubicle wall. "I had to work a case with her last year, and let me tell you, she's a piece of work! How'd you get stuck with her?"

"Lowest man on the totem pole?" Mercury asked. It was true he was one of the more recent hires in the department, and he certainly had one of the lowest-level positions, but it was also true that she had been assigned the case, and Mercury was the most knowledgeable analyst on the topic.

"Look, my advice is do whatever she says, no matter how stupid. It'll keep her from yelling at you." Cheng was grinning at Mercury as he spoke, no doubt glad that he hadn't been chosen. "Once the case is resolved, you just have to fill out the paperwork to transfer out of the field department and back to the cubicle farm. She's had so many partners over the years that HR is probably used to it. If she didn't get slam dunks with just about every damned investigation she was put on, she'd have been out the door a long time ago."

Mercury nodded, taking in the gossip with half an ear while he shut his computer down.

"Any other advice?" he asked after glancing at his watch to see that he still had another minute before Valerie would consider him late.

"Take up drinking?" Cheng asked with a laugh. "You'd better go."

Mercury waved goodbye and headed to the elevator to meet with potential doom, apparently. He couldn't believe he had gotten stuck with such a hard-ass, especially one who didn't respect him solely because of his species.

Valerie was waiting for him in the lobby, her foot tapping impatiently as she glared at the elevators. Many of Mercury's coworkers were giving her a wide berth as they headed past her into the building.

"There you are," Valerie snapped the second Mercury stepped out of the elevator. "It's a forty-five-minute drive. I hope you have gas in your car."

"I don't drive," Mercury replied, already flinching in anticipation of her reaction. She glared at him, her eyes narrowed and lips pinched, but she changed direction in the parking lot to head toward a rusty clunker tucked awkwardly in the back corner. It didn't look like a car that could safely be taken on the highway, let alone survive a forty-five-minute drive.

There was a better, magical option that would ensure they actually made it to the scene, but Mercury didn't think Valerie would ever agree to let him transport them with a spell. She already hated him. Would it be any worse if he didn't ask for her permission first? Probably. Yet, as they walked closer to Valerie's very dead-looking car, Mercury honestly believed that it was still the better and safer option.

"What's the address?" Mercury asked. Magic fizzled through his fingers as he began to build a transportation spell around them. Valerie didn't notice, but she rattled off the address after a quick glance at one of the papers sticking out of the bag she was rifling through for her keys.

Mercury added the address to the spell and felt it lock on. He jogged up to Valerie, looped his arm through hers, and let his magic pull them both away.

The parking lot vanished, and magic swirled in its place for a brief moment before a debris field manifested around them. Mercury let go of Valerie and took a step back to look around, but before he could see more than broken wood and shattered brick scattered on the ground nearby, Valerie's fist caught him in the stomach.

He groaned and fell to the ground, his hands automatically coming up to protect his stomach as he wheezed for breath. Valerie stood over him while he gasped, glaring down.

"Owwie," Mercury whimpered when his diaphragm finally relaxed enough that he could take a full breath.

Valerie's lips twitched involuntarily, and Mercury winced and wondered when he had acquired Alloy's vocabulary.

"I have seven kits," he grumbled in explanation.

Valerie's attempted smile grew for a brief moment—Mercury thought he could call it an actual grin—but it faded just as quickly as it appeared.

"Don't you ever use your magic on me like that again!" she snarled. Her hands were in fists as she glared down at him. He could tell that she wanted to hit him again, but at the same time she knew she shouldn't have attacked him in the first place. It wasn't professional. Then again, she was known for having trouble keeping partners.

"You hit me!" Mercury grumbled back, which had her freezing in place.

"Everything all right here?" another voice asked before Valerie could retort. Mercury stumbled back to his feet with a suppressed groan. He was going to have a bruise there! Dane would be so angry, but he would also get the chance to kiss it all better tonight, so Mercury wasn't too upset. Besides, Mercury was kind of enjoying needling Valerie. He would do the same if any of his kits were in a bad mood, and she had almost cracked an actual smile for a second there, so maybe he was getting through her growly shell.

"Just a little dizzy from the transportation spell," Mercury explained, turning toward the man approaching them. "I slipped on some of the debris. Are you in charge here?" he added, quickly reaching into his pocket to pull out his badge.

The man was a plainclothes police officer. His suit fit him better than Valerie's fit her, but he hadn't yet perfected the stony cop's face that she wore all the time.

"Captain O'Simmons is in charge," the officer said once he had looked at both Mercury and Valerie's badges. "He knows you're stopping by to have a look. He's right over here." He waved toward a grouping of officers, some in uniform and some not, standing near a squad car and ambulance that were blocking the road from commercial traffic. Mercury and Valerie walked in that direction.

They had landed just outside the crime scene tape that surrounded the blasted area, which was the purpose of the simple wards that were cast on every roll of the tape. The officer led them around the perimeter toward the squad car. Mercury followed, but he also looked at what was left of the building.

Only one wall was still standing of what appeared to have been a two-story structure. The rest of the building was scattered around the street and the parking lot. Nothing was smoldering, although soot was heavy on the ground and the debris. He was in a commercial area of town that had seen better days. The shops on either side of the destruction zone were empty, their windows boarded up. The asphalt underneath his feet had been cracked and pitted with age before the destruction had made it even bumpier, and rivulets of water and firefighting foam made it slippery to walk on. The wind was blowing gently and Mercury smelled the usual city scents of old cars, filth, and muck, but he also caught the slightest whiff of gunpowder underneath the stench of char, which was decidedly odd.

The inside of the standing wall came into view as they neared the squad car. Mercury had been feeling melodramatic and, quite frankly, pissed off when he had finished destroying the water dragon lab where he and Nickel had been held and had etched "Let My People Go" into the small bit of that lab that was still standing. It had gotten his point across fairly strongly, he had felt at the time, and the connection to biblical slavery and incarceration had been poignant.

"Is that paint?" he couldn't help exclaiming after studying what the impostor had done.

"Meant to look like blood, I think," one of the officers milling around grunted in agreement.

Mercury's lip curled, and he let out a growl of disgust. "The original Quicksilver used magic to etch that saying into the brick or stone of whatever lab he had just finished destroying. Red paint is the work of an amateur."

"Valerie Robertson, FBSI. This is my partner, Mercury Chicago," Valerie stated, flashing her badge. Mercury flashed his too, manfully not wincing when she mentioned his last name. It was a result of the foster system arbitrarily handing him a last name when they had to put him into the system. He had wandered into a suburb of Chicago as a kit, and that was the name they had stuck him with.

"I'm Captain O'Simmons," one of the men said. He strode forward with his hand out for Valerie to shake. He was wearing a uniform, but the extra shiny bits around his badge told Mercury that his uniform was a mark of his rank while the other officers wearing their uniforms were the peons. It was a complicated way to divide ranks, but since it worked for the police, Mercury wasn't going to question it. O'Simmons looked clean-cut with a military-style buzz for a haircut, sharp brown eyes, and he fit in his uniform nicely with defined shoulders and a trim waist. He smelled like a normal human, although Mercury probably shouldn't be relying too much on his nose, given the acrid stench of burnt building and firefighting foam that encompassed the entire area. O'Simmons turned to Mercury with his hand still out and so Mercury shook it too, hoping the bronze scales on the back of his hand didn't freak the man out.

"Any leads so far?" Valerie asked, turning to survey the scene as she spoke.

O'Simmons grunted. "Nothing. Had one of my boys look up the graffiti and he pinged off of your database, so we had to call you in. How many unsolved Quicksilver cases does this make so far for the FBSI?"

Captain O'Simmons might not have a problem with Mercury being a dragon, but he did have a problem with the SupFeds swooping in to steal his case. It was typical inter-departmental rivalry, Mercury knew, but it was still fun to see firsthand. Mercury let Valerie answer.

"There have been three bombings like this one that can be attributed to Quicksilver and a fourth we're fairly certain he was involved with even though the site was missing his usual signature. This is the fifth Quicksilver case I've investigated."

Mercury didn't know Valerie was the lead investigator on his criminal activities. It must have rankled a good bit to be forced to work with the guy she had been trying to put behind bars not too long ago.

"Five unsolved cases?" O'Simmons said with a mocking whistle of disbelief. "I'm sure glad they sent you my way then."

"She never said they were unsolved," Mercury couldn't help interjecting. "The FBSI are fully aware of the circumstances surrounding the first four bombings and have exonerated the culprit." At least, he hoped they had. Mercury didn't want to accidently put himself behind bars while looking for the impostor.

"With a judge and jury?" O'Simmons asked sarcastically.

"You know full well that's not how some things work," Valerie snapped back. "So we've got a copycat, and we need to find out who and why before he or she attacks again."

"You're so certain it's a copycat," one of the plainclothes officers standing behind O'Simmons asked, his tone just this side of polite. He was apparently taking cues from his boss instead of being civil.

"Like I said, the paint is the work of an amateur. The real Quicksilver has enough magic that he doesn't need to resort to cheap tricks," Mercury explained. "The place also smells like gunpowder, which is another cheap trick Quicksilver would never have to use to destroy a building."

"Sounds like you think the bastard's a hero or something," the officer said warningly.

Mercury shrugged. "Maybe I do. I'm a dragon, and Quicksilver was destroying evil places where evil people were hurting dragons. Or maybe I want to go do my job and your nattering is pissing me off." He smiled widely at them, just being friendly, except he was also showing off his sharp teeth.

"Tell me about this scene," Valerie snapped when the men shifted around slightly as if unsure whether they should be grabbing their guns or their security blankets.

O'Simmons stepped forward, aggressively muscling his way past his own men and past Valerie as he walked toward the crime scene tape as if he needed to prove to everyone present that he was still top dog. "We've only had access to the scene for a few hours; fire and rescue had to cool off all the hot spots and the bomb squad had to declare the scene secured before my team could move in, and that took all fucking night. Our bomb technician tells me that whoever set the bomb most likely found instructions on the internet. It wasn't a high-tech build. Quicksilver set it off, ran for it, and returned with his paint to graffiti what was left."

"The fake Quicksilver," Mercury grumbled under his breath. He ducked underneath the tape and started walking around the scattered debris in the parking lot in front of the building.

"Had to be a bomb with a lot of pop," Valerie said as she followed Mercury. "Most internet sources aren't strong enough to blow out entire walls. They'll kill anyone close enough and cause major damage, sure, but this looks more like a missile hit than an internet bombing. I'm going to speak with your technician. Is he still here?" O'Simmons pointed toward the large crime scene vehicle parked next to a fire truck on the far side of the debris field. Valerie nodded. "I'll be over there. Don't make a mess, Mercury."

Mercury just growled in reply, frowning at her when she turned and walked away.

"She's a piece of work," O'Simmons remarked. Mercury held back his scathing reply of asking whether O'Simmons knew he was obnoxious, too, and instead walked toward what was left of the building.

Aside from the lone standing wall, the rest of the two stories were scattered on the ground in various states of charcoal. There was a hole in the ground in the shape of the building, what was left of the basement. It looked like the bomb had been set down there because the basement ceiling was missing, too, and Mercury could see a crater in the center.

Mercury walked to the edge of the basement and dropped down, hiding a smirk at O'Simmons's exclamation of surprise. There was a ladder set up off to one side for everyone else. He walked around the bomb crater, careful of the people still snapping pictures of the scene, and headed toward one of the hallways. He wanted to find the suspected jail cells first.

There wasn't any evidence of destroyed lab equipment shattered on the floors. In fact, aside from the pieces of the building itself, Mercury didn't see any other debris. The place must have been totally cleaned out before it was attacked. Or it was never a lab to begin with because the impostor had nothing to do with dragons.

Whatever. Mercury refocused on his surroundings instead of worrying about the various what-ifs.

Stockton wouldn't have known that there were rooms that could have been cells on the upper floors after the bombing, which meant the area where any dragons might have been confined was somewhere still standing. There was only one hallway on his side of the basement, so he wandered down it.

Four broken doors lay haphazardly on the ground. The walls they were supposed to be attached to were a soggy, half-burnt mess. Most of the basement was built from wood, but for some reason it felt like these particular walls were a later addition. Mercury didn't want to get his nice clothes dirty; he stayed outside of the soaked wood perimeter and leaned as far over the mess as he could to look inside.

He didn't see the small bed or toilet he remembered from Zinc's horrible cell inside the first door. It didn't smell like a dragon either. In fact, underneath the overpowering stench of gunpowder and firefighting foam, it smelled kind of like wet dog. Mercury wrinkled his nose and backed away from the first room.

The second room also smelled like dog and like old blood. The same smell repeated in the last two rooms as well. There was no sign a dragon or anything with a human form had been kept captive in the building. Beyond the hallway was another large room with the remains of what looked to Mercury like a fighting ring in the center.

"This was a dogfighting operation," Mercury called loudly so everyone above could hear him. His stomach rolled with disgust, but also with relief that he wasn't looking at any more dead dragon kits. He had seen enough of that horror to last for the rest of his very long life.

"A what?" Valerie asked from somewhere above his head.

"Dogfighting. The whole place smells like dogs and blood, and this looks like a fighting ring to me."

"So the impostor blew up the wrong building?" Valerie asked sharply. "Get up here so I can look at you properly when you're talking!"

Mercury sighed, but obeyed. He didn't think there was anything more to discover in the blasted basement anyway. Unless someone discovered a trap door that led to cells or a lab even farther underground, Mercury was done searching.

He couldn't jump out of the basement the way he had jumped down, and the walls were muddy so he didn't want to climb them. Instead, Mercury hopped up the ladder and then jogged over to where Valerie was waiting impatiently with O'Simmons near the lone standing wall.

"There hasn't been dogfighting in this town ever, and I don't expect there to be any now," O'Simmons was insisting to Valerie as Mercury got close enough to overhear.

"It smells like wet dog down there, and I'm pretty sure the ring in the far room was where they fought them," Mercury interrupted. "You've got dogfighting in your town now. I thought this was supposed to be a bombed government facility?" he asked Valerie.

"Ex-government facility, and only through a technicality," she grumbled. "It was declassified thirty years ago and sold to a developer who went bankrupt before the property could be dealt with. We have no idea what squatters might have been doing with it in the meantime."

"Apparently, they used it for a dogfighting operation, blew it up, and put Quicksilver's catchphrase on the wall," Mercury muttered. He looked up at the lone wall and the paint staining it. "Maybe someone who likes dogs did it?" he asked jokingly.

"Or a werewolf?" Valerie added thoughtfully. Although their initial meeting had been terrible, Mercury didn't think she was a bad partner. She was just gruff and a little bit mean. He had a feeling her attitude had gotten her paired with the least capable of partners, Mercury included, and the worst assignments. Maybe she deserved it, Mercury thought unkindly with an awkward shuffle of his feet in the wet muck, but sometimes a bad reputation was also caused by bad luck. Maybe she didn't deserve it, Mercury insisted to himself. He stared down at his wet shoes, wondering if Chrome had ever returned his second pair so he had something dry to wear tomorrow. Everything was wet and yucky thanks to the firefighters' efforts to put out the fire. Mercury's shoes and pants cuffs were suffering.

Everything was wet from hose water, except for the paint.

Mercury rushed closer to the wall, staring incredulously up at the paint.

"What now?" Valerie sighed with exasperation in her voice. "I don't see any dog hair in the paint."

"Why isn't the paint washed away?" Mercury asked. "It couldn't have been dry by the time the firefighters arrived, and the hoses should have been strong enough to wash at least some of it off."

"Yet, it's pristine," Valerie finished. She spun on O'Simmons. "When did you first notice the paint?" she asked sharply, her intense eyes pinning O'Simmons in place as if he were a bug on display.

"First the firefighters had to get the fire out; then the bomb squad had to clear what was left," O'Simmons hedged shiftily. "We didn't secure the scene until five o'clock this morning," he finally admitted.

"And the bombing occurred at, what? Six o'clock yesterday evening?" she continued scathingly. It had happened early enough to make the morning paper, Mercury knew, which should have been more than enough time for O'Simmons to take control. That he hadn't meant he was either incompetent or was colluding with the bomber or the impostor. "Which means the paint might have been added well after the bombing, and you didn't have the scene secured enough to know?" She swore at O'Simmons and ran a hand through her hair, dislodging it from its hair tie. "So sometime after the firefighters finished putting out the burning building, someone entered the scene and added the paint."

"That's my guess," Mercury replied with a shrug. The curl of one letter was low enough that Mercury could touch it. How wet the paint still was would let them at least estimate at how long ago it had been added. Mercury reached upward and felt the trap spring into action, magic igniting inside the paint to freeze his fingers in place.

"Uh-oh," he gasped.

There was magic in the paint, and he hadn't noticed. Mercury called himself an idiot as he yanked on his hand. He wasn't quite touching the paint, but his fingers were stuck. His own magic flared from his fingers in ineffectual sparks as every spell he tried failed to free him.

"What did you do?" Valerie snarled, glaring at him again.

"The magic caught me," Mercury replied through gritted teeth as yet another spell failed to free him.

The paint flared again, and a second spell formed around his hand. Mercury groaned as it set into place and his body tried to shift form without his permission. Sweat broke out on his forehead as he fought the magic internally.

"What's it doing?" Valerie snapped. "Talk to me!"

"Trying to force me to change shape," Mercury gasped out.

"And that's bad?" she asked, sounding skeptical.

"I'll destroy the entire crime scene and squish you, O'Simmons, and most of the adjacent building if the spell wins," he growled, sending more magic through his fingers to fight the spell.

Valerie spun on O'Simmons, who was backing away from Mercury with a dawning look of horror on his face. Maybe he just hadn't known that Mercury was a dragon when they shook hands, and that was why he hadn't acted prejudiced.

"You have a witch on staff or on call?" Valerie asked him sharply.

"There aren't any witches in this town," O'Simmons replied with a touch too much pride in his voice, as if that was a good thing. Idiot.

"Just like you don't have any dogfighting operations?" Valerie scoffed. "You're terrible at your job; I hope you know." She turned back to Mercury. "It'll be at least forty-five minutes for the FBSI witch to get here. Can you hold on that long?"

Mercury growled. He could feel the spell working through his body, picking at his muscles and bones, tugging on tendons and ligaments, and scratching down his scales. It hurt so very badly and Mercury just wanted to give in and change shape, but he knew he couldn't. There was a reason the spell had been triggered by his fingers, why someone had set a spell for a dragon in the paint, and he wasn't going to allow them to win, but he could only hold out maybe another five minutes and there was no guarantee the SupFeds witch could even help.

"I have a better idea," Mercury gasped out. His free hand dove into his pants pocket, and he pulled out his phone. It took a few seconds to key in Dane's cell phone number and hit send. Mercury could only hope Dane was in a part of the forest where there was service. Dane picked up on the second ring.

"Hello!" Dane seid, sounding cheerfully stressed as if he was trying to make the best of a difficult situation. Mercury didn't have time to worry about Dane at the moment as the spell intensified suddenly as if sensing he was about to get help.

"I'm a little stuck right now. Some sort of magic caught me, and I can't break free. I was wondering if you or Lumie might be able to get me out." He rattled off the address, then had to pause when yet another pulse of magic flared though him. His body shuddered, but he held his human form. This time. He might not be able to next time.

"I'll be right there," Dane finished, ending their call abruptly. Mercury tucked his phone back into his pocket and tried a different spell to get his hand free. He failed.

"Who was that?" Valerie asked. "You can't just call in an outsider like that! If you don't follow the protocol, you'll get us both fired."

Mercury didn't bother to answer. A second later, the air shimmered next to him and Dane appeared. Lumie was clutching at his leg. They were inside the perimeter supposed to be maintained by the warded police tape.

Valerie jumped and swore. O'Simmons went a little white in the face. Dane ignored them all, immediately rushing forward and putting his hands on Mercury's shoulders. Mercury felt a block fall into place as Dane erected a magical wall between Mercury's body and the spell trying to force him to change shape.

"This is a nasty bit of work," Dane murmured as Mercury sagged against him in relief.

"Nasty, nasty," Lumie echoed, staring up at where Mercury's fingers were still stuck. "Daddy's silly."

"I know, Lumie. I need to look before I touch," Mercury replied with a grin.

Lumie nodded imperiously, something both adorable and hilarious coming from a five-year-old kit, and held his hands out for Dane to pick him up. Dane lifted Lumie high into the air until he could reach Mercury's hand. Lumie danced his fingers across Mercury's own fingers, and with a loud pop, Mercury's hand slipped free. Dane's wall faded away slowly. The part of the spell forcing Mercury to change shape had also vanished the moment Mercury was released.

Mercury's magic was depleted. He felt sweaty and gross, and a little stupid. It was idiotic of him to not double-check the paint before reaching out and touching it. Dane let Lumie drop to the ground and wrapped his arms around Mercury. Lumie wandered off to eagerly check out his first real crime scene.

"Give the paint a whiff," Dane grumbled. "I really hate that smell."

Mercury obeyed and then wrinkled his nose at the first sniff. It smelled like paint, burnt building, and firefighting foam, but underneath all of that Mercury could smell tainted dragon magic. It was faint, and it was also entirely possible that it hadn't been discernable until after Mercury had stupidly activated the hidden spell.

"The enemy was here," Mercury growled. "So either they bombed the building and then set the trap, or they took advantage of someone else's criminal act and trapped the paint when the firefighters were still working."

"It's the first solid lead we've had in months," Dane replied eagerly. "The kits should obey their tutor for at least five more minutes. Let me dig at the layered spell in the paint for a bit."

"Why were you home?" Mercury asked since Daisy was supposed to be watching the kits while Dane searched through the woods. Then he thought of an even more serious worry. "What did you bribe the kits with?"

Dane blushed slightly. "Candy after dinner, but only if their tutor says they behaved." So the kits would be sugar high before bed. It made things a little more difficult, of course, but it was better to have happy kits than surly ones when it came to baths and pajamas. It only became an issue when Alloy decided to savor his candy, fell asleep with it still in his mouth, drooled all over his pillow, and woke with it on fire. "Daisy's son bit his teacher today," Dane added, sounding forcefully okay with how his morning had apparently turned out. Dane might not have a problem with the kits destroying his home or with a half-dozen things that drove Mercury mad, but he was desperate to find the missing dragons before the enemy did and losing the chance because Daisy had to leave work early again was enough to push his button. "Her husband took a half day at work, but he can't leave until noon. Daisy promised Lumie she'll be back in time for our picnic, but until then I'm stuck making sure the kits don't kill this week's tutor." He sighed heavily.

"Wait a second!" Valerie retorted, interrupting Mercury before he could voice his sympathy. "Don't you dare contaminate the crime scene! Mercury, you know better than to invite someone arbitrarily into a case like this!"

"Ah," Mercury said, turning to look at Valerie. "May I introduce Dane, from the Supernatural Consulting Firm. The FBSI uses his services regularly."

"And you think we have the budget to hire him?" Valerie steamed, her face growing red as her eyes narrowed in fury.

Dane grinned over his shoulder at Mercury. "He'll pay me at home tonight. Don't worry about your budget."

"What?" Valerie hissed, her face growing even redder. "I'll have your badge for this, Mercury!"

"He's my mate," Mercury said with a happy shrug. Valerie couldn't take his badge, and Mercury seriously doubted she had the pull to get someone higher up to do it. Besides, it was such a cliché thing to say to an officer, Mercury knew she was just venting anger without actually thinking first. "We've been together for five years, so he'd come running if I called even if I didn't promise a kiss afterwards."

She gaped at them both for a brief second before storming off toward the basement. She was probably going to see if there was any truth to Mercury's claim that the building had been used for dogfighting. He also hoped she took a few minutes to calm down.

"Okay, bored now," Lumie rumbled. He threw his arms around Mercury's legs. "You won't forget, right?" he asked Mercury's knees.

Mercury glanced at his watch and was astonished to realize that it was already eleven o'clock. Where had all the time gone? "In two hours, I'll come home so Dane and I can go on your picnic," Mercury promised. He would drag Valerie kicking and screaming back to the office for lunch if he needed to.

"You'd better," Lumie sighed. He squeezed Mercury's legs one last time before letting go and running after Dane. He slammed into Dane's legs, causing Dane to swear and catch himself on a large piece of rubble so he didn't hit the ground. "Time to go," Lumie said with a wide grin up at Dane, who lost his responding scowl quickly under Lumie's cheerful onslaught.

"See you in a bit," Dane called over to Mercury, who smiled and nodded. Dane and Lumie vanished, leaving Mercury to return to work.

Chapter Three

Mercury arrived home at exactly one o'clock, looking harried, yet also exhilarated. He didn't mind his desk job, Dane knew that, but there was nothing quite like tracking down the enemy on foot. It got the adrenaline pumping, and it was why Dane had chosen to open his consulting firm in the first place. He didn't need the money, and while he enjoyed helping people, Dane didn't need to be so open about it, but he loved the job and he had a feeling Mercury now did too.

Although, that angry partner of his would need to even out her temper and attitude first. Dane knew he shouldn't interfere, but he did want to pull her aside and read her the riot act, something Mercury would kill Dane for if he ever found out.

"Any luck?" Dane asked. There had been murmurs about the enemy over the past five years. Dragons like the mother and kits Dane was searching for who were running from the enemy were the most frequent. The trap Mercury had triggered was the most overt the enemy had been since the warehouse earthquake trap they had engineered five years ago. Dane and Mercury couldn't find them, which infuriated Dane to no end. The enemy had at least one dragon held prisoner that Dane knew of, an air kit named Platinum, but Mercury and Dane were very worried that the enemy had gotten more and was torturing them too while Dane and Mercury essentially twiddled their thumbs.

Mercury sighed. "I think Valerie finally browbeat Captain O'Simmons into at least looking into the possibility that someone was holding illegal dogfights in that building's basement. He's still insisting that there's no way his quiet town would have something as terrible as that, but when he said that, he used the same amount of derision as when he happily told us there weren't any witches in his town either. Which means that Valerie is also sending a request to the FBI to have O'Simmons's unit investigated for racist hiring practices and racist policing. She's hoping a more open-minded and progressive person will take O'Simmons's place in time for us to make some progress on the case, but I'm not holding my breath."

"So no one is looking into the magic imbedded in the paint?" Dane asked, wondering if he could cut lunch short and go do some more digging on his own. He hadn't wanted to step on Mercury's toes by butting into his investigation, and Dane had needed to get back to the kits and their long-suffering tutor anyway, so he had left before he was able to get more than a cursory look at the spell.

To Dane's relief, Mercury grinned conspiratorially. "I put a ward over the paint so O'Simmons's bumbling wouldn't destroy the evidence and contacted the SupFeds' in-house witch. She's agreed to be at the scene this afternoon whether O'Simmons likes it or not."

Dane shared Mercury's grin, glad that Mercury was happy, but turned around when Dane heard Lumie grunting behind him. Lumie was dragging a wicker picnic basket as long as he was tall. It was huge and it looked heavy. What had the little scamp actually made? It looked like there was enough food in there to feed an army.

The basket *was* heavy, Dane realized as he hurried forward to take it from Lumie before he hurt himself. Daisy was in the kitchen feeding the rest of the kits. Lumie waved goodbye and scurried back so he wouldn't miss his own lunch.

"Shall we?" Dane asked, gallantly holding out his arm—the one not dragged down by the heavy basket—out for Mercury to take. He wrapped his arm around Dane's.

"Let's go."

Dane let his magic pull them away, reappearing in a familiar enough location. The clearing was a little more overgrown than it had been five years ago when five kits had been trying to nurse their sick father back to health. The three trees that had fallen still made a nice little cave off to one side, but they also let in a lot of sun and new trees were slowly growing to take their place. Dane was able to find a flat enough bit of grass and scrub to lay out the blanket Lumie had helpfully included.

Mercury grinned at Dane, no doubt recognizing the location and Dane's attempt to be sentimental, but then he looked at the basket Dane had set down next to the blanket and remembered why they were actually here. "How bad do you think it is?" Mercury asked, his face set in a worried frown.

"Knowing Lumie?" Dane joked before pulling open the two halves of the top of the basket. A wave of heavy cinnamon scent practically exploded from inside. "Knowing Lumie, it probably has cinnamon in it," Dane sighed.

Mercury and Dane slowly unpacked the basket. First was a bowl of what appeared to be potato salad, except the potatoes had been turned a funny shade of reddish orange by the sheer quantity of cinnamon Lumie had added. Next was a plastic-wrap-covered plate of sandwiches. Dane was pretty sure they were chicken-salad sandwiches, but the mayo Lumie had doctored for the salad had the same off-color tinge as the potatoes. There was a bowl of leafy greens mixed with other chopped vegetables coated with... Dane sniffed it expectantly to double-check his worst fears and found them confirmed. There was cinnamon-flavored salad dressing completely coating every inch of lettuce, carrot, and tomato.

"He included dessert," Mercury groaned. His hands were rubbing his face tiredly, but he peeked between his fingers just in time for Dane to pull out a covered pitcher of cinnamon iced tea. Dessert was, predictably, cinnamon cheesecake.

"Lumie isn't allowed to cook for other people ever again," Dane grumped, staring incredulously at the food Lumie expected them to choke down.

"You still have the number for the pizza place?" Mercury asked. He was looking at the food as if he might be sick.

Dane immediately pulled out his phone and, predictably, there wasn't any signal in the middle of the forest. "Let me see if I can get a few bars. If not, I'll pop into town and order one there." Dane bent over to press his lips against Mercury's, but he pulled away a few moments later with a grimace.

"Everything reeks of cinnamon. I can't even enjoy you with that stench in my nose," Mercury whined.

Dane couldn't help laughing at Mercury, and Mercury grinned along with Dane because it was hilarious. Dane pecked Mercury on the end of his sensitive nose before getting back to his feet and heading across the clearing. Dane's phone resolutely told him there were zero towers nearby as he walked around in an awkward shuffle with his phone held out in the air, desperately hoping the little bar would appear in the corner. He made it all the way to the far tree line before he found even one bar of signal, but it flickered out before Dane could pull his phone to his ear to make a call.

A touch of magic to augment the signal would solve the problem. Dane much preferred to do that and spend the twenty minutes it would take for the pizza to cook sitting with Mercury than standing around in the store. He called on his magic, letting it form slowly between his fingers, and jumped about a foot in the air when his magic informed him that it had found dragons.

Dane hadn't ended the spell he had been using when Daisy called to let him know she was taking a few hours off. It gleefully told Dane that there were three dragon kits tucked under a bush just three feet to his left.

"Damn it, Lumie," Dane grumbled under his breath. He must have known there would be dragon kits here. Couldn't he have just told Dane that instead of sending Mercury and Dane on the excuse of a picnic? Then again, it was Lumie, and he probably thought that was exactly what he had done.

Dane tucked his phone back into his pocket and waved to Mercury to let him know something was up. Mercury immediately came to attention on the picnic blanket instead of lounging indolently. His magic flared briefly as he called it to his fingers in readiness.

It wasn't hard for Dane to keep his feet from making any noise while he crept over the heavy autumn-leaf debris covering the three feet of ground to where the dragon kits were hiding. The bush was big enough that a casual observer might miss them, but it was starting to lose its leaves, too, and Dane could make out the occasional flash of red scales as he got closer.

"But it smells so good!" one of the kits whined.

"Mama said to stay hiding until she comes and gets us," another admonished in reply.

"But I'm hungry!" the first replied, his whine grating and high-pitched. After wincing through that noise, Dane knew that even had Mercury and Dane remained on the blanket with an edible picnic they would have noticed the kits eventually.

Dane peeked under the bush behind them. All three kits were in dragon form, their oversized and currently flightless wings tucked close to their backs so they could fit underneath the bush. Two of them were staring at Mercury and the picnic basket avidly. The third was looking at Dane with dawning fear in his widening eyes.

"Hello," Dane said amicably, hoping this would go well. Except he was dealing with dragon kits, and there was no way this would go well.

The two kits that hadn't noticed Dane yet screeched in surprise and accidentally lit the bush on fire. The one who had seen Dane jumped to his feet and dashed into the clearing to get away. He forgot about Mercury, though, and was caught a brief moment later.

Dane doused the bush with a touch of magic and used his larger size to herd the other two kits after their brother.

Mercury rumbled at them, his human throat making the soothing dragon noise without trouble. "We've been looking for you," he explained gently. "Come have some lunch."

"You're not the bad guys?" the second kit Dane had heard speak asked sharply. He tried to be as menacing as Dane knew Nickel could be, but he lacked the serial-killer aura Nickel had learned during his time trapped and experimented on in a lab before killing the scientists in order to escape. Dane reached out and smoothed the scales on his head.

"We're not the bad guys. Your father told us where to find you," Dane explained, stretching the truth just slightly. Their father had asked for Dane's help finding them, but he hadn't known where his mate had fled.

"We have a lot of food that I'm sure you'll love," Mercury said as he gently steered the kit he was still holding onto toward the blanket. "It was made by a fire dragon kit just like you in the hopes that we would have something for you when we did find you."

"Once you've eaten, we'll take you to your dad," Dane added with a smile. "Do you know how far away you left your mom behind?"

One of the kits was sniffing the potato salad, and another was clawing off the plastic wrap around the sandwiches.

"Human form, please," Mercury instructed firmly. "This is food you eat with hands, not claws."

The kits grumbled, but one by one they shifted forms. They were naked and unconcerned about that fact, of course. Wild kits often didn't know anything about clothing or the social mores that dictated what people wore. The fact that Chrome consistently wore clothing, as ripped and dirty as it was, was the result of a lot of hard work on Daisy and Mercury's part. Dane didn't say anything, but made a mental note to wash the picnic blanket before it ended up back in the hall closet.

It only took a few minutes for all the food Lumie had made to vanish. The kits ate voraciously, as if they hadn't had a proper meal in days. Dane honestly doubted they had any clue what they were actually putting in their mouths—potato salad and cheesecake didn't occur naturally in the wild—but they enjoyed it all the same. Lumie was apparently an excellent cook, as long as he was feeding fellow fire dragons.

Had their mother been anywhere nearby, she would have come rumbling out of the forest to protect her kits from strangers. Either her kits had wandered off a long way while she was fighting the enemy, or she had been captured and the enemy hadn't had the resources to keep her subdued and track down the kits at the same time. The enemy would be back in these woods soon enough to search for the kits, and Dane would be waiting. He suppressed an evil grin and shared a sidelong look with Mercury, whose eyebrows were drawn. He looked tense as he watched the kits and the forest surrounding the clearing. Mercury was on the same page as Dane.

They needed to get the kits out of this forest and safe with their dad as soon as possible, but they also had to do it without alarming them. The kits would fight back if they were rushed or made to feel wary. Lumie's trick with the food had helped a lot, and now all Mercury and Dane had to do was to get the kits to trust them enough to transport them somewhere.

Before Dane could come up with a plan, one of the kits yawned. He was immediately echoed by both of his siblings.

"We've been running all morning," the first kit to yawn explained tiredly. "We're gonna take a nap now."

All three kits curled up amid the remains of the picnic lunch and dropped off to sleep without a care in the world. It was no wonder the enemy had been able to gather as many kits as they had, given how trusting and innocent they were.

Mercury and Dane waited a few minutes to let the kits fall fully to sleep. They quietly repacked the picnic basket so none of the local wildlife got accidentally poisoned from licking remnants of all the cinnamon in the bowls. Once Dane was certain the kits were dead to the world, Mercury put one hand on Dane's shoulder and Dane bent over so he could touch all three kits at the same time. His magic pulled them all away.

They reappeared in the middle of a burgeoning village. The kits were lying in the middle of a wide dirt road. Six two-story houses stood on each side of the road. The houses were almost identical in design: each had different-colored siding and shutters and they had porches of different sizes, but the basic blueprint was the same. Two more houses were in various stages of construction farther down the street. A young man with bright-red hair was sitting awkwardly in a chair in front of the house that was little more than foundation and framing.

Mercury and Dane both straightened up. Yelling for attention and waking the kits would be a bad idea, so Mercury headed over to the sitting man. A breeze rustled the leaves overhead, and one of the kits rolled over so he could snuggle close with his siblings. Of course he also managed to plant his elbow into his brother's face with the unerring accuracy of siblings across the world.

With a squawk of outrage, the kit woke up. Dane cringed, used to his own kits' eruptions when something bad happened, but the kit got in a good look around him before he started screeching and flaring fire. He let out a different sort of squawk, this one full of fear and confusion, until he caught sight of the man who had been sitting alone.

"Daddy?" the kit asked softly. The man stood awkwardly when he caught sight of the kits, one of his legs encased in a thick cast to help the severely broken bone heal correctly, but he grinned and held out one of his hands. "Daddy!" the kit shrieked, waking his siblings as he dashed down the road. The other two kits echoed their brother, screaming and running at their father, who had to collapse into his chair to hold them all.

There was a lot of babbling and some loud crying. Pretty soon, Mercury and Dane weren't the only ones standing in the middle of the dirt road. Three-dozen dragons and kits lived in the tiny town, and it felt like more than half of them came outside to investigate the noise. An air dragon who inexplicably called herself Martha, even though that wasn't her real name, walked over to Mercury and Dane.

"The construction crew just left for their lunch break," she said softly. "The house will be ready to go before winter sets in. It's nice to see it will be a full house. Some of us were getting worried you wouldn't find the rest of the family. I'm happy to add all three kits to the school roster." Martha was the unofficial mayor and the official schoolteacher of the town. She had been one of Dane's first finds when she and two kits she had rescued from the wild had come to him directly for aid.

Dane had just put the word out that his consulting firm was particularly interested in helping dragons in need. She hadn't been fleeing from the enemy, but she was a fully trained elementary school teacher with a Master of Education and two particularly articulate kits. No one would hire her because they didn't trust a dragon with the rest of the kids in the school. She wanted somewhere she could teach and be happy, so Dane suggested they build a town exclusively for dragons in need.

It wasn't anything like how dragons lived in the wild. Kits had both parents with them for a while after they hatched, but within five or six years the father would need to return to his old territory to keep from fighting with his mate just as the mother would be forced to send her kits away when they grew large enough to fly. Something about living in the town in a house where everyone was able to carve out their own space and keep it separate from the rest of the dragons living there allowed real family units to form and stay together. That permanence meant that kits could go to school like regular children and adults who loved each other enough to have kits could stay with each other happily.

By the time the town was done raising the first generation of kits, they would have highly educated and socially aware young adults to send out to the world and maybe begin disproving the widely held view that dragons were only wild creatures.

There would have been much more of an outcry had the enemy been experimenting with pack magic, for example, and stealing young cubs from werewolf mothers for their experiments. Werewolves worked and lived openly and happily in nearly every community, unlike dragons.

Martha ran a hand through her white hair, cropped short so it stuck up in spikes. "Any word on the mother dragon?"

"I'm going back to look for her. She sent her kits on ahead, so I'm going to backtrack down their trail and see if I can locate her," Dane answered.

"I'll pass that information on as soon as things quiet down," Martha agreed.

Dane smiled at her and nodded before turning to Mercury, who was looking at his watch and frowning.

"My lunch hour's almost over," he sighed regretfully. "I'll have just enough time to grab a sandwich from the cafeteria and get back to my desk."

"I'm sorry Lumie's picnic didn't go well," Dane said with a laugh.

Mercury shook his head. "I think it went exactly how Lumie thought it would. I wish he would just tell us why he did things instead of doing them and us only finding out why once the results become obvious."

"Lumie change?" Dane asked, with a laugh. "Not a chance."

Mercury laughed in agreement. "I'll see you tonight?"

"Of course," Dane replied immediately. "Can you get through the wards around the town?" He had ensured that a place where a lot of dragons were congregating was well protected, but sometimes those protections messed up transportation spells.

"I think I've got the hang of it." Mercury leaned forward to press his lips briefly to Dane's, and then Dane felt the swirl of his magic before he vanished from sight.

Dane followed, his magic taking him back to the clearing where he would hopefully find the kits' trail and their mother alive at its end. Hopefully.

Chapter Four

Mercury had barely finished unwrapping his sandwich and popping open the bag of chips that came with it when Valerie stormed up to his desk.

"Where the hell have you been?" she snarled.

Mercury wasn't going to miss out on his lunch because she was in a tizzy. He was allowed to take an hour for his lunch on occasion if he wanted, no matter what Valerie might say. He took a big bite of his sandwich and shoved a handful of chips in afterward, then stared at her expectantly.

Valerie spluttered for a long moment while he chewed, crunching loudly. He couldn't quite make himself chew with his mouth open, but the impulse was there.

"We have a case?" she asked slowly and very sarcastically. "Work? You ever heard of those? We don't get lunch hours when there's so much still to do!"

Mercury took another large bite of his sandwich.

Valerie puffed up with air, her face red and her lips pressed tightly together. "I've laid everything out in the conference room when you're done, Your Highness," she snarled before spinning sharply on one heel and marching off.

"Oh, man. That was beautiful." Cheng popped up to hang over the shared side of their cubicle again, and he was grinning widely. "Seriously, I've never seen her that mad, and I was her partner for an entire week! You two are a match made in heaven."

"I have Dane," Mercury said after he swallowed. "I don't need any more matches."

Cheng laughed and waved his hand as if he needed to clear the air. "Not a love match, a work match. You don't take any of her shit or grovel whenever she gets all authoritative. That's exactly what she needs. Listen, I know I hate her guts, but she's a hard worker. You and her figure out how to actually work together with a lot less snarling, you could be good."

Mercury took another bite of food and was gratified to see that his new tactic worked on Cheng too. He didn't wait for Mercury to swallow again before returning to his own cubicle. If only that trick would work on his kits, but he doubted it would deter them.

He finished his sandwich before heading to where Valerie was waiting impatiently. She was leaning aggressively over the conference table, her hands planted in front of her while she stared at the documents that covered half the surface. Her scowl hadn't faded in the least, but Mercury refused to let her scare him.

"So, it was definitely a trap," Mercury said as he entered the room. Valerie immediately turned her glare on him.

"Set for you specifically?" she finally asked when her glare didn't automatically make him wilt. She needed to meet 'Ron in a snit. No one glared and grumped like 'Ron. Maybe that was why he was so impervious to her attitude. In fact...

"You want to come to my house for dinner tonight?" he asked with a smile. "The rest of my kits would love to meet you."

Her scowl vanished, replaced with an openmouthed look of incredulous shock. "You want me to what? Why?"

Mercury shrugged. "I think my kits would like you, and I know they'll want to meet you when I tell them about my day during dinner." And Valerie might learn that her angry and antagonistic ways wouldn't have any effect on him for a very good reason. Working with a partner who was surly all the time would get very old very quickly. "So, six o'clock? I'll come to your place to pick you up?"

"Will it get you to shut up and focus on the case?" she asked. At Mercury's nod, she sighed. "Fine. Six o'clock. Now tell me about the trap."

Mercury pulled forward a picture of the paint from the scene and tapped it with one finger. "The evidence points to the fact that the paint was added sometime after the fires were out, but before the police were actually able to secure the scene. When I attempted to get a closer look at the paint, a spell was activated."

"When you tried to disturb the evidence, you mean," Valerie said pointedly.

"Yeah, okay, no touching strange paint decorating a wall from now on," Mercury agreed. "Anyway, the spell must have been keyed to a dragon. It immediately encircled my hand, making it impossible to move away from the wall, which gave the second part of the layered spell the time it needed to coalesce."

"And the second spell was trying to force you to change shape?" she asked.

Mercury nodded. "That's how I know it was keyed to a dragon. Werewolves and other shape-shifters utilize a different form of magic than dragons to change their shape. Their bones, muscles, and everything else inside their body move around, elongating, or shortening depending on what new shape is needed. Dragons simply are one form or they are another. It's difficult to explain, but it's like both forms exist simultaneously and we consciously decide which one we want to wear in any given moment. That's how our magic works, and the spell was designed to call to that magic to force me to change shape."

"And if you had changed shape?"

"Well, I would have destroyed the scene entirely and probably accidentally squished a few people since my claws would still have been stuck in place. I wouldn't have been able to get myself out of the way. So I called for backup."

"We have to have a talk about bringing outsiders into potentially confidential crime scenes," Valerie grumped. "You'll get us both fired."

"But it worked," Mercury shrugged. That was all that mattered to him.

"So, you called your partner and a child, and they were able to save you?" she asked, quickly changing the subject as her frown grew. She had apparently learned that starting an argument with him wasn't going to work.

"Dane put up a block between me and the spell, and Lumie was able to get my hand free. The part of the spell that was trying to force me to change shape needed me to stay in one spot for it to work, so it faded away."

"So it won't have any negative effect on the FBSI witch we're taking to the scene in an hour?" she asked.

Mercury didn't know the answer to that. "She won't be affected by the spell that attacked me, but I have no way of knowing whether there's another spell keyed to a witch in the paint."

"She should be strong enough to tell," Valerie replied.

"Okay. So what do we need next?" Mercury looked over the many different papers strewn across the conference table, wondering if the answer was hidden somewhere inside. This was his first field investigation, so he didn't know how these things worked.

"We need to know who actually set the fire, which means I have to get that idiot O'Simmons off his ass and into gear. He's still insisting that there hasn't been any evidence of dogfighting inside his jurisdiction. I'm wondering how many reports did actually come across his desk that he ignored for political reasons. O'Simmons's boss holds an elected position, and I'm certain he appreciates not having major crimes or scandals marring his reelection."

"Yikes." There were so many potential layers to the problem that he had never considered. He had thought O'Simmons was just a bad cop, not that he was corrupt.

"I've got the FBI on that, since it's their jurisdiction. They're supposed to red flag me on anything relating to dogfighting that they might come across. They're also going to have a look into why there aren't any witches or other magical creatures living there, but racism and discrimination is a separate department."

"So we just have to wait?" Mercury sighed.

"Wait and read through what we do have to double-check we didn't miss anything," Valerie agreed. "You really don't know who might be impersonating Quicksilver?"

Mercury pulled out one of the chairs around the conference table and sank into it. "Not a clue of who they are specifically, but I know what they want and why."

"You think it's the same people who were kidnapping dragons and doing terrible experiments on them," she said evenly. Mercury couldn't tell if she believed him or was being sarcastic, so he chose to go with the former. "Look," Valerie added tersely, "I was at each scene, and I saw the broken eggs and dead bodies that were uncovered. I tried to fight back when all my evidence and my findings were classified, which made me unable to pursue the case like I wanted to. It's one of the reasons I'm one more failed case away from being fired, although I think Director Stockton is aware that I got stonewalled by his predecessor. He's giving me a chance to reopen those cases with all my old notes and files unclassified again."

Mercury sat up straight at her words and stared at her. "Do you think I could read all your old notes sometime?" he asked. There could be a clue to the enemy in there. He needed to know who they were and where they were hiding. Platinum and the other dragons they were still experimenting on needed to be saved.

"If you're right and the same people who operated those terrible labs are the ones who set your trap, then there might be a connection somewhere. I'll pull everything I can find." She jogged off.

Mercury flipped open a folder in front of him and began reading. While he had been away at lunch, Valerie had apparently typed up all their findings into an official document. At his desk job, Mercury compiled dozens of reports exactly like Valerie's; he couldn't make himself feel guilty that he had made her do this one. Unfortunately, Valerie's report didn't outline anything he didn't already know. Mercury pushed it aside and pulled another folder forward. This one contained photographs of the scene. He browsed through them, but didn't find anyone looking shifty while carrying a bucket of paint hidden in the background.

There were a number of shots of Mercury and Valerie, which confused him. Very few of the photos were captured as part of the larger scene. Most of them were close-ups of his and Valerie's faces. He knew the police liked to get shots of the rubbernecking crowd because oftentimes the criminal liked to return to see his or her handiwork, but he had never heard of needing to purposefully take pictures of the responding officers. The last picture in the pile was another one of Mercury and Valerie. A white halo was standing next to Mercury, holding up a red haired child. The halo was Dane—he didn't show up on regular photography thanks to his heritage—and the child was Lumie. It only showed the back of Lumie's head and his hand as it reached up to free Mercury, but Mercury swallowed hard in fear all the same. That photograph proved to the enemy that Lumie wasn't a regular dragon, that their crazy experiments had been a success.

Mercury had put Lumie in grave danger all because he couldn't control himself at a crime scene. Admittedly, the enemy would have a devil of a time catching Lumie and an even harder time keeping him confined, but that wouldn't stop them from trying. Mercury sighed—there really wasn't anything more he could do to protect Lumie than he already was—and forced his focus to Dane's image instead.

Dane could control himself for long enough to take a picture when he tried. It was how the photo hanging next to Mercury's work computer had been taken. He couldn't suppress the halo when he was using his magic, which was why he was so bright in the picture. Just beyond him, Mercury could just barely make out O'Simmons's face. O'Simmons looked beyond furious, as if Dane and Lumie's arrival had ruined his life. The reaction wasn't in proportion to the general inconvenience they had caused by barging into a crime scene.

Valerie came back a moment later carrying a laptop. It was open and she was typing into it one-handed as she walked, but she put it down on top of the papers so Mercury could see the screen too before taking her own chair.

"Have you seen these pictures?" Mercury asked her, unwilling to let himself get pulled into the past cases on the computer when the present still held so many questions.

"You mean all the pictures of you and me? I wish my badge had a picture as nice as some of those," Valerie grumbled. "I also wish O'Simmons would give me the photographer's name so I could figure out who paid him or her to get pictures of the responding officers instead of the actual scene. Now that I know the trap was set for you, I'm going to get that name if it kills me and follow that money trail until I get you some answers."

"Did you see this picture?" he asked, passing over the final picture with Dane and Lumie.

"I'm sorry they caught a picture of your kit," she said, sounding truly apologetic even though it hadn't been her fault. It was the first emotion he had seen from her that wasn't anger in some way. It transformed her face from harsh to youthful and pretty. All she needed to do was cool down, and she would get a totally different reception from her coworkers.

"What about him?" Mercury asked, tapping the photo just above O'Simmons's head.

Valerie bent over the picture and squinted. Her frown returned with a vengeance when she saw what Mercury had found. "He's just pushing all my buttons. I need to figure out what's making him tick. You catch up on all the reading while I make some phone calls." She walked to the far corner of the room while poking at her cell phone. Mercury pulled over the next folder and started the lengthy task of catching up on years of Valerie's hard work.

*

Mercury let his spell bring them into the foyer of his home. Valerie was clinging to his arm, her nails digging in slightly as if she was afraid she might fall off midtransport and be lost forever. The air smelled faintly of cooking chicken and potatoes roasting in herbs. Mercury had texted Daisy ahead of time to warn her he was bringing a guest, but he wanted his kits to be surprised.

"Daddy's home!" 'Ron shrieked from the top of the staircase above them. "He brought a girl home!"

Valerie jumped, but she suppressed her scowl. Mercury could see the effort it cost her in her clenched fists, but her lips remained in a slight frown as she looked up at 'Ron. Doors slammed, upstairs and down, and the scent of dinner suddenly grew stronger as a half-dozen pairs of footsteps stampeded toward Mercury.

'Ron was closest, and she ran directly into Mercury's chest, making him oomph out a breath of air. Her arms wrapped around his waist, and she squeezed happily. Two impacts against his legs that he could feel, but not see, thanks to 'Ron, told Mercury that Lumie and Alloy were saying hello. Nickel, Copper, and Zinc were more sedate. They were older, but no less excited. Mercury had little doubt they had also run into the room, but they were content to wait for their turn. Chrome, on the other hand, whined and pushed 'Ron out of the way so he could get his hug in. She pushed back, and Mercury had to take a few seconds to dispel the fight before it got out of hand.

"Everyone," Mercury said once all the hugs had been given. "This is Valerie. She's my new partner at work. She wanted to meet you all."

A chorus of hellos and one "You're so tall!" from an admiring 'Ron echoed around the room. Mercury made introductions.

"So you're not cheating on Dane, then?" Zinc asked. She tried for nonchalant, but Mercury could see the anxiety in her eyes. She had some lingering separation issues from her time locked away in a cell. After being left behind to die and separated from her biological brother Platinum, she was always slightly worried that Mercury or Dane would do something similar. Usually that fear was banked, but every once in a while it reared its ugly head.

"Not a chance," Valerie answered before Mercury could. "Sorry, Mercury, but I think I'd kill you if we had to live together."

The kits all nodded sagely, as if this were the word from a god. Although, since they didn't treat Dane with nearly the same reverence, Mercury might have been better off thinking of the kits' rare moment of silent agreement as a lucky fluke. He should just enjoy the moment instead of analyzing it.

"How was the picnic?" Lumie asked from somewhere around Mercury's knee. Mercury gently moved 'Ron aside so he could kneel next to Lumie and Alloy. He hooked an arm around Alloy but looked sharply at Lumie.

"Lumie, you could just tell Dane or me about these things instead of tricking us into it. It's not very nice, and if Dane had known where those kits were this morning, he could have picked them up hours earlier and been searching their back trail for their mother all afternoon."

Lumie shrugged and grinned. "But this way was more fun. You found the kits though." He turned away and toddled off in the direction of the kitchen before Mercury could resume trying to scold him. Mercury sighed, standing up with Alloy in his arms.

"So, how many of you are supposed to be helping Daisy cook or set the table?" Mercury asked. A couple of kits looked shifty-eyed for a second; then Chrome, Zinc, and Copper hurried off. 'Ron followed, but she had cleaning-up duties and probably only wanted to show Daisy her new dress. "Is Dane home?" Mercury asked Nickel as he walked slowly after his kits.

Nickel shook his head. "He stopped by the office to pick me up, but he said he had one more place to check and he'd be home in time for dinner." They talked about homework as they walked to the kitchen, Mercury trying to explain a history question Nickel had to answer for one of his mandated practice exams for his GED. He was going to graduate early at the rate he was going, while the rest of Mercury's kits would be lucky to graduate before they were twenty. Valerie trailed placidly behind them as they entered the kitchen.

"There ya are," Daisy called happily. "I've had the kits set the dining room, since ye've brought a guest. Everything needs another five minutes, which is just enough time for y'all to wash yer hands." She smiled at Mercury and Valerie absentmindedly as she untied her apron and gathered her purse. "I'll be here on time in the morning. The husband's taking the day off so I don't have to."

Her son had bitten his teacher, Mercury remembered. "If you need to bring him here..." he began.

Daisy laughed. "Not a good idea." Her words were punctuated by a crashing noise from the nearby bathroom followed by the laughter of a number of Mercury's kits. "I'm worried they'll get along a little too well. Have a good night."

"You too," Mercury called as she swept past him gracefully. He heard the front door close a few minutes later as she headed down the drive toward the transportation circle those who didn't have personal magic to transport them needed to use.

Mercury put Alloy down. "Why don't you show Valerie where to sit and then go wash your hands?" he told Alloy and Nickel. Alloy smiled eagerly up at Valerie, grabbed her hand, and dragged her off toward the dining room. Mercury found some oven mitts and began pulling dinner out of the oven. He put all the heavy dishes onto one big tray and carried it out to the dining room.

They didn't eat at the dining room table often; the kits were far too messy and destructive for it, and it was easier to deal with them in the confines of the kitchen. Still, they ate formally often enough that everyone had an assigned seat. Dane sat at the head of the table with Mercury to his right. Nickel usually sat across from Mercury, but he had surrendered his spot to Valerie for the night. He sat on Valerie's left and Zinc sat on his other side. 'Ron sat next to Zinc, and the final chair belonged either to Lumie or Alloy depending on how they were feeling that day. Copper sat next to Mercury with Chrome on his other side, followed by either Alloy or Lumie. Tonight it was Lumie. Alloy slid into his seat across from Lumie, his hands still dripping wet, as Mercury set the dishes on trivets on the table.

Copper and Nickel helped pour water into the younger kits plastic cups while Mercury dished chicken, potatoes, and tarragon green beans onto each plate. He did remember to let Valerie take her own food, but it was a near thing. Half of his attention was on his kits chattering about their day. The rest was focused toward the rest of the house for the first sign that Dane had finally made it home.

The kits asked Valerie all sorts of invasive questions, which made Mercury grin involuntarily.

"What about your boyfriend?" 'Ron asked eagerly. She had turned very girly girl as she grew up, indulging in dresses and dreaming of the day Mercury allowed her to try makeup, but aside from Daisy and Becky, she didn't really have any adult female role models in her life. She was milking Valerie for all the information on what being an adult female was like, including the mysterious concept of wanting a boyfriend. At nine years old, 'Ron was just starting to figure out that boys weren't necessarily an "eww" concept.

"I don't have a boyfriend," Valerie replied. Mercury caught Chrome's eye and pointedly held his fork in a proper grip. Chrome grumbled and rearranged his fingers around the utensil so he was no longer eating like an uncultured caveman.

'Ron gasped in shock, a piece of chicken falling off her fork and back onto her plate as she stared incredulously at Valerie. "No boyfriend? Why not?"

Valerie shrugged. "I haven't found the right one yet. I don't want a boyfriend just to have a boyfriend. I want a man who means something to me."

'Ron cooed. She had put down her silverware in order to clasp her hands under her chin cutely as she gazed in wonder at the mature woman who didn't need a boyfriend to define her life. Which meant, of course, that now Mercury was going to have a feminist dragon haranguing Chrome for being such a slob instead of an empty-headed teenybopper haranguing Chrome for being such a slob. Neither were necessarily a bad thing for 'Ron to be, but she excelled at being annoying at whatever she did. Mercury was looking forward immensely to 'Ron being finished with puberty, although the flip side was that when 'Ron began to grow out of puberty, Lumie would be starting it—and that was a basket of eggs Mercury really didn't want to drop. Ever.

As dinner progressed and his kits took seconds and thirds, Mercury reserved a piece of chicken and a scoop of all the sides for Dane on his plate. Dane could heat it up whenever he got in. When everyone was finished eating, Mercury supervised the kits clearing all the dishes. He would clean the kitchen later, but first Lumie toddled into the dining room with the basket that contained dessert inside. He already had a Cinnamon Bomb in his mouth, stretching out one cheek. The basket was passed around, and everyone took their favorite candy. Valerie hesitated when the basket reached her and glanced up at Mercury for advice.

"Take whatever you want. The basket gets refilled regularly." Mercury reached across the table and took one of Nickel's blue rock candies.

Valerie took a Cinnamon Bomb, which made Mercury wince—he hated the things—and Lumie giggled happily. It didn't take long for the candy to vanish. Mercury tried not to glance at the door while everyone happily got sugar high. It wasn't like Dane to be so late, especially when he had told Nickel he'd be home before dinner. Maybe he had found the mother dragon and was having some trouble getting her settled in to the dragon village, but he would have called to tell them he would be late if that were the case.

Mercury was very worried that something else had gone wrong. But Dane was the son of a god. His magic was unbelievably powerful. It did take a while to amass for larger spells, but there were very few creatures on earth that could match him or keep him confined. There was no reason he shouldn't have been home on time.

Still, Mercury didn't want to worry his kits. He caught Lumie's eye, then Copper and Chrome's. "Bath time," he insisted. Lumie groaned and Chrome rolled his eyes. Copper would stoically obey, although he didn't like the water any more than Lumie did. The other kits would bathe themselves without issue, even Alloy, who sometimes hated the water as much as Lumie and other times loved it as much as Nickel.

With dinner over, the kits all ran off in different directions. Mercury did hear water start to run upstairs in at least one of the bathrooms, so someone was obeying him. Probably Zinc or Nickel. Hopefully one of them had grabbed Lumie or Alloy to take a bath together. His two youngest kits were capable of bathing themselves, but it was usually a messy process without supervision.

Mercury headed to the kitchen with Valerie to clean up.

"I'm sorry I can't drop you home right away," Mercury apologized as he pulled open the dishwasher to begin stacking the dinner dishes inside. "I don't want to leave them alone right now, and with Dane not home..." He shut his mouth quickly before his worry could leak out, but Valerie caught it immediately. She was a good investigator, and he had little doubt that she hadn't missed the few times he hadn't been able to stop himself from glancing toward the door during dinner.

"Where is Dane?" she asked. Her tone was gentle instead of sharp. The kits had done a number on her permanent scowl, easing it into a mere frown as she studied him.

Mercury leaned his weight on his hands where they were pressed against the edge of the counter. "I don't know," he forced out. "We've been helping dragons together for five years now. The enemy is still capturing dragons for their cruel experiments, so whenever we hear about one under attack, we respond immediately. A male dragon sent a message to Dane a few weeks ago saying his family had been attacked. He had held the enemy off while his mate and their three kits escaped, but he was badly injured. He couldn't look for them, so Dane promised we would, instead."

"So Dane was out in the woods tonight searching for those missing kits?" Valerie gasped. Her eyes were narrowed in thought. "These are the same guys who placed the trap in the paint? They must be," she continued, answering her own question before Mercury could speak. "They were trying to draw you out at the crime scene, maybe catch you and Dane and keep you both from interfering with their dragon capturing."

"We found the kits this afternoon while I took my long lunch," Mercury explained. "They're safe, but their mother was still unaccounted for, so Dane went back to the woods this afternoon."

"He had one more place to check," Valerie remembered, echoing Nickel's words prior to dinner. "Since he's not back yet, it might be safe to assume his one last place was the right one and he might have run into some trouble." She paused to look at Mercury as he continued to stack dishes. "You need to go after him, just in case. I'll stay and watch your kits."

Mercury looked at her in shock. Valerie's personality was so grating at times; he didn't think she was capable of handling any of his kits, should they get in a snit. Yet, at the same time, he wanted to run after Dane to double-check that he was safe.

"My sister's got a set of rambunctious triplets that I babysit. I can handle a few hours with your kits, especially when they'll all be in bed soon. Go."

Mercury took her at her word. He gathered his magic and directed it into a transportation spell. The kitchen vanished around him, replaced by the familiar clearing. Mercury hurried over to the bush where Dane had found the kits and then paused. Dane would have left magical markers for himself to show where he had already searched. They were keyed only to Dane so no one except Dane could read them. But Mercury knew enough to be able to find them, and he knew Dane well enough to be able to tell which markers were positive indicators and which were negative.

It took a few minutes of searching with his magic before Mercury found the first one. It was high in a tree where only the birds and squirrels would ordinarily find it, but once Mercury located it, the rest almost blazed against the touch of his searching magic. Each marker felt subtly different as Mercury followed them through the forest. Some simply indicated that Dane had traveled in this direction while others told stories of failed searches off to the west and his eventual return to the original path.

Mercury was walking south. Every once in a while, he saw what Dane must have been looking for: the scratch of scales or claws against the bark of a tree, the disturbed leaf litter where the kits had stopped to play or nap. The markers flashed by as Mercury increased his speed. Every moment he dawdled admiring how much difficult work Dane had accomplished in one short afternoon was another moment that might mean he was too late.

Mercury's stride ate up the miles quickly. He knew where the clearing was on a map, northeast of Dane's office in the Berkshires, and that he was paralleling Route 87 south toward New York City. The spot where the mother dragon was separated from her kits couldn't be much farther. The kits had been alone for not even five hours, and they hadn't been walking steadily for the entire time.

When Mercury finally reached the marker that felt like a stopping point, he paused to catch his breath. This was where Dane had paused in his search to go pick up Nickel from the office; Mercury could sense the remnants of Dane's transportation spell as he left and then returned again shortly after. Mercury was still in the middle of a forest with only trees and the deepening twilight surrounding him. The sounds around him were normal as the creatures of the day bedded down and the creatures of the night woke up. Dane had gotten Nickel just after five o'clock and dinner had been served at six. That gave Dane an hour of time before Mercury was certain something had happened, then an hour while dinner had been eaten, and forty-five minutes of Mercury following Dane's trail. So Dane should be within a three-hour radius of the point where Mercury was standing. Mercury would continue to follow Dane's trail until he found Dane or found traces of another transportation spell, at which point he would regroup.

Mercury proceeded at a slightly slower pace, double-checking with each marker that he was on the right trail. He was still moving faster than Dane must have been since Mercury didn't need to search the ground for minute clues of a dragon's passage. Mercury also didn't need to divert from the path to run off in one direction or another to check over a ridge or under a fallen tree for more clues, which saved him a lot of time. Within fifteen minutes of walking, the forest began to quiet around him. The hoot of waking owls and the scurry of squirrels and mice as they found their nighttime dens faded away, replaced by an ominous air.

There was a strange sort of weight to the wind as it rustled the leaves around him. It was tainted in the disgustingly familiar way of stolen dragon magic. Mercury called on his own magic and weaved it into an intangibility spell. True invisibility was impossible—someone would notice the strange distortion around him as he moved—so he instead used a spell that kept people from looking at him at all.

Dane's markers faded away, but Mercury didn't need them any longer. He followed the tainted magic until he found the source.

Two trees had been utterly shattered; splinters poked out of the ground and were embedded in nearby trees. The air smelled faintly of smoke and some of the splinters had charred ends, but over all of that was the stench of tainted magic.

"Can we get a helicopter here or not?" a voice snarled. No one answered, but a second later the voice continued. "Tell them we're transporting an elephant that escaped from the zoo!"

Mercury peeked cautiously around a tree, trusting that his spell would avert anyone's eyes from him. An adult red dragon was lying on the ground only a few feet to Mercury's left. She was alive, but she had been liberally wrapped in heavy iron chains and then covered in dragon's bane. The flower was similar in size and shape to wolf's bane, the petals an odd mix between a bell shape and a winglike shape, but these flowers were the pearlescent white that was poisonous to dragons instead of the lavender-colored kind that hurt werewolves. Mercury didn't doubt that this was the mother dragon Dane had been searching for and that without the dragon's bane holding her immobile she would still be destroying trees.

Dane was lying unmoving next to her on the ground. For a heart-stopping moment, Mercury was afraid Dane was dead. Mercury clutched at the tree he was hiding behind and forced back a whimper so he didn't give himself away. Then he saw the slow rise and fall of Dane's chest, and he sagged in relief. Mercury wiped a stray tear away and took a few deep breaths to slow the shaking. Dane was unconscious, or he was pretending to be. Mercury caught the gleam of one blue eye peeking out from underneath his lid and felt the wind blow past him. A handful of the dragon's bane flowers blew off the mother dragon, vanishing harmlessly into the forest behind them. Dane was okay, Mercury reminded himself, so it was time to refocus on saving them all from the enemy.

The rest of the area had been turned into an impromptu campsite. Someone had built a fire in a clear spot to ward off any autumn chill as the sun set. Three men and one woman were standing close by, the flickering light illuminating their faces. Mercury recognized three of them from the bomb scene that morning, and he knew he was looking at crime scene techs and at least one police officer. Mercury memorized their faces to tell Valerie later now that he had tangible proof that the bombing case was connected to the missing dragon.

Another gust of wind blew through the trees and another large handful of dragon's bane vanished. The people by the fire edged closer to it, as if they sensed that the wind could become dangerously cold in a mere moment. They didn't notice that it was Dane's magic affecting them and luckily also weren't alert enough to notice Mercury.

Mercury wasn't as allergic to dragon's bane as most dragons, but even he couldn't go near that much without having a reaction. Instead of trying to help Dane with the dragon, he slowly crept closer to the man snarling into his phone.

"Yes, I have the authority to requisition a Black Hawk helicopter should the need warrant it!" the man was yelling. "Tell them of course they haven't heard about an elephant escaping the zoo! It was kept quiet to reduce panic. No, I don't have any idea how an elephant would get from the zoo all the way out here. Make something up!"

Mercury's magic fizzled between his fingers. He didn't know what magical defenses the guy must have put in place with his tainted dragon magic, so Mercury would have to be careful.

Suddenly, the man spun and stared out into the forest as if he sensed someone watching him. Mercury froze in place, unwilling to move and give away his position. Another gust of wind blew, distracting the man from the forest. He looked toward the fire as if he wanted to join his comrades, but the phone call was more important. The fire lit up the side of his face, making him look particularly evil with the flickering red light contrasted against the shadowed half of his head. It also gave Mercury a glimpse of his features, and Mercury had to stifle a gasp of recognition when he saw O'Simmons's familiar face. Mercury should have known that bastard O'Simmons was neck-deep in the entire thing. He wasn't just corrupt or a bad cop. He wasn't just in someone's pocket. He was running the entire operation!

After the enemy lost their foothold with the SupFeds, they must have wanted to solidify their ties with some sort of law enforcement. Who better to recruit than a racist police captain? O'Simmons was probably highly interested in the idea that magicless humans could become stronger than their supernatural counterparts. He hadn't smelled like tainted magic at the crime scene—Mercury would have noticed that smell immediately and tracked it down—which meant he hadn't used the magic since his last shower and change of clothing. That was far more devious than Mercury would have attributed to O'Simmons, but then he also hadn't expected to run into the man in the middle of the forest.

"Fine!" O'Simmons snapped into his phone before pulling it away from his ear and hitting the button to end the call. With the face to match to the voice, Mercury didn't understand how he had missed recognizing O'Simmons earlier. Although Mercury did have to admit he had been more concerned with Dane and the captured mother dragon than with specifically who he was about to fight against. O'Simmons abandoned his search of the surrounding forest, probably brushing off his feelings of being watched as that of an overactive imagination. "I need to go to the hangar directly. They won't take my credentials over the phone," he explained to the other four people.

The woman nodded, apparently in charge while O'Simmons was away. There was a swell of tainted magic and O'Simmons vanished. Mercury frowned as the magic slowly dissipated through the air. Elemental dragons couldn't form a transportation spell like that. Their magic was restricted to their respective elements of fire, water, air, and earth. Only precious dragons like Mercury could use spells outside of those parameters, which meant that somewhere the enemy was siphoning off the powers of a precious dragon for use in their magical cocktail.

But that was a problem for another moment. Dane's eyes flashed open briefly again, and Mercury knew he was checking that Mercury would be ready to act at the same moment Dane did.

The wind roared through the trees. Colorful leaves were ripped from their stems and blown up off the ground, circling like a terrible, obscuring cyclone. The fire went out with a puff of acrid smoke, and the four humans began to shout at each other over the noise of the wind. Tainted magic swelled from them, but Dane batted it aside effortlessly. Mercury had little doubt that Dane had been gathering as much magic as he could hold while pretending to be unconscious.

Mercury shifted forms, his dragon scales shoving trees out of the way to make room for his girth. He roared, adding his own magic to Dane's, and was echoed a moment later as the fire dragon shook off her chains and lifted her own voice into the wind. Dane wouldn't let the enemy leave the scene by transporting away, holding them in place while their magic fought against Dane's and Mercury's combined forces. He felt Dane weaving something extra into the magic and recognized the antideath spell he was adding to the wind. In their last confrontation with this tainted magic, Jacobson had died before he could be questioned, thanks to an extra touch of evil added to his concoction of stolen magic; Dane wasn't about to allow that to happen here.

It took a while before their struggles diminished as one by one their borrowed magic ran out. If the concoction ever made it to the black market, Mercury knew it would be as bad as any addictive drug. Powerful one moment, helpless human the next. Addicts would do anything to get their hands on more magic. Mercury didn't doubt the four who were sitting on the ground gaping at their hands as they tried and failed to call up a spell were experiencing the desolation of withdrawal.

The wind slowly died away. Mercury pulled his magic from the air as Dane's powers dissipated with the breeze. The woods were silent except for the soft rustle of leaves settling back down to the ground. Mercury shifted forms, smoothly losing his claws and scales for his clothed human shape as he strode across the clearing.

"They had the same death spell on the end of their magic?" he asked Dane.

Dane grunted. "Bitch of a spell, but I got rid of it this time."

"Where is it?" the woman moaned, flinging her hands out as if she were casting some sort of spell. "Where did it go?"

"They didn't tell you it was a finite supply when they doped you?" Dane asked scathingly. He knelt in front of the woman to try to catch her gaze, but she wouldn't look away from her hands as she tried spell after spell to no effect. Mercury had once heard Dane compare the stolen magic to a spool of string. It was strong and felt infinite, but it wasn't renewable. Eventually the users reached the end of the spool, and suddenly there wasn't any magic left at all. The absence was apparently shocking, given the way the woman was babbling.

"What should we do with them?" Dane asked, frowning down at the group. The men were in just as bad shape as the woman, although they weren't being as vocal about it.

"We can't stay here. O'Simmons will be back," Mercury replied.

"And I need to run after my kits before they get hurt in the woods," the red dragon rumbled. She didn't look particularly steady on her four legs. She was probably still suffering the effects of dragon's bane poisoning; plus, she had thrown her magic in with Dane's to stop the enemy from escaping.

"Can we take them to the SupFeds?" Dane asked Mercury thoughtfully before turning soothingly toward the worried mother. "We found your kits earlier today. They're safe with your mate. If you wait a moment, I'll bring you to them."

Mercury dug his phone out of his pocket and dialed the number Valerie had left him. It rang twice before she answered.

"Hello?" she gasped, sounding winded.

"Hey, what's the protocol for bringing criminals to the FBSI building for interrogation?" Mercury asked, pushing aside his worry over why she sounded so out of breath.

"Have you formally arrested them?" she asked, suddenly sounding very businesslike.

"Not yet. I don't want to do it wrong. They're not exactly coherent enough to understand Miranda."

"Okay," Valerie interjected before Mercury's worries took over their phone call. When all this was over, he was going to take a class on being a field agent. He didn't want to be caught floundering again. He needed to take whatever classes the SupFeds offered if he was going to continue working with Valerie so this situation was never repeated. "I've got Stockton's home number. I'll give him a call, and you bring your criminals to the office since we can't send cars to the middle of the woods to pick them up. Have the guards at the front door security desk help you bring them down to interrogation. One person per interrogation room. I assume you found Dane, so when you come get me, he can take over with the kits, and I'll make the formal arrests and read them their rights. See you in a bit." She hung up.

"I'll get our mama dragon settled and then head home," Dane said when Mercury pocketed his phone. He had apparently been listening to the conversation. "I'll watch the kits for tonight, so take as much time as you need."

Mercury began gathering his magic. He needed more in order to weave a spell that would transport everyone to his office.

"I'm going to try to convince them to go after O'Simmons too. I have a feeling he's hiding a dragon lab in his precinct, and I want to use the SupFeds' resources to find it before O'Simmons is tipped off that we're on to him."

"Call when you have word," Dane agreed with a small smile. He gently took the mother dragon's arm and they vanished. Mercury let his own magic loose, pulling all four captives along with him as they headed to the SupFeds office.

*

Valerie should be one of the top field agents the SupFeds had ever trained. Mercury had no doubt about that fact, and he really hoped that after their case came to a successful end she would finally get the recognition she deserved. By the time he arrived outside his office building, she had already informed Stockton that something important was up, had alerted the appropriate people that Mercury was bringing criminals in for questioning, and had begun planning their next move. All Mercury needed to do was hand over all four criminals, turn around to get Valerie, and then be present as Valerie's partner when she outlined their investigation to Stockton and the other bigwigs that had been called in.

The bigwigs all seemed to be familiar with the case in question. Mercury didn't doubt that they all had to be, given they had probably been investigated along with Jacobson, their previous boss, when Jacobson's connection to kidnapping and cruel experimenting on dragons came to light.

"So, what do we have on this Captain O'Simmons?" Stockton asked when Valerie finished her explanation about why everyone's evening had been interrupted.

"Just what the FBI's been able to find so far," Valerie replied immediately, digging in the stack of papers she had brought to the meeting and pulling out a woefully thin manila folder. "They've run a background check on him as a civilian and as an officer of the law, and they're not impressed. His bank account has quite a number of unexplained deposits of exactly nine thousand dollars."

Which was just under the ten-thousand-dollar minimum amount that had to be reported to the IRS for tax purposes and a clear sign that he was doing something shady. "He has two vacation homes, one in Florida and the other in Hawaii, which he shouldn't be able to afford even on a captain's salary. His wife is unemployed, he hasn't won the lottery, and he didn't inherit any money or property. As captain, he has been diverting police funds to a warehouse that's billed as an evidence warehouse, but there aren't enough cases in his relatively small precinct to actually warrant the space."

"A warehouse?" Mercury asked curiously, leaning forward to read the papers over Valerie's shoulder. "The last place they were holding dragons captive was a warehouse on the Chesapeake Bay."

"Where the magical earthquake attack hit five years ago?" a woman asked. Mercury hadn't caught her name. She didn't work for the SupFeds, and Stockton had acted very differentially toward her when she had walked into the room. Maybe she was from the State Department?

"That's correct, Madame Secretary," Valerie replied. Or she was the Secretary of Defense and Mercury had better damn well learn her name if he wanted to keep his job. "O'Simmons was recorded trying to requisition a Black Hawk helicopter from the local air base to return an elephant that had wandered out of a local zoo. When no proof could be found that an elephant had actually escaped the zoo, his request was denied. He must have realized by now that Agent Mercury has interrupted his planned capture of a fire dragon and apprehended his coconspirators." Mercury wasn't officially an agent yet, just an analyst, but he appreciated the promotion since he was doing an agent's job with Valerie at the moment. He also appreciated the fact that she hadn't used his last name. "We need to move on that warehouse immediately before O'Simmons has the chance to shut everything down."

"He'll most likely kill whatever dragons he's holding captive if he doesn't think there's time to move them," Mercury added to emphasize that time was of the essence.

Madame Secretary stood up and tapped the table sharply. "Get it done," she informed them. She nodded to the room before striding out.

"What do you need?" Stockton asked Valerie the second the door had closed behind the Secretary.

"O'Simmons is using stolen dragon magic, so I'll need as many witches we have on staff as well as SWAT to move in. It would be nice if we could hire the Supernatural Consultant as well—"

"But he'll need a babysitter first. And he'll bring Nickel, which I'm not sure the FBSI would agree with," Mercury interrupted.

"Nickel's only thirteen!" Valerie gasped, turning to glare at Mercury for suggesting they bring a minor along.

"He's the Assistant Supernatural Consultant," Mercury explained to Valerie and the rest of the room. "And he can hold his own in a fight."

"What kind of babysitter?" Stockton asked.

Mercury blushed and Valerie let out a small chuckle. "Someone with a lot of energy and a lot of patience," she said.

Stockton looked thoughtful for a brief moment, then nodded. "I'll make the phone calls. Be ready to go in a half hour." He departed the room, too, leaving behind the strike team he had assembled for the job.

Valerie pulled a folded piece of paper out of her stack, unfolded it, and pointed to the blueprints of the warehouse in question. "This is what we're aiming for, but be prepared for O'Simmons to have changed the layout."

Mercury let Valerie do the rest of the talking. He was way out of his element. He knew how to break into a building, take out the enemy, and rescue everyone inside, but he didn't know how to do that legally. Valerie did, and he hoped to learn a lot from her, but every second that passed while the humans prepared was another second that they might be too late to save the dragons O'Simmons was holding captive. He bit his lip and told himself to endure the wait and hope the result was a good one.

Chapter Five

The kits were all hyped up from the new experience of having a babysitter, an occurrence that had never happened before, and by Valerie's abrupt departure after only an hour. They knew something exciting was going on and wanted to hear every detail. Dane was hounded for information from all sides, including above, as Chrome had decided to shout his own questions into the melee while flying around their heads in dragon form. It took Dane a half hour to calm everyone enough so they were willing to climb into bed. It was another half hour after that before Dane stopped hearing excited rustling and the occasional additional question shouted down the hall toward where he was attempting to relax in the sitting area between the two wings of his house.

Only once it was actually quiet did Dane finally relax. The armchair was soft underneath his butt, and he relished the comfort even as he let his brain run through how his day had gone. Dane's legs hurt from all the walking he had been doing while searching through the forest and then from an hour of lying on the ground pretending to be unconscious.

Allowing himself to be captured was a risky move, one Dane didn't think he would be repeating any time soon. He had made the decision based on a few facts. First, because he would need time to amass enough magic to fight against five humans using tainted dragon magic.

Second, if Dane stayed hidden out of sight while he amassed that magic, he might be too far away to act should the enemy hurt the poor dragon they had captured. She'd been alive for the moment, but Dane had no way of knowing how much longer that might last.

Judging by the destroyed state of the forest, it had taken quite a while to actually subdue her. She had been fighting to protect her kits, and Dane had little doubt that desperation had given her fire more heat and intensity. The enemy had found her sometime in the morning, Dane didn't know exactly when, and she had kept them engaged for long enough they hadn't been able to chase after the kits and keep her contained. Given what Dane knew about how quickly very young kits could move, which was pretty damned fast, combined with how easily they got distracted, which was unbelievably easy, his estimate was a two-hour battle, plus another hour to actually get the chains and dragon's bane in place.

Theoretically, that should have left the enemy the entire afternoon to take their captive away and subsequently return to look for the kits. One of the reasons Dane hadn't wanted to go too far away from the scene was because he honestly couldn't figure out why they had spent the entire afternoon just sitting around with their captive. Then O'Simmons had appeared.

O'Simmons's actions quickly established in Dane's mind that he was the leader of the group and he apparently made all the decisions. Dane knew that O'Simmons had been stuck at the crime scene Mercury was investigating all day and had probably barely had a moment to check his phone messages, let alone sneak off to deal with a captured dragon. His team had waited for him instead.

Dane felt Mercury's magic prod at some of the markers he had left behind to mark his trail not long after. Mercury would join him soon, since his mate could read the markers. Dane would allow himself to be captured, giving him the time he needed to gather his magic and to begin freeing the dragon from her bindings. It would also give Mercury time to get close enough to back Dane up, but just in case O'Simmons decided it was time to move before Mercury arrived, Dane would be ready to stop him.

Luckily, Mercury arrived in time and the battle went well. Dane brought the dragon to her family, and Martha was helping them settle in. When he returned home, Mercury would probably scold Dane for scaring him by not calling when Dane knew he was going to be late and by pretending to be captured, but Dane enjoyed the way Mercury's face looked when he got serious. Mercury had the same fiery eyes when he was growling playfully at Dane as he did when in the middle of battle. Which could explain why his serious moments usually led to a rousing evening with his mate. He'd start with some candlelight and chocolates. Then...

Dane told his romantic thoughts to shut up. There was no way Mercury was going to be home in the next few minutes to help him make his straying thoughts into reality. Mercury was out saving dragons; Dane needed to keep his mind on his own tasks, instead of on wishing Mercury was already here with him.

A rustling noise forced Dane's attention back to the present. He looked up from where he had been staring unseeing at his clasped fingers just as Nickel settled into the chair across from him. Nickel was dressed in rough jeans and a T-shirt rather than his pajamas. The little scamp had made all the same motions of going to bed as the rest of the kits, but instead of actually going to sleep, he'd come to bug Dane.

"There's something happening," Nickel said quietly so the other—actually sleeping—kits wouldn't hear that he was still awake. "Tell me."

Dane told him. From the first moment Mercury had made Dane take Nickel along to a raid to save the air dragons, Nickel had always been an active participant in their goal to save the dragons from the enemy. Nickel might still be young in body, but his psyche was that of a man twenty years older, and Dane trusted Nickel to have his back.

"Darn. So they were able to catch a precious dragon," Nickel sighed. "That's real magic to the humans."

"Elemental magic is real magic too," Dane admonished. Nickel wouldn't be the first person Dane knew to bemoan the fact that their magic was too specialized to have a broad use. Mercury could cast any spell he wanted as long as he knew it and had the power for it. Nickel could only use magic that pertained to water.

"If you know how to use it properly," Nickel replied easily. He clenched one fist, which squelched slightly as if he were holding a water balloon, and his smile grew a touch more deadly. No, Dane didn't have to worry about Nickel. He did have to worry about greedy humans who would see elemental magic as weak in comparison to a precious dragon's and who had the technology to try to warp their stolen magic even further. "So when do you think Stockton's going to give you a call? If they're raiding a lab with humans using tainted magic, he's going to want the strongest magic user in the area working with his team."

With just a few moments of thought, Nickel had figured out why Dane was still in the sitting area instead of preparing for his own bed. Mercury might not be able to call Dane to his side in this case, but Stockton could and would.

As if Dane's cell phone were just waiting for Nickel's cue, it rang. Dane let it ring twice, carefully cupping his hand over the speaker to keep the noise from echoing so it wouldn't wake anyone.

"This is Dane," Dane said politely into the phone. "I assume you got this number from Mercury's emergency contact form?"

Stockton laughed on the other end. "Good guess. You probably also know why I'm calling. I've arranged for a babysitter to watch over your kits. We'll pay her rates and yours. If you could come to the FBSI offices as soon as she arrives?"

The front door downstairs popped unlocked, and Dane leaned to the side in his chair to look over the railing to see who was coming inside. Daisy's distinctive green skin was visible through the window as she tucked her key away again and pushed the door open.

"That shouldn't be a problem," Dane replied. They both hung up. Dane got to his feet and headed down the stairs to say hello to Daisy, Nickel tight on his heels.

"Ya know, Boss, ya didn't need to get some head honcho to call me if ya needed me to stay here a few extra hours," Daisy said playfully as she took her light coat off to hang in the hall closet and stashed her purse below.

"You're moonlighting as a babysitter for difficult children?" Dane asked, trying to keep his own tone playful. "Clearly I'm not paying you enough if you need to go elsewhere for money. Nickel, remind me to double her salary when we get home."

Daisy was still gaping in incredulity at Dane when Nickel's hand landed on Dane's shoulder, and Dane's magic pulled them away. Dane focused on Mercury, letting his magic take them to Mercury's side. They appeared inside a conference room that Dane felt safe assuming was somewhere inside the SupFeds' regional office.

There were a few exclamations of surprise, and one man instinctively unhooked his gun holster at their sudden appearance.

"Not the usual method of entering our premises," Stockton called above everyone else's noises of surprise. "We prefer if you were cleared by our security team downstairs first." Dane had slipped through the wards the SupFeds had around the building to prevent people popping in like Dane had, and he didn't even look winded for the effort. Nickel got a few odd looks as well, but since no one commented on him, Dane assumed Mercury had warned everyone.

"This is the warehouse we think the dragons are being kept in," Mercury said. He slid a piece of paper across the table toward Dane. Nickel picked it up and held it so they both could see.

"They couldn't build underground in this neighborhood, even if they just stuck to below the warehouses," Nickel said thoughtfully. "Even with magical reinforcement, there's too much chance they would open up a sinkhole underneath someone's house and give away their position."

"So we're looking at an aboveground assault." Dane agreed with Nickel's assessment. "O'Simmons's magic was powerful enough that he could transport himself to other places, but he couldn't transport something as large as a dragon. He's definitely a threat, but I'm more worried about him combining his magic with others. That could be deadly." Dane had used a lot of magic earlier in the day, and his stores were depleted. However, one of the benefits about his lineage was that he couldn't get exhausted from using too much magic. Dane just had to replenish his stores. Magic came easily to Dane's call as he slowly, but steadily, began to prepare for the coming fight.

"SWAT goes in first. We would like you with them, Dane," Valerie said. "You have the magic to combat any attacks that the SWAT witches can't handle, and if they find the dragons, you'll be able to calm them."

Nickel was the one who answered, even though Valerie was speaking to Dane. Dane didn't have a problem with that, given Nickel would be joining whichever group Dane was assigned. "That would work. Getting doused in water would certainly throw the enemy off their game, and Dane and your witches can follow up. This O'Simmons guy has had at least an hour's head start on us. We should go to the warehouse now."

"The longer we wait, the more chance we'll miss him entirely," Mercury agreed.

Dane took in another large gulp of magic and let it settle before asking for coordinates of where they were meeting in the town. Dane's problem with working with the government was their need to follow so many regulations. Every *i* had to be dotted and *t* crossed on dozens of forms before anything could happen. Plans had to be made and double-checked. In a way, Dane did understand why. Should someone get injured or die during a raid, no one would get in trouble, thanks to every single properly filled-out form. It was sad that the government had to work that way, and Dane hated the delay it caused, but liability suits were ugly. Gregory, Dane's lawyer, would kill Dane if he had to handle one of those simply because Dane had rushed the SupFeds and something bad happened.

Yet every second they dithered over red tape and preparation, Dane grew a little more impatient. If it were just Mercury and Dane, they would have already infiltrated the warehouse and been saving the dragons. Having backup was a nice change—Dane couldn't deny that—but if it meant harm would come to those poor dragons... Dane didn't really want to think about it.

Magic crackled under his fingers, and Dane reeled it back in. Wasting magic just because he was getting antsy was stupid, and starting a raid with his being stupid was not a good omen.

"You're to stay behind a shield at all times," the burly guy apparently in charge of the SWAT team insisted to Dane and Nickel. Dane quirked an eyebrow, wondering just what he needed a shield for—he could stop bullets and spells equally with his magic—but he nodded just to keep the proceedings moving along.

"All right, that's enough stalling," Valerie snapped. She slammed her hands down on the table to get everyone's attention. "We've all run an operation like this before. We're all trained and prepared. Let's stop talking over the what-ifs and move to actually doing. We have lives to save."

"Well said," Stockton agreed. "This is high profile, people. The Secretary of Defense wants these terrorists stopped before they escalate to higher-profile targets. Let's move out!"

Higher profile, as in people more important than dragons. The mindset that dragons were wild and untamable needed to be changed in order to keep something like this from ever happening again.

Nickel growled at Stockton, who looked suddenly chagrined as he realized what his words implied while speaking in front of two dragons and some other people who might remember his insensitivity and potentially deny him a future promotion. But he didn't apologize, instead turning to Dane.

"Can you transport all of us to the rally point?" Stockton asked.

"If we're finally ready to go?" Dane couldn't help adding his own disapproving growl—a lot less impressive than Nickel's since he didn't have the proper vocal cords for it, but still strong enough to emphasize his own unhappiness. "Everyone who's going needs to stand up and come closer to me."

Dane sucked in more magic and then let it flow around all the people gathered. It took a second to weave them all into his usual transportation spell—without them touching him, he needed extra effort—and then the conference room vanished around them.

They reappeared in a small parking lot about four blocks around the corner from the warehouse. The area was a mix of industrial and residential with apartments above crumbling storefronts directly adjacent to the warehouse. It wasn't a great part of town, another strike against the façade that the warehouse was being used to securely house police evidence, but the increased police presence would hopefully keep everyone safe until they could leave again.

Things moved quickly once everyone was present and accounted for. Nickel and Dane were placed in the middle of the SWAT team breaking through the front door. A second team was circling the back of the warehouse with Mercury and a pair of witches. Everything was timed so Dane's team arrived at the front door at the same time that Mercury's was arriving at the back. The man in front of the group holding the battering ram stepped forward on time to match the man with the same job at the back door. He swung, and the ram hit the door with a hollow gong. Runes flared brightly along the length of the ram as the man pulled it back and thrust it forward again. This time when it hit, the runes swirled and slammed into the door along with the more mundane metal. Dane smelled a whiff of tainted magic as the runes fought against whatever was protecting the door.

The battering ram held an amazing bit of spell work. Dane hadn't seen the like in at least two decades, but the height of runic spell work had come and gone before the advent of Christianity. Still, the runes destroyed the spell placed on the door. It popped open easily, and then the runes faded from sight. SWAT poured inside; Nickel and Dane went with them like pebbles caught in a strong current. Dane was feeling a little superfluous at the moment. SWAT had infiltrated the evil lairs of bad magic users plenty of times before without his help; that they had included him with them this time was probably only because the SupFeds had insisted.

Dane forced his attention back to the task at hand as SWAT began to spread out and search the building. The warehouse itself was fairly large, larger than the one on the Chesapeake that Mercury, Nickel, and Dane had tackled five years ago. It wasn't nearly as high-tech, though. Off to the right he could see heavy plastic sheeting hanging from the ceiling where a clean room had been set up. He could see some machines behind the plastic, but

Dane didn't want to get closer to investigate. To the left were clapboard walls that didn't reach the ceiling. SWAT members cleared both rooms while Nickel and Dane stood ineffectually near the door with their guard.

The air felt heavy with magic. Since Dane wasn't doing anything else, he sent a tendril of his own magic out to investigate why. Magic could build up in the air from frequent usage or from big spells like the runes impacting against the door ward, but this felt different: like an active spell, but it was unlike anything Dane had ever encountered before. He might have been impressed with what the otherwise magicless humans had managed to come up with if he hadn't also been so utterly disgusted by their methods.

"It's something like Zinc's magic," Nickel warned, glancing around the room. He strode forward, and Dane followed, their guard hissing at them to remain still before he trotted after them too. "It's the bad magic, though."

"So someone here is using tainted air magic?" Dane asked, although his own magic was confirming what Nickel had told him. This was a great educational moment for Nickel. They weren't being actively attacked, so Dane could take a few seconds to let Nickel parse out what he had already surmised. Dane let his magic flow through the warehouse and began to pluck and tug at the suffocation spell that blanketed the building. It was difficult to force the tainted magic to change to what Dane wanted it to be, and it took far more magic than he wanted to use.

"Don't touch that!" Nickel shouted, suddenly dashing forward. He ran through the corridor between the clean room and the clapboard room and vanished around a corner. Dane followed more sedately while the guard growled about the difficulties of protecting two people who wouldn't damn well listen.

Nickel was squatting over a grate set into the floor, carefully not touching it. It was wide enough for an adult human to fit through when the metal bars were removed, and for those who knew that the last facility had been underground, it was the perfect trap.

"Let me," Dane told Nickel. He squatted at Nickel's side and let his magic flare between his fingers. The suffocation spell was waiting for someone to touch the grate, either by foolishly walking over it or by trying to pry up the bars to investigate underneath. Dane let his magic hit it first, and the grate shuddered as he started unweaving the spell. The air felt suddenly heavier, like a weight was trying to push down and force everyone to fall to the floor. The guard swore and spread his feet out to brace himself. Dane's magic continued to nip and push at the spell, tugging the strands apart.

He felt Nickel jump to his feet and then felt Nickel's magic flare, but Dane needed to get this spell unraveled more than Nickel needed his help. Water splashed in Dane's face, and he heard the echoing bang as multiple guns fired. Someone screamed, someone else gurgled as they choked on water, and the suffocation spell collapsed below Dane's hands.

The air felt lighter as he stood to see what he had missed. Nickel was standing in the center of a large puddle of water, somehow still in human form. Three bodies lay at his feet, dead. Their guard and three other SWAT members were staring at Nickel. Dane could see that their mouths were hanging open in surprise even through their mostly opaque helmets.

"What happened?" Dane asked curiously, watching as Nickel stepped through the puddle and around the dead bodies nonchalantly.

"We broke a concealing spell in our half of the warehouse," Mercury called from somewhere out of sight. He was apparently close enough to overhear Dane. "Three of them slipped past us. We've got O'Simmons in cuffs, but I could use your help on these cages."

Cages? Although now that Dane thought about it, the warehouse wasn't exactly set up for proper cells. Nickel and Dane both hurried farther down the corridor, passing another two plastic-sheeted clean rooms before they found an open space with two large cages. O'Simmons was being helped to his feet by three SWAT members. He looked furious, but at the same time he had the slightly bewildered look Dane recognized from his colleagues that had been drained of magic in the forest. Apparently even O'Simmons hadn't realized just how dangerous a drug he had ingested. Although, since he didn't have the death spell at the end of his spool of magic, Dane couldn't help wondering if they had managed to catch a big enough fish that they might finally get the information they needed to begin dismantling the operation.

Inside the cages were two dragons. The closest cage held a little boy approximately Lumie and Alloy's age. He had very long golden hair, unkempt and dirty from lack of care, and he was using it as a curtain to hide behind. Dane could see the gleam of his golden eyes through his hair as he stared worriedly at them. Mercury was kneeling next to the other cage, and one glance told Dane why. Lying there was a woman with dirty silver hair cut as if she had fought with whoever had the knife, so the result was uneven and ugly. Her stomach was bulging, and she was snarling and gasping for breath.

"We're going to get you out of there and somewhere safe," Mercury was insisting as Dane hurried to his side.

Nickel knelt down next to the boy's cage to try to coax him to sit up.

"They won't have my kits," the woman growled semicoherently. "I'll die first."

"They won't," Mercury replied reassuringly. "You'll have your kits among other dragons and raise them as a dragon should."

The lock was a simple padlock that a pair of bolt cutters should pop open easily enough, except Dane's fingers tingled with magic when he touched it. Unless the bolt cutters were covered with the same runes as the battering ram, they would be turned into scrap metal. Dane pulled in more magic from around him and formed it into a hammer. The woman didn't have time for him to carefully unravel the spell; she needed to get to help now. Dane's magic hitting the lock made an echoing clanging noise. The woman shrieked, then clutched at her stomach with a groan. He banged again, harder, and the lock broke in two with a screech.

Mercury had the door open in seconds, and he climbed inside the cage to help the woman awkwardly crawl out. She clutched at Mercury's arm desperately, sobbing.

"She needs medical care," Mercury insisted to the SWAT leader who had joined them at some point. "Let me bring her somewhere where she can get help. You can get her statement after she's given birth."

The SWAT leader backed away with his hands up in the air. "Take her," he insisted. Apparently womanly troubles like babies weren't his forte, and he must have understood that a regular human hospital probably wouldn't be able to help a dragon lay her eggs.

Mercury wrapped his arms around her to support her. Dane felt his magic flare as he built his transportation spell. The young dragon apparently felt it too. He screamed, one hand reaching through the bars of his cage desperately.

"Not without Goldie," the woman gasped, turning around toward the kit's cage.

Dane hurried over to the lock, pulling more magic so he could get Goldie out. It took two tries while Goldie continued to whimper, but once Dane had pulled the door open, Goldie dashed toward the woman. His legs were shaky and he mostly crawled, but within seconds he had his arms wrapped around her leg, much like Dane had seen Alloy do to Mercury.

Before leaving, Mercury caught Dane's eye, then looked around the cage area once more. Dane could see what he was thinking: Platinum, a dragon they knew was being held captive by the enemy, wasn't here. The battle to save the dragons wasn't over yet. Mercury altered his spell to account for one more, and then all three dragons vanished from sight. Nickel and Dane stood, and they both walked over to the SWAT leader's side. The situation felt anticlimactic to Dane. Yes, he had unraveled a big trap spell and he had gotten two dragons safely away, but he hadn't captured the enemy or really fought at all. Most of his time had been spent standing around waiting for something to do. Still, no one on their side had died, and the mission had been accomplished. Dane shouldn't complain.

Nickel, on the other hand, had fought against three magic users and won. He might only have access to water magic, but he was turning into a very formidable creature.

Apparently, the head SWAT guy agreed. "When you turn eighteen, send your resume my way. My team could use a guy like you," he said to Nickel.

Nickel smiled, clearly flattered by admiration for his hard work. "Sorry," Nickel replied with a shrug, "but I've already got a job waiting in Dane's consulting firm. Feel free to give me a call if you need my help, though."

Stockton walked around the clean room partition as Nickel finished speaking. "You'll blow your quarterly budget if you do that," he called. His grin said he thought the expense to be worth it. Dane would see what Stockton said after he saw the rate Dane charged to hire both Nickel and Dane, but for now he was glad to know the SupFeds and Dane were going to continue working together on occasion. Their money kept Dane's household flush with Cinnamon Bombs, which kept Lumie happy, which kept the rest of them sane. That was important.

"We done here?" Dane asked. He was tired from all the magic he had worked today, and Nickel needed to get to bed.

Stockton nodded. "The evidence technicians and some federal agents I trust are coming by car to take over the scene. They're about ten minutes away. If you'll transport those of us who need to return to the office when they arrive?" Dane nodded and tiredly started pulling in a little more magic from around him. He could do one more big spell before collapsing into bed and sleeping for twelve hours straight.

Nickel yawned beside Dane, so Dane threw an arm over Nickel's shoulders to pull him close. He leaned against Dane, his head barely coming up to Dane's chest, and rumbled tiredly. Copper was the tallest of Dane's kits, but only because he had already hit one growth spurt.

Dane had a feeling that in a few months Nickel might be taller than him. He certainly had the bone structure for it.

And Dane's mind was wandering, but admittedly thinking about his kits was far more interesting than watching people scurry around a crime scene.

Finally, the backup crew arrived, and Stockton organized everyone who needed a magical lift to the office. Valerie grinned at Dane, her demeanor utterly changed from the first time he had met her. Apparently running a successful operation after years of stymied preparation agreed with her.

When everyone was ready, Dane let the spell take them away, the warehouse vanishing to be replaced with the conference room they had left just hours ago. The Secretary of Defense was sitting in one of the chairs. She had her phone held up to her ear, but she ended the call when they appeared. Stockton nodded politely to her, but he was listening to the SWAT leader's report. She got to her feet and walked purposefully in Dane's direction.

Dane blinked at her. She glanced from him to Nickel, who had fallen fully asleep while they were waiting to leave. "Dragons are certainly very strong," she said softly, apparently cognizant of the fact that Nickel was sleeping. "I wish we had more like Mercury Chicago on our team." She hadn't phrased her sentence like a question, but Dane could sense the banked curiosity there.

"Think of it this way," Dane replied. He couldn't let this opportunity pass by. "You have a homeless, migratory population with no access to formal education or health care, no Social Security number or any formal identification. The average lifespan of a dragon is only twenty-six years, not because they have short lives but because they are killed in the wild by other predators or by the elements. And when a dragon attempts to rectify that situation by entering human society, they're often ignored. I believe Mercury is the only dragon working for any federal agency."

"So there's no way to change that?" she asked sharply.

"I didn't say that." Dane's smile had a bit of an edge to it. "All the dragons need is a place to call home where they have the resources to prevent territory disputes and where doctors and educators can work with them. I'm attempting to create such a place, but some additional funds to build a proper school and hospital would help. As would some sort of national campaign to help change the negative mindset people have toward dragons. They're not lamias, but they're often treated the same way, and you might be able to change that."

She wanted to have dragon magic available to help fight wars and to bolster local police and federal forces. Dane wanted dragons to have equal access to colleges and jobs nationwide. She nodded thoughtfully to him.

"We'll have to speak again later, at a better time," she said.

Dane agreed. "Stockton has my number. Have a good night." He let his magic pull him and Nickel away.

They reappeared in the sitting area between the two wings of Dane's house. Daisy was kneeling on the ground, talking softly to Lumie. The second they appeared, Lumie dashed around Daisy and hurried over to Dane.

"Where is he?" Lumie asked suddenly, his red eyes looking around Dane as if someone might be hiding behind Dane's legs.

"Who?" Dane asked. Daisy clucked in exasperation and gently took Nickel from Dane's arms. Nickel grumbled incoherently, but allowed himself to be led to his bed.

"The golden dragon," Lumie replied in a tone that said Dane was being stupid for not already knowing the answer.

"Goldie?" Dane asked, wondering what the heck Lumie was up to now. "He went to the dragon village."

Lumie sighed. "I'll have to go there, then."

"Not tonight," Dane said firmly. "You and Goldie need to sleep, and Goldie needs to settle in first."

"Fine," Lumie grumbled. He turned and headed for bed. Dane gratefully headed for his own. Daisy would leave once Nickel was situated. Dane hoped Mercury could come home soon too, but he had a feeling Mercury would be with the pregnant dragon for a few more hours.

Dane washed his face in the bathroom, changed into pajamas, and was asleep before his head hit the pillow.

Epilogue

Mercury stumbled his way home long after the sun had risen. Daisy was cheerfully preparing breakfast for the kits starting to take their places around the kitchen island. Zinc and Copper were the only two not present.

"How's Goldie?" Lumie chirped when he caught sight of Mercury. He looked wide awake, which made Mercury jealous.

"Scared out of his wits and feeling lost," Mercury sighed.

Martha had needed to separate Goldie from the pregnant dragon rapidly going into egg fever. Goldie had freaked, screaming and crying, which had attracted the attention of the rest of the village. A dozen curious kits had tried to talk to Goldie, who had run off in absolute terror. The poor thing had probably never seen another dragon until the soon-to-be mother had been captured, and he had attached himself to her. It had taken a while to find Goldie hidden underneath the porch of one of the houses and even longer to coax him out. Only Martha's promise that he could see his companion and her four eggs had gotten him moving, and he had vanished into the room and couldn't be budged again.

"He's going to need a lot of time to heal," Mercury tried to explain. Lumie nodded, looking disappointed for some reason. Daisy served him a plate of eggs in the nest, an oddly appropriate dish given how Mercury's night had gone, and Lumie was distracted enough that Mercury could leave the kitchen and head upstairs. His bed was waiting for him.

Dane took one look at Mercury when Mercury walked into their bedroom and winced. He dropped the socks he had been about to pull on his feet and instead hurried into the bathroom. Mercury heard the sound of water running a moment later. Dane returned with a damp washcloth. Mercury took it gratefully, glad to wash the sweat from his face. He undressed and slid into bed.

"I spoke to Zinc," Dane said as he took the washcloth back from Mercury. "I let her know that we will keep looking for Platinum, and that your boss is helping now too. She's upset, but she'll be okay." Mercury could only nod, grateful Dane had talked to her.

Dane smoothed the covers, then sat beside him on the bed before continuing. "Stockton called. He let me know they've gotten a search warrant for just about everything O'Simmons owns. If there's something to find about dragon experimentation, Stockton says they'll find it, and he'll make sure we're both kept in the loop. Valerie was put on point for the investigation, and you're still her partner."

"So I'm being promoted to agent," Mercury found the energy to reply through a wide yawn. He was fading fast. Helping a dragon who had gone into egg fever shift forms and then safely lay her eggs was extremely taxing on mind and body. Plus, having to track down the panicking Goldie in the middle of it all hadn't helped. "That's probably going to mess up my working hours."

"I'll let Daisy know we might need her for babysitting after dinner on occasion, but I'll also see if I can shorten my hours at work. We'll figure it out—we always have—so don't worry."

Mercury nodded, glad to hear his new job wasn't going to cause any problems at home. He blinked, but his eyes took a few seconds to reopen. They slid closed again almost immediately.

"See you later," Mercury heard Dane say softly. Dane pressed his lips to Mercury's forehead. "Sleep well."

"No more picnics," Mercury mumbled in a last-ditch effort to stay awake for his mate.

They needed to talk about the aftermath of the warehouse and what it meant having the SupFeds so deeply on board, but it wasn't hard for Mercury to realize that he was far too tired to remember anything they spoke about at the moment. When he woke up again, he and Dane—and probably Nickel too—would have to sit down and figure it all out together.

Dane laughed. "I'll tell Lumie. I'll also call your office and tell them you'll be in tomorrow for any follow-up. Get some sleep."

Mercury pried his eyes open one last time so he could smile at Dane and then let the soft pillow and mattress do their jobs. He was asleep before Dane left the room.

DRAGON

DILEMMA

Chapter One

Saturday-morning breakfast was always chaotic. With seven kits running around, it was inevitable, and Daisy—the babysitter/housekeeper who helped to look after the kits—had weekends off. Daisy somehow managed to corral all the kits into line for breakfast, lunch, and dinner and got them to their lessons with their tutor on time. Dane, on the other hand, was lucky he still had a standing kitchen.

Lumie and Alloy were chasing each other in circles around the kitchen island, yelling excitedly about something. Their words were too garbled for Dane to catch. Lumie's red hair kept flashing by, followed by Alloy's mix of blue-and-red hair. Copper and Zinc were yelling at each other from opposite sides of the island. Their argument stemmed from something that had gotten spilled in the bathroom, which might also explain why Copper smelled particularly flowery this morning. Copper would probably smell like that for days; as a fire dragon, he avoided proper baths as much as possible. Even though he was eight years older than his youngest siblings—much too old to be skipping baths—his hair was the same shade of red as Lumie's and Alloy's. Zinc was an air dragon the same age as Copper. Her hair was white and she kept it in one long braid down her back to avoid getting it tangled in her magic.

Chrome and 'Ron were also arguing—this time about frogs. Why? Dane couldn't even fathom a guess. The answer might scar him for life. Over the last year, 'Ron had cut her brown hair into long spikes and had traded frilly dresses for sparkly pairs of jeans. She was still cleaner and more put together than Chrome, whose brown hair was actually longer than hers and usually contained a few sticks and leaves tangled in his curls, but she was more willing to go frog hunting now. Or frog dissecting. Again, Dane really didn't want to know.

Luckily, Mercury was at the stove calmly flipping pancakes on the electric griddle. His bronze hair was long on his collar and still sleep mussed. Dane had to hide a grin because he knew exactly what had caused Mercury to look so disheveled this morning, and it wasn't a kit-friendly topic.

"Kits who aren't sitting quietly don't get pancakes." Mercury didn't say it loudly, but he didn't have to. Copper, Zinc, Chrome, and 'Ron immediately shut up and took their seats around the island. Lumie stopped by the spice drawer to pull out the extra-large bottle of cinnamon before he and Alloy also settled quietly into their places.

The threat of being denied pancakes was a serious one. Dane went to the pantry to grab the syrup—another extra-large bottle, because dragons were sugar fiends—and set it in front of his seat as he took his own spot at the island.

"I'm going to have to shovel the driveway this morning," Dane said into the quiet kitchen. "I'd appreciate everyone's help." Copper, Lumie, and Alloy looked immediately interested—they could melt the snow with their fire magic as long as they didn't leave puddles of water that would eventually turn the driveway into a skating rink. Nickel, the only kit who had been sitting quietly the entire time, nodded to tell Dane he was in too. He liked playing with frozen water just as much as unfrozen. Nickel was the only full water dragon living under Dane's roof, his blue hair and bright blue eyes a stark contrast to the other kits'. Alloy had been genetically altered in the egg to have both fire and water magic, but he spent most of his time with Copper and Lumie, so fire was his preferred method of choice.

None of the kits made a peep of agreement or disagreement. The pancake rule was still in effect, apparently, but at least Dane wouldn't be shoveling his driveway on his own.

Mercury brought the plate over and the steaming scent of buttery pancakes enveloped the table. Chrome was actually drooling, Dane thought, but he didn't look too closely. There was a sudden popping noise and a sealed envelope appeared directly on top of the stack.

Dane knew that spell. Hell, he knew the handwriting on the envelope, just as he also knew that the sender had chosen to have it materialize on the food on purpose. Mercury pulled it from the stack of pancakes and read Dane's name on the front, then held it out for Dane to take with a quizzical look on his face. Dane's hand wasn't shaking when he forced it to reach out and take the envelope from Mercury. It wasn't, he reassured himself, but he wasn't breathing either.

"I'm starving!" Chrome moaned. Mercury smiled at him and grabbed a fork to begin filling everyone's plates. The syrup disappeared with alarming quickness while Dane was staring at the cramped cursive. That handwriting was so familiar and so damned frightening.

"Who is the letter from, Dane?" Mercury asked.

Dane looked up just in time to see Lumie liberally coat his syrup-drenched pancakes in cinnamon. Copper and Alloy each had their turn with the cinnamon before Dane remembered that Mercury had asked him a question.

"It's from my mother," Dane said as unemotionally as he could. If he didn't suppress what he was feeling, he might start screaming or crying.

Mercury put his fork down on his plate, which was just as drenched in syrup as his kits', and stared at Dane with his bronze eyes. "The one who's a god?" he asked. Dane was the child of a god, something he had told Mercury before they became mates, but Dane had never gone into specifics. Mercury had seemed to sense that it was a difficult topic for Dane and had never asked for more detail.

"No," Dane replied. "My mother is one of the few witches in the world strong enough to summon a god, though." At Mercury's blank look, Dane sighed. "The Isle Crone?"

Mercury's jaw dropped. "Your mother is the Isle Crone?" he gasped.

"Who's that?" Zinc asked curiously.

"We have a grandma?" 'Ron added. She bounced in her seat with excitement. Mercury's lips tightened and Dane had to hide a wince. It wasn't Mercury's fault that dragons in the wild had to abandon their kits so they didn't inadvertently end up killing them over a territory dispute. Mercury didn't have the first idea of where to find his parents or any of his siblings. Dane had a mother who was the Isle Crone and a father he had never met and probably never would.

"She's not the cookie-baking type," Dane tried to explain to 'Ron. She was more of the biblical-smiting type. She was the territory leader of the British Isles, and she ran her territory with an iron fist. No one dared to challenge her because she was that powerful and that ruthless. For all that, she wasn't evil. Mostly she was controlling, and no one was allowed to live their lives outside of how she dictated. It made her one of the more well-known territory leaders in the world.

Dane had left her house as soon as he was old enough to get away. Actually, *escaped* her house was probably a more accurate description. He had traveled all the way across the ocean to flee from her, but that hadn't been nearly far enough, thanks to the more modern and less taxing innovations to basic transportation magic. Luckily, she wasn't more powerful than Dane, so she couldn't force him to return with her magic, but she had made her displeasure known many times since then.

His favorite instance was when she had instructed the largest witch coven in England to curse him. He had managed to counter it before he found out what exactly it was supposed to do to him, but the end result, according to his mother, was supposed to have been him crawling back to her for help and falling under her thumb again. She had sent a letter much like the one he was holding to tell him how disappointed she was that he had managed to avoid that fate.

That, along with a number of other difficulties she had caused throughout the years, was why he hadn't spoken to her in at least a decade and had hoped to go a few decades more before having to even think about her again.

"What'd she write?" Chrome asked through a mouthful of food.

"Don't talk with your mouth full," Mercury immediately scolded. Chrome frowned but obediently shut his mouth.

Dane gritted his teeth as he slid a finger into the envelope and began ripping it open. One piece of formal stationary slid out when he tipped the envelope over. His mother's careful cursive only filled the first third of the paper.

I will be visiting this Sunday to meet my grandchildren, she wrote. *I am very disappointed that I had to learn of their existence through rumor and gossip. We will be having a discussion about your communication skills when I arrive.*

She hadn't signed it, but she didn't need to.

Dane passed the letter on to Mercury to read and turned to his own breakfast. Luckily he didn't need more than the dregs of the syrup bottle to sweeten his pancakes, because that was all the kits had left him. Dane forced himself to cut his pancakes into bite-sized pieces and then to chew and swallow. It was tasty enough—Mercury knew what he was doing in the kitchen—but it sat in Dane's stomach like a nauseating brick.

Once everyone's plate was clean, Mercury clapped his hands to get their attention. "Grandma is coming to visit tomorrow. That means the house needs to be spotless. Copper and Lumie, help Dane with the driveway and then come inside and clean your rooms. Zinc and 'Ron, I need the bathrooms cleaned and organized. All of your toiletries need to be put away; you can't leave them on the counters. Chrome, the carpets need to be vacuumed, and then your bedroom needs to be unearthed from the disaster area you've created. Alloy, you need to clean the schoolroom. And, Nickel, you need to help me get a guest bedroom ready."

The guest bedroom. Shit. The last time Mother had visited, Dane had put her in the master bedroom in the other wing, mostly to keep her as far away from him as possible. That room had been transformed into the kits' classroom when Mercury had moved into Dane's bedroom with him. Dane wasn't about to change the room back over and put her in the same wing as the kits. He didn't want any crying kits. Which meant she would have to take one of the bedrooms in Dane's wing of the house. He could already hear the complaints.

She would have a bathroom to herself, but it was in the hall instead of attached to her room. The room was smaller than she was used to and didn't have a sitting area. Plus, she was coming with a bad mood already in full force. It was going to be an awful visit.

Dane cleared his plate and helped the kits get theirs into the dishwasher before Copper, Lumie, and Dane went to go get their winter coats. When Dane walked outside with his coat zipped tight and a shovel in his hands, Copper and Lumie were already busy melting snow in their dragon forms. Red scales appeared between snowdrifts as they burrowed and melted. Fire flared and water sizzled, evaporating into a low-lying fog. Dane called a gentle wind to blow the fog away, burrowing deeper into his coat as the additional windchill made his nose ache. He followed after his kits with his shovel, cleaning up the edges of the drive and scooping up the piles of snow they missed.

The driveway was two miles long, although Dane's protective ward around his house only covered about a mile and a half. They weren't going to clear even that much, though. All they needed was to clear from the transportation circle to the front stoop so Daisy and any other visitors with permission to enter Dane's wards could safely make it inside. The rest of the driveway was never used. Dane didn't have a car, and no one ever drove to his house. In fact, he wouldn't be surprised to learn that the far end of his driveway where it met with the main road was overgrown. He should probably walk down there in the spring to double-check.

It didn't take long to clear the driveway. Dane felt bad that Nickel couldn't join them. He was a serious kit often more interested in getting his work done than in playing, which was the exact opposite of the rest of Dane's kits. One of the few occasions Dane could get Nickel to play was in clearing the snow. Getting the driveway safely plowed was technically a chore, but Nickel was willing to unwind and toss himself through the snow like his siblings for the half hour it took. Dane really hoped it snowed again soon.

"Come on, kits!" Dane called to the left of the driveway, into the yard where Copper and Lumie had vanished beneath the untouched snow, as he shoveled the last bit of leftover snow off the drive. "There are more chores that need to be done."

A wet glob of snow hit Dane on the back of the neck with a splat. He dropped the shovel in surprise and spun around. He heard giggling, but whoever had thrown the snowball had burrowed beneath the snow again. Another snowball hit his jacket from behind, accompanied by more giggles. And then, suddenly, the air was full of snowballs as all seven of his dragon kits and Mercury let their ammunition fly.

Some snowballs missed and Dane deflected others, but at least two hit him square on the nose. It was on! Dane dove into a snowdrift on the side of the drive for cover and began forming his own snowballs for return volleys. His magic swirled around him and three large snowmen grew, their stick arms quickly and firmly pressing together snow and letting it fly as the kits soared by.

Their efforts to clear the driveway were destroyed within minutes, but Dane was smiling and the kits were giggling incessantly. Mercury popped up out of his snow bank for a few crucial seconds, his snout wide in a toothy grin, and Dane popped him on the nose with a snowball. A second snowball hit Mercury moments later, and Mercury squealed, then growled playfully when Nickel gave a loud laugh. He vanished back beneath the snow.

Dane had to refocus on his own survival as Zinc whipped a snowball around his snow bank with a jet of air. He dodged and one of his snowmen sent a ball back her way. This was fun, a much-needed distraction from the impending cloud of doom heading their way, and much more fun than their very first snowstorm together, nine months after Dane and Mercury had chosen to start sharing the same room. At the time, Dane and the kits had come to some sort of understanding: they liked him and therefore they would try not to destroy his house.

The snow, their first winter together, had been slow in coming. Flurries dusting the ground through November and December had been the only snowy weather, so this was the first time a heavy snow had fallen. Dane's windows were full of kits staring out at the front lawn as the big, fluffy flakes of snow fell and the browning grass quickly vanished beneath a blanket of white.

The older kits—Nickel, Copper, and Zinc—had seen snow before. They had lived in the wild for long enough to experience trying to survive in the ice and chill when hunting was minimal and being outside a cozy den was dangerous. The younger kits hadn't, and Lumie and Alloy had never seen snow at all.

Light was fading outside as the sun set through the heavy clouds overhead. Mercury was in the kitchen getting dinner ready. Some of the kits were supposed to be helping him, Dane knew, but the novelty of the snow had pulled them away, and Dane couldn't make himself put his foot down and send them back. The snow had drawn him to the window, too, and he wanted to go outside and stick his tongue in the air and catch some flakes. He also wanted the kits to be able to experience that.

"Come on," Dane called as he headed toward his front door. Cold air rushed in as he pulled it open and stepped outside. Kits piled out behind him. Two pairs of arms wrapped around his knees as Lumie and Alloy grabbed him. They peeked around his body and stared out into the twilight. Nickel let out an uncharacteristic giggle as the snowflakes landed on him and quickly melted. Copper breathed out a touch of fire and then grinned when a large swath of snow collected on the ground sizzled away in moments. That was all the rest of the kits needed. They ran out into the snow; even the two gripping Dane's legs dashed off.

It didn't take long for the kits to vanish into the growing gloom. Eventually all Dane could hear was the giggling of kits and the flare of fire or swirl of water that gave away their locations.

"What are you doing?" Mercury hissed into Dane's ear. "We agreed that they couldn't go play until after their chores are done."

"It's snowing?" Dane said with a questioning lilt to his voice, feeling guilty. Mercury was right, and Dane had forgotten. Teaching the kits responsibility as they grew wasn't going to be an easy task. For most dragons, responsibility was a nonentity. They lived in the wild where the only thing they had to worry about was finding food and a safe place to sleep. Once a dragon built their den, they didn't worry about much else. Mercury wanted the exact opposite for his kits. He wanted them to care about a home and one another, which required that they take responsibility for keeping things clean and helping each other out. Working with Mercury to prepare dinner and set the table for everyone was just one aspect of that, and Dane had let the kits skip it for a bit of snow.

"Dinner is going to burn if someone doesn't come set the table," Mercury yelled into the snowy lawn. Heads popped up like gophers as the kits froze in place and turned to look at Mercury. The novelty of snow warred against the lure of food. Food won. After only a few seconds of thought, a stampede rushed past Dane, flinging snow high into the air around him as they galloped through it. Mercury frowned at Dane before following. In mere moments, Dane was the only one outside. The cold air and the chill as the snow landed on him were a sharp reminder that he had failed yet again as a parent and as a partner.

He would have to work harder, Dane decided. He would have to remember about chores and bedtimes even when something as unique and beautiful as the first *snowfall of the season distracted him. Dane couldn't let himself get swept up by the kits' eagerness either. He was the adult and they were the kits, and he had to help them learn, not dance to their tune.*

Mercury was right to be mad.

Dane had cleanup duty that night, aided by Nickel, 'Ron, and Alloy. Mercury was upstairs getting everyone else bathed and into bed. By the time Dane had finally gotten all the dirty dishes into the dishwasher and cleaned the rest of the dishes that needed to be washed by hand, Mercury should have been getting ready for bed too. Except when Dane walked into their shared bedroom, Mercury wasn't there. The light was off, the bed was cold, and there was no sign that Mercury had come and gone. Dane had messed up badly, and he was really worried Mercury wasn't going to come to bed at all.

A snowball hit Dane right in the face, sending a cold shock up his nose and making his eyelids clench tightly in protective reaction. He shook his head to clear away the snow and brought up a mittened hand to wipe his eyes clear.

The memory had been so vivid, as if it had barely happened a few hours ago instead of years ago. It wasn't the first fight Mercury and Dane had ever had, or their last, but it was one Dane would always remember. It was the moment when he had finally decided to take his own responsibility for the rearing of the kits. Instead of fretting about it like the memory had seemed to imply just now, he had gone to find Mercury and apologize. Mercury had come to bed like usual, and their relationship had progressed unhindered from there.

Dane knew of only one person who could take a memory, warp it slightly to her own design, and pop it back into her victim's head without them noticing the change.

"Mother, you're here a day early," Dane said loudly so he could be heard over the squealing and screaming of happy dragon kits. Both Mercury and Nickel heard him and understood the implications. They froze in their tracks, Nickel with a snowball packed tightly in his hand that he let drop to the ground. It took the other kits a few more seconds to realize the game had stopped, but when they did, they dropped their snowballs, returned to human form, and gathered around Dane and Mercury.

A woman stepped out from behind the trees. She stood tall, her back unbent despite the evidence of age in the wrinkles on her face and the streaks of white through her otherwise black hair. She was scowling, which only emphasized the sharp blade of a nose she had passed down to Dane.

"Dragons, Dane? Really?" she murmured. Her voice was soft, but disdain dripped from every word. Her heavy British accent underscored her dislike as her consonants became even more clipped. "I had heard the rumors, but I did not wish to believe you had done something so utterly foolish."

She stalked forward through the messy driveway, daintily avoiding the clumps of snow from the snowball fight. She didn't have a speck of white on her severely black dress.

"Mother," Dane said, hoping to cut her off before she offended one of the kits. That would end badly, either through tears or when a kit attacked her and she retaliated. "This is Mercury. He's my partner. And these are our kits. Nickel, Copper, Zinc, Chrome, 'Ron, Lumie, and Alloy. Kits, this is my mother, Kendra the Isle Crone."

"Nice to meet you?" Nickel tried to state, but it came out as more of a question.

"We shall see about that," Mother replied firmly, luckily not taking Nickel to task for being indecisive. She strode closer, then stopped a few feet away to study Dane's family. Her scowl didn't abate in the least.

'Ron slipped out from behind Mercury and walked over to Mother. She tilted her head as she studied Mother. "Why do you talk funny?" 'Ron asked suddenly. Dane had to force himself to remain still instead of jumping in between them. Mother didn't handle disrespect easily, and he refused to let 'Ron get hurt just because 'Ron didn't offer respect to many people. Still, if he jumped in he might accidentally escalate the situation, which would be even worse.

There was a brief moment of surprise when Mother's eyes widened slightly, but then they narrowed even further. "You are Iron, correct?" she asked. She didn't wait for a response. "Have you ever pondered the fact that perhaps it is you who are speaking oddly? The English language is a very precise one, and the various American accents pollute it horribly. It is no wonder none of the witches on this continent are capable of performing strong magics, considering their garbled tongues."

Dane scrambled to think of some way to separate them before Mother really got started. It took 'Ron a few moments to parse through what Mother had said, which wasn't nearly long enough for Dane to formulate a viable plan. 'Ron shrugged in answer. "I'm 'Ron, not Iron,

Grandma, and I don't need to use words for magic, so it doesn't matter how I talk." She threaded her arm through Mother's and started pulling her past Dane and the rest of the family.

"You may refer to me as Grandmother, Iron," Mother stated. She tried to plant her feet in the ground to keep 'Ron from pulling her, but 'Ron had the momentum. To save her dignity, Mother finally rearranged her arm in 'Ron's so it looked like 'Ron was guiding a willing visitor into the house.

"Nickel just put new sheets on your bed, Grandma," 'Ron continued, blithely ignoring Mother's futile attempts to stop her.

Dane let them go. 'Ron had diffused the situation better than Dane could have, and Mother had apparently chosen to be cordial today. He would keep an ear out for them, just in case, but he didn't think 'Ron was in imminent danger any longer.

This must be the first time Mother had interacted with dragons, Dane realized. He held in his snicker until after 'Ron had closed the door behind them. Mother had absolutely no idea what she was in for. Her proper ways and beliefs were about to be shattered. 'Ron gleefully dragging Mother through the house was just one example of what Mother was about to experience. Although, if 'Ron went too far, Mother wouldn't hesitate to punish her, which was unacceptable. She wouldn't be allowed to lay a hand on any of his kits. Dane did not want to have to confront her, but he knew that her visit was going to quickly be reduced to a battle between who was more stubborn: Mother or the kits. That wouldn't end well for anyone, so he suppressed his laughter and hurried into the house after them.

Chapter Two

Mercury directed the kits to set the formal dining room for lunch. He had a feeling Grandma Kendra wouldn't appreciate sitting around the kitchen island. She certainly hadn't appreciated her accommodation, nor the willy-nilly way the kits helped Mercury cook their grilled cheese sandwiches. Kendra located a set of cloth napkins she insisted on using with the table settings, but luckily she didn't insist on putting out Dane's good china. She had enough common sense to understand the kits needed plastic plates and cups for a few more years, although Mercury wasn't certain how much sense she had about anything else. If she continued to call 'Ron Iron for much longer, she was liable to have a small avalanche dumped on her head.

Then again, she was the Isle Crone, so it was very likely that anything 'Ron sent her way wouldn't harm her in the least.

Nickel had willingly given up his spot around the table at Dane's side for her. Everyone settled in and Mercury began dishing individual sandwiches out to each plate. Dane brought in a soup tureen—Mercury hadn't known they even owned one until Dane pulled it out of a top cabinet—and began ladling tomato soup into everyone's bowls.

Kendra's grilled cheese sandwich had three different kinds of cheese in it—she had scoffed at the quality of the cheese in their fridge, but had taken four different slices anyway—and wafer-thin slices of tomato and red onion. She daintily cut her sandwich into bite-sized pieces as she ate with a fork and knife and took careful sips of soup with her spoon. It looked almost as if she had never eaten a sandwich dripping with gooey cheese and was attempting to figure out the correct etiquette on the fly. The kits, on the other hand, didn't care about etiquette in the least. They happily dipped their sandwiches whole into their soup, disdaining the use of a fork, knife, and spoon entirely. They gobbled up the dripping cheese and soup before the bread disintegrated. Mercury dipped his sandwich too. He wasn't going to change his eating habits just because Kendra didn't approve. However, he ate considerably more neatly than all of his kits, except Nickel.

Dane took one look at Kendra's frown and reached for his silverware. His hand hesitated over his fork; then he swallowed firmly and, instead, reached to pick up his sandwich by hand. He didn't dip his sandwich into the soup, but he ate it like a normal person despite, or perhaps because of, his mother's disapproval.

Kendra tasted the soup, grimaced, and looked along the table. "Aluminum, please pass the salt."

Lumie ignored her with the intensity only Lumie could manage. The salt grinder sat just in front of him.

"Aluminum, it is unbearably rude to ignore someone when they are speaking with you." Kendra's scowl deepened. Alloy was sitting across the table from Lumie and the salt. He glanced at the salt grinder, then at Lumie, and quickly reapplied himself to his sandwich. Alloy might be the oddest looking of Mercury's kits, but he was a smart cookie. Grandma Kendra was an unknown quantity—Alloy didn't know how she might react—but he did know Lumie, and the prudent thing would be to stay out of Lumie's way.

Mercury wanted to open his mouth to tell Kendra to knock it off. He glanced over at Dane to double-check that it was okay to say something to his mother and saw Dane's own indecision. They both wanted to defend their kit, but were unsure if their interference might actually make it worse. It was Lumie who eventually made the decision for Mercury. His eyes were gleaming in a way that told Mercury he was enjoying being harassed by Kendra or, more likely, was really going to enjoy making her look like an idiot.

Lumie could take care of himself; Mercury did know that. It was just hard to remember sometimes since Lumie was so young and all Mercury wanted to do was wrap him in a blanket and give him a big hug. Only Alloy and 'Ron willingly submitted to that out of all his kits. Lumie was more likely to run off on some sort of mysterious adventure. Kendra bothering him about the salt was probably just another bit of fun for him, so Mercury decided to keep his mouth shut and let Lumie handle it.

Kendra's frown grew even more as Lumie continued to ignore her, something Mercury didn't think was possible given how deep her frown had been from the first moment she had walked out of the woods. The salt grinder shivered on the table for a brief moment, then floated upward. It drifted over Lumie's head, and the grinder turned.

Salt fell like snow, but before it came close to Lumie's head, it flared with bright yellow flames and vanished. Lumie didn't even look up, but Kendra's eyebrows lifted slightly upward in surprise.

Kendra didn't know anything about dragons, Mercury realized. Even Dane had known something before he came to their rescue. Mercury didn't think Kendra had ever spoken with a dragon. She probably assumed that dragons were wild, untamable creatures. That was what most people thought about them. Having one speak to her and then another beat her cruel joke with his magic had to be astonishing to her.

Regardless, enough was enough, even if Lumie was enjoying this far too much. "Lumie, would you please pass the salt?" Mercury asked.

Lumie finally looked up. He caught Mercury's pointed look, sighed, and plucked the saltshaker out of the air. He passed it down the table toward Mercury, who took it and passed it over to Kendra.

"Thank you, Alum...Lumie," Kendra said slowly. Saying Lumie's preferred nickname instead of his full name must have been a big concession for her, but she said it without her scowl changing in the least. Lumie had impressed her. Mercury couldn't help wondering what he and the rest of the kits had to do to prove themselves to her as well.

Lunch finished quickly after that. The kits didn't engage in their usual babble. Epic tales of the snow fight should still be echoing through the house, but they were unusually quiet. Kendra's scowl didn't invite the idle chatter the kits were so good at.

Mercury pushed his chair back and stood. He was about to ask the kits whose chores included cleanup duty to come help, but his words were swallowed by a hollow booming sound that rattled the dishes and made 'Ron shriek.

The boom sounded twice more, almost as if someone were knocking on the door, except much louder.

"Someone is banging on the wards around the property," Dane hissed, jumping to his feet. Nickel, Copper, and Zinc immediately followed. The four of them dashed toward the front of the house. Mercury turned to the rest of the kits.

"Clean up, please," he said calmly, even though he wanted to growl. Magic trembled under his fingers, and he fought it down. Were they under attack again? The enemy hadn't tried Dane's wards after their first failure years ago, but if they amassed enough power, Mercury knew they would try again. He wanted to run after Dane, to guard his back, but he needed to be with the rest of the kits to ensure their safety.

'Ron and Chrome grabbed the plates from the table and stacked them in Alloy's arms. When he was holding all he could carry, Alloy rushed into the kitchen. It was frenetic energy, born of fear and excitement. They wanted to bite and attack, to get in on the action, but they also knew that they would only get in the way. Nickel had been fighting for far longer than them, and Copper and Zinc were at least old enough to know how to hold their own. They couldn't compete with Nickel, of course. They didn't have his drive or his willingness to kill, but they could, and did, watch his back.

Alloy returned empty-handed and began taking bowls and drinking glasses from Chrome, scurrying back and forth every time his arms were filled. Lumie had vanished, but he would be fine wherever he had run off to. It was the other three kits Mercury needed to remain behind to protect. Mercury gathered the heavy serving dishes, his teeth clenched to keep his growl hidden. Dane and the older kits would be outside by now, carefully running across the snowy lawn toward the intruder. Any moment now, Mercury would begin to hear the sounds of battle: the roaring of dragons and the shiver of magic in the air as Dane let loose.

Mercury was trained to handle an intruder the same as Nickel. He had dealt with the enemy before, and his work as a field agent with the Federal Bureau of Supernatural Investigations had prepared him even more. But someone still had to watch over the rest of the kits. It wasn't the first time Mercury had been left behind. He knew the necessity of it and that it wouldn't be the last time either.

"Dane's coming back, right, Daddy?" Alloy asked softly. He was curled in Mercury's lap, just a few months out of the egg and still timid at how bright and new the world was around him. He was the opposite of Lumie right out of the egg, but Alloy's hesitance wouldn't last long. Mercury enjoyed the chance to cuddle with Alloy while he still could, but with half his mind occupied by the reason for Dane's absence, Mercury found he couldn't enjoy the experience as much as he wanted to.

"Of course he is," Mercury replied firmly. He refused to believe anything else. Besides, Dane was unbelievably strong, and he had Nickel guarding his back. They would return unscathed, and the dragon they were hoping to help would be freed.

"Good," Alloy said with a nod. He yawned and curled into a tighter ball on Mercury's lap. Alloy was the main reason Mercury had remained behind instead of helping Nickel watch out for Dane. Sometimes when

Alloy cried, it started raining inside the house. When Alloy was angry, couches caught on fire. He had very little control over his powers; someone with stronger magic needed to be around him at all times to stop him. Daisy didn't have the magic to handle Alloy, nor did any of the older kits. Only Dane and Mercury could do it, which meant Mercury had to stay behind.

But Alloy wasn't the only kit who needed Mercury to stay. They had all wandered into the bedroom he shared with Dane to say hi or ask a silly question over the last hour. Even Copper had spent five minutes sitting in the chair across from Mercury, indirectly asking for whatever reassurance Mercury could give while pretending he was only there for Alloy's sake.

Mercury hated being left behind—there was no denying that—but he understood the necessity. When Dane came back Mercury would have to yell at him for leaving him with the kits.

Yell at him? Mercury remembered greeting Dane with a warm, relived hug when Dane and Nickel had returned unscathed. After Nickel and Dane had regaled the family with their adventure, Mercury and Dane had put all the kits to bed and then very eagerly fallen into their own. Mercury couldn't remember any yelling, and there shouldn't have been any bad feelings at all in that memory. Could he be remembering wrong, or was there something weird going on?

"Daddy, the table's clear. Chrome and Alloy are loading the dishwasher. Do you think we have to run it before dinner?" 'Ron asked.

Mercury blinked and looked down at her, wondering when his mind had wandered off. "Let me check," he said, picking up the soup tureen and then following 'Ron into the kitchen.

The dishwasher was full from their breakfast and lunch dishes. Mercury took over the hand-washing before too much water got on the floor, then started the dishwasher when he was done. The whole time he was working, he was also straining his ears for the first sound of fighting. He couldn't hear anything over the water in the sink, but it was also possible that Dane had kept his wards up and couldn't engage with the enemy. There was no way to know what was happening out there from inside the kitchen.

Mercury dried his hands when the dishes were clean and dripping in the drying rack and then headed out of the kitchen, to the upstairs. There was a nice seating area in between the two wings of the house that overlooked the large front window. He could see the front lawn and a fair way down the driveway from that vantage. 'Ron, Chrome, and Alloy followed, settling into the couch on either side of him. Kendra was already there, sitting in a cozy armchair with a book propped open on her knee. She seemed utterly unconcerned with what was going on. Mercury was straining his eyes to try to see farther, but the edge of the wards was out of sight of the house. He wouldn't be able to see Dane or the kits unless they took to the air. That didn't stop him from looking, though.

Another very long ten minutes passed before Mercury saw anything. He spotted Dane, Nickel, Copper, and Zinc immediately. He didn't recognize the three people walking with them. Everyone was picking their way through the snow-covered driveway. When they reached the partially cleared area near the spell circle, Mercury could begin to make out expressions. Dane and Nickel were tense, but not upset, which meant the newcomers were definitely a threat, albeit not an immediate one. They weren't being coerced or forced into allowing the visitors into Dane's territory—not that Dane could be forced—but Mercury didn't see any signs of distress.

He abandoned the couch and hurried downstairs to the front door. Mercury pulled it open and stepped onto the front stoop. Magic tingled along his fingertips as he studied the visitors. The man in front, walking next to Dane, was very dark skinned, especially against the white glare of the snow, and well over six feet tall. He didn't seem to even notice Nickel stalking behind him. That was a mistake as far as Mercury was concerned, but it could also mean he was powerful enough that he didn't feel he had to worry about Nickel.

The other two visitors were walking with Zinc and Copper. The woman was chatting happily with Zinc. Her hair was almost as blonde as Dane's, but it looked like a good dye job to Mercury rather than her natural color. She was short, maybe only five feet, but it was hard to guess after gauging the first man's significant height. The third person was a man. He was round and genial-looking at first glance. A second glance revealed his hard eyes and firm chin beneath a layer of fat. Copper was sticking close to him.

It didn't take long for them to reach Mercury. Dane stepped to the side so he could see everybody and make introductions.

"Mercury, this is Henri," Dane said with a wave to the tall black man. "He controls the territory to the south of me and lives in New Orleans."

"Don't bite him," Lumie added sternly as he stepped out from behind Henri. All the visitors jumped in surprise, even the ones who should have been able to see Lumie hiding behind Henri's back. Lumie could literally be holding Mercury's hand and Mercury wouldn't know he was there unless Lumie wanted him to. The visitors were getting a crash course on Lumie's quirks right from the start. Mercury caught Nickel rolling his eyes at Lumie, but he wasn't surprised in the least. "He's got something weird in his skin that will make you sick."

Henri was the first to mask his surprised expression. His face slid into a wide grin as he looked down at Lumie. Mercury could see that his canines came to unnaturally sharp points. It was still daylight so Henri wasn't a vampire, but he had to be something similar.

"That's probably very true, Lumie," Dane agreed quickly before Henri could say something. "This is Jessica. She controls the Appalachian Mountains to the Mississippi River. And this is William. He controls Canada."

Mercury wanted to ask if Dane meant all of Canada as that was an awful lot of territory for one man to control, but the cold look in William's eyes told Mercury that William didn't share well. Lumie slipped between Mercury and Dane and went inside.

"Hi, Grandma!" Mercury could hear Lumie yell.

"Keep your voice down inside." The door opened wider, and Kendra stepped out.

Henri had been about to step up onto the front stoop to follow Lumie into the house. He froze in place with his leg in the air and stared with his mouth open at Kendra. He had apparently run into her before.

"Get inside before we all freeze to death," Kendra snapped. Henri obeyed with alacrity, and everyone else followed just as quickly. Mercury was the last one inside, and he closed the door behind him.

Mercury had seen how cautious Dane was being around Kendra, and now he had evidence that she scared the other territory leaders as well. Just how powerful was she? Mercury would have to ask Dane if they had a moment of free time that night.

He followed everyone into the entranceway where Nickel, Copper, and Zinc were helping everyone with their coats, and couldn't help worrying. Kendra, plus three other unknown territory leaders, who had come to visit for some mysterious reason, were all under the same roof as his kits. Something bad was bound to happen; it was inevitable. Mercury would just have to somehow ensure that Dane and all their kits came out unscathed.

Chapter Three

Dane didn't know what to expect as he hurried toward the edge of his wards. The booming sound that had come from the area near where the wards intersected with the driveway had almost sounded like polite knocking, but it could just as easily have been from someone trying their own strength against his. Dane wasn't willing to take a chance that it was the enemy instead of a friend, and neither were the kits at his back.

Zinc had shifted into dragon shape. She was the farthest back. While her power over the wind was certainly strong, it also made her really fast. Zinc always took on the role of lookout, and if it seemed Dane needed extra firepower, she was the one to run to get Mercury. The wind bolstered her wings until it was impossible to keep up with her. She stayed as far away from the fighting as possible to keep her escape route to Mercury's side clear.

Next in line was Copper. He had fought before and done well for himself; plus, he trained fairly often against Nickel. Their fire and water powers canceled each other out strongly enough that they didn't do too much damage to Dane's lawn, and they both learned a lot about fighting by squaring off against their magical opposites. Copper knew his role was backup. If he was needed, he would jump in to help, but otherwise he was just there to bolster the numbers fighting at Dane's side. Luckily Copper and

Zinc had previously practiced this maneuver, and they knew their roles well enough that they wouldn't interfere with each other and restart their ongoing feud.

Closest to Dane was Nickel, the one dragon kit Dane trusted at his side in a fight. The rest were certainly trustworthy enough, but Nickel had more than proven himself in previous fights. Dane didn't need to worry about Nickel like he would about Copper if Copper felt the need to jump in.

Dane had moved the edge of the wards as far into the forest as he dared after the enemy scientists had attacked not long after Dane had taken in the kits. His mistake at that time had been allowing the wards to be close enough to his house that anyone could stand outside them—and therefore outside of his magical awareness—and see his house and its occupants clearly. Now the wards were more than far enough away that no one could get a clear glimpse of his house from the edge, although the winter-bare trees did make it a bit easier to see than Dane would have liked.

He sucked magic into his body as they walked, filling his reserves slowly. Those reserves were nearly bottomless, so it took a lot of effort to fill them. He shouldn't have any problem defeating whoever was on the other side of those wards with what he had stored. However, it didn't hurt to be extra prepared.

They passed the spell circle that allowed entrance to Daisy and anyone else keyed to his wards, and moved from the snowball-fight-mussed drive to the completely unplowed portion. It was harder to walk through the piled snow, but Dane didn't let their pace slow. The driveway vanished into the cover of the trees as they followed it. Dane kept a careful watch on his surroundings. He hadn't felt anyone breach his wards yet, but it was always better to be careful in case of an ambush.

After another few minutes of wading through the snow, the wards came into view. Three people stood patiently on the other side. He didn't feel any magic in the air around them, nor did they appear to be waiting to attack. As Dane and the kits finally walked close enough so Dane could make out facial features, he understood why.

Henri, Jessica, and William each controlled one of the territories directly adjacent to Dane's. He had never seen Jessica in person before, but he recognized her from pictures. She had only taken control of her territory seven years ago and had therefore missed the meeting of territory leaders that occurred every ten years. None of the three would have come to Dane's house inside Dane's own territory for a simple social visit, so something must be up. Dane whispered that fact to Nickel, Copper, and Zinc, who nodded to acknowledge they understood, and then Dane plastered on a welcoming smile.

"It's been almost ten years!" he called across the wards when he had gotten close enough. "There's another few years until the next conclave of territory leaders. I hadn't expected to see any of you until then."

It wasn't a question, but he also wasn't being rhetorical. Henri was the one who smiled, echoing Dane's own plastered-on welcoming grin, and answered.

"Something has come up that we felt we needed to speak with you about at once," Henri explained, sounding as genial as Dane had. "We thought it best to come to you instead of forcing you to travel away from home and your family."

"I see," Dane said slowly. He couldn't help thinking that the chance to see Dane's family might have been the real reason they had decided to come to Dane instead of setting up a meeting in a more neutral location. Dane forced away that thought to prevent his smile from turning into a frown; he didn't want his visitors to know he might be onto their scheme. "Well, I certainly don't want you to stay out in the cold. Please follow me to my house." He waved his hand at the wards. He didn't need the gesture for his magic to work, but it was always good not to give a potential enemy too much insight into how his powers functioned.

He opened a hole in the wards that was just large enough for all three people to step through, and once they were on the other side, Dane made certain the wards were closed and secure again.

"This way," Dane added as he turned to lead the way to his house. Everyone fell into step behind Dane, following him through the snow. Nickel chose to stick close to Henri, which meant something had indicated to Nickel that Henri was the most dangerous one of the three. Zinc and Jessica started chatting almost immediately. Dane had no idea how some girls were able to do that, although Valerie, Mercury's work partner, wasn't nearly as talkative. Copper stuck sullenly close to an equally stoic William.

It was interesting that Nickel had chosen Henri to keep a close eye on. Dane would have pegged William as the most dangerous of the three. He controlled all of Canada, not just one or two provinces, and a man didn't run that much territory without the power to back it up. Not everyone had an almost unlimited store of power like Dane did. Dane's territory was his because there wasn't anyone willing to or capable of challenging him over it. For other territory leaders, keeping control was often about being more brutal than their opponents as much as it was being stronger. William was definitely more brutal than Henri, but Dane trusted Nickel's judgment.

It didn't take long to retrace his steps back toward the house. They crossed the line where the driveway had been cleared before the snowball fight had destroyed it. The front door opened as they approached, and Mercury stepped into view. Dane was still smiling, but it gained a touch of sincerity at the sight of his mate. Introductions were made and everyone trooped into the house.

There were kits everywhere. 'Ron was sticking close to Mother's side, talking a mile a minute even as Mother was tucking the book she had been holding into the bag she had left by the door.

"Nice place," Jessica said after a long glance around the entrance hall. After Mercury had shattered the windows five years ago when enemies had attacked them, Dane had replaced them with stained-glass dragons flying through the sky. The kits hadn't managed to break them yet, so it was a glorious sight. Dane loved the new windows and was glad to see Jessica did too. She controlled one of the smallest territories in North America, and everything he had heard about her made her seem like a fairly easygoing territory leader. She was still a leader, though, so he couldn't discount her just because she seemed to be a bit friendlier than the other two.

"Chrome," Mercury called. Chrome froze midstep—he and Alloy had started a game of chase once it became clear there wasn't going to be any fighting—and turned to look at Mercury with a slightly guilty look in his eyes. "Have you finished cleaning your room?" Mercury asked with a lifted eyebrow.

Chrome whined, but he didn't argue. He tromped up the stairs and vanished around the corner.

"Zinc, Copper, 'Ron, Lumie, Alloy, please come help me make up three more rooms for our guests." The kits sighed heavily, but stopped whatever they were doing to follow Mercury upstairs. Alloy followed with his own whine when Nickel gave him a gentle shove toward the stairs. That left Dane, Nickel, and Mother with their three guests.

"Can I get anyone something warm to drink?" Dane asked. He led the way through the house, everyone following along behind him, and held open the door to the dining room. It had been cleaned up from lunch while he was gone.

"Tea for me," Mother said immediately.

"That sounds fine," William agreed. He was shrugging out of his heavy, fur-lined coat. He hung it from the back of an empty chair and then sat in the chair next to it.

"And for me, thanks." Jessica also hung up her gray peacoat. Henri hadn't bothered to dress for the weather and also didn't bother answering.

"I'll get it and be right in," Mercury said as he stepped into the doorway behind them, no doubt having hurried back downstairs once the kits were safely settled. He vanished again, so Dane took his seat at the head of the table. Nickel took his usual seat to Dane's left; he wasn't going to give it up to Mother during a meeting. Mother didn't even bat an eyebrow, instead simply walking farther around the table and taking the chair at the foot.

Mercury returned with a teapot and enough cups for everyone. He had only grabbed tea bags, which made Mother huff, but William and Jessica seemed happy enough. Henri didn't take anything, but Dane didn't mind holding the warm cup as his fingers were still slightly chilled from the long walk to the edge of his wards and back.

Dane waited until everyone who was having tea was set and Mercury had settled into his chair across from Nickel, then turned to look at Henri and William.

"Why are you here?" Dane asked. He was trying to sound cautiously curious. He didn't want to give away the fact that he was concerned, although having three territory leaders appear at his house unannounced would cause concern for anyone.

"You should know," Jessica insisted when no one else spoke for a few long moments. "This thing you're doing with the dragons is encroaching on our territory. You can do whatever you want inside your own territory, but the second you started messing around with ours, we took notice. When I realized you were encroaching on more than just my territory, I contacted Henri, who already had some concerns of his own. We spoke with William and made the decision that all three of us should speak to you. We made provisions for our second-in-commands to take over for a few days, packed, and headed here."

"How have I encroached on any of your territories?" Dane asked, honestly confused. He had an open policy that any dragons in need could come to him for help, but he had never crossed territory lines. The enemy scientists that were kitnapping dragons in the wild and conducting cruel experiments on them didn't discriminate on location. Mercury had taken down three labs—the water, earth, and fire labs—outside of Dane's territory before coming east to Dane to find the air dragon lab. Together they had succeeded in shutting down the air lab and had brought the matter to the attention of people in high places who could really help shut down those scientists.

Mercury now worked for one of those agencies: the Federal Bureau of Supernatural Investigations, also known as the SupFeds. On occasion, he and the SupFeds did travel outside Dane's territories. Dane didn't even consult with the SupFeds whenever that happened because he didn't want to be seen as overstepping.

Jessica let out a little snort of laughter. "The first one I noticed was when Mercury Chicago disdained the leader of his own territory to instead travel here to you."

Jessica's territory included Chicago, where Mercury was originally from and how he had gotten his last name, so she was talking about herself. Apparently she had been offended by Mercury's choice of coming to Dane instead of her. At the same time, Jessica didn't have the reputation for helping people that Dane did. Those who had only heard of what his powers could do called him the Genie of the East. He was known as the Supernatural Consultant by anyone who knew about his consulting firm. Mercury had come to him because he had heard of his work and had hoped that Dane would be able to help. Jessica might be the leader of her territory, but she didn't have anything close to Dane's reputation. He was proud of what he had accomplished since he had earned his reputation thanks to a lot of hard work. Jessica's only reputation was her role as leader of her territory, and Dane thought she sounded a bit jealous of him.

"That's only one aspect of our issue," Henri continued. "Certainly I've had a number of my own people turn to you instead of me, which is quite infuriating, but worse is the moment you physically overstepped the boundaries of your territory."

"When have I ever done that?" Dane asked incredulously. He certainly couldn't think of a time he had left his territory without first being welcomed by the person whose territory he was visiting.

"The warehouse you destroyed was on my side of the Chesapeake Bay," Henri snarled.

Dane couldn't help being surprised at the level of vehemence in Henri's voice. He sounded incensed that Dane had dared to take out the lab where air dragons had been cruelly confined and experimented on. Dane constructed a mental map of his territory lines and placed that warehouse on the map. The border was a straight east-west line, but the Chesapeake Bay curved in a north-south direction, which meant large portions were in Dane's territory and other portions were part of Henri's territory.

The warehouse had certainly been close to the border, but, according to Dane's mental map, it was still on his side.

"It wasn't," Dane disagreed. "Jessica, Mercury came to me because I've made a name for myself in the business of helping people. I don't know if he even knew you existed, let alone where to find you for help. Besides, he had already taken care of the three labs in your territory. The fourth was in my territory, so it was only natural that he come to me for help finding and destroying that fourth lab."

"It was not in your territory! It was in mine!" Henri insisted.

Mercury jumped in. "Jessica, I didn't need the help of a territory leader to find the three labs I destroyed. I was told that getting your help required a tithe of money and a minimum of a year of indentured service to you in return for your aid. That wasn't a price I was willing to pay, so I did not bother wasting your time. When I chose to leave your territory to follow the scientists to their next lab, your jurisdiction over me ended. Even if I was once based in Chicago, in your territory, I am not beholden to you for the rest of my life. Henri, I can pull up maps and news articles on a computer if you would like. I can prove the warehouse was entirely in Dane's territory. He hasn't left his territory once in all the years I've known him."

"If what Mercury and Dane are saying is true," William interjected thoughtfully, "and I'm not confirming whether I believe it is or not, then none of us have the right to have left our own territories to invade Dane's." He paused to look around the room.

Mother looked totally disinterested in her chair at the far end of the table, as if she would rather be anywhere else. Since she had technically invited herself to the meeting, she could leave at any time. It was strange that she hadn't, which meant that for some reason she was actually interested in the proceedings. He couldn't fathom why, but then Dane didn't really want to delve into the mysteries of his mother's mind. He knew it was probably a dark and dismal place that would eat him alive the second he tried to understand it.

Henri was also an unknown quantity. He was snarling to himself, his lips pulled up in a growl that revealed his pointed canine teeth, and the threat they implied. Dane couldn't understand why someone as smart and ruthless as Henri suddenly couldn't read a map.

Dane didn't know Jessica as well as the other territory leaders. She was a human with access to some sort of power—he didn't know what—and she had taken the role of territory leader only seven years ago. He hadn't met her before today, although they had corresponded as neighboring territory leaders a number of times. She didn't feel threatening in any way. In fact, her jealousy that Mercury hadn't gone to her for help made her seem petty. Dane had doubts she would last a full decade as leader.

William's glance around the room ended at the same time Dane's did. Dane wished he could read William's mind to figure out what he had been searching for in that long glance, but mind reading wasn't one of Dane's powers.

"Jessica, it seems to me that you had zero jurisdiction the moment Mercury stepped outside of your territory. Implying that he should have still come to you when the difficulty he was facing was inside of Dane's territory tells me that you were the one looking to overstep your boundaries. Henri, I do need to see a map to confirm, but I suspect that since Jessica's claims are invalid, yours might be as well. Who told you the destroyed warehouse was inside your territory?"

"Get a map first," Henri replied with a low and dangerous-sounding growl, "before you start accusing me of gross incompetence."

Dane nodded and stood. "I'll go grab a map and my computer, where I've saved all the data I collected on the warehouse."

He headed toward the door just as a loud crash sounded overhead. Giggling echoed from upstairs as Dane pushed the dining-room door open.

"It might take a few minutes to sort that out first," he grumbled. "I'll be back in a bit."

Dane didn't want to leave Mercury and Nickel alone with the group, but he had already gotten up, so he might as well go police whatever his kits had broken this time. Besides, they were both more than capable of taking care of themselves. Dane headed upstairs. He didn't have to search for long before he found the scene of the crime. The giggling had vanished, as had the kits that caused the destruction, but the glass from the guest bathroom mirror in Dane and Mercury's wing of the house, where all their guests would be staying, was in glittering pieces on the hallway floor.

"Does anyone know why the mirror is shattered?" Dane asked. He added a touch of magic to his voice, making it echo down the hall and all the way to the other wing of the house where he had a feeling the guilty kits were hiding. How they had gotten the mirror off the wall and into the hallway, and why they had bothered, was something he didn't think he really wanted to know.

Only after his voice had echoed back down the hall to him did he remember that he had guests who might not be as amused as Mercury to hear him scolding their kits. It was too late to be embarrassed about it, though. He could hear doors slowly opening down the hall and feet creeping across the carpet.

"So, what happened with the mirror?" Dane asked, his voice back to a normal volume. Copper, Zinc, Chrome, 'Ron, and Alloy all slunk into view and then stopped a few feet away from him, as if they wanted the extra space for a good head start if they needed to make a run for it.

"We were finished cleaning the rooms," 'Ron began hesitantly, "and Zinc thought we ought to double-check the bathroom, and Chrome thought the mirror looked smudgy, so Copper said we should clean it, and Alloy asked how." She paused guiltily, which told Dane all he needed to know about who had suggested they move the mirror instead of going to find some paper towels and cleaning spray to bring to the bathroom.

"Are the beds all made and the rooms dusted and ready to go?" he asked, instead of continuing to let 'Ron hedge.

The kits all nodded, looking eerily like living bobbleheads.

"Let's have a look." Dane led the way to the nearest bedroom. He was aware he was keeping the territory leaders in his dining room waiting for him, but his kits came first. The mess downstairs was important—leaving Henri to stew was probably a very bad idea—yet his kits were what was really important in his life, not whether he had breached a territory leader's borders, especially since he knew he was innocent. Mercury would explain what was going on if anyone left downstairs got impatient.

Mercury had given Mother the room closest to their own in order to keep her as far away from the kits as possible. That room would be fine, as Mercury had supervised its cleaning earlier that day. Dane thought he would make sure Henri got the next room along the hall. He went into that one first and was impressed by what he saw. The bed was made with fresh sheets, the dresser and nightstand dusted and ready to go. He straightened a pillow, surreptitiously checking to see that there was a fitted sheet and top sheet underneath the comforter.

The kits were all clustered in the doorway, watching him with wide eyes. Dane nodded to the room, satisfied with what they had been able to accomplish, and slid between the kits and back into the hallway. The next room along the hallway would be William's. Dane did the same check and then moved on to the last room in this wing of the house. It was closest to the sitting area that separated the two wings, and Dane hoped Jessica didn't mind being close to the kits when they woke up in the morning and started making noise. All the rooms were ready to go, so the kits apparently hadn't gotten creative until the bathroom. Although he hadn't actually checked to see whether the beds were short-sheeted or not. Oh well.

Dane walked back into the hallway and to the bathroom. Even that looked shiny and clean. The kits really had been trying so hard. Dane waved his hand for emphasis and a light breeze blew through the hallway. The pieces of glass glittered and then vanished. 'Ron ran to check and gasped in the bathroom doorway at the oval mirror hanging, unblemished, over the sink.

"It's like we never broke it," she said with a wide grin. "Cool!"

"Don't go breaking things just because I can fix them," Dane quickly warned before she got any ideas. "I'll let you all off with a warning this time because you did such a great job getting the guest rooms ready. If you all do your chores tonight without complaining, I'll completely forget you broke the mirror, and no one will lose their dessert privileges."

The kits all nodded eagerly, this time looking like bobbleheads given a violent shake. Candy was serious business, as Dane well knew. They would behave for the rest of the night.

Dane went into his office, the small room in between his and Mercury's and Mother's, to grab his computer and an old map he kept folded in the bottom of one of his filing cabinets. He returned to the hallway that was now devoid of kits and stopped. He did a mental count in his head, frowned, and turned toward Zinc. She was sprawled comfortably on one of the couches in the sitting area between the two wings of the house. Three miniature cyclones were dancing in a circle around her head.

"Have you seen Lumie recently?" he asked. Lumie hadn't been with the rest of the kits, and he should have been. He was the hardest of the kits to pin down, which meant it was doubly important to make certain he was getting his chores done.

Zinc shrugged. "I'm sure he's around. He wouldn't sneak off to the dragon village when we have people visiting. Have you checked the dining room?"

She had a good point. Dane thanked her before heading downstairs.

The dining room was quiet when Dane stepped back inside. It didn't appear that anyone had continued where their argument had left off while he was gone. Small talk didn't feel right for the situation at hand either, so they had all simply sat in silence. Luckily, no one seemed upset that he had taken a few extra minutes to get his kits situated.

Dane set the folded map and his computer on the table in front of his chair, but instead of sitting, he followed Zinc's advice. He walked around Nickel and checked the empty chairs next to him. Henri and William were staring at Dane incredulously as he quietly stalked past them to check the rest of the empty chairs. Halfway along the table on Mercury's side, Dane saw a little foot peeking out from underneath one of the chairs. Dane bent down quickly, grabbed Lumie's ankle, and pulled.

Lumie slid out from under the table easily and dangled from his ankle as Dane stood up without letting go. He let out a yawn around the thumb tucked in his mouth, totally unconcerned about the fact that he had been discovered and was hanging upside down.

"Oh, Lumie," Mercury sighed. Dane could hear the suppressed laughter in his voice, but he doubted anyone else could.

"Why are you in here?" Dane asked. He wasn't mad; he honestly should have expected something like this from Lumie after the stunt he had pulled jumping out from behind Henri at the front door. The problem was precedence. Dane and Mercury had told the kits to help out by getting the guest rooms ready, and instead of helping, Lumie had hidden under the dining-room table. If Lumie got away with skipping his chores once, he would feel like he could get away with it whenever he wanted. That was a damned slippery slope, particularly since Lumie was the kit involved.

"Nickel's in here," Lumie whined. "Why can't I be too?"

"Nickel is working while you're purposefully avoiding your chores," Dane explained. No one pouted quite like a six-year-old fire dragon being held upside down against his will. Lumie had the art of pouting down to a science, but Dane didn't let Lumie faze him.

"Nickel's only been sitting there the entire time. That's not working," Lumie whined some more. He knew he was in trouble. He had allowed his concentration to wane, which was how Dane was able to find him when Lumie could have easily remained hidden, and now that he had been caught, he was going to have to face the consequences. Lumie absolutely did not like consequences.

Mercury stood from his seat and walked over to Dane and Lumie. He reached out to grip Lumie under his arms and spun Lumie around until he was upright and cradled gently in Mercury's arms.

"You haven't worked a day of your life, Lumie," Mercury sighed. "How would you know what Nickel's been up to?"

"I haven't worked yet," Lumie grumbled under his breath. Nothing Lumie said could ever be taken lightly. Dane didn't know if he was supposed to have heard yet another of Lumie's cryptic pronouncements, so he ignored it. Mercury ignored Lumie too.

"You made all the other kits do your portion of today's chores. If you want to have any candy tonight or for the rest of the week, you'll go apologize and you will help each kit with one of their chores to make up for skipping out on them."

"But Daddy!" Lumie whined as Mercury walked to the door.

"Get to it," Mercury said as he opened the door and deposited Lumie on the other side. He shut the door on Lumie and returned to his seat. Dane hurried back to his own chair and the waiting laptop and map.

The room was quiet for a few more seconds while Dane opened up his laptop and hit the power button. The silence didn't last long, however.

"Out of curiosity," William asked, "what do you mean that Nickel is working at the moment? He's clearly too young to be involved with this discussion. I'm honestly wondering why he's here at all."

Dane focused on his computer instead of answering. Nickel was capable of handling himself, and Dane was more than happy to leave him to it. Nickel turned his head slowly to look at William. He was smiling widely, giving the room his cold, cutest-little-serial killer grin that always sent a shiver of fear running down Dane's spine.

"I am here to make sure everyone stays civil," Nickel replied simply, but with enough of a growl in his voice to imply that he could back up what his smile promised with equal strength. It was a touch too theatrical for Dane's taste, and he knew Nickel was hamming it up for the audience, but it was effective.

William didn't respond, only nodded mutely. He didn't look afraid of Nickel, but it really wasn't possible to contradict Nickel after seeing that horrible smile. The room remained silent except for the chime as Dane's computer logged into his secure wireless server. He quickly pulled up the relevant documents and activated the spell that would only let his visitors read those specific files. Dane passed the computer to Nickel, who then passed it on to William since he was closest. William tilted the screen and started reading.

Dane unfolded the map next. "The border between our two territories is here," Dane said to Henri as his finger traced the straight border through Maryland. It was just below the Mason-Dixon line, not many miles into Maryland, but far enough that Dane did have control of some of the Chesapeake Bay. The line Dane was drawing showed just how difficult it would be to discern the boundary from the ground. The northern border between Maryland and Pennsylvania, which the Mason-Dixon line followed, wasn't a straight east-west line. It went from southwest to northeast, but the territory lines were based on the land itself, not on the state's borders, and remained firmly east-west. That was why Dane had control of some of Maryland and only half of Delaware.

"Here's the line on a better map," William agreed, tilting the computer screen so Henri could also see from a few seats away. "The address for the warehouse is here," he continued, tapping the dot Dane remembered adding to the map in question. He had made certain the warehouse was inside his territory before attacking it and had left that map on top of the open files for William to see.

"But that's…" Henri closed his mouth sharply before whatever thought was on his tongue could escape. He glared at the computer screen, but didn't open his mouth again to refute Dane's proof. "You're supposed to inform me whenever your activities come close to our shared border," he finally finished petulantly. Dane had a feeling Henri would be pouting like Lumie if he thought he could get away with it.

William frowned at Henri before Dane could formulate a response. "Now you're just splitting hairs. I for one am quite disappointed. I was told there was irrefutable evidence that Dane was trying to take over two adjacent territories and that it was only a matter of time before he also turned his attention to mine. My goal," he added with a glance at Dane, "was to bring your machinations to an immediate halt. We hoped that the three affected territory leaders would be able to subdue you, Dane. It appears to me that Henri, Jessica, and I have instead invaded your territory without appropriate provocation. We must discuss how our misconception occurred and what reparations we need to make."

Dane nodded slowly in agreement, but he couldn't help wondering what was going on. Someone had incited all three territory leaders to leave their own territories and invade Dane's. That the duplicity had been uncovered was good—Dane really didn't want to have to fight against the combined strengths of William, Henri, and Jessica in order to keep hold of his territory and his home—but the fact that the accusations had grown to the point that the territory leaders felt they had to intervene was very worrying to Dane.

Dane didn't care about reparations. Finding out what was going on was far more important, but Dane glanced over at Mercury only to see that Mercury was frowning down at his watch. Dane glanced at his computer as William returned it to him, and the clock in the upper corner of the screen told him how late it was getting.

"We definitely have some things to discuss," Dane agreed, "but if we don't start making dinner, the kits will literally start eating the furniture.

Mercury nodded in agreement and pushed back his seat so he could stand.

"It's fettuccini alfredo night," he said to the table. "It'll be ready in a half hour."

Mercury left the room and could be heard calling for the kits to come help. Dane stood as well.

"There are going to be kits in here in a minute to set the table." And they wouldn't be shy about shoving the visitors out of the way to get their chores done as quickly as possible. It was a recipe for disaster. "How about we take a break until after dinner?"

It took a few moments for everyone to stand and head out of the room. Dane called on his magic, letting it fizz through his fingers. Mother glanced sharply at him, but no one else noticed as the magic tapped a mark onto Henri, William, and Jessica's shoulders. Now he didn't have to have them watched while he was busy helping the kits and Mercury get dinner ready. He let his guests wander freely, aware that if they went anywhere suspicious he would know. Dane left them to it and hurried to Mercury's side in the kitchen.

Chapter Four

Mercury knew to stand back and let the kits have at it. Fettuccini alfredo was a dish the kits had long ago memorized the recipe to, and he was more than happy to supervise. Zinc and Alloy were in charge of the stove where a gigantic pot of boiling noodles bubbled away. A second, equally large pot was melting together the cream and butter for the sauce. The kits knew when to start adding the cheese to the cream and to stir the pasta so the noodles didn't stick.

Lumie was slinking around the kitchen with his shoulders slumped, helping Chrome and Copper set the table as part of his reparations. 'Ron, Nickel, and Lumie had cleanup duty, which meant Lumie would probably still be working to make up for missing his chores for the next few days.

"Don't forget the pepper," Mercury called when Zinc hesitated over the boiling pot of cream and cheese. She nodded and grabbed the pepper mill to grind a lot of pepper into the mix.

The oven beeped, so Mercury walked over to remove the crescent rolls and let them cool on the counter. He would have preferred homemade rolls, but the processed ones out of a cardboard can were pretty good, and it was much easier to make four-dozen rolls that way.

Mercury got out of the way quickly when Zinc and Alloy hurried to the sink to drain the pasta. The only safe place was the kitchen island, so Mercury sat on one of the stools. A gust of wind blew the large plastic bowl off the top shelf of the cabinet. It flew past Mercury's head and into Zinc's hands. She held it steady while Alloy dumped the pasta from the strainer into the bowl, then headed over to the stove to finish the sauce.

"It's amazing how capable your kits are," William said softly as he sank onto a stool a few feet from Mercury. "It's unusual, I believe?"

Mercury nodded, but a flash of alarm had him wondering just where William was going with the conversation. Too many people were overly enamored with the kits' powers, and the last thing Mercury wanted was to have to fight off William to keep his kits safe.

"It's taken years of setting out rules and ensuring they follow them," Mercury explained when William's continued stare demanded some sort of answer.

"But how do you control them so well?" William asked sharply.

There was something more to his question. Mercury thought he sensed a sort of desperation hidden in William's tone, as if his question wasn't just mere curiosity. It made Mercury want to answer, but he couldn't help still feeling cautious.

"You can't control a dragon," he replied slowly, carefully watching William for his reaction. "They're free spirits that need the chance to explore and experience on their own. That's how they learn about the world around them and grow. Kits especially need that space. They get an idea in their heads, and they need the chance to run with it until it explodes spectacularly in their faces."

"But clearly you've managed to exert some sort of control over your dragon kits. They're cooking dinner like regular people, for god's sake."

Mercury knew he wasn't imagining or misinterpreting the desperation in William's voice. He looked earnest, as if the answer was the most important thing he might learn that day.

"Tell me about your own dragons, and I'll see if I can help," Mercury said, guessing about William's motive. He wasn't wrong. William's shoulders slumped slightly, and his mouth twisted with an odd mix of shame and consternation.

"I have two of them. Just kits, maybe a little older than Lumie and Alloy," William began softly. Mercury leaned closer to hear, knowing that William wouldn't want to admit to whatever shame he had over his kits where anyone else might hear. "They were just playing in the river, but the water swelled to flooding proportions. They were threatening the dam and the village in the valley below. But they were so young! I scolded them instead of punishing them, and then when I found out they were alone in the woods without a parent or anyone to take care of them, I took them home."

"How many times have they flooded your house?" Mercury asked, knowing from his own kits' mishaps that William had no doubt had some problems with his.

"Twice," William groaned. "And it would have been more if I hadn't caught them. They run away to play in the rain or the nearby lake. They terrorize my household, yet at the same time everyone that meets my kits falls in love with them.

"I had to sedate them before I left," William continued sharply. His voice deepened as the shame he felt for his actions overcame the joy that had filled his voice just moments before. "I couldn't leave them alone without me there to stop their powers from getting out of control. It was my only damned option!"

His voice rose almost to a shout, but it went unheard over the clatter of the kits as the finished fettuccini alfredo and the rolls were moved to serving bowls. Zinc was quickly throwing together a salad as the food and drinks were being transferred to the dining room. Mercury only had a few minutes to explain.

"Dane and I needed to keep an almost constant watch on Alloy when he was just hatched because he couldn't control his powers. Don't feel bad that your kits are the same. What you have to understand is that you can't control or restrict dragon kits, especially young ones. They need to make messes in order to learn about themselves as dragons. Your house getting flooded was inevitable, to be honest. The difference between your kits flooding your house again and not flooding your house is a combination of bribery and consequences. You saw Lumie today. He shirked his chores and thought he could get away with it."

William nodded. "I saw. I also saw him calmly accepting that he had to make up for missing his chores by helping the other kits with theirs, but I could never make my own kits do something they didn't want to do like that. Even if I could get them to do chores in the first place, they certainly wouldn't take on more responsibility if they failed the first time."

"You missed the part about Lumie not getting dessert if he didn't help the other kits," Mercury explained. "That's where bribery comes in. Dragons are sugar fiends, and I'm certain your kits are as fixated on candy as mine. When you go home and wake them from their sedation, I suggest you offer them a basket filled with as many different blue-colored candies as you can find. They'll fall in love with one candy in particular. Lumie loves cinnamon bombs, and Nickel loves blue rock candy, for example. Once you know what their fixation is, you can use it as leverage. You'll get a piece of candy after dinner only if you clean your rooms. You made a mess—clean it up, or you won't get your candy tonight. Do you see where I'm going with this?"

"Obviously it works," William said, glancing at the parade of dragon kits heading eagerly toward the dining room. Dinner was ready.

Mercury stood and waited for William to join him before following the kits.

"It works. They're all going to graduate from high school; they accomplish their chores, and they sometimes even stop to think before they make a big mess. Not often, but enough that our house is still standing. If you want, you can bring your kits here. Meeting Nickel and seeing an older and controlled water-dragon kit might help ground them a bit."

"I've never heard of a kit as calm and controlled as your Nickel," William admitted.

"Nickel's a special case," Mercury replied, purposefully not explaining just what had happened to Nickel to make him so different. They didn't have time for the story at the moment, and Mercury didn't know what William would do with the knowledge, so he kept quiet. Still, it wouldn't hurt to let William know he wasn't alone. "There's a village in Dane's territory where a lot of young dragon kits live. There's a school and adult dragons to keep an eye on them. If Dane agrees and your kits are interested, they can visit."

William looked pensive, but he nodded. "I'll think about it."

They walked back into the dining room. Dane and Kendra were already there along with all the kits, sitting in the seats they had taken during lunch. Henri and Jessica had been relegated to the far end of the table, so William went to join them while Mercury took his seat next to Dane. As the various bowls were passed around, the room filled with the noisy sounds of kits eating.

It didn't take long for the bowls and plates to empty. The recipe was one Mercury had found in a cookbook when he was living on his own in Chicago and had embellished over the years. It was damned good and there were never any leftovers. It also didn't leave room for much dinner conversation since everyone's mouth was constantly full. That was probably for the best, Mercury knew. The kits didn't exactly understand delicacy, and at this point William, Henri, and Jessica didn't need blunt inquiries into the mistakes that had led them to Dane's doorstep. Kendra wouldn't appreciate it either, but she seemed content with glaring at the way the kits were holding their forks.

Pasta was hard to keep on a fork, so Mercury let the kits eat however they wanted for this particular meal. Some, like Nickel, had figured out that it was actually easier to eat neatly when he held the fork correctly, but Mercury had a feeling Chrome would still be eating with his hands for a few more years. Kendra's glaring certainly wasn't going to have any sort of effect on whether Chrome ate properly or not.

The kits in charge of cleaning up hurried to collect the plates when everyone was finished eating.

"Can I get anyone some coffee or tea?" Mercury asked. Dane was supposed to supervise cleanup—that was how they split their own chores—but Mercury volunteered himself so Dane could stay with their guests. Dane would make it up to him. Mercury was smiling to himself as he stood and reached for the bowl that had held the salad.

"I doubt you have any real tea, considering what you served this afternoon," Kendra said with a dismissive sigh. "I suppose you can bring me whatever you have and I'll choose."

"Decaf coffee for me, thanks," William said with a smile.

"Same," Jessica added, and Henri nodded in agreement.

Mercury picked up the bowl that had held the fettuccini and carried his two bowls into the kitchen behind his kits.

'Ron was already at the sink rinsing dishes so Lumie could stack them in the dishwasher. Nickel was bringing the last of the dishes in from the dining room. Mercury stayed out of their way, instead going to the cabinet across the room where the newly discovered soup tureen was kept. Next to the tureen was a small teapot with a strainer inside for loose tea. Mercury rinsed it using the instant hot spout when 'Ron gave him a bit of space at the sink, then filled it with hot water. The teapot and one of their teacups with an unchipped saucer went onto a tray. Nickel saw what Mercury was doing and headed toward the cabinet where they kept their tea. With that taken care of, Mercury headed to the coffee maker.

There were two varieties of loose tea, which Nickel added to the tray. At one point there had been more types, but Zinc liked to dump loose tea into her baths and had been slowly working her way through their stash. Nickel added a few different flavors of tea bags to the tray just in case.

"Ask her if she wants cream or sugar," Mercury called as Nickel picked up the tray and headed to the dining room. Nickel nodded to show he'd heard as he walked off.

The coffee maker was spitting happily by then, so Mercury got everything he needed to serve the coffee arranged on his tray.

"She wants milk, not cream, and two lumps of sugar," Nickel told Mercury with a roll of his eyes as he strode back into the kitchen.

Mercury rolled his eyes too. "She wouldn't accept anything less, I guess," he joked. They had a small pitcher that went with the personal teapot. Mercury rinsed it, then filled it with milk. There was also a bag of sugar lumps in the back of the pantry. Dane had no doubt purchased it the last time his mother had come to visit, and the kits had somehow not noticed the sugar in the interim. Mercury found another saucer, placed two lumps on it, and added it all to the tray of mugs. Nickel took that tray back into the dining room.

"The dishes are done," 'Ron said happily. The two pots that needed to be hand-washed were still on the stove, but that was Mercury or Dane's job tonight. He would get to it after dessert.

"Go on and make sure our guests are entertained," Mercury said. "I'll be in once the coffee is ready."

'Ron and Lumie ran off. Nickel stopped in briefly to return the tray, but the kitchen was otherwise blessedly empty and quiet. Moments like this were few and far between in their house, and Mercury cherished every one. Still, he had five minutes to kill while the coffee dripped; he quickly washed the two pots and the baking sheets the rolls had been on. By the time those were dripping in the drying rack, the coffee was done. Mercury went to the top of the fridge where the candy basket was kept, pulled it down, then collected the coffee pot and headed to the dining room again.

"Are you a horse?" Mercury heard Kendra's scathing voice ask as he pushed open the door and stepped inside.

"I'm not a horse, I'm a dragon!" 'Ron declared, sounding scandalized that someone could make that kind of mistake.

"Well, only horses eat sugar lumps raw. Dragons may only have them in tea," Kendra finished.

Mercury held back a smirk. It appeared Kendra had finally figured out 'Ron and was handling her at least a little better than before. He started pouring coffee while Kendra tested a sip of her tea under 'Ron's watchful eyes. Once everyone who wanted coffee had it, Mercury brandished the basket.

The kits all sat up, eagerly staring at the basket. Mercury went to each of them one by one, letting them choose one candy from the stash. William was watching the process very closely as Mercury was hoping he would. Lumie hesitated for a moment over the basket, glancing up at Mercury to make sure it was okay.

"You're trying very hard to make up for your mistake," Mercury told him gently. "You can have your candy tonight, and if you keep working hard, you'll get it tomorrow too."

Lumie smiled, eagerly dug out a cinnamon bomb, and popped it into his mouth with a happy sigh.

Once the kits had chosen, Mercury moved to their guests. Kendra declined, but the other three each took something. The rock candy came in packs of blue and green and Nickel only ate the blue ones, so both Dane and Mercury took a green rock candy for themselves.

Silence again reigned as mouths were kept full. Candy was a serious subject for the kits, not to be debased with idle chatter or other distractions. Only once their mouths were empty again did they start talking. One glance at his watch told Mercury he had better start getting them moving, or they would keep chattering for hours.

"Bath time," Mercury said sternly.

The kits all froze in their seats and looked shifty eyed, Lumie and Copper especially. Zinc sighed and got to her feet. She caught Alloy's hand in hers and tugged him out of his chair and after her out the door. 'Ron hopped up after them, bopped Chrome on the head, and hurried off. That was two bathrooms taken; Zinc would help get Alloy scrubbed before taking her own shower while 'Ron used the other bathroom.

Chrome yowled and dashed after 'Ron. There was a crashing sound in the kitchen, then thumping footsteps as they fought on their way up the stairs. Whether Chrome would actually get in the tub was doubtful, but at least 'Ron had coerced him into heading in the right direction.

Lumie, Copper, and Nickel were the only kits left. Mercury knew that Nickel would get in a shower before bedtime without prompting. Instead, Mercury gave Lumie a look. Lumie, who already knew he was in the doghouse, sighed and wandered off in the direction of the door. Copper followed, but Mercury knew better than to believe that either of them would hurry into the bath.

Dane didn't need Mercury's help keeping the other territory leaders in line. Being the less powerful person in their relationship was a fact that he had long ago come to terms with. He refused to relive that memory at the moment even though it was suddenly in the forefront of his mind—not in front of the territory leaders and not when the possibility of their bathrooms being flooded over their heads was imminent. Mercury resolutely pushed his thoughts about being second in power, but first in Dane's heart, aside as he stood, smiled politely to everyone, and followed his kits upstairs.

Besides, Dane might be powerful, but Nickel was ruthless. Nickel would make sure nothing happened in the dining room that Dane hadn't engineered.

Mercury thought he saw Kendra looking at him sharply with an almost thoughtful look on her face, but he didn't stop to double-check as he pushed through the dining room door and entered the hallway. She could wait; his kits were much more important.

Chapter Five

"Where do we start?" Dane asked everyone still sitting around the table. Mother took another sip of tea, but he hadn't missed the way she had been looking at Mercury. Hopefully, she wouldn't try playing with his memories, like she had with Dane. Although Dane was surprised at how well-behaved she had been so far. He was waiting for the other shoe to drop and was honestly surprised it hadn't yet.

"How did this misunderstanding happen?" William asked. "Jessica, you brought his actions to my attention."

Jessica looked up from her mug of coffee and grimaced. "Only because Henri called me."

"He blew up a warehouse inside my territory," Henri insisted. "I refuse to believe his maps are telling the truth. You doctored them," he accused, turning toward Dane with a snarl.

Dane didn't bother answering that. Anyone who had seen the maps he had shared knew they were accurate. The real question was how Henri had managed to misread his own maps and come to the conclusion that he needed to gather all the relevant territory leaders to stop Dane. William shot Henri a sharp look that said he should shut up before more of his stupidity showed. Henri shut up.

There were only a few people powerful enough in the world to tell someone to shut up with just a look. William was one, Mother was another, and some did consider

Dane to be on that list. Others, however, thought he was a pushover because he spent his days helping people via his supernatural consulting firm instead of ruling them. Henri wasn't anywhere near that list, but Dane thought he shut up because he was embarrassed to have been proven wrong and ignorant in front of an important audience.

"Dane gave the wrong address for the warehouse, then," Henri continued after a long moment gathering his courage again. "I bet if we compare the address for the actual warehouse you'll see differently."

"Fine. Let's compare," William replied agreeably. "What is the real address for the warehouse?"

Henri spluttered for a moment. Dane thought he was trying to come up with an excuse for not answering, and he was right.

"That isn't important," Henri finally said with a dismissive wave of his hand.

"But you just said it was important," William replied. He sounded gently curious, but the hard look in his eyes said otherwise. Dane could tell he was very ticked off that he had been dragged to Dane's house for this farce.

Henri didn't answer, and after a moment, William sighed heavily and turned toward Dane.

"I don't know what any one of us was thinking, but clearly our reasons for invading your territory continue to be false. The charter set forth to keep peace between territory leaders dictates that all three of us owe you reparations for it. I am willing to provide one million dollars from my own personal funds. Jessica?"

Jessica gaped at William. "Where the hell did you get that kind of money?" she asked sharply. "I can't match it."

That didn't make any sense to Dane. He had researched the way she ran her territory, and if anyone wanted her aid, they had to pay for it. She should have been flush with cash. Then again, it wasn't his concern where her money was going. She could run her territory however she liked. It was nice to know she was willing to abide by the charter, a set of guidelines put together two hundred years ago when the old Native American territory boundaries were replaced by the current ones. Dane had had a hand in writing some of the guidelines. The territory leaders loosely followed it. In situations like this where honest—and sometimes not so honest—mistakes were made and all those involved wanted to remain on friendly terms, it was easiest to follow what the charter said to do: make reparations.

"How about I send some of my deputies to your territory? They can be your servants for five years. They'll help out at your detective business or do your laundry." Her tone implied that she knew just how much laundry he must go through, which was true, but completely rude to note. "Whatever you need them for, I'll pay their salaries."

It was a generous offer, but also very intrusive. Dane couldn't accept the possibility of her agents trying to sabotage his territory; for all he knew this was a ploy for her to expand her own. She wouldn't be the first leader hoping to emulate William and control all of America.

"Henri?" William asked sharply.

"I don't owe him anything for a misunderstanding," Henri insisted.

"It was at your word that I attended this meeting," William snarled, his voice low and menacing. "If I must pay, you must too."

Dane decided to jump in before the argument turned into an actual fight. Nickel was eyeing both William and Henri as if trying to decide if he could take them both.

Dane thought Nickel could probably take on Henri, but there was no way he could handle William, at least not yet. A few more years of training and he might be able to, but he was still too young at the moment. The last thing Dane wanted was for Nickel to get hurt, so he was going to stop the fight before it started.

"I don't need money," Dane cut in quickly before Henri could reply. "And I don't need any help with my laundry. Thank you very much for the offers."

"What do you want?" Jessica asked shrewdly.

"Information. As you know from my emails, there is a group of scientists kidnapping dragons from the wild and conducting horrible experiments on them. I want to stop them. Any information you can find on them will help me destroy those scientists for good."

"Anything I find, I'll tell you," William replied immediately, which had Dane mentally raising an eyebrow. Why would William be so interested in helping dragons? Dane would have to ask Mercury whether he had noticed anything.

"Dragons?" Henri scoffed snidely. "Well, it's easy to see you have an interest in them, but that's a little excessive."

"I can tell you like dragons and all, since you adopted a bunch, but it's definitely weird to be so obsessed," Jessica agreed, although she didn't sound nearly as rude as Henri. "Dragons are wild animals. What do you care what happens to them?"

"Do I look wild to you?" Nickel asked softly. He didn't sound offended, but then Dane knew that Nickel had heard it all before and was probably numb to it.

No one answered—Jessica looked away from Nickel as if she was embarrassed that she had insulted him—but

Dane smiled at Nickel because they both knew that dragons were wild and crazy, but not in the derogatory way Jessica had meant.

"So, information?" Dane asked Jessica and Henri.

Jessica sighed. "If I hear anything, I'll let you know." She didn't sound the least bit sincere, but she probably thought it was a fool's errand. Dane would have to keep in contact with her regularly to see if she had heard anything, because he doubted she would remember to volunteer the information.

Henri just nodded jerkily, agreeing without looking like he was giving in. Dane would take it.

There wasn't much to say after that. They sat in silence for a long moment until Jessica let out another sigh.

"Since we're all here anyway, why don't we discuss some of the stuff that has been going through the territory leaders' email chains," she said. "The one about the werewolf kidnappings occurring up and down the Eastern Seaboard sounds pretty serious. How can I help you three combat the kidnappers before it spreads west into my territory?"

Dane knew he wasn't going to get any more answers tonight. Henri wasn't willing to explain his false reasoning, and both Jessica and William seemed happy to let the misunderstanding fade. They wouldn't appreciate Dane trying to force the issue. Besides, Dane had gotten what he wanted: more allies, no matter how reluctant, in the fight against the evil scientists. Dane let it go. His territory was safe, which was what mattered, and he needed to start doing something about the kidnapped werewolves anyway.

*

It was long past bedtime before Dane was finally able to head upstairs. Dane was always reminded just how young Nickel actually was whenever Nickel stayed up past his bedtime. Nickel was stifling a yawn behind a clenched jaw as they showed each territory leader where their rooms were and where the shared bathroom was. Mother harrumphed at the arrangements, but didn't otherwise complain.

Once everyone was situated, Nickel headed for the kits' wing of the house.

"Go to sleep," Dane said pointedly. He knew Nickel might take a shower and get in pajamas to placate Dane and then stay up all night on watch instead of sleeping. "Mercury and I will keep an eye out tonight, which means we'll need you to be sharp in the morning."

Nickel nodded. Even though he was only fourteen years old, he understood what Dane was instructing. Nickel would go to sleep, but he would be ready to react instantly should something occur.

Dane left Nickel alone, instead heading to check on the rest of the kits. 'Ron and Zinc were curled in their beds. Dane didn't know when 'Ron had found big pink bows or why she had decided to thumbtack them to the wall over her bed, but it made for an interesting sight. Zinc's long hair was unbraided and spread around her head on the pillow like a white halo. That was two kits accounted for.

Copper and Alloy were also happily asleep in their beds. Their room had a slightly burnt smell to it, almost like an unpleasant aftertaste that lingered on the back of Dane's tongue. It was acrid, but the kits didn't mind it.

Alloy was half water kit and half fire kit, but thanks to Copper and Lumie's influence, he preferred his fire half most of the time. Whatever had burned in the room had no doubt made Alloy perfectly happy. Sometimes Lumie bunked with Alloy, preferring the fiery room to the room he shared with Chrome, but Alloy was alone in his bed tonight.

Lumie and Chrome's room was a disaster area. Dane remembered Mercury telling Chrome to clean his room as part of his chores, but Chrome had evidently chosen to forget that. There wasn't a clear path on the floor amid Chrome's clothes, books, shoes, and what randomly appeared to be dishes from the kitchen. Chrome would be cleaning for most of the morning—Dane would make sure of that.

The top of Lumie's bed was the only clear space in the entire room—even Chrome's bed was covered, and Chrome was happily nested beneath the mess—and Lumie was nowhere in sight.

Dane sighed. Lumie vanished regularly, but he knew the rules about bedtime and that he wasn't allowed to leave the house after dark. It was entirely possible Lumie had decided not to brave Chrome's mess and had found somewhere else to sleep, but he usually ended up sleeping with Alloy when that happened. Dane walked down the hall to double-check the bathroom and the schoolroom at the end, but found them both devoid of Lumie.

Instead of continuing to search, since Lumie would only be found if he wanted to be, Dane turned around and headed down the hall to the room he shared with Mercury in the other wing. They had the room that mirrored the schoolroom in the kits' wing. It was large, with a king-sized bed, two dressers, a small sitting area with a table and chairs, a fireplace, and a private bathroom. Mercury was just coming out of the bathroom when Dane walked inside.

Mercury's bronze-colored hair was still damp from his shower, and his pajama pants were slung low on his hips, showing off his bronze scales that covered most of his chest and stomach. He was beautiful and Dane's thoughts instantly dissolved into babbly mush at the sight. Mercury's responding grin said he noticed and appreciated Dane's attention.

"Love you," Mercury said as Dane stepped closer to pull him into a hug.

"Love you more," Dane replied instantly before Mercury pulled his head down into a kiss good night.

*

Mercury was already settled into the sitting area between the two wings of the house when Dane finished his shower and dressed in a clean pair of jeans and a sweatshirt. Snow was falling outside, highlighting the evergreen trees in the distance and making Dane wish he and Mercury could take the time for a late-night stroll. It was beautiful, but they had much more important things to focus on.

Mercury put the book he had been reading aside. Dane sat on the couch next to him with a sigh. At least the snow provided something interesting for them to look at as the long hours passed until dawn. Dane opened his mouth to speak, but then paused when Mercury looked pointedly at the nearby armchair.

Lumie was curled up on the cushion, snoozing happily with his thumb in his mouth.

Dane rolled his eyes, but lowered his voice to a whisper before he spoke. "What are your impressions of our visitors?"

Mercury grimaced. "I'm not really sure. I think I like William. Oh, I have to tell you about the conversation I had with him while the kits were making dinner. Apparently he rescued two water kits and has been taking care of them. He wanted some advice on how to keep his house standing."

Dane held back a laugh so he didn't wake Lumie. That explained why he was so interested in helping Dane. Dane had no doubt that William's life had been turned as upside down by his new kits as Dane's had and that William was loving and utterly exasperated by every moment of it.

"I gave him some pointers, but don't be surprised if he comes to you for more advice."

"William needs the shake-up," Dane replied, still holding back laughter.

Mercury frowned. "How long has he been territory leader? He seems like a regular human, but a regular human wouldn't be able to control all of Canada like he does."

"My first thought when I saw him on the other side of the wards was that he was here to try to take Maine and the other northern parts of my territory away from me," Dane replied thoughtfully. "He's been known as the most ruthless of all the territory leaders in North America for well over fifty years. The only reason you probably haven't heard of him before is that he keeps to himself unless he notices a problem and then the problem vanishes. Poof, gone, along with all the instigators and aggressors. I don't believe our enemy has dared to set up a lab in his territory for fear of what he might do to them."

"Maybe they would have before you got involved," Mercury joked, "but they're so afraid of your repercussions they didn't dare involve another territory leader. So, if William isn't human," Mercury asked in a much more serious tone, "what is he?"

"You know that people sometimes call me the Genie of the East because I'm so powerful?" Dane asked. He waited for Mercury to nod before continuing. "I think William might actually be a genie, and he's hidden his power behind a human façade."

Mercury nodded thoughtfully when Dane finished speaking, clearly glad to have some sort of explanation.

"I think he's trustworthy when it comes to dragons, at least," Mercury said. "I want to help him get his two water dragons settled."

"Another powerful advocate for the treatment of dragons can't hurt," Dane agreed.

"I assume he's given up the idea of taking over Maine, then." Mercury rested his head on Dane's shoulder tiredly. "How did the talks go while I was getting the kits ready for bed?"

Dane snorted in disgust. "Henri refuses to admit he made a mistake, and I couldn't get him to explain how he managed it. Luckily, William took control of the meeting. None of them wanted to be the first to offer a concession, but they all knew that they owed me something. William made sure they offered."

"Are you talking about money, territory?"

"William offered me money and Jessica offered me some of her personal staff to help me run my territory." Dane shook his head to let Mercury know he hadn't agreed to either. "I was able to convince them that they owe me information about the scientists. I'm hoping they'll actually look and then send what they find to me, but I think only William will without my reminding him that he agreed to help."

"I don't think you'll have any problem with William. The others?" Mercury shrugged. "No idea. I can't even figure out how Jessica took power. She can't be a genie too, right?"

That was something Dane had been wondering too. She didn't exude power like Henri or hide it like William and Mother. "Not a genie, but there's got to be something—" He froze in place and held up one hand to silence Mercury when he started to ask what had caught Dane's attention.

One of the magical markers he had placed on his visitors was moving.

"Henri has decided to test my patience," Dane murmured once he had figured out which marker. "He's going onto the roof." The marker had climbed out the bedroom window and continued upward. Dane waited to see whether Henri was heading toward Dane's office and bedroom, or toward where Dane and Mercury were sitting. Henri chose the latter, and Dane sucked in a little magic from the air around him to bolster what he already had stored.

When Henri was directly overhead and continuing onward toward the kits' rooms, Dane let his magic flare. He yanked downward with both his magic, and his fist and Henri's body fell through the ceiling. Henri hit the floor with a thud and scrambled quickly to his feet with a fang-baring snarl.

"Taking a stroll?" Dane asked, surprised that his voice still sounded genial when rage was flaring inside. How dare Henri try to attack his kits!

"Thought I would see the sights," Henri replied, but he didn't sound genial in the least bit. Instead he sounded dangerous, his voice low and his accent menacing. Dane had to keep himself from rolling his eyes. Henri was a vampire, albeit a powerful one, but was no match for Dane in the long run. Had Dane been in any way interested in expanding his territory, taking over from Henri would have been far too easy. Admittedly, Dane hadn't quite figured out how Henri had managed to be out in daylight, but that was a mystery for another day. That new ability wouldn't hinder Dane in any way.

"Feeding from a dragon will only give you a stomachache," Lumie said through a yawn. He sat up on his cushion, and Dane saw Henri immediately focus on Lumie. It was easy enough to guess that Henri had probably been heading in Lumie's direction on the roof. "It won't give you special powers like the dhampir you've been keeping locked up in your basement does."

And that explained the mystery of Henri's ability to walk in daylight. A dhampir was a hybrid, a child with a vampire father and a human mother. They had the protection from the sun thanks to their human half and a plethora of vampire powers thanks to their father's. Dane hadn't known feeding from a dhampir would give a vampire those human-granted abilities, but apparently Henri had figured it out.

"And how would you know that?" Henri asked scathingly.

Lumie shrugged. "I had a dream. It was a very long dream. Your dhampir escaped about an hour ago, and by the time you get back to the territory, he'll be the leader, not you." Lumie recounted his dream with nonchalance, as if he were only describing a painting instead of seeing the future. Dane didn't doubt his words; he had too much experience with Lumie to believe anything less than what Lumie was saying.

Dane turned to Henri and couldn't stop the cold grin from showing on his lips. "For your attempt on my kits' lives, I banish you from my territory. You have six hours to get across the border before I take action. I suggest you hurry if you want to actually stay in power," Dane added frostily. "And, territory leader or not, if you step inside my territory again I will end your existence."

"You dare threaten me?" Henri snarled. "I'll call the whole territory leader council and have you removed!"

Dane just let his smile grow at the threat. "Since you won't be a territory leader in a few hours, I'm not worried. Now go away." Dane waved his hand at Henri even though his magic didn't need the direction. Magic swirled around Henri for a brief moment, then sent him away with a pop of displaced air. Dane felt Henri land in the snow just outside of the wards around his house.

Lumie yawned again and slipped down from the armchair. He wandered down the hall and stopped in front of Copper and Alloy's door.

"Lumie," Dane called. "I'm going to make sure Chrome cleans his room. You don't have to help him with any chores tomorrow, because he didn't complete the chores he was assigned today either." Lumie grinned at Dane—no doubt he already knew that Chrome would face consequences for the disaster he had left—and let himself into Alloy's bedroom.

Mercury waited until the door was closed before letting out a sigh. "That was interesting," he grumbled.

Dane couldn't help agreeing. "I'm wondering if Henri made up the whole thing with getting his maps mixed up just so he had an excuse to get inside my wards and attack our kits. I haven't kept it a secret from the territory leaders council that I'm raising some very powerful dragons."

Dane paused to think that through before continuing. "I'll bet he was going to be facing some serious challenges for territory leader in the near future, more than just the dhampir that's taking over his territory right now. Since he was able to absorb the dhampir's power, maybe he thought he could absorb Lumie's as well? I'm glad we stopped Henri before he could try to touch Lumie."

They shared a grin, both knowing how poorly that would have gone for Henri. Henri should consider being banished from Dane's territory and dumped outside in the snow as lucky in comparison.

Dane was about to settle back onto the couch with Mercury when one of the doors down his wing of the house slammed open. William rushed into the hall, saw Dane standing in the sitting area, and ran to him.

"The wards around my compound just fell. I need to get home now. Let me out of your wards," William gasped. His jeans weren't buttoned and the shirt he had thrown on was inside out.

"You need any help?" Dane asked immediately.

"Of course not," William scoffed. "Now let me out." Dane nodded and let his magic fly. William vanished from sight a second later.

"Two territory leaders under attack on the same night?" Mercury mused aloud.

Dane nodded his agreement. Something fishy was definitely going on. Dane sent a little more magic into his own shields, just in case someone thought to try him as well. Someone taking over Henri's territory wasn't too odd. Henri was very powerful for a vampire, but most territory leaders were closer to the caliber of Dane and William. Henri might have thought he fit in, but he really didn't compare. It was only a matter of time before someone stronger stepped in.

Someone attacking William was serious and also worrying however, which was why Dane had offered his help. It was William's territory, though, and his problem to deal with, so once the offer was denied Dane had to accept that fact. Still, someone with enough power to attack William would have no qualms going after Dane. He would need to keep an extra pair of ears open to any possible chatter about an attack on his own territory and make certain he spoke to William about it after William had finished stopping the attackers.

"Jessica doesn't seem to be having a problem," Mercury continued thoughtfully.

"Whoever's attacking might only be going after the leaders on the Eastern Seaboard," Dane answered. Or the two attacks had nothing to do with each other. Henri's dhampir might have simply escaped his confinement and decided to take power instead of running, and it might simply be a coincidence that someone else was trying to attack William on the same night.

Dane hated coincidences.

"Let's hang out here for a few more hours, see if Jessica or my mother have similar issues," Dane sighed.

Dane retrieved his computer from his office so he could start double-checking anything he could access about his territory via the internet, and Mercury returned to his book. As the hours passed, they took turns dozing on each other's shoulder. When the sun started peeking out above the horizon, Mercury left to start getting ready for the day. It was the weekend; the kits would be up soon. Dane and Mercury couldn't get them up on weekdays when they had to be ready in time for the tutor, yet on the weekend they were up at least an hour earlier than their weekday alarms. The kits made no sense to Dane. Instead, he was just glad to find a pattern of behavior he could follow. Although, with Copper, Zinc, and Nickel hitting puberty now, there was no telling what might happen.

He resolutely pushed that terrible thought from his mind and refocused on the report he was writing for one of his cases at his detective agency while a territory search ran in the background. A woman's husband had gone missing. The woman was more interested in retrieving the three million dollars her husband had also taken than in finding the man himself, which meant Dane was crunching numbers and talking to offshore banks. It was taking much longer than usual to close the case, but that meant he could charge her more for his time. He had to keep the candy basket full or face a mutiny, which meant the woman would be paying through the nose for his troubles. She could afford it, of course. He only charged what his customers could afford to pay.

He got in another twenty minutes of work before the first kits woke up.

"Wow! More snow!" 'Ron cheered. Cold air blew through the hallway a few seconds later, followed by Zinc's yelp.

"Close the window!" Zinc yelled. There were sounds of a scuffle, and then the breeze abruptly vanished. 'Ron came rushing out of her room. She dashed past Dane and headed straight for the stairs and the front door that would let her out into the snow. Her thin sleeping pants and T-shirt—which looked like it had been stolen from Chrome at one point—were entirely inadequate for the weather.

Dane sent out a lasso of magic and caught 'Ron before she could get too far down the stairs. He pulled her back to the sitting area and sternly pointed back to her room.

"Pants and a sweatshirt first," he admonished. "Then find your coat, scarf, and gloves."

"But I'm going to change shape to play," she whined immediately. Her scales in her dragon form would protect her from the cold, but it was very possible that she would want opposable thumbs or hands in general to fling snow around and shift to her underdressed human form without thinking about how little she was wearing. Dane continued sternly pointing toward her room until she growled and slunk off to get changed.

Nickel emerged next, fully dressed in warm clothes and looking ready to go outside. Apparently Nickel had decided that if the kits were going out to play in the snow before breakfast, he was going to be their guard for as long as their visitors were still on the premises.

Dane quickly filled Nickel in on Henri and William's absences while the rest of the awake kits got dressed.

"I can't believe you made me miss all that!" Nickel grumbled, his face twisting into an unhappy pout.

"But now if something happens today, you'll be better prepared than Mercury or I to handle it. We need someone to always stay sharp; you know that."

Nickel didn't look the least bit placated by Dane's explanation. He growled deep in his throat as he stalked past Dane and headed down the stairs. Dane heard the hall closet open and close as Nickel got his coat and then watched over the balcony as Nickel walked out the front door. Seconds later, a blue dragon slunk through the snow, quickly vanishing from sight as Nickel called on his magic to use the wet snow as cover. He would be extra vigilant thanks to Dane's warning about someone daring to attack William in case they might eventually turn their attention toward Dane as well.

'Ron reappeared properly dressed this time with Chrome, Zinc, and Alloy hot on her heels. Copper and Lumie weren't as interested in the snow as the rest unless they got to melt it, so Dane wasn't surprised when they decided to stay in bed instead.

Mercury laughed when he emerged from their bedroom and saw the snow fight going on outside. The kits were being loud enough that their remaining guests wouldn't be able to sleep through it. Oh well.

"You go get dressed. I'll get breakfast started. When you're done, go wrangle the kits who are supposed to be helping me," Mercury said. He bent and pressed a lingering kiss to Dane's lips before heading downstairs.

Dane was grinning to himself as he put his laptop away and went to go shower and get ready for the day.

*

Jessica didn't seem to be in any hurry to leave. When Mercury asked her about it, she said she was waiting for William to return and wanted to see if Henri's usurper would send a representative. She seemed to think there was more for the leaders to talk about, although Dane had assumed they would all be leaving after breakfast. Dane would have thought she would be more concerned than she was acting after hearing that two territories had been attacked overnight and would rush home to ensure hers was still okay. It was what Dane would have done before he had Mercury at home to reassure him over the phone that the territory was still in his control. Perhaps Jessica also had someone at home? Or she had some other plan in mind that required she stay put. Not knowing what was going on in her head was starting to become infuriating, but at the same time Dane didn't quite dare to send out feelers into her territory to see if he could find anything out. He had already been accused of overstepping his boundaries once; he didn't want to give her an opening to accuse him again.

Mother was also an enigma. She got up when the kits' noise couldn't be ignored any longer, didn't complain about the unusual wakeup call, and then placidly went downstairs. That was not normal, and it was making Dane feel a bit twitchy.

Dane walked outside into the snow fight that even Copper and Lumie had been coerced into participating in. Snowballs, wind-whipped snow banks, tree branches, and anything else the kits decided was usable as a projectile were flying through the air. Dane let his magic flare and anything that was airborne froze in place.

"Any kits who are supposed to be helping Mercury with breakfast need to go inside now," he called.

A series of groans met his pronouncement, and the kits slunk out of the snowy forest toward the house. Even the ones who didn't have chores decided to come inside. The last thing they would want was to be late for breakfast.

Dane let everything he had caught in the air drop to the ground as the kits filed inside. Nickel slipped in after them, but Dane doubted he had participated in the fun of the battle. Another shame; Nickel needed to relax and playing in the snow was one of the best ways for that to happen. Until their visitors finally left, Nickel wouldn't allow himself to let go like Dane knew any kit his age really needed to. It wasn't fair and Dane hated the necessity of it, but he also knew Nickel wouldn't be happy living as carefree as the rest of the kits. He needed the responsibility just as much as he needed a chance to let loose.

Mercury had breakfast well in hand, especially now that his help had arrived. Dane headed into the dining room where Mother was enjoying a cup of tea on her own. Mother would yell if he didn't act like a good host and entertain her, although she hadn't actually griped much at all since meeting his kits. He took the seat next her.

"How are you?" he asked tentatively.

Mother took a long sip of tea, carefully arranged the cup on the saucer, and then turned to look at Dane.

"I am feeling my age, I'm afraid," she sighed.

Dane had no idea how to respond to that. She was almost four hundred years old. Carrying the son of a god when she had been thirty years old had changed her, mostly by slowing her aging process greatly. Only in the last fifty years had she started looking like she was in her seventies. Dane estimated she aged ten years for every hundred she lived, which did mean she was starting to actually get old.

"I usually have a skilled apprentice with me when I do spell work these days, Dane," she continued. Her voice sounded bland, but Dane could infer from the context that she was hiding a great deal of pain. "I found a young man who is particularly strong at the craft. I was planning to introduce you two and entice you to leave your territory and take over mine with him. I would have spoken to your father about helping the young man stay young and powerful if you had liked him too, but obviously that is moot now."

She had probably made a lot of extravagant plans to trick Dane into leaving his territory and taking over her own. Except she would only really relinquish her power upon her death, which meant her replacement could never actually say they were a territory leader. Mother would rule from behind the curtain instead of in front of it. Dane wouldn't have been able to abide that, not after running his own territory for so long. He had left her side with the ships to the New World at his first opportunity and hadn't looked back.

He had only been territory leader for about a hundred and fifty years, waiting until after the Native American leaders of old had passed on and a new one hadn't been available to take their place. The territory borders had been redrawn as the United States subsumed the old Native American boundaries, and Dane had carved out his niche and was sticking to it no matter what his mother insisted.

"Dragons usually die young," Mother said after the silence between them had gone on too long. "St. George killed all the dragons in England before you were born, and everything I have heard since indicated that most dragons do not even reach adulthood."

Dane opened his mouth to explain the territory urges that forced dragon parents in the wild to abandon their kits for fear of accidentally killing them. He also wanted to tell her that he was working to change that by building a village where dragons and kits were learning about homes instead of territories and that sharing was more than possible. Dragons weren't always controlled by their bestial nature. It wasn't something that came naturally to them, but once they were shown the alternative, every single dragon Dane had ever met had eagerly embraced it.

She didn't give him the opportunity to speak, talking over him quickly before he could formulate the words he wanted.

"Have you asked your Mercury how old he actually is?" Mother asked him softly, almost as if she didn't want to cause problems. Since Mother usually loved to cause problems, Dane decided it was better not to answer. Apparently it was a rhetorical question anyway, because Mother went ahead and answered it for him. "I would put your Mercury at somewhere near a hundred."

Dane gaped at her in shock. Mercury didn't look a day over thirty, and that was if Dane was being ungenerous. He had always known dragons were a long-lived species, despite the fact that so many died young, and Mercury had said over and over again that dragons didn't die unless they were killed, but Dane had never put two and two together. Sure, Dane was almost four hundred years old. Unlike his mother, who was only a few decades older than him, his aging process had completely stopped; he didn't look a day over twenty-five. Dane knew that was due to the powers he had inherited from his father, as gods were generally immortal; while he could be killed, Dane wouldn't die until the day he asked his father to take him to the other realm. His mother's lifespan had been influenced by that power while she carried him to term, but it was starting to fade as the years caught up with her.

Mercury didn't know when he was born. Dane did know that. After being abandoned by his mother around ten years old, when he had first started to fly, Mercury had lived in the wild for a long time. For some reason Dane had always assumed that a long time meant five years; Mercury hadn't had a calendar to keep track of the days so he couldn't say for certain how long. He had still looked young enough to be considered a child when he had emerged from the wild in Chicago and had been placed in the foster system. But what if Mercury had only looked young? What if he had been in the wild for ten or even twenty years and the humans' inexperienced eyes saw an early blooming teenager? Certainly Mercury's ignorance of how the human world worked would have played in his favor with his inexperience making him seem younger.

After the foster system, Mercury had put himself through college and then lived in Chicago for a while before being kidnapped by the enemy and getting embroiled in saving the dragons from the scientists bent on experimenting on them. Dane did the math of just Chicago: at least five years in the foster system, another five to finish college, and approximately five of living on his own. That, plus the past six years living together combined with at least fifteen years of living in the wild told Dane that Mercury must be pushing forty even though he looked much younger. A hundred wasn't possible.

"Are you sure?" Dane finally asked Mother.

She nodded curtly. "I had a quick look at one of his memories of his relationship with you after lunch yesterday, and by the end of it he had retaken the spell from me. I made a second attempt yesterday evening and couldn't even entice him into his memories. He's far stronger than you or I originally believed and, to be quite honest, I can't help thinking that he might actually be a suitable partner for you. Now, your kits, on the other hand..." She sighed with an exasperated shake of her head.

"They're kits," Dane replied with a shrug.

"Some of them are," she agreed, but her look was sharp and pointed as she spoke. "Copper, Zinc, 'Ron, and Chrome are perfectly normal. Alloy, well, even I can see that something isn't quite right with him, but he is a normal kit in comparison to Lumie and Nickel. There is something severely wrong with Lumie and Nickel."

"I know, Mother," Dane said.

"No, I don't believe you quite do," she snapped. "They're not dragons like you or I would think of dragons any longer. They're different; their power is different. Your Mercury might be long-lived and very powerful, but they are different even from him. Most of your kits are regular elemental dragons. Mercury is a normal precious dragon. Lumie and Nickel are a strange hybrid of both with something else also running through their veins."

"I know," Dane repeated. "Mother, Mercury and I didn't find our kits in the wild and decide to keep them. We rescued them from horrible labs where human scientists had been experimenting on them in order to steal their powers. The older kits—Nickel, Copper, and Zinc—were taken first, and something happened to them that made all three far more powerful than they ought to be. Nickel, unlike the other two, has chosen to hone his power to the highest possible level. He has surpassed every expectation and continues to grow. Alloy and Lumie were experimented on while still in the egg. Alloy is certainly more normal than Lumie in that he only hatched with fire and water powers. We have no idea what they did to Lumie, but yes, he is different.

"But, Mother, different or not, they're still my kits." Dane had never been able to glare as intensely or scornfully as his mother could, but he was certainly trying.

Mother was unaffected, of course. She looked thoughtful instead of intimidated. "That is why you declared that any dragons in need could approach you and asked for information from the other three territory leaders. You are trying to help the dragons those scientists are still trying to experiment on."

Dane nodded. "We're pretty sure they don't have any more organized labs now. They're underground with only a few dragons kept captive. We want to keep them from getting their hands on any more dragons and stop them once and for all."

"Is it safe to assume that the incident on the Chesapeake Bay that Henri was so concerned about was one such battle?" she asked, but she didn't wait for him to respond. "I find it curious that they would focus on that to attempt to unseat you and that Henri and William are under attack simultaneously. You must realize that someone is behind these problems."

"I know, Mother," Dane sighed.

She nodded. Mother hadn't raised Dane to be blind. He had noticed what she was just figuring out, as had Mercury and Nickel.

"Henri isn't going to return. I'm hoping William will." The kits started drifting into the room to take their seats as Dane finished speaking, which meant breakfast was imminent.

Dane let the conversation with his mother end. They hadn't spoken about anything he didn't already know, and Mother was smart enough to figure out the rest on her own. He got to his feet and headed to his chair at the end of the table as Mercury emerged with a large bowl of scrambled eggs. Zinc followed, holding a basket of sliced bagels, and Copper came in after her with containers of cream cheese and orange juice. The table was set quickly, and Jessica was called from the sitting room she had settled in. Breakfast was passed around.

Dane looked at his kits, wondering what Mother saw that had her so worried. Yes, Copper, Zinc, 'Ron, and Chrome were normal enough kits. They were wild and rambunctious, but that was typical kit behavior. Nickel had always been far too stoic and more concerned with becoming strong enough to fight the enemy than in playing. It was something Dane regretted that Nickel felt was necessary, but he trusted Nickel to have his back in a fight in a way he wouldn't the other kits. Alloy and Lumie were just as odd as Mother had said, but it was what made them unique and interesting. Maybe Mother was seeing something more than Dane was able to discern. He would have to ask his mother about it, but waiting until after Jessica was gone would be best.

Instead of dwelling on the kits, Dane turned his thoughts to Mercury. He knew Mercury hadn't lied about his age or his powers; he was open about everything. He didn't know how long he had lived in the wild after being abandoned by his parents, nor had he kept track of how many years he had lived in Chicago. Dane hadn't actually looked at any of the paperwork about Mercury entering the foster system to see what the corresponding dates were, but that was probably the only way to know for certain. Mercury acted like a mature adult. He didn't make messes like the kits or cause destruction simply because he didn't know any better, but Dane had to remind himself that Mercury was still a dragon and sometimes dragons didn't practice linear thinking the way humans did. Telling Dane how old Mercury was probably hadn't even crossed his mind, and Dane needed to stop worrying about it.

Dane forced himself to think only thoughts about breakfast. His bagel was warm, the cream cheese soft, and the eggs cooked perfectly. Good, yummy eggs.

He brought his fork, filled with eggs, to his mouth and ate, hoping that by the time breakfast was finished his mind would be clear again, and he could focus on the more immediate problems.

Chapter Six

Mercury let Dane supervise the cleanup. Dane looked like he needed a break from being the territory leader for a half hour. The way Dane had been staring at his plate like the bagel there had all the answers to his problems told Mercury that his brain was too full of thoughts and worries. Dane needed a moment to get his head screwed back on straight, and watching to make sure the kits didn't decide to flood the kitchen or chuck dishes at each other like Frisbees might give him that opportunity.

Jessica wandered off again, and Kendra didn't seem to be interested in conversation, so Mercury left the dining room and headed into the kitchen. He settled out of the way on one of the kitchen stools.

Dane was elbow-deep in bubbles as he washed dishes at the sink. 'Ron was giggling loudly as Dane playfully glared at her, so Mercury felt it safe to assume the excess of bubbles was her fault. She was standing on the stool next to the sink taking the dishes as Dane finished cleaning them and stacking them on the drying rack.

"How dare you!" William's voice boomed through the kitchen as the man in question slowly appeared next to the island where Mercury was sitting.

Dane stilled at the sink and his eyes went sharp as he focused on William's form shimmering into view. 'Ron stopped giggling immediately, hopped off her stool, and ran out of the kitchen. Nickel and Zinc rushed in a moment later, and just as William's form finally solidified, Copper joined them.

The sharp smell of magic filled the kitchen. Mercury's own magic was sparking lightly against his fingertips. He also sensed Dane's magic flaring dangerously. The three kits were no doubt ready as well, but the strange magic William was using was so unbelievably strong that Mercury couldn't even sense Nickel's water magic. The way Dane was staring almost searchingly at William told Mercury that William had somehow managed to get through Dane's wards. The only person Dane had ever met who could do that as far as Mercury knew was Lumie.

"How dare you!" William repeated.

"How dare I what?" Dane asked. He reached out to take the dish towel hanging over the oven to dry his hands with an apparent nonchalance that Mercury knew Dane didn't actually feel.

"My kits! Where have you taken my kits?" William sounded incensed, but he also sounded scared.

"Someone took your kits?" Mercury interjected, his words jumping in between William's glaring match with Dane.

William let out a growl that lifted the hairs on the back of Mercury's neck. It was a bestial sound, yet it felt almost more primordial than fanged. There was death there, Mercury's shaken nerves insisted.

"Walked right through my compound to their room, packed them up, and escaped over the border into your territory without any hiccups," William snarled. "But you already knew that, didn't you, since I told you about them just yesterday."

"Where?" Dane snarled, and his voice suddenly held the same note of danger that William's still spouted. Zinc zipped away, a quick gust of wind rushing out of the kitchen. She didn't go far, just to the junk closet where one of the kits had stashed the map left behind in the dining room last night before dinner. Zinc returned in another rush of air and spread the map out on the kitchen island.

William was still glaring incredulously, but he jabbed a finger at the border where Canada met with Vermont.

"Nickel?" Dane said. Nickel immediately stepped to his side and placed a hand on Dane's shoulder. Mercury didn't even have to be told to join them. With William ready to attack at any moment, Dane needed Mercury at his side in the fight instead of Copper and Zinc. He hurried around the island to Dane and gripped Dane on the elbow.

"Be good," Mercury warned Zinc and Copper, who would be the most responsible people left in Dane's house. Mercury had a feeling Kendra would keep the kits from destroying too much. "Coming?" he added to William.

William hesitated for a long moment, no doubt shocked at their reaction. Dane's magic flared as his transportation spell took hold. William reached out quickly to grip Dane's other shoulder, unwilling to be left behind. The kitchen vanished around them, immediately replaced by trees.

Much of New England was forested, but this land was primal and untouched. The trees overhead towered above them, giants in a land of giants. Mercury felt tiny in comparison. Even the sun struggled to penetrate the bare branches overhead to reach the snowy ground below. Mercury shivered, wondering if there was time to jump back home, grab coats, and return. One look at William's incensed glare as he backed away from Dane told Mercury that suggesting that wouldn't go over well.

"I can sense where you used your magic in my territory," Dane said as he turned and started walking, his feet leaving behind deep holes in the snow. Mercury couldn't tell why Dane chose that direction instead of any other, but he followed along with Nickel. "This is where you cast a searching spell." Dane stopped walking abruptly, as if there were a wall in front of him. The thick snow on the ground made it impossible to make out any trail markers, but Mercury knew that Dane was absolutely aware of where his territory ended and he wasn't going to take a single step over the line without permission.

"Any trace of the kidnapper vanished the second they stepped into your territory, as you well know," William snarled. "Stop fucking with me and give me back my kits!" His voice boomed with power, violently echoing through the trees around them. Winter birds screeched overhead as they erupted into the air and flew away in fright.

Mercury was focused on something else, though. There was a smell in the air that he recognized. It almost felt like dragon magic, but it was grossly tainted and sick-feeling. Only the enemy scientists trying to capture dragons for their experiments used that type of stolen magic.

"You smell it?" Mercury asked softly. Nickel nodded, his shoulders tense as his eyes scanned around them. "How long ago were your kits brought through here?" he asked William.

"I tracked them to the border not even an hour ago, ascertained that some sort of dragon magic had been used, and came for you," William replied. As each second passed, he was losing a bit of the ire that had been sustaining him. Worry was starting to crease lines on William's forehead. Whether his kits were a means to more power or if they were simply wards in his home, William clearly did care for them.

Mercury sniffed the air again, and the stench made his stomach twist in disgust. The tainted magic wasn't strong enough to have been used for a transportation spell. It felt like a concealment spell instead. Besides, if the kitnappers had been able to use a transportation spell, why would they be walking through untamed forest? They could have instantly taken their prize to their destination without worrying about being chased.

Which brought up another question. Why had the kitnappers chosen to come into Dane's territory? He doubted William's compound was any nearer the border with Vermont than to Minnesota. In fact, the chances that his compound was actually in Quebec, the province closest to Dane's territory, were probably pretty slim. Territory leaders tended to choose headquarters in the center of their territories. That was why Dane had built his house in Massachusetts and Jessica was located in Ohio. There were exceptions to the rule, of course. Henri had chosen New Orleans as his headquarters because he loved the city rather than for its strategic importance. If the new leader of that territory was smart, he would move his headquarters to somewhere in Georgia, much farther away from the crazy leader of Texas Mercury hoped to never meet. William seemed like a smart man rather than a sentimental one; he would have built his home compound in northern Manitoba or Saskatchewan, a cold but defensible location, which meant it was unbelievably out of the way for the kitnappers to come all the way to Vermont.

The easiest explanation, and the one William had apparently come to, was that the kitnappers were delivering their cargo to Dane. It was a little too easy an explanation, Mercury knew. They were being set up.

Mercury didn't need to say his suspicions aloud. Dane and Nickel were both smart enough to have already figured it out, and William would come to the same conclusion, too, once rationality overcame his fear.

Had the kitnappers assumed William would attack first and ask questions second? Were they planning to pit William and Dane against each other and then take out the severely weakened and possibly injured winner? If that was the case, they had underestimated William and Dane.

"Any sign of them?" Mercury asked.

Dane was the one who answered, although Nickel must have magic running through the snow around them searching for the kits. "They're traveling east along the border." He pointed and then started walking in that direction. Mercury followed behind with William tight on his heels. Nickel drifted off to the side, deeper into Dane's territory.

The snow crunched underfoot, soaking Mercury's socks and sending shivers up his spine. He couldn't sense what Dane and Nickel could, but he was ready for whatever was at the end of the trail they were following.

He didn't expect to find two water dragon kits carefully propped up against a fallen tree branch, gently wrapped in a blanket and left alone in the snow. Their blue hair was long and unkempt, falling over their closed eyes and thin faces. Asleep they looked angelic, but they were just a little older than Lumie and Alloy, so Mercury knew better.

William gasped at the sight of them, quickly dashing forward to move to their side. He ran into the arm Dane held up, stopping his forward momentum abruptly.

"Careful," Dane insisted when William turned on him with a snarl. Dane wasn't looking at the kits. Mercury followed the direction Dane was eyeing and saw a faint line carved in the deep snow just in front of William's toes. The line continued in a circle around the fallen branch, completely encircling the sleeping kits.

"Trapped," William spat in disgust. He was looking at the line too, but his gaze was more calculating than Dane's. With a grunt, William sent a blast of magic at the line just in front of his toes. It was a ball of unformed power of such intensity that it should have incinerated the forest around them. The line merely flared brightly as the spell hit it. There was silence for a brief moment during which Mercury fervently hoped William had overwhelmed the tripwire spell with his own immense powers, but then he heard a strange creaking noise. Snow fell from the branches around them, landing with wet plops, and Mercury looked up just in time to see one of the tree branches bend like it had an elbow and reach for him.

Mercury yelled and dove out of the way, only to be forced to jump when a root popped out of the ground from a second tree to trip him. Flashes of light from William's magic and the sound of Dane swearing under his breath were only distractions as Mercury called on his own power to try to combat the suddenly live trees.

The stench of tainted magic in the air was almost unbearable. That line must have only been a tripwire, waiting for someone to step over it or to send magic over it for the trap around them to spring. All of the trees that circled the clearing were moving in their direction. Mercury dodged a reaching tree limb and stumbled as another thick root thrust up from beneath the snow to catch his feet. He shot a spell at the root, freezing it in place and ensuring the tree couldn't move from that spot. Mercury hit every root that appeared with that same spell. Dane and William caught on quickly and the moving trees slowly came to a halt. That didn't stop their branches from attacking from overhead, though. Mercury continued to dodge and weave, but it was easier when he didn't have to watch what was attacking his feet as well as his head.

"Got it," William yelled suddenly from across the clearing. A swell of magic erupted through the forest, and the trees abruptly froze in place as if Mercury's spell had been large enough to encompass all of their gigantic forms. They shivered as if they were fighting against William's power and the stench of tainted magic increased.

"No, I got it," Nickel snarled. Mercury couldn't see Nickel through the churned snow and trees, but he recognized the hard and deadly tone in Nickel's voice. There was a cracking thud of two hard objects hitting each other from the direction of Nickel's voice. Nickel walked into the cleared space where the two kits were still sleeping peacefully and dropped the body he was dragging into an empty swath of snow.

"Anyone recognize her?" he asked.

The woman's head was tilted at an awkward angle, attesting to how Nickel had killed her. Her hair was bleached blonde and her skin the unnatural shade of orange too much time spent in a tanning bed provided. Mercury didn't recognize her, and one look at Dane's blank face told Mercury that Dane didn't know her either.

William walked around the body to get a closer look and swore when he saw her face. "That's Jessica's lieutenant. She's the one who came to my compound to tell me about Jessica and Henri's concerns. She must have converted one of the humans that work for me and convinced them to take my kits while some other magic-using humans attacked my compound as a distraction."

"And we left Jessica unwatched inside our house!" Mercury gasped, spinning toward Dane as he realized what could be happening at home. "We need to catch her before she attacks."

Dane grunted. "We're too late for that. Someone just tried to breach my wards from both the inside and the outside. Jessica's making her move."

She had probably started the moment William's spell had activated the trap in the trees. Mercury didn't doubt that she had already managed to accomplish whatever she had wanted to inside the house and was only now realizing that she needed Dane's permission to leave his wards.

"I'll take the force outside the wards if you'll go to the house and rally the kits," Dane said to Mercury. "Nickel, I don't want to leave William alone with his kits without someone to watch their backs until we're certain we've stopped the attack." Nickel didn't look happy, but he nodded sharply anyway. "William, I'll contact you the second my house is secured again. If you have Nickel with you when you transport in, my wards will let you through." William also nodded, but he turned toward his sleeping kits.

Mercury called on his magic and felt Dane doing the same at his side. The transportation spell pulled him away from the forest, the trees vanishing from around him. Mercury's spell wasn't as smooth as Dane's. The transition from forest to the windows of the upstairs sitting room was slower, and he felt a little stretched until the spell was complete. When his chilled and damp feet were firmly placed on carpet, Mercury let out a loud roar. His dragon's voice echoed through the halls of the house and out onto the snowy lawn.

It took a few seconds for his voice to fade away, and then he heard silence. The only time the house was this quiet was when everyone was asleep. Even when the kits were playing outside, their voices and explosions still penetrated the walls. This quiet was unnatural, and it made Mercury feel like his heart was lodged in his throat.

Then he sighed in relief at the sound of a door slamming open and two sets of feet pounding toward him. Chrome and 'Ron appeared from the direction of Mercury and Dane's bedroom.

"Dane's office let us hide there," 'Ron gasped as she dove forward to slam into Mercury's middle with a hug. "She couldn't get to us there, but she grabbed Alloy!" The wards around Dane's private office were so strong that Mercury couldn't breach them with his strongest spells. Only Lumie could go in there without Dane's express permission, but apparently Dane had set the wards to let the kits inside in case of an emergency. "Copper and Zinc went after her."

"Which way did Jessica go?" Mercury asked. He was still being held tightly by 'Ron and was gripping one of Chrome's hands so it wasn't easy to move, but he got all three of them heading back to Dane's office.

"Jessica?" 'Ron asked, sounding confused. "Grandma grabbed Alloy and tried to grab Lumie, but we all ran so she only got Alloy."

"Grandmother Kendra?" Mercury asked sharply, unsure if he was hearing her correctly.

'Ron frowned but nodded. Chrome growled. "Her voice didn't sound right. She didn't talk weird like usual."

Was she possessed? Had Jessica done something to her? Mercury let out his own growl.

"Stay here where it's safe," Mercury said as he gently pushed 'Ron and Chrome back through the wards and into Dane's office. "I'll see what's up with Grandma."

If Dane's mother couldn't walk right through Dane's wards as she had done when she arrived at Dane's house on Saturday morning, then there was something seriously wrong with her.

Mercury hurried back down the hallway and into the sitting room. There were windows on both sides of the space, letting Mercury see into the front and backyard. Flashes of fire from Copper were visible on the driveway, so Mercury hurried down the stairs and out the door.

The driveway still had a coating of snow on it from last night's bad weather. The gray sky overhead told Mercury that more snow was imminent, but he had more important things to focus on. There were patches of ice where Copper's fire had melted the snow, and it was quickly refreezing. Mercury slid a few times before he snarled and shifted into his dragon form so his claws could give him some traction on the ice. It was a long walk to where Dane had set the wards, but on four paws Mercury reached the end quickly.

Kendra was slumped on the ground at Jessica's feet. Mercury couldn't tell whether she was unconscious or dead. Jessica was holding Alloy by his ankle. Alloy's eyes were open, but he wasn't blinking. He wasn't moving at all, but the stench of tainted magic was strong around Jessica. Alloy had hopefully only been placed under a stasis spell of some sort. Copper and Zinc were both in their dragon forms. They were still adolescents and therefore smaller than Mercury, but their respective bright-red and white scaled forms with the spikes growing in along their backs were a threatening enough sight.

Jessica held Alloy in the air as Mercury approached. "I can kill him before you even try to attack me," she yelled. Her voice was high and shrill as if she was running on panic alone. Mercury doubted she had any idea what a dragon could do if attacked before today, but now that Copper and Zinc had shown her, she was regretting her actions.

Mercury shifted back to human form. "You can't escape the wards," Mercury called. "Let Alloy go." He was trying to sound calm to keep Jessica from hurting his kit. His voice was authoritative, yet he kept it soft to avoid startling her. If Mercury allowed himself to start yelling, he wouldn't stop; fear for Alloy would overtake his rationality, and he would start begging for her to put him down.

Alloy was his baby, the lone kit who would still peacefully curl up with him on the couch. He was their anomaly and loved all the more for his quirks. Copper, who had taken to raising Alloy since he hatched, must be frantic, but he and Zinc had stepped back to let Mercury take point. If Copper could stay calm, Mercury could, too, no matter how hard his heart was pounding in fear or his gut clenched in worry.

Dane wasn't visible on the other side of the wards, but Mercury hadn't expected him to be. There were two men standing there. They had their hands pressed against the ward and were trying to force their tainted magic to break through and allow Jessica to get out. The wards were invisible to the naked eye, but were revealed by touch and magical sight. The men apparently had to be in physical contact with the wards to be able to discern them. Dane was no doubt ready to take both men out, but wasn't willing to commit until after Mercury had gotten Alloy to safety.

"I think you're going to let me go to ensure I don't kill him right now!" Jessica threatened. Her free hand pointed at Alloy as if a spell was on the tips of her fingers ready to kill Alloy if Mercury didn't comply.

"The wards weren't built in a day. It'll take me a few minutes to get you through them," Mercury cautioned, trying to stall for time while hoping she made a mistake. His hands were up in front of his face to show he was unarmed as he stepped toward her. His fingertips were tingling with the magic he was holding back; it was as riled as his emotions, and it was taking far too much of his concentration to hold it steady too.

"Stay where you are!" Jessica snapped. She jerked her arm back, and Alloy flopped in the air like his body lacked bones or muscles. Her free hand waved and the stench of tainted magic increased. Alloy's body writhed like a fish caught on a hook even though he was unconscious. Copper moaned softly behind Mercury as Mercury froze in place, his hands still in the air.

"Fine, fine," Mercury breathed, not moving any part of his body. "Let me see what I can do about the wards." He very slowly stepped back and then to the side, edging around the far side of Kendra's crumpled form on the snowy ground until he reached the boundary. Mercury could step through it easily, but he couldn't key it to allow someone else entrance. He could physically carry someone through the wards, but besides the fact that Jessica wasn't about to let him get close enough for that, he was still stalling for as much time as he could.

The stolen magic Jessica and her two cohorts were using was finite, and the leader of the scientists, whoever he or she was, didn't bother to inform the peons of that fact. Over and over, Dane and Mercury had fought battles where waiting for the enemy to exhaust themselves was the key to victory. There was a death spell hidden at the end as a safeguard against any of the peons getting captured and talking about where they got the magic, but Dane had grown proficient at stopping it since his first encounter. And yet, Jessica was a territory leader. She wasn't a scientist and was completely unlike anyone they had fought before.

"How did you win your territory?" Mercury asked. He was curious and wanted answers, of course, but he hoped that distracting her would give him enough time to form a complicated knockout spell. Nickel would have killed her by now, and Dane, with his superior magic, would have already incapacitated her. Mercury wanted to capture her for questioning. He was a federal officer; he preferred capture and interrogation to killing, although as a dragon he understood the necessity of destroying the enemy.

Jessica frowned at him. "Focus on getting the wards down," she hissed.

"I need to know something more about you in order to weave you into the ward," Mercury lied.

She looked skeptical, but she answered anyway. "I'm a witch, one of the strongest in North America." Her boast made Mercury want to scoff in disbelief, but he held himself in check. If she had actually been a strong witch, she would have been a territory leader years ago without the need to supplement her powers with tainted magic. Mercury let her keep talking without voicing his skepticism. "I killed the stupid mouse in charge of the central territory and have been getting stronger ever since. Does that help your spell?" She sounded as suspicious of Mercury's request as he was of her actual abilities as a witch. Still, he nodded to uphold the facade.

He almost had enough power gathered and formed to take her out. He had his fists clenched at his sides to keep the power surging on his fingertips from escaping prematurely. Most battles he fought were a litany of spell after spell as he attacked and defended. Those snap spells were weaker than what he was looking to cast now, and he was better at those, but he could do this too. Mercury just needed a few more seconds to get the spell formed correctly.

A few more seconds.

Lumie appeared behind Jessica in his dragon form. He was easily half the size of Copper, but just as red. The spikes on his back were still nubs just starting to grow in, but his wings were large enough to carry him in flight. He couldn't actually fly yet, and he wouldn't for at least four more years, but they were an impressive sight flared behind him as he dove forward and bit down hard on the arm still holding Alloy aloft.

Jessica screamed, and Alloy went flying as she jerked her arm out of Lumie's mouth. There was blood everywhere, running down her arm in rivulets and dripping from Lumie's sharp teeth. Lumie turned and ran toward Alloy's crumpled body. Jessica screamed again, but this time there were garbled words mixed up in her pain as she cast a spell.

Mercury threw out his hands, and his magic flew free. His incapacitation spell wasn't quite formed, and it unraveled as the magic traveled from him to the space between Jessica and Alloy and Lumie. Mercury had wanted to create a shield between his kits and Jessica's spell, but there was too much magic, and too much of it had already been formed. Something was going to go wrong with it, Mercury could tell even as the spell was leaving his hands.

"Get down!" he yelled.

Copper and Zinc ran backwards, not taking their eyes off Jessica even as they obeyed him. Lumie crouched over Alloy, ducked his head, and braced himself.

Mercury wanted to send more magic toward his kits to protect them, but he had put everything he had into that incapacitation spell. There wasn't anything left in his reserves to cast now.

The two spells collided in midair with an earth-shaking boom and a bright flash of white light. The concussive force of it made Mercury stagger back a few feet. His ears rang, and he saw spots. Copper and Zinc were fine, far enough away to have been unaffected. Lumie was still crouched protectively over Alloy, as untouched by the violence of the two spells as he was by any magic. Jessica staggered back to her feet, her bleeding arm held tightly to her body. More words Mercury didn't understand fell from her lips as she built another spell.

He didn't have enough magic left to combat her, but that didn't stop him as he shifted back into dragon form and charged. Jessica didn't notice him. Neither did Kendra.

Kendra pushed her body upward in an awkward one-armed pushup. She flung her free arm toward Jessica and yelled something as incomprehensible to Mercury as what Jessica was saying.

Mercury heard a strange crunching sound through his ringing ears as both Jessica and Kendra fell silent at the same moment. It was a sound like one of his kits stepping on a full bag of chips, crushing every morsel inside into a powder. Jessica's body jerked, then dropped to the ground in a heap. Blood dripped out of her nose, eyes, mouth, and ears.

Kendra's smile was full of cold satisfaction as she let her body relax back down on the ground.

The instant Jessica's body hit the ground, Mercury also saw Dane dash out of the woods. His hands clamped on each of the two men on the other side of the wards. Their bodies twitched for a few long seconds like Dane was pumping electricity through them as he yanked their stolen magic out of their bodies, and when they fainted or died—Mercury couldn't tell which—Dane let their bodies drop to the ground. He stepped through the wards, hurried around what was left of Jessica, and crouched at Lumie and Alloy's side. Mercury was only a beat behind him.

Lumie stepped back from Alloy looking pleased with himself. He damned well should be, Mercury knew, and would be getting extra candy for saving Alloy's life after Mercury finished scolding him for getting involved with the fight when he wasn't trained for it.

"It's just a sleeping spell," Dane sighed in relief. Mercury echoed him a moment later when Alloy yawned and opened his eyes. He looked around the driveway, saw the bodies and everyone who was standing over him looking worried, and yawned again.

"I guess I missed the fun," he grumbled. He got to his feet slowly, a little too shakily for Mercury's peace of mind, and threw himself into Mercury's arms. Alloy's body was shaking, though, as if his nonchalance was faked. Mercury held him close, cuddling his baby kit.

Dane moved away now that the most important concern was taken care of. "Mother, you didn't have to kill her," Dane admonished as he bent down at Kendra's side.

"Oh, yes I did," she replied. She sounded winded, and there was a quaver in her voice that spoke of age and exhaustion. "She was a hodgepodge of different magics. That's how she overpowered me. Her own witch power, the power she stole from dragons, and a dark magic steeped in blood and selfishness. I had to kill her. If she had a chance to share her dark knowledge with anyone, we would end up with another witch-burning. I couldn't allow that to happen."

Justifications aside, they now had a dead and bloody body, two bodies that Mercury wasn't sure were dead or not, a bunch of traumatized kits, and the territory to Dane's west was now leaderless.

"I'll call Valerie and see if she can set up a task force to go have a look at Jessica's home. If we can get there before whoever gave Jessica the tainted dragon magic does, we might be able to get some good information." Mercury stood with Alloy still cuddled in his arms and waved to the rest of the kits to head to the house. Dane and Kendra had caused the bodies—they could deal with them. Besides, Kendra needed a moment to collect herself after fighting off whatever spell Jessica had used on her and subsequently casting a killing spell of that caliber. She didn't need an audience of curious kits trying—and failing, because his kits were better at getting in the way than helping—to get her back on her feet.

Valerie could handle the logistics. They were work partners, field agents for the Federal Bureau of

Supernatural Investigations, and Valerie didn't have much of a social life. She was gruff, stubborn, and so prickly that most people couldn't get along with her. She wasn't nearly as crazy as his kits, so Mercury enjoyed working with her. They had been partners for a year, the longest Valerie had ever stayed with one partner. She would honestly be happy to go into work on a Sunday morning to handle the massive operation Mercury was about to dump on her. She wouldn't even be upset that he couldn't join her until later. Valerie had babysat for the kits a few times and understood completely where Mercury's priorities were. They were perfect working partners.

He walked into the house with his kits, calling loudly so 'Ron and Chrome knew it was safe to come out, and went to find his cell phone.

Even with seven kits trying their hardest, his weekend couldn't get any stranger at this point. Mercury couldn't help smiling as 'Ron and Chrome galloped down the stairs. Yes, it was over for the moment. Once he called Valerie to get the ball rolling, they might finally be able to find a lead that would help them destroy the enemy once and for all.

Epilogue

It took three hours for the kits to start calming down. 'Ron and Chrome spent the time running around the house, working off their nervous energy. They weren't ever going to be fighters, but that didn't mean they enjoyed having to hide like scared rabbits. Dane hadn't heard any crashes or the bang of bodies bouncing off walls for at least ten minutes, so he felt it was safe to assume 'Ron and Chrome were finally settled down somewhere. Although having assumptions when it came to the kits was stupid. Dane knew that; oh boy, did he know that. Sometimes silence could be just as ominous.

Zinc and Copper were outside somewhere. Dane hadn't bothered to check on them, but he had a sinking feeling they were trying to emulate Nickel by walking around the perimeter inside his wards. It was a waste of their time, since Dane had already ensured his wards were still sound, but Dane wasn't about to stop them. As long as he didn't see any trees catching fire or getting blown down, he was happy to leave them be. Mercury had checked that they were bundled up properly for the weather before he let them go. That was enough for Dane.

Lumie was off being Lumie. He had bitten Jessica, gotten her blood all over him, and then wandered off again. Mercury had tried to find him, yelling about Lumie brushing his teeth to get the blood off, but Lumie had vanished completely as only Lumie could. Dane knew

Lumie spent a lot more time in the dragon village Dane was helping to build than he or Mercury actually realized; Dane wouldn't be surprised if that was where Lumie had gone.

Which left only Alloy on Dane's mental checklist. Nickel was still with William, but Dane had called William as soon as he had finished dealing with the bodies and William had promised to have Nickel back home around lunchtime. That was any minute now, Dane knew without having to find a clock to confirm. His stomach was growling, which meant the kits would start swarming the kitchen soon. Dane was waiting for his wards to ping to tell him Nickel was back before he started figuring out what to make. Mac and cheese would probably be best. Given the day they were having so far, the comfort food could only help.

Alloy was attached to Mercury's side. Dane hadn't seen the two of them separated by more than an inch while he was running around over the last three hours. Dane had been dealing with the bodies, making sure Jessica hadn't left any booby traps in the house, double-checking the integrity of his wards, and locating his computer. He'd use that to start what would be a lengthy search of the central territory by Mercury's people at the SupFeds and by Dane—without leaving his own territory, of course. Mercury had been coordinating with Valerie on the phone almost the entire time. Dane preferred to handle the bodies, especially since it gave Mercury and the SupFeds a chance to go on the offensive against the enemy scientists.

There was no way of telling whether it was Alloy or Mercury who didn't want to let go. They were both completely freaked out by the attempted kitnapping and each equally unwilling to be separated from the other. Mercury had walked around for an hour with his phone held to his ear and Alloy held in his arms. At the moment, they were both curled up together on the couch in the upstairs sitting area. The phone was dark on the table in front of them as they waited for Valerie to call back with an update. Aside from the addition of the phone, seeing them cuddled together was a sight Dane remembered often from five years ago when a newly hatched Alloy had escaped from Copper's overbearing clutches and crawled into Mercury's lap almost every evening.

Mother was resting in her bedroom, recuperating her strength after being attacked and casting such a terrible spell. She had decided to leave first thing in the morning now that she had her answer as to whether Dane would be willing to leave his own territory and take over hers when she retired. Since the answer was a resounding no without any room for negotiation or coercion, Mother was leaving peacefully. Dane had a feeling she would be visiting again soon enough. 'Ron had really taken a shine to her, and Dane had little doubt that it wouldn't be long until she was be begging to have Grandma visit again.

Thinking about Mother brought one of the other issues she had mentioned to the front of his mind. Dane sat in one of the chairs in the sitting area, glad to be off his feet for the first time in hours, and turned to Mercury.

Mercury was running his fingers through Alloy's red-and-blue hair, mixing the colored strands together between his long fingers. Alloy had his eyes closed and his head resting in Mercury's lap. He seemed content and halfway asleep. He wouldn't be disturbed if Dane asked his question.

"Mercury, do you know how old you are?" Dane asked softly. Alloy didn't twitch at the noise, so maybe he was completely asleep.

Mercury frowned in thought, then shrugged carefully so he didn't dislodge Alloy. He didn't seem upset about the question, which meant he wasn't hiding it from Dane; rather, he just hadn't bothered to bring up the subject. "I'm not really sure. I know I'm older than the paperwork the government has for me says."

"How long were you in the wild once your parents left?" It was a sore subject for Mercury—for every dragon, really. No child should have to grow up without their parents, and that terrible experience had scarred Mercury deeply.

Mercury shrugged again. "Maybe twenty years? I honestly don't have any idea. When I got to Chicago and child services picked me up, they guessed that I was only fifteen, although I think there's still a question mark next to my birthdate on the birth certificate they had created for me. I'm still not sure why I was taken in instead of being sent back to the wild like most dragons, but I was in their system for the next seven years until even the broadest-minded foster homes couldn't continue to believe I wasn't eighteen yet. I don't think I looked much older than fifteen until I managed to complete high school on my own, which took a few years. Then I put myself through college, and afterward I spent maybe fifteen years living on my own before the enemy grabbed me."

All of their kits looked their age. Nickel was only fourteen at the moment, but he had been growing steadily like any normal child. Dane didn't think Nickel would continue to look fifteen years old when he was twenty and older. It didn't mean that their kits were aging faster than

Mercury. Rather, Dane thought it might have something to do with the conditions in which they grew up. Being small and quick in the wild helped keep dragons safe from predators, something his kits didn't need to worry about. It was also harder to find food in the wild, which meant inhibited growth. Mercury's body had probably spent those seven years in foster care trying to catch up. Once his body had reached its prime, somewhere in its late twenties while Mercury had been in college, it had settled down. He had looked the same for all the years they had been living together, as unaged as Dane was.

"Mother told me she thought you were nearly one hundred years old," Dane explained. Mercury hadn't asked why Dane wanted the answer to his question, but Dane wanted to tell him anyway. "She said she came to visit because she thought she found a suitable mate for me, someone whose magic was strong enough they wouldn't leave me behind in fifty or so years. She had no idea that dragons were practically immortal too."

"How old are you?" Mercury asked, his curiosity piqued.

"I am almost four hundred," Dane replied. It was an easy enough answer. Like Mercury, Dane had grown to the point where his body reached its peak, then had stopped aging. He didn't get older every century like his mother.

Mercury nodded, but didn't say anything more. Four hundred years was a lot of time to get his head around, Dane knew, as was the idea that they could be together, loving each other and raising their kits, for centuries. Mercury's fingers hadn't stilled in Alloy's hair while they spoke.

Dane waited, trying to pretend that he wasn't holding his breath in anticipation. Mercury knew how long he would live, and now he also knew how long Dane would live. Their mere six years together was not anywhere close to six hundred. Dane was willing to give it a try, but was Mercury?

Mercury's hand finally stilled in Alloy's hair. He looked up at Dane, and his bronze eyes sharpened. Mercury hadn't missed Dane's anxiety.

"There's going to be a lot of candles on our birthday cakes, aren't there?" he murmured. A second later, a smile grew on his face. "We'll just have to pick out bigger cakes to accommodate them."

He said "we," as in together forever. Dane let out the breath he was holding and returned Mercury's smile. He shifted forward in his seat, intent on leaning across the divide between their chairs and taking Mercury's lips with his. Which was the exact moment his wards alerted him that Nickel was home and had brought company.

"Lunchtime," Dane explained when he pulled away. Mercury's grin had an edge to it as he also pulled back. Dane felt a shiver of anticipation run up his spine. He knew what that look meant when they finally had the privacy.

"Better start cooking," Mercury agreed. His hand returned to petting Alloy, and his suggestive smile faded to a more innocent one as he looked down at his sleeping kit. Dane nodded in agreement and headed downstairs.

*

Dane could sense Nickel as Nickel walked into the house and headed directly to the kitchen. It was lunchtime and, like all the kits, Nickel knew that the best place to find one of their guardians was in the kitchen. He had two bouncing satellites circling him as he hurried over to where Dane was standing in front of the stove.

Dane had to stifle a grin at the sight. William's two water dragons had clearly never seen an older and more experienced water dragon like Nickel. They had glued themselves to Nickel's side, and it didn't appear they were going to give Nickel space any time soon. Nickel appeared to be flattered by the attention. William, who had walked in after the kits, looked like he was calculating how he could use his kits' adoration of Nickel for his own benefit. Dane had a feeling visiting Nickel was going to become some sort of reward for good behavior.

"No ambushes or any further sign of the enemy," Nickel reported. Dane nodded to show he had heard, but the milk in the gigantic pot he was standing over had finally started to boil, so he had to add in the cheese.

Dane felt a tug on his pants leg and looked down to find that one of the kits had detached from Nickel and was trying to get his attention.

"Uncle Willy said we could stay for lunch if we asked nicely," the kit said.

Nickel took the spoon from Dane's hands to continue stirring the sauce, so Dane bent down to look the kit in the eye.

"How do you ask nicely?" Dane asked.

The kit frowned and looked distressed when an answer wasn't readily forthcoming.

"Oh, I know!" the other kit said, jumping up and down on Nickel's other side. "Uncle Willy said you have to say 'please'!"

The first kit's face brightened into an eager smile. "Please?" he asked.

"Thank you for asking. You are more than welcome to stay. What's your name?" Dane asked.

"I'm Aqua and that's Rios," the kit chirped. Mercury walked into the kitchen carrying Alloy, and Aqua was immediately distracted at the sight of another kit. He hurried off, and Dane stood back up to reclaim the spoon.

"I know they're not traditional dragon names, but the kits couldn't remember their own names and don't mind the ones I gave them," William explained, sounding somewhat sheepish at the admission.

"If it makes them happy," Dane said, knowing he didn't need to elaborate for William to understand. "You'll keep an eye out in your territory for other dragons in need?"

"Absolutely," William replied immediately. "I already was going to once my kits finally started to settle in. Now that I've seen how you've corralled your kits, I don't think it would be a problem to help out a few more. Mercury mentioned something about a village you were setting up?"

Dane nodded, but the timer he had set for the pasta went off before he could explain. "I'll tell you later," he said as he went to find a strainer.

The lure of imminent food drew the kits to the kitchen from wherever they had spent the rest of the morning. The ones whose chores were to help set the table quickly took stacks of dishes to the dining room. With the addition of William and his kits, they didn't have enough room in the kitchen. Alloy finally detached himself from Mercury and was happily introducing himself and his family to Aqua and Rios, which meant when Lumie appeared Mercury could grab him in a hug.

Lumie was fine and he protested being dragged upstairs to brush his teeth. Mother came downstairs with them once Lumie was clean and everyone settled down for lunch.

Their family was large and crazy, Dane knew as the kits fought over who got mac and cheese first. He didn't even mind that it was growing steadily as new friends were made, and Mother actually joked with 'Ron about which cheeses were better for mac and cheese.

Mercury's hand crept into Dane's under the table, and they shared a grin.

It was all worth it. They were building their family together, and that made it perfect.

About the Author

When Mell Eight was in high school, she discovered dragons. Beautiful, wondrous creatures that took her on epic adventures both to faraway lands and on journeys of the heart. Mell wanted to create dragons of her own, so she put pen to paper. Mell Eight is now known for her own soaring dragons, as well as for other wonderful characters dancing across the pages of her books. While she mostly writes paranormal or fantasy stories, she has been seen exploring the real world once or twice.

Facebook: www.facebook.com/MellEightFiction

Twitter: @MellEight

Website: www.melleightfiction.weebly.com

Other NineStar books by this author

Ge-Mi, Part One
Ge-Mi, Part Two

Supernatural Consultant Series

Dragon Consultant
Dragon Deception
Dragon Dilemma
Dragon Detective
Dragon Soldier

Also Available from NineStar Press

Connect with NineStar Press

www.ninestarpress.com

www.facebook.com/ninestarpress

www.facebook.com/groups/NineStarNiche

www.twitter.com/ninestarpress

www.ingramcontent.com/pod-product-compliance
Lightning Source LLC
Chambersburg PA
CBHW051605100726
47898CB00001B/237